THE SAWDUST PILE

THE SAWDUST PILE

Growing Up in Southwest Georgia

A Novel by Don Mobley Adams

iUniverse, Inc.
New York Lincoln Shanghai

THE SAWDUST PILE
Growing Up in Southwest Georgia

iUniverse books may be ordered through booksellers or by contacting:

iUniverse
2021 Pine Lake Road, Suite 100
Lincoln, NE 68512
www.iuniverse.com
1-800-Authors (1-800-288-4677)

ISBN-13: 978-0-595-36011-6 (pbk)
ISBN-13: 978-0-595-80462-7 (ebk)
ISBN-10: 0-595-36011-4 (pbk)
ISBN-10: 0-595-80462-4 (ebk)

Printed in the United States of America

Dedication and Foreword

When I started writing this book, I began in anger, determined to expose the human weaknesses I had seen in others. I wound up exposing myself, mainly, and I hope I've done away with most of the anger.

When it comes to a dedication, there is only one qualifying candidate: Ellen, my former wife. I realize writers dedicate books to their spouses all the time, and I've read such tributes with my usual cynicism. Yeah, sure, I've said, the rascal's just buying a little peace in the family, throwing a crumb to the poor soul who's had to witness the agony of creation. But, at least with me, there's nothing to dedicate without Ellen. Without her unfailing encouragement and criticism, this project would have languished in the computer, in some misplaced files in cyberspace, and maybe that's where it really belonged. But, it's not there; it's here for the reading, and whatever merit it has, I owe to Ellen. So thanks, Ellen for all the things you did to make this book come alive. It was a lot!

And finally, Gentle Readers, if you have the time, patience, and pluck to read on, I'm grateful. I hope that you may find a few tidbits worth keeping.

DMA

❦ ❦ ❦

And many thanks to Ro, for bringing this book and me to life again!

DMA

Prologue

What is it about funerals? Jeremiah Goodwin asks himself.

Something has to be done, he knows, to show respect for the dead and sympathy for the living. But over the last thousand years, it seems to Jeremiah, homo sapiens should have been able to devise some better ritual. At least something better than the south Georgia variety. Something more benign—something without the awkward greetings, hollow gestures and vapid eulogies. He feels trapped by the convention. He has always manufactured excuses—sometimes good ones, sometimes not—to avoid funerals, but some funerals just can't be avoided. He faces two of those today. *Two* funerals for two very different people on the *same day*! What a shitty prospect!

As Jeremiah sits alone in the den, eating raisin bran, he watches the 5:00 a.m. television newscast. He winces as he hears the TV announcer getting into the same stuff about Alex again. How many times would they keep airing the gruesome mess? Still shots of the room, the walls and mirrors splattered with blood. The video of the motel scene, Alex's Mercedes surrounded by police. The same old tired interview with the deputy sheriff. Why couldn't they let it rest? He knows the answer, of course: human beings have a morbid, inexplicable fascination for things like this—never tiring of watching members of our own species destroy themselves. We are irresistibly drawn to stories about death and depravity, fascinated by the lurid details—like buzzards around a carcass.

But with the TV running the same scenes over and over and *over* like this? He wonders how much pain a family can take? Are there no limits?

Sarah is not going with him to Shrewsbury Crossing. "They're *your* people," she had snapped at him the night before, "*you* go bury them!" And that had ended the discussion. Sarah does not do much of anything with Jeremiah anymore, and he can't blame her—especially since the San Francisco episode. No wife could forget something like that. But it's much more than that, he tells himself; the distance between them has been growing for years. Thirty-seven years of marriage, and bonds that held them together—the emotional and physical ties—are now almost gone. Like an FM station drifting out of range, there's too much interference now, too many alien noises crowding out the signals. The music is fading, fading fast, and Jeremiah wonders if it'll ever come in clearly again.

Shortly after five, Jeremiah turns the ignition key and cranks the Jaguar, simultaneously punching the remote for the three-car garage. The engine purrs with the deep-throated roar he loves as he turns onto Johnson Ferry Road. Minutes later he finds himself on Roswell Road, and soon I-75, moving south toward downtown Atlanta. Not much traffic this time of morning. He can enjoy the ride through town, seizing this somewhat rare chance to take his eyes off the road and savor familiar landmarks: the historic steeple of the Georgia Tech campus on the right, the Varsity to the left with its multi-colored pennants fluttering in the breeze. Then the Olympic village apartments, standing a dozen stories tall, somber, austere and lifeless, looking as though they had been erected as barracks for troops rather than for the cream of the world's athletes. The blinking airline sign with temperature and time comes into view just as the road veers to the left to miss the central downtown complex of towering hotels and office buildings.

In early December of 1996, most traces of the Summer Olympics—the Centennial Olympics—are gone: no more banners on the interstates or over-sized billboards hawking everything from Coca Cola to Nike. Just beyond the state capitol, the two stadiums loom, one soon to be demolished after a short life of thirty years, and the new one just built, the Olympic stadium, to be renovated to remove seats so the Braves will have the assurance of playing to capacity crowds. But they needn't fear as long as the Braves keep winning, he thinks to himself; the crowds will always come so long as they win.

Jeremiah punches the cruise control and locks in the speed for seventy, but he can't get his mind off the things going on with the stadiums he has just passed. He reflects on the absurdities of the human condition and marvels about the strangeness of his own species. The human animal—what a bizarre creature! Spending enormous sums to destroy perfectly good structures, while people go hungry four hundred yards away. Jeremiah remembers the fanfare in the sixties when the old stadium was built—state-of-the-art, they said, built to stand forever. What a joke, but nobody seems upset about it now. What is it in our nature that accepts change so readily, yet drives us inexorably in the attempt to create permanence? And we always fail. That's the hell of it. We always fail. Stadiums, monuments, marriages, empires—everything begins with great expectations, and nothing really endures. Nothing—absolutely nothing—makes it in the long run.

South of Macon, Jeremiah pulls off an exit to fuel the Jaguar. The sun is just rising. He is making good time, very good time. After coffee at a convenience store, he returns to the interstate and soon passes signs that read "Valdosta 150 miles," and a mile-marker labeled 164—that many miles to the Florida line. He sets the cruise control on seventy-eight now—fudging as much as he thinks he can over the seventy-mile-an-hour speed limit without drawing the state patrol's attention. Suddenly, he inhales deeply and begins to relax, for he knows that he will reach Shrewsbury Crossing well before noon, early enough to spend time with his mother in the nursing home.

The first funeral is scheduled for noon. He doesn't want to get there early. Arriving just as the service begins will allow him to avoid superficial embraces and some of the tears. It will be a quiet, private affair, not more than a few dozen people, he figures—an awkward situation, to say the least. God, what a mess! No way that Alex's casket will be open. It was a grisly scene, the face beyond repair, even by the expert morticians Annie probably hired in Tallahassee. Actually, he's going to this one *only* because of Annie. Dear, sweet, precious Annie. Once *she* knows he is there, he will have served his purpose.

The other funeral will be in the First AME Church, beginning at three p.m. Jeremiah has attended other Negro funerals before, but this one is special. In fact, Beagle was special, a terrific human being. So much of Beagle's life wasted, not just because of his death, but because an ugly, despicable caste system forced Beagle to fight for his manhood all of his life.

Jeremiah knows the sanctuary will be packed, people everywhere—outside on the walk, the grass, the parking lot. There will be lots of crying, singing, shouting, calling to Jesus. Jeremiah will be at this one because he *has* to be there. It is a moral imperative, and he knows he *must* attend. Beagle deserved no less, so Jeremiah must join the hundreds of people who will pay tribute.

And afterwards he will go through Albany on the return trip to Atlanta—not much out of the way. He absolutely *must* visit Ethan, his dearest friend on earth. What an injustice! Ethan—perhaps the noblest, the most honest human being he has ever known—winds up in jail. The guilt gnaws at him—knowing that Ethan has been in an eight-by-ten cell three months now, and Jeremiah hasn't even visited. Jeremiah hopes he can absolve himself from at least some of the guilt this afternoon.

He leaves the interstate at the Ludlow exit and heads toward Shrewsbury Crossing on the four-lane that winds into Florida and expedites the trip from the central part of south Georgia to the Florida panhandle. Twenty miles later he passes the city limit sign for Shrewsbury Crossing. On the left is a sprawling shopping center. With new apartments, offices, strip malls, the town is bulging with a booming economy. The area has changed here unbelievably since he was a boy.

But on the right side of the four-lane, squatting behind dilapidated public housing, are the decaying remnants of the old sawmill, vestiges of tin-covered stoops which had once, many years ago, sheltered freshly cut two-by-fours and four-by-fours stacked to weather and dry. The sight evokes vivid childhood memories: the smell of turpentine and pine slabs burning to fuel the boiler. He can picture the smoke and steam rising through hot summer air as though it were yesterday, and he can almost hear the screams and laughter of the other boys—Alex and Beagle taunting each other and Ethan's unforgettable giggles. Fighting to be king of the mountain, pushing, shoving each other off. Jostling for supremacy, for dominance, for control, and Alex always winning. He can still see Alex now, standing at the summit, legs spread, his hands on his hips, grinning, sneering, daring someone to challenge him. Not the last summit Alex would conquer either, as things turned out.

Jeremiah checks his watch, then slows the car and turns down an abandoned lane leading to the sawmill, pot-holes and dog fennel marring what was once a respectable asphalt road. Wincing as he hears dried weeds, briars and dead tree limbs scratch the underside of the Jaguar, he curses himself for having done this and abruptly stops. Opening the door, he stands beside the car. The mid-morning sky is brilliantly clear, a December coolness in the air, but no trace of a breeze alters the stillness of the scene before him. He sees the faint outline of the ancient sawdust, once towering thirty-five feet over the flat southwest Georgia landscape but now just a slight brownish hump, decayed and desolate behind the rotting wood and rusting tin—ants, termites and scorpions, now the only tenants.

Bulging conspicuously from the surrounding leaves and debris by the side of the sawdust is an oblong bank of fresh dirt. He sees tattered scraps of yellow crime scene ribbon strewn in places, some shreds snared by brambles. *My God!* he thinks, sucking in his breath, that's the *grave*! That's where Beagle was buried; it's where they dug him up.

Could you say it all started here, he wonders, and that it ended here? Could eight-year-old boys from the backwoods of Georgia ever have imagined that their lives would weave such a yarn, a tale of such rich and tragic depth, a story that would conclude here in such a place? Could it be that this pitiable mound of rotting dust and wood shavings is alpha and omega—a full cycle, a beginning and an end?

Jeremiah removes his glasses and rubs his eyes. He stands transfixed by the scene, motionless, overcome by the stillness. Pursing his lips, he gets back in the car. He puts on his glasses and sits there a moment before turning the ignition key. Shuddering slightly and taking another deep breath as he places the car in reverse, he keeps a foot on the brakes and gazes toward the remains of the sawdust one last time.

Two funerals await him, but for the moment, there is only the intense, overwhelming reality before him—revelations of time, vivid recollections of the past, indelible memories of himself and Beagle and Ethan and Alex.

And of the many summits they fought over and climbed.

PART I

1934–1964

CHAPTER 1

Brass Tacks

"Birth, and copulation, and death.
That's all the facts when you
come to brass tacks."
T. S. Eliot, *Sweeney Agonistes*

Jesse Wayne Rumpkin worked nearly thirteen hours at the Shrewsbury Crossing sawmill that April day in 1934 when his wife gave birth to his son. Even though it was early Spring, the weather was already ungodly hot in southwest Georgia when word came late that afternoon that Jesse's wife had delivered the child. His daughter, Christina, age five, came running to the mill to bring the news from the shack where they lived a few hundred yards away. Jesse happened to glance up as she approached, so he moved toward her, away from the noise of the mill, and heard her say, excitedly and breathlessly, "Paw, the baby's been bornt: it's a boy and he'll be my brother! I'm gonna take good care of him, Paw. You'll see!"

"Shore you will, Tina," Jesse said, wiping sweat from his brow. "Shore you will, honey. How's yore mama?"

"Awful weak, Paw, awful weak. Granny says to tell you to get home *now*. Mama ain't got no color or nuttin in her face. Is she gonna die, Paw?"

"Course not, baby. She's a strong woman—a real strong woman," Jesse said, staring at his daughter with a vacant look on his face. "And 'sides, Granny's with y'all now. You just run back to the house and help take care of yore mama and baby brother. I'll be comin' in 'long 'bout quittin' time."

"But, Paw, Granny needs you *now*! Please come home *now*." Tina pleaded. Her lips quivered and tears glistened from the large brown orbits of her eyes. Wearing a faded pink dress, two sizes too large with the hem sagging to her ankles, she carried a ragamuffin doll with stuffing protruding from both elbows. Again she begged, "Please, please come home, Paw. Granny's skerred. I'm skerred too. I'm skerred mama's gonna die."

"Cain't come right now, baby," Jesse said without emotion. "Yore mama'll be all right. I gotta stay on the job and make money to feed you and the new youngun." Patting the child on the head, Jesse gently but firmly took her shoulder and pointed her up the hill toward home. "Like I said, you run along now."

Returning to his place beside the giant planer, Jesse watched Tina walk slowly up the road. She looked back frequently, futilely hoping that her father might change his mind and follow her; but he had resumed his labors and was no longer watching as she moved toward the ramshackle gate leading to the Rumpkin house.

Jesse had been married for nearly five years. He and his wife had both been eighteen at the time of the wedding. A sharecropper's daughter who had dropped out of school in the sixth grade to work in the fields, she was a simple-minded, good-natured girl, who had been smitten by Jesse's good looks and charm when they met at a church social in 1928. She had been pregnant—carrying Christina for seven months—when Jesse took her for his bride in 1929.

For over two years now, Jesse had been what was known as a "slab-toter" at the sawmill. Twenty-three years old, a strong, handsome boy, Jesse stood by the huge saw that planed the giant pine logs. His job was to pick up the slabs thrown to the side of the spinning blade and carry them several yards away to a pile where they would be later burned as fuel for the enormous boiler that produced the steam power for the mill. On the far side of the planer stood the other slab-toter, Jesse's closest friend and co-worker for two years, Erasmus Bonobo. "Rasty," Jesse and others called him. The two men—along with the foreman—were the only white workers at the mill. The heaviest labor—cutting down and hauling the giant pines, moving them to the conveyor, and stacking the freshly cut lumber—was left to Negroes.

All work at the mill was tedious and exhausting, drudgery worsened by the humid heat that dominated the southern part of Georgia most of the year. The monstrous engine and pulleys for the mill sprayed grit and dust-filled steam everywhere, coating the workers' unprotected bodies and eyes, saturating their nostrils and lungs. Constantly bathed in turpentine tar, the workers used kerosene as a cleaner, the odor worse than the turpentine itself. The callused hands, the smells, the unsmiling faces, everything was a reminder that these were mill hands. Jesse's world was harsh and the news that day for him was that he had another mouth to feed. He could think of no reason to celebrate.

The workday at the mill began soon after dawn and continued until seven p.m. when the mill whistle gave a merciful blast to proclaim quitting time. Except for a thirty minute break at noon for a meal of hunks of cornbread, syrup, and smoked sausage, the hours of hot, grueling labor hammered away relentlessly at the men. Wages were seventy-five cents for the long day's work, but in 1934 Jesse could buy a five-pound sack of flour for a quarter and a decent pair of shoes for two dollars. As with most things, there was a silver lining.

But Jesse rarely saw the lining. As he sought sleep each night, the whine of the planer and the noise from the engine and the giant pulley belts continued to ring in his ears. He drank away most of his earnings, leaving scarcely enough money to buy food. His wife had helped out by taking in washing for middle class families, but she had been forced to stop two months earlier because of her second pregnancy. Jesse had been an unwilling, sometimes frightened observer of her terrible ordeal, which had involved severe bouts of nausea and vomiting. He had listened through endless nights to her hacking cough, and watched as she struggled for breath while drawing smoke from the cigarettes she constantly dangled from her mouth. It would probably be weeks or even months before she could work again, and everything—the baby, Christina, cooking for the family and caring for a sickly wife—would be on Jesse's shoulders. In a word, his prospects were bleak: years of backbreaking labor, poverty, turpentine, kerosene, depression, and ringing ears.

So when the mill whistle sounded quitting time on this April day of his son's birth, Jesse mulled over two choices. He could go home to a whining, often demanding, five-year old daughter; a half-witted and sickly wife; a crying newborn; and a shrewish mother-in-law. The other option was that he could go with Rasty to the Night Owl pool hall, about two miles from the mill near the Shrewsbury Crossing colored quarters.

It wasn't much of a choice. Jesse figured that his wife was probably too weak to give much of a damn whether he came home or not, and his mother-in-law could take care of everything until he got home later. Besides, he told himself, he wouldn't stay very long, and he needed a little break somewhere. With that thought, he motioned to Erasmus, raising an imaginary glass to his lips. Rasty understood the signal, nodded in agreement, and with no words exchanged between them, the two men threw down their last armloads of slabs, brushed themselves off, and trudged up the dirt road past Jesse's house, beyond rows of other tenements and the Shrewsbury Crossing water tower to the Night Owl saloon.

Negroes were allowed in the Night Owl—the only place in town where the races mingled freely with each other outside the workplace. Jasmine, a fair-skinned Negro, was the waitress: she was a stunningly beautiful girl of nineteen with an exquisite figure set on a medium-sized frame. Her facial features were fine and proud, her cheekbones high, and her nostrils flared slightly. Large buttocks lent emphasis to her small waist and full thighs.

"What'll you two boys have?" Jasmine asked, smiling softly as Jesse and Erasmus sat down.

"Bring us some soda water and a little rotgut," Jesse said. "It's been a hell of a day, and I need me some unwindin'." Even though Prohibition had been repealed, alcohol was still illegal anywhere in south Georgia in the thirties, but a ready supply of moonshine was available and was regularly served to trusted customers of the Night Owl.

"I hear yore old lady done had another youngun," Jasmine said, looking directly at Jesse. "Ain't you done figured out what makes babies, Jesse? You oughta keep yore pants buttoned."

"I figure you might want my pants *un*buttoned, am I right, Jasmine?" Jesse said, winking at Erasmus and jabbing him on the arm.

Jasmine did not answer, but threw her head back and smiled broadly as she walked away from the table. Jesse was one of the waitress's favorite customers among the whites. He had always treated her with respect and dignity, and she had reciprocated with warm banter and knowing smiles, never insisting upon full payment on those frequent occasions when he was broke. Jasmine was always good company for Jesse, and he needed good company tonight. Especially on this night his spirits needed lifting.

But other spirits were at work. After a few minutes, the liquor changed Jesse's personality. Normally shy and withdrawn, full of self-doubt and feelings of inferiority, Jesse became outgoing, moving through the saloon confidently, telling jokes, slapping backs, and watching Jasmine out of the corner of his eye as she dallied with other customers.

Rasty began a game of pool in the rear of the bar with one of the Negroes while Jesse leaned over the juke box, his forearm and elbow resting on the glass. He picked out a Bob Wills song, and when it began playing, he turned and saw a scowl on the black face of Erasmus's pool partner—not surprising, since Negroes routinely abhorred hillbilly music. But he didn't care, and besides, it was his nickel and he would damn well play whatever song he pleased.

Time slipped away for Jesse and after a while, alcohol buried his worries—the oppression of the day's work, the unbearable heat, the tedium and boredom, his despair about supporting his growing family. Suddenly, his life had promise. Didn't he have a good friend in Rasty? And wasn't he lucky to have a new baby, a son? Lots of men wanted sons, and he had one, didn't he? He started thinking about the new baby: what would they name him, he wondered, and would he favor his daddy? Maybe he and the boy would become real buddies, like him and Rasty. That would be nice, and for an instant, it occurred to him that maybe he should just go on home. But just then, he glanced up to see Jasmine's radiant figure coming toward his table. Shouldn't leave just yet, he thought: he had worked hard all day at the sawmill and needed more time to himself.

Jasmine stood next to his table, her hands on her hips, and said: "Mind if I set a spell?"

"Shore, take a load off!" Jesse answered.

Jasmine sat down. Raised voices suddenly came from the pool table. Erasmus's shot had knocked a ball to the floor, and his opponent was arguing loudly about the proper penalty. Jesse sensed that there could be a fight, so he got up, walked over to the table and placed his arm around Rasty's neck. "Come on over and set down with me and Jasmine," he said under his breath, pulling on Rasty's arm.

Erasmus stood glaring at the Negro, his hand tightening on the pool stick. "Boy, you gonna git in a pile of trouble," he said, grimacing.

"You wants to go outside and finish this up?" the other man asked.

"Simmer down now, Rasty," Jesse whispered in his friend's ear. "Hell, ain't nothing worth gettin' stabbed by a drunk nigger."

Erasmus muttered a profanity as he threw down the stick and moved with Jesse away from the pool table. They walked back to the table where Jasmine still waited and seated themselves, Jesse next to the girl, Erasmus facing the couple across the table. The waitress sat close to Jesse, her legs crossed and her foot brushing lightly against his leg. Jasmine had brought a quart jar of moonshine to the table, and Jesse poured a half-glass and handed it to Erasmus. Jasmine talked with the men a few minutes, then got up to wait on two customers who had just entered the tavern.

"You kinda sweet on that nigger gal, ain't you?" Erasmus asked.

"Naw, hell naw!" Jesse said. "She ain't bad to look at, but I ain't one for race mixin'. If'n I'm nice to her, I figure she might feel me up a little. What's wrong with that?"

"Nothin', Jesse, but I been around you too much. If that little colored gal gets to feelin' you up, y'all gonna be screwin' 'fore it's over. Hell, I know you. You'll fuck a water moccasin with a little moonshine in yore belly, and Jasmine is a hell of a lot better lookin' than any damn snake."

Jesse laughed and slapped his buddy on the back. "Shit, Rasty, you're just jealous 'cause you fancy pokin' her yoreself, ain't that so?"

Erasmus winced and huddled over his glass. "Hell naw! I don't mess with niggers, Jesse. I like white women."

Jesse cast his gaze down at the splinters in the table top. He liked white women too, but Rasty was right. He couldn't stop himself when he was drunk. He knew it wasn't right bedding other women when he had a wife—but damnit, sometimes he just did it. "Just hush up, Rasty," Jesse said. "I ain't tryin' to get in her britches, and 'sides, I ain't feelin' too good right now. Sometimes things just pile up on me. Everything seems real heavy right now. Know what I mean?"

"You ain't got nothin' to complain about, Jesse," Erasmus said. "Yore wife's just given you a baby boy, and you got a good job. Yore life's turnin' out fine, I reckon. Lots of folks' would wanna be in yore shoes."

"You just ain't got no idea, Rasty. You don't know nothin' 'bout my problems," Jesse said. "Man from the bank came to the house last night and said he'd be back at the end of the week to take my Model-T. With the old lady sick and not able to take in washin', I done missed the last two payments. Besides, the damn thing won't run. 'You gonna have to pull it in,' I told him, 'it needs a overhaul and a new set of plugs,' but he says, 'never mind, I'm comin' for it with a tow truck day after tomorrow,' and I 'spect he'll show up. Don't know what we'll do without no way to go. The old lady has to pick up and deliver her washin' in that car, if she ever gets able to work again."

"Aw, you'll work it all out some way," Erasmus said, patting Jesse on the back. "That damn bank rather have yore money than that old wore-out car. They gonna work with you when it comes right down to it. That banker's just tryin' to scare yore ass."

Jesse managed a weak smile as Jasmine returned to the table and sat down. "What's ailin' you, chile? You looks sorta down in the mouth," she said.

Jasmine snuggled closer to Jesse, her shoulder brushing lightly against his arm. She had sat with him on other nights. As Erasmus babbled with a story about his great grandfather in the Civil War, Jesse fixed his eyes on Jasmine, studying her profile, her shapely nose and the rich fullness of her lips. Her presence seemed particularly beneficial to Jesse tonight. She looked radiant, and it dawned on him that she had no blemishes to speak of, save a small wart the size of a pea about one inch from the left side of her mouth. If Jasmine had been white, Jesse thought to himself, she would have long ago been married off to the son of a rich, white landowner or a department storekeeper. But as it was, he figured her color would mean that she would sleep around, have a half-dozen children, get fat, lose her teeth, and become a field hand or a maid in some white family's house. What a cryin' shame, he thought to himself, what a damn shame!

"How long you gonna be here tonight?" Jasmine asked. "We gettin' ready to close."

Jesse checked a clock above the bar. Eleven o'clock, pretty late, he thought, and the morning mill whistle would sound early. Maybe he should go.

"Tell you what, sweet thang," Jesse said, "I'm gonna have another sip of this likker, and then I'm gonna amble my weary way home. Have another one with me, all right?"

Erasmus had left the bar without a word to either of them. Only the bartender and one other customer lingered over drinks. Jesse started telling Jasmine about a trip he and Erasmus had taken to Mobile the previous summer.

"I'll tell you straight, Jasmine," Jesse said, "that was the damnedest time I ever had. Rasty got so shit-faced drunk he started peein' in the middle of the damn street with people walkin' by. I tried to make him put his pecker up when I seen a cop comin'. 'Rasty,' I said, 'you gonna get us both locked up,' but all he did was laugh and giggle and keep right on pissin'. He was a sight that night, I'm tellin' you."

"Did y'all finds any women?" Jasmine asked.

"My God, did we find us some *women*!" Jesse exclaimed. "We had three ole ugly gals hangin' on us when we closed down this joint that night, and we didn't have a fuckin' cent. All our money was gone, but these gals wanted to fuck us Georgia rednecks whether we was broke or not."

"Was they whores?" Jasmine asked.

"Hell, I don't know—naw, don't think so," Jesse said. "Them gals was too ugly to sell it. Shit, one was harelipped. I 'spect they'da starved to death tryin' to sell it."

"Warn't you worried about yore old lady back home?" Jasmine asked, one hand resting on the inside of Jesse's thigh, the other hand stroking the back of his neck. "She wouldn't cotton to you messin' with them women."

"I warn't thinkin' 'bout her." Jesse slowly shook his head. "Just like I ain't thinkin' 'bout her now. I figured she ain't got nobody else to depend on. 'Sides, ain't nobody but me can satisfy her."

"I 'magines you could take care of me," Jasmine whispered, nibbling his earlobe.

"Goddamnit, gal! You just 'bout drivin' me crazy." Jesse twisted, jerking his head away. "I reckon you're right. I oughta be thinkin' of my wife and newborn baby at home right now, but I ain't! What's wrong with me? Why cain't I git my mind right?"

"Boy, you ain't thinkin' nothin' but what you was made to think." Jasmine slid her hand further up his thigh. "Come on," she said, "le's go where I stays."

Jesse had no resistance. With the half-empty liquor jar in one hand and the other around Jasmine's waist, he stumbled from the building and walked eratically with the girl up a dusty road leading to Jasmine's shack. For a quarter-mile, they sang and laughed as a bright moon emerged from a cloud cover, illuminating a row of tenements to their right. Jasmine tugged on Jesse's arm, pulling him gently toward her shack, the first house on the row. As they limped up the steps and entered the one-room cabin, Jasmine threw herself on the bed, rolling over and tossing her shoes to the floor in the same motion. Jesse took off his shirt and pants and lay down beside her still-clothed body. Propping her head on a pillow, Jasmine struck a match and lit the kerosene lamp on a crate by the bed. The beauty of her face in the soft glow of the lantern astounded Jesse.

He kissed her long and passionately, all the while unbuttoning her blouse. She pulled down her flimsy skirt and giggled as he touched her breasts. She wore no underclothing and she sighed loudly as his hands explored her body. She gave forth an odor of rich femininity, and Jesse was overwhelmed by the poignant musk from her workday sweat mingled with the heavy, rank sweetness of cheap perfume. Abruptly, she sat up with her back against the headboard and coyly looked at Jesse as she lit a cigarette.

Jesse leaned on an elbow as he watched Jasmine inhale the smoke. Then he took the cigarette from her mouth and placed it on the crate where the lamp stood. Savoring her body, he studied the contours of her cheeks, the gentle furrows below her stomach, and the smooth angles of her hips. He ran his finger along the side of her nose and around to the nape of her neck where he detected faint vestiges of sweat below the hairline. Her body was magic to him, and, in a hoarse, shaking voice, he said: "Jasmine, I love you."

"There, there, chile," Jasmine said. "You cain't love Jasmine. You just thinks you loves me. White boys cain't love no colored woman. What you loves is this cottony sweetness 'tween my legs, but you can have it, baby. It's here for you."

Jesse eagerly took the invitation, but as their bodies melded together, his rapture was too intense to endure. He quickly rolled over exhausted, and she pulled him to her, guided his head to her chest, and whispered that he should rest. Minutes passed and his breathing slowed. He stirred again, then moved his mouth down to her breast, cupping a nipple between his lips. Jasmine began to moan softly and stroked the back of his neck. "Now, baby," she said, "if you feels like it, you can take care of Jasmine. Put yore lips on me?"

For a flicker of time, Jesse hesitated. Then, as Jasmine's breasts trembled beneath the touch of his outstretched fingertips, he moved down, kissed her stomach and pressed the tip of his tongue on the rim of her navel. With his head between her hands, she churned his hair, pushing his face further downward. Holding his head and face firmly against herself, Jasmine twisted and pressed hard against him, her nostrils flaring as she screamed uncontrollably.

Sleep came for the couple like a dead calm on water for the next four hours. Jesse awoke to hear Jasmine urinating in the pot in the corner of the room. His eyes blinked as he stared toward the unfamiliar ceiling and he coughed uneasily as alien odors invaded his nostrils. His mind, still blurred and deadened from residual alcohol, urged him to rise and flee, but instead he turned his head and saw Jasmine's beautiful, naked torso in the dim light on the far side of the room. As she stood up, she saw that he was awake, and she smiled and moved toward him. Instantly, Jesse was again overcome with the seductive beauty of her body and his titillating realization that the two of them had just shared each other's arms and the last few hours of sleep.

Returning to the bed, Jasmine detected Jesse's excitement. Pulling back the sheet, she straddled him. This time, her position allowed her to control the coupling, and her heart quivered with the exhiliration of knowing that she was now dominant—at least for an instant—in a world of overbearing white rule. Suddenly, blackness and whiteness were gone as the union of their bodies obliterated any other reality and only their humanness remained as their souls blended in the primal, surging, sacred act of intimacy and creation. They quivered in disbelief, then lay silently, side-by-side, taking short breaths in gentle rhythm with each other.

They did not sleep again. The faint light of daybreak soon broke through the ragged sheet covering the window.

"Reckon I better get home," Jesse said, clearing his throat nervously. "It'll be time to get to the mill 'fore I know it." He rose to his feet, shifting his weight unsteadily by the bed as he pulled on his pants and shirt, and then he sat down again to put on his shoes.

Jasmine remained motionless in the bed, saying nothing. She stared blankly at the ceiling and made no effort to look toward Jesse as he disappeared through the door.

Jesse's mother-in-law railed at him as he crossed the threshold of his house. "Where you been, you no-count bastard?" she screamed. Jesse went to a water bucket near the stove, filled the dipper, and took a drink. "If I was a man," the woman yelled, "I'd take a wood ax and cut off yore head! Out drinkin' and carousin' while my baby's been lyin' up here all night at the point of death. I hope you burn in hell forever!"

Jesse could not look his mother-in-law in the eyes. He said nothing as she yelled out: "Soon's my girl's able to get outta bed, I'm gonna take her and Christina and this new baby as far as we can go away from you and yore worthless hide. I knowed you warn't no damn good when she married you." Jesse nodded weakly. Too nauseous to offer any defense, he managed a sick smile as he mumbled words to the woman, saying that she was right, that his wife would be better off without him, and that he should go to hell for all he'd done. Then he heard his wife crying in the bedroom. He went in, glanced over at the crib and the son he had never seen, stepped to the bedside of his wife and knelt down, reaching for her hand.

"Where was you, Jesse?" his wife said. "Where was you all night? I been needin' you so bad. I'm real sick, cain't breathe good, and my chest hurts more'n you can imagine. Why ain't you been here? Don't you care nothin' 'bout this baby I give you?"

"Well, I'm here now, sweetheart, and I'm real sorry," Jesse said. "You cain't ever know how sorry I am. I'm a sorry excuse for a husband—a sorry excuse for a man."

"Looks like you coulda' come home last night," his wife said, her voice breaking. "You know I try not to say nothin' when you stay gone so much, but

I coulda' *died* last night, Jesse. Didn't Tina tell you how bad off I was? Didn't you know that?"

"Baby, I'm gonna do better, I swear!" Jesse's blood-stained eyes swelled with tears. "You gonna see. I'm gonna work hard and make you proud of me. You ain't gonna have to worry 'bout me bein' here no more."

"Don't go to work today, Jesse," his wife begged. "I need you beside me today. They can get along without you at the mill. Please stay home."

"Got to, baby. Ain't got no choice. You know the old man'll fire me at the drop of a hat if I don't show up for work. Cain't afford to lose my job; we need the money."

With those words, Jesse kissed her on the forehead and turned the kerosene lantern down to a flicker. He patted her hand gently, and she grabbed his arm, gripping his wrist until her nails cut into the skin. Jesse shook his head and forced his arm away, saying "Now, now, baby, you got to let me go." His wife whimpered as he walked to the cot where Christina was sleeping. He stroked his daughter's forehead softly, taking care not to wake her. Moving to the crib, he stood for an instant gazing at the newborn infant, then shook his head sadly as he left the room.

Returning to the kitchen, he sat in a chair by the table. For a moment, his wife's mother eyed him contemptuously, and she opened her mouth as if to speak, her whole body shaking with rage. But she said nothing. She only grimaced and shrugged her shoulders, rolled her eyes upward, and walked back to her daughter's bedside.

Hollow-eyed and his brain throbbing, Jesse sat facing a window revealing an ever-brightening sky. He stared down at the floor with knotholes the size of silver dollars through which frigid winds of winter had entered the house. He gazed at shelves holding pathetic blackened pots in which his wife cooked, and the pile of chipped dimestore plates on which they ate. A picture of Jesus, hands outstretched, hung by the cupboard. He looked down at his own hands, callused and scarred, stinking of turpentine from the pine slabs he had carried for endless hours in the unbearable heat for an endless succession of days. Another such day—indeed, a lifetime of such days—loomed before him.

Jesse's head felt swollen, the night's events spinning through his brain, beyond his control like an unreal dream. What was he thinking when he left the mill yesterday? Why couldn't he have gone home to his wife and children? Was it worth the torment he felt now to have gone drinking with Rasty? And, for God's sake, how *could* he have slept with a Negro? Even going *down* on her? What kind of man was he? Not a decent one, for sure: a decent man—an honorable man—would have been home with his family, caring for them, seeing to their needs. Jesse shuddered and buried his face in his hands. Nothing about his life made sense. He was sick of himself, sick of living, sick of the struggle.

In an instant, Jesse realized what he had to do. He stood, unhooked a latch, and opened the cupboard. From the top shelf he took the thirty-eight caliber pistol his grandfather had given him for his tenth birthday. Placing the gun in his belt, he left the house and walked toward the sawmill. It was after five-thirty and other mill hands would arrive soon.

Walking at a surprisingly brisk pace, Jesse breathed deeply, letting the morning air provide an invigorating infusion of oxygen for his lungs. The bitter, pounding pain of his hangover lingered, and he still felt nauseous but his mind was clear. He reached the mill just minutes before his boss would arrive to check the boiler and to sound the whistle which would call the sawmill hands to work, and by which everyone on the eastern side of Shrewsbury Crossing marked the beginning of the day.

Jesse went directly to the sawdust pile standing twenty feet high behind the smoke stack of the mill. He noticed a patch of dogwoods blooming in the edge of the woods beyond. He glanced wistfully at a chinaberry tree where he and Erasmus had sat eating syrup and sausage during many noonday breaks. He saw that new seedlings had sprouted under the tree, but most seemed to be wilting and dying while three or four seemed capable of reaching up to the sunlight and surviving.

Then Jesse placed the barrel of the gun in the roof of his mouth, pulled the trigger, and blew a half-inch hole through the top of his skull. Fragments of bone and flesh—replications of his essential being—splattered in crimson drops on the sawdust. With a brutal finality, leaving no semblance of an explanation or apology, and with an emptiness that characterized his entire life, Jesse Wayne Rumpkin completed the final moment of his twenty-three years. With a short burst of gunpowder, Jesse had expurgated his guilt and despair, and in that instant, he had ended his unique role in the enigma of human life.

But Jesse had not failed in one respect: he had succeeded in achieving what living organisms are designed to achieve; a part of himself had been preserved—he had deposited his seed in vessels for the future. One was Christina Patricia Rumpkin, a daughter, born five years earlier; another was an unnamed son, born yesterday.

CHAPTER 2

A Prophet and a Dreamer

"If there arise among you a prophet,
or a dreamer of dreams…, thou
shalt not hearken unto the words of
that prophet, or dreamer…."
Deuteronomy, Ch. 13, v. 1-3.

Melissa Goodwin's water broke shortly after a February midnight in 1937. A bitterly cold wind—unusually cold for Shrewsbury Crossing, Georgia—whipped around and through the small frame house where she lay in bed. Remnants of coals in the fireplace emitted smoke but no heat or light. A kerosene lantern flickered on a chest of drawers near the fireplace and threw dancing shadows on the ceiling. Melissa drew blankets tightly around her neck as the first contractions set in, and she moaned softly but loudly enough to wake her older sister sleeping ten feet away on another bed.

"What's happenin', Sis?" Pink asked, sitting up. "You all right?"

"I think the baby's comin', Pink," Melissa said. "I'm feelin' pretty bad; I'm feelin'…."

"Is it the contractions? Are they startin'?"

In the pale light, Pink could not see it, but Melissa was sweating profusely. The fluid from her amniotic sac had soaked the lower half of her feather mattress, the wetness aggravating the deep chill of the unheated room.

Pink felt Melissa's forehead, then reached under the blanket and discovered the condition of the bed covers and mattress. "We got to get you some dry clothes and moved to the other bed," she said. "You'll freeze to death the way you are."

Melissa strained to sit up on the side of the bed. Pink pulled off her wet clothes and swabbed her with a dry towel. From the chest of drawers, Pink took a fresh nightgown and slipped it on her sister. Then, holding Melissa by the waist, Pink helped her across the room to the dry bed where Pink had been sleeping.

"Let me build the fire up," Pink said, "it's terribly cold in here."

"I ain't sure there's time," Melissa said, holding both hands on her swollen stomach. Pink leaned over the bed and patted her sister's forehead lightly with a cloth.

Melissa Goodwin and Pink Allday were more than blood kin: they were devoted friends. They had been constant companions all their lives, playing together as children, working in the fields side-by-side, and sharing their deepest feelings, hopes and dreams. They sang together in the church choir, Melissa, the alto, and Pink, the soprano. The women were bright: both had completed high school, and Pink had been the valedictorian of her class. And even though both had married young—in their teens—the sisters had been fortunate to marry good, God-fearing men. Melissa's husband, Jim Goodwin, was the hardware manager for a department store and sold and repaired radios on the side. Pink's husband, Ezekiel Allday, owned and operated the Shrewsbury Crossing cotton gin. In February of 1937, Melissa was twenty-nine and Pink thirty-one, and both women had been childless until now.

"Don't you reckon I better go fetch the doctor?" Pink asked. Melissa and her husband had not been able to afford a telephone.

"I believe so," Melissa said, "but I cain't stand for you to get out in this cold. Jim's gone in our car to Alabama, and you'll have to walk. And you got your own baby to worry about. You ain't in no condition…."

"Aw, pshaw, a little cold weather ain't gonna hurt me," Pink said. "'Sides, that's why I'm stayin' with you while Jim's away. My baby ain't due for months yet. I ain't hardly showin'."

"Dr. Willingham may not come in the middle of the night like this," Melissa said, "and he might not be at home…."

"Just hush, Melissa, hush. You worry too much. He'll come. You know he'll come," Pink said, patting her sister gently on the arm.

"But what if he won't?" Melissa was hysterical, and the pain in her abdomen was growing more intense.

"You know how I am, Sis, I ain't takin' 'no' for an answer," Pink said. "Dr. Willingham will come if he thinks you need him. Pshaw, I seen him callin' on sick folks in mud up to his knees. He's just like that." Pink was bringing the fire to life as she spoke; the kerosene-soaked kindling caught quickly and soon the pine logs began to blaze.

Sitting in a rocker near the fireplace, Pink pulled on her shoes over two pair of heavy woolen stockings. A thick sock cap covered her head. Standing, she put on a navy blue sailor's jacket her uncle had worn aboard a merchant ship in World War I. She tied a scarf around her neck, and said: "Now, don't you worry none, Melissa. I'll be back 'fore you know it with the doctor." She opened the door to the front stoop of the house, shutting it quickly as she left, stopping the blast of cold wind that tried to sweep in. Once outside, and even though Melissa couldn't hear, Pink whispered: "Pshaw, I'll be back with the doctor 'fore you know it," this time trying to persuade herself.

Melissa's house on the outskirts of Shrewsbury Crossing was slightly over a mile from the placid street lined with brick homes near the center of town where Dr. Charles Robert Willingham, his wife, and two children lived. As Pink made her way toward her destination, blustery cold wind pierced her clothing, blowing with such force that she slipped several times on patches of ice. She never fell, however, and the urgency she felt for her mission gave her added strength and quickened her pace. She carried no lantern, but a sliver of a moon and newly installed gaslights along the streets in Dr. Willingham's distant neighborhood were enough to help her find her way.

A half-hour later, nearly frozen, Pink stumbled up the steps to the doctor's porch, found the door and rapped lightly with her fist, too faintly to be heard by anyone within the house. Seeing the clapper, she took it and knocked loudly, shouting "Doctor, doctor!" as she did.

A light came on in the foyer. Pink could see the outline of a moving figure through the stained glass of the door, and suddenly the door opened. Wearing a felt robe and slippers, Dr. Willingham asked, "Who's there?"

"Oh, thank Jesus," Pink said, spitting out her words. "Doctor, thank goodness it's you. I was scared you wouldn't be home. Please, please come quick. My sister's baby's comin'. You know, my sister, Melissa. Her water broke 'bout an hour ago. Please hurry!"

"That you, Pink?" the doctor asked, squinting with his hand on his forehead. "I can hardly see."

"Yessir, it's me, Pink—Pink Allday." She had worked with Dr. Willingham several months earlier on a fund-raising drive to provide surgery for an orphaned child.

"Here, come in out of the cold," the doctor said. "Let me get dressed and I'll be right back."

The doctor soon returned fully dressed to the foyer where Pink waited, still shivering from the cold. Buttoning his coat, he reached for a black satchel under the coat rack by the door, placed a hand on Pink's back, and guided her through the door to the porch. "I hope she's gonna be all right," Pink fretted. "She's had an awful lot of trouble carryin' this child. Feelin' real bad when I left."

"Oh, she'll be fine," the doctor said. "Let's get in the car. Melissa lives over near the sawmill, doesn't she? Not far from the gin?" Before Pink could answer, he added: "Yeah, I know her street. We'll be there in a minute."

The doctor's 1936 Packard was parked in the driveway. As the couple seated themselves, Pink was struck by how cramped the doctor looked in the driver's seat. Even though the car was a large, four-door model, one of the newest and most luxurious in town, the doctor's massive, muscular frame—well over six feet—barely allowed him room to fit behind the wheel. He had strikingly large hands, long, bushy eyebrows, and thick, black hair that distinguished him physically from practically everyone in Shrewsbury Crossing. He could be spotted from a distance at church, at high school athletic events, or on the streets of the town. Most people recognized him on sight, and spoke to him almost reverently when meeting him on the street.

As he drove rapidly through the dark streets toward Melissa's house, Dr. Willingham asked: "Where is Melissa's husband tonight? Why didn't he come for me?"

"Well, he couldn't, you see," Pink said, "he had to go to Dothan to sell radios yesterday. Didn't want to go with Sis ready to deliver, but they needed the money and I promised I'd stay with her and all. He's supposed to be back tonight."

Jim Goodwin sold Zenith radios part-time to supplement his income, especially during the winter when things were slow at the department store. An Alabama state fair was being held just over the Georgia line in Dothan, and Jim had rented a booth back in October to display the latest models—a decision he had not realized at the time would conflict with his wife's last days of pregnancy.

With the headlights outlining the Goodwin's modest frame house, Dr. Willingham brought the car to a stop and cut off the engine. Slamming the car doors, Pink and the doctor walked quickly up the wooden steps and, in an instant, the doctor had crossed the room and stooped down by Melissa's bedside. He stroked her cheek gently with his huge hand. She trembled, moaning softly: "Oh, doctor, I'm so glad you're here. I'm hurtin' all over, please help me…."

"There, there now," Dr. Willingham said. "You're going to be fine."

The doctor turned to Pink and asked her to get linens. After listening to Melissa's heartbeat, he lifted the blanket and sheets and placed a stethoscope on her swollen stomach. He then examined the birth canal, swabbed away wetness, and replaced the bed clothes. Standing, he moved toward the fireplace, motioning Pink to follow.

"Is she gonna be all right?" Pink asked, eyes wide.

"Yes, I think so," the doctor said, hesitating. "There is more bleeding than I would like, though. We're going to have to watch it closely. Too much blood loss could complicate everything."

"Maybe we ought to try to get her to the clinic," Pink said.

"I think it'll be better to keep her here for now. You and I can handle things." Pink smiled faintly, proud to hear that the doctor was counting on her assistance.

Pink added wood to the fire as Melissa stirred. Dr. Willingham returned to the bedside and pulled a rocking chair close. "You know, Melissa, about all I can do right now is wait for you to do the work," he said, holding her hand and smiling. "I'll be timing the contractions and listening with the stethoscope to the baby's heartbeat, of course, but we have to let nature take its course. You understand that, don't you?" Melissa nodded her head weakly.

The labor was long and severe. The hours crept by, and the glow of daylight finally appeared through the window panes. The wind outside had subsided, and Pink's diligent stoking of the fire had brought the temperature of the room to an almost comfortable level. As the first rays of sunshine filtered in, Melissa sank into fitful periods of sleep. Dr. Willingham sat in the chair next to Melissa's bed, and Pink sat across the room near the fireplace. As time passed, the doctor and Pink took catnaps, but both woke quickly when Melissa stirred or moaned.

Shortly after eight a.m.—nearly eight hours after labor had begun—the doctor walked over to where Pink was dozing. Taking his car keys from his coat, he said: "Pink, I need to ask you to do something for me. Here, take my car and drive into town to the clinic."

"Gosh, Dr. Willingham," Pink protested, "I cain't drive your car. What if I was to wreck it or something?"

"Hush now," the doctor said, patting her gently on the shoulder. "You won't have an accident, but I want you to go to the office and tell my nurse to call all my patients who have telephones and cancel today's appointments. Tell her I need to stay here with Melissa, and that if there are any emergencies, she should come and let me know. I'll deal with them as best I can."

Pink did as the doctor asked and returned to the house within an hour. "How's she doin'?" she asked, as she stepped through the door.

"Better, I think," the doctor said. "The bleeding has slowed a good bit, but there is still some spotting. Unless my nurse comes for me with some extreme emergency, I intend to stay here so I can watch her. We're going to have to take this a step at a time and wait. It's about all we can do."

"Dr. Willingham," Pink said, seating herself in a rocker by the fire, "you must get terribly tired gettin' called out like this at all hours. You know, you bein' the only doctor in town and all. I bet there's times when you wish you hadn't been a doctor."

The doctor rose from Melissa's bedside and walked toward Pink. He propped an elbow on the chest of drawers and stood before Pink, his massive frame seeming to dwarf everything in the room. Then he smiled broadly and said: "Not really, Pink. I'll never regret becoming a doctor although I certainly get weary at times. But it all comes with the territory. When I entered medical school, I decided that no sacrifice would be too great if I could help other human beings. Fact is, I almost became a minister, but I don't think I'm very good at public speaking; it's something I intend to work on."

"Oh, Dr. Willingham, I don't agree," Pink said, firmly. "I heard you give the devotional one night in church and you just thrilled my heart with your message."

"You're too kind, Pink," the doctor said, blushing. "For some reason, I decided against the ministry but I came to believe that God wanted me to attend to people's physical needs, and maybe—just maybe—in the process He would let me do something for their spiritual welfare too. I like to think it works out that way. The way I see it, I'm sort of a missionary. If I can treat people's bodies, maybe their souls will benefit too. I guess that's my reward."

"Well, yore reward's gonna come a lot quicker'n you think if you don't quit haulin' outta bed in the middle of the night to help the sick," Pink said. "Everybody in town knows how hard you work, and your nurse told me just a while ago that you never stop. You just cain't keep goin' like you been doin' for the last five or six years."

"I realize I can't keep this up, Pink, and I don't plan to. Tell you what, I'll share something with you I haven't told many other people. I have three young doctors joining my practice next month. Imagine, *four* doctors in Shrewsbury Crossing! Can you believe it?" The doctor's face glowed with excitement.

Melissa stirred briefly, coughed, then drifted off to sleep again.

"How'd you ever talk three doctors to come to a dinky little place like this?" Pink asked. "Looks like they could make more money most anyplace else."

"They probably could, Pink. They probably could." The doctor paused. "But these are bright, young physicians, top of their class, and human beings are frequently driven by things other than money."

"Like what?" Pink asked, cocking her head.

"In the case of doctors, the opportunity to do research, to pioneer new medical advances, to gain prominence within the profession—the respect of other doctors. You know, I'm not boasting, but I've become fairly well-known in medical circles for the success I've had treating asthma. Patients seek me out from all around the area, and I've done some writing in the medical journals. Others have written about my work. Somebody even got carried away and labeled me a 'genius' in one of the periodicals. We all got a big laugh out of that at the clinic. In fact, my nurse put a sign on my desk that says: 'Quiet! Genius at Work.', however far that may be from the truth, these three young doctors have decided it might enhance their careers to spend a year or two in practice here. You know, feathers in their caps."

"That's just wonderful, Dr. Willingham," Pink exclaimed.

"This is just the beginning, Pink. You'll probably think I'm loco—lots of folks do—but I have a vision of making this little town a nationally recognized medical center. One that will attract the best, brightest physicians and research experts from around the country. I mean to make it happen. I'm renovating my offices now to make room for the new doctors. *Four* doctors in the Willingham Clinic! How's that sound?"

"Unbelievable, just plain unbelievable," Pink said. "But if anybody can do all that, you can. I bet you wind up with ten—maybe even a dozen—doctors 'fore you're through."

"I don't think there are any limits, Pink, no limits at all," the doctor said. "Very few people in this country realize how medical science—all kinds of science, in fact—is growing by leaps and bounds. If you can see far enough ahead, and if you've got the commitment and dedication, you can become a leader. And I aim to—no, I don't *aim* to—I *will* become a leader, recognized everywhere in the medical profession."

"You got some kinda' inner voice that tells you all this, don't you?" Pink asked.

"I don't mean to sound vain, Pink, but God has *chosen* me to do this work. He put me here in this place and time to do what I'm doing. I know it as sure as the sun rises every day."

"Doctor, tell me," Pink said, "what do you make of folks that says people come from monkeys? Ain't that the most foolish thing you ever heard? People like that must be atheists or infidels, don't you think?"

"They're certainly misguided," the doctor said. "I don't see how they can ignore the beauty and harmony of the natural world. It's all too magnificent to have just come into being on its own through some unconscious force. Fact is, Pink, I believe the Bible, and it says we're made in God's image."

"Right! Absolutely right," Pink said. "And God don't look like no monkey, does he?"

"I wouldn't think so," Dr. Willingham said, chuckling. "That makes me think of the story of the first grader who was busily drawing at his desk when his teacher stopped by. 'Johnny,' she said, 'what are you drawing?' 'A picture of God,' the boy answered, beaming proudly. The teacher was amused, but said: 'That's nice, Johnny, but you must realize that no one knows how God looks.' The boy responded with a smug grin: 'Well, they will when I get through with this picture.'"

"Oh, that's so cute," Pink said, laughing. "Where'd you hear that?" Melissa moaned from her bed. "Oh, my goodness," Pink said, "I'm makin' too much noise, ain't I? I'm gonna bother Melissa."

"Yes, we should both speak more softly, I guess," the doctor said. "I don't remember where I picked up that little story, but my point is that we human beings too often try to paint God in our own image, try to fit Him into a box where we think He belongs. I believe it's arrogant—perhaps even *blasphemous*—to confine the Almighty to human dimensions. The closest revelation of God, in my view, is through the Holy Book and Jesus Christ."

"That is so well *put*, Dr. Willingham," Pink said, tears welling up in her eyes.

"As for evolution," the doctor added, savoring the adulation he saw in Pink's face, "I have the feeling the Darwinians can't see the forest for the trees. Instead of digging around endlessly in fossil records, measuring skulls of long-dead apes, they would be better off focusing on the living world all around us—praising the mystical powers of the Creator by blessing His work and living our lives in His service. I've studied the human body in every detail, seen numerous autopsies, watched newborns take their first breaths. Something deep inside me says clearly—unequivocally—that it didn't all just happen through some process of natural selection. There had to be a designer, a 'watch-maker,' and I call that being 'God.'"

Pink listened in rapture to the doctor's words. She had heard him speak publicly a number of times, and—like many of the citizens of the small town—she was smitten with the handsome young doctor. But here he was talking directly to her, and his magnetic eloquence, all concentrated on Pink, was overwhelming. "You amaze me, Dr. Willingham," Pink said. "You have a wonderful gift of understanding. We're all so *blessed* that you came to us here in Shrewsbury Crossing."

❧ ❧ ❧

The hours passed slowly, but late that afternoon, Melissa's contractions became more frequent—about three minutes apart. Screaming with pain, Melissa squeezed the doctor's hand, her nails leaving indentations on his wrist. The doctor stroked her brow and listened for the baby's heartbeat. Shortly before six that afternoon, Melissa shrieked in anguish. Labor had continued for over seventeen hours, but moments later the baby was delivered.

Dr. Willingham stayed by Melissa's bedside for three more hours. Finally, with the mother and infant sleeping, he gave Pink parting instructions and left for home. Pink stood by the window and watched as he walked down the steps and got in his car.

Awakened by the slamming of the car door, Melissa called softly from the bed, "He's a fine baby, ain't he, Sis?"

Pink turned toward her and answered: "He shore is. *Shore* is. And a big youngun too, over nine pounds, the doctor said. What you gonna name him?"

"I ain't sure. Jim ought to be back soon and we can decide, but I think he's gonna want to call him 'Jeremiah.' That's Jim's favorite prophet, always quoting from that book of the Bible. Said several times he would favor that name if the baby was a boy."

"What about a middle name?"

"I know what I'd pick," Melissa said weakly, "and I think Jim'll go along. 'Willingham' would be my choice. That man's a saint, ain't he?"

"He shore is," Pink said, placing a piece of wood on the fire. "He just proved that last night, didn't he? Comin' out in the freezin' weather, and stayin' right with you all that time. Wouldn't leave 'til he knew you was all right. Ain't many doctors would do that. Lots of stars gonna be in that man's crown."

"Maybe that's what it will be," Melissa smiled broadly for the first time. "'Jeremiah *Willingham* Goodwin,' how's that sound?"

"Sounds like a preacher's name," Pink said. "Fact is, he might be a preacher someday, you reckon?"

"That's a nice thought," Melissa said. "Yeah, a preacher, his life dedicated to the Lord and the Lord's work. I kinda' like to think it could happen. Even a prophet maybe? Maybe he'll even be a prophet of sorts?"

CHAPTER 3

King of the Sawdust Mountain

"All kings is mostly rapscallions."
Mark Twain, *The Adventures of Huckleberry Finn*

The afternoon commenced—as lazy, summer afternoons frequently did—with a rendezvous in Aunt Pink's kitchen. Crouching behind a row of towering camellias, Jeremiah tiptoed around the back of the house to the stoop leading into the kitchen and caught Ethan, sitting at a table with his back to the window, eating chocolate cake and drinking milk.

"Hands up! Gotcha' covered!" Jeremiah yelled, pointing his finger at Ethan, and jumping with a loud thump through the doorway.

"Pshaw! You ain't skerred me none. I seen you comin'," Ethan said, even though he had not seen his cousin coming. Jerking his head around instinctively when Jeremiah yelled, he had spilled a forkful of cake on the kitchen floor. "I was expectin' you," he said, regaining his composure. "C'mon in and set down. Want some cake?"

In June of 1945, Jeremiah Willingham Goodwin was eight years old—eight years and four months, to be more precise. Jeremiah was the only child of Jim and Melissa Goodwin, hard-working, church-going people immersed in religious and ethical beliefs of white Southern Baptists. Jeremiah's father, now in his late thirties, managed the hardware section of the town's largest department store, and he sold and repaired radios on the side to supplement the family's income. Even though he worked long hours, seven days a week, Jim Goodwin made time for his son, especially after supper or on Sunday afternoons when they would sit together and discuss world events; in particular, Jeremiah would listen spellbound as his father described the wars raging in Europe and the Pacific.

During the previous summer, the summer of 1944, a transforming event had occurred in Jeremiah's life when his father took a part-time job as a radio announcer at a station in Ludlow, twenty miles away. Each night, the boy would stay glued to the small Zenith radio, frequently crackling with static and interference from thunderstorms, and listen to his father's five-minute newscasts, which were aired on the hour and half-hour until the station's sign-off at 10:00 p.m. During those nights, Jeremiah followed closely his father's accounts of such matters as the Normandy Invasion, the assassination attempt on Hitler, and the liberation of Paris. One of his father's newscasts had been recorded by the station manager, and the 78 rpm record was brought home where Jeremiah replayed it so often that it finally wore out, but not before Jeremiah had memorized its contents. Anytime he could find an audience, he would proudly recite his father's words:

> "Adolph Hitler, in a speech broadcast throughout Europe today, left no doubt that German homefront morale is sagging badly. At first he sounded tired and old, but he gradually warmed up to his old themes of castigating democracy and the Jews. He warned that Allied air raids were having no effect on German resistence, and that it was even ridiculous to think that Finland would make peace…."

Jeremiah adored that broadcast: in his mind, his father's delivery imbued the report with importance and he had looked up every word he didn't understand: words like "castigating," "morale," and "resistence." He was puzzled that Hitler seemed to hate democracy and the Jews, but his father explained that the dictator was a madman and that's why the war had to be fought in the first place. But the fact remained that Jim Goodwin's radio announcing served only to intensify the unbounded curiosity with which Jeremiah viewed the world.

Even so, the boy was inwardly shy and insecure and he wanted, more than anything else, to be accepted and respected by his peers—the white cousins and the black friend with whom he romped and played in the woods and fields on the outskirts of Shrewsbury Crossing. Untainted at this early stage of life with cynicism or despair, and as World War II drew to a close during the summer of 1945, Jeremiah Goodwin was a fascinated observer of people around him. His first cousin, Ethan Allday, who sat eating cake this June afternoon at Aunt Pink's kitchen table, was one of those people.

As he sat down, Jeremiah gave Ethan an affectionate jab on the shoulder. "What you wanna do this afternoon?" Jeremiah asked, his lips smeared with crumbs and chocolate frosting. "Alex is comin' too. Where's Aunt Pink? Why don't we do somethin'?"

Alex was the two boys' distant, older cousin. Jeremiah and Ethan frequently roamed the woods and fields by themselves, but having Alex join them was rare and special: he invariably brought an element of excitement to their games.

"Mama's gone to get groc'ries," Ethan answered, "and I'm glad Alex is comin', ain't you? What you reckon he'll wanna do?"

"Well," Jeremiah said pensively, cupping his chin in his hand, "I reckon we could go dig some worms and head for the creek. Want to? I bet the red-eyes' ll bite this afternoon! Or, tell you what, we could walk the banks and do some tight-line fishin' for war-mouth perch. Want to, Ethan? Me and my daddy does that all the time. It's fun."

"Doubt we got enough time, and 'sides, the worm-diggin' warn't too good last time I tried. I think the niggers dug 'em all up."

"Guess you're right," Jeremiah responded, "and Alex ain't into fishin' too much no way. Says it bores him." "I know," Jeremiah went on, eyes wide, "we could play Japs and Germans!"

"Aw, we done whipped the Germans," Ethan said, "Ain't gonna be no fun in that. They say ole' Hitler's dead. Good riddance, ain't it?"

"Yeah, shore is, but we still gotta beat the Japs," Jeremiah said.

"We'll lick them pretty quick too." Ethan took a big swallow of milk.

"I ain't too shore we will," Jeremiah said. "They fight crazy. Fly them suicide planes into boats and all that. I'm thinkin' it's gonna be a long time before we whip 'em."

"Might be," Ethan said, "but I still ain't wantin' to play Japs today, and 'sides, you and Alex ain't never willin' to be a Jap. Alex always winds up makin' me be one."

Ethan Allday would have his eighth birthday in early July. Inseparable friends now, Ethan and Jeremiah had been thrown together since they were toddlers. Their mothers—Melissa Goodwin and Pink Allday—were sisters and spent much of their time with each other, shopping, sewing and cooking—leaving their two boys free to play in the nearby woods on the outskirts of town. Alike in many ways, Ethan and Jeremiah were also quite different: Ethan was unusually quiet and methodical whereas Jeremiah was frequently compulsive. Ethan never spoke without giving considerable thought to what he was about to say, and he never became hurried. The epitome of a boy growing up in the rural South of the 1940's, Ethan was tousle-headed, buck-toothed, with freckles scattered indiscriminately over his body. Yet any of Ethan's traits and physical characteristics that might arguably have been considered imperfections were themselves so perfectly integrated with his personality that they only reinforced the sense of balance and equilibrium that others—especially Jeremiah—saw in him.

"I know what," Jeremiah said, slapping his hand on the table. "Why don't we go play around the sawmill? Alex'll love that. You know how he likes to mess around the sawdust pile on Saturday when there ain't nobody gonna know we're down there, with the mill shut down and all. Alex'll wanna do that, I bet."

"Yeah, you little turds, I heard one of you say my name. You talkin' about me?" Alexander Wayne Rumpkin loomed in the kitchen doorway. "Aw right, now, which one of you was it?"

Three years older and nearly a foot taller than the other boys, Alex was their distant cousin—a third or fourth cousin, Jeremiah could never remember which—although his mother had outlined Alex's branch of the family tree many times. Even though he was malnourished and emaciated, Alex had ruddy good looks, a winning smile, and a gift of gab. He had skin of unblemished ivory which tanned perfectly in the Georgia sun. Generally well-proportioned, his worst physical features were a neck that did not provide adequate separation between his head and his body; narrow, slanted eyes; and a nasal twang in his voice caused by adenoids that should have been surgically removed when he was a baby.

Alex had a natural, ready-made following in Jeremiah and Ethan. The age and height difference accounted for some of his influence, but he was also a born leader. The younger boys paid rapt attention when he spoke, and they marveled that he could be so confident about life, especially considering the rather bad cards he had been dealt. His father had died the day after his birth and his mother had struggled to survive by taking in washing and doing house cleaning. Also, Jeremiah and Ethan had overheard gossip—stories they didn't quite understand—that Alex's mother was a sinful woman, entertaining men at night. At times, the younger boys felt sorry for Alex, but he never appeared to feel sorry for himself: he was cocky, boastful, and sometimes arrogant, seldom indicating that he was worried about anything.

"We was just sayin' how you like to mess around the sawmill on Saturday, when the mill's shut down." Jeremiah said, shifting his eyes toward Ethan. "You wanna go down there and play some now?"

"Maybe," Alex said, "Just maybe I might. I'll think it over, but right now I want some of this cake and milk. If the mood hits me right, we'll go down to the mill. I'll let y'all know when I'm ready. Any problem with that, boys?"

"Alex! Ethan! Lookit me. I'm king of the mountain," Jeremiah shouted from the summit of the pile of wood shavings and sawdust. He had run to the top of the sawdust pile while Alex and Ethan were preoccupied, attempting to blow the steam whistle on the sawmill boiler—a futile effort since the boiler had cooled overnight. Looking down from the top of the pile, hands on his hips, Jeremiah taunted the other boys. "Did y'all hear me? I'm *king* of the mountain," he repeated.

For many years—since the early thirties—the sawdust pile had been growing to its present height of over thirty-five feet as shavings from the planer, a saw over three feet in diameter, were sucked up and blown through a large duct to an area sixty yards away. In the early forties, the sawmill's operations had intensified, culminating with a seven-day-a-week operation in 1944 and through the spring of 1945. Only during the last two months, a slight drop-off in demand for lumber from the U. S. war machine had led to a shutdown of the mill on weekends.

Shrewsbury Crossing, Georgia, was like thousands of towns across America that formed the matrix of the massive war effort. Settled by English immigrants in the 1840's and named for the place of their origins—Shrewsbury, England—the small town was located several miles north of the Florida line, in a hot, steamy climate that caused long-needle pines to thrive. While dispatching dozens of its young men to fight and sometimes die in alien places like Okinawa, Corregidor, Palermo, and Bastogne, the town and the surrounding area also supplied the materials of war: food and produce, chemicals, textiles and lumber from its sawmill. While the demons of war killed and maimed thousands, they also had the paradoxical effect of transforming the economy of the sleepy little town and enriching a number of its citizens. One such individual was Erasmus Bonobo, known locally as 'Rasty,' a former sawmill laborer who had scraped together enough money in 1938 to buy the mill. Erasmus had lost two brothers in the war: a B-29 pilot over France and a Marine in Bataan, but he now owned a sawmill which produced lumber in ever-increasing quantities as demand and prices soared because of the war.

On this Saturday afternoon in June of 1945, the idle sawmill and the huge pile of sawdust was the setting for the game playing of Jeremiah, Ethan and Alex, who were oblivious to the rolling thunder of distant battles and the fact that thousands of their species were at that very moment reenacting ancient rituals of domination and death. The three boys were unconcerned about raising battleflags on meaningless peaks in nameless islands of the South Pacific. Their only concern this Saturday was settling the dispute over who would be king of this particular sawdust mountain.

"I'm comin' up there and bust yore ass, you little turd," Alex yelled as he climbed toward Jeremiah. Ethan followed from a distance.

"I'm gonna throw y'all *both* off," Ethan yelled. The threat drew derisive laughter from the other boys, since Ethan's fifty pound body was no match for either of his companions. It was not a matter of courage: Ethan often weighed into fights with boys twice his size, but he just didn't have the muscle to push Jeremiah off the top of the pile, not to mention the much bigger Alex.

A mismatch also existed between Jeremiah and Alex. Even though he was skinny and seldom ate properly, causing his ribs to stand out like limbs of a tree on his torso, Alex was fifteen pounds heavier than Jeremiah and considerably stronger. The boys had engaged in the ritual many times before: even if one of the younger boys got to the top of the pile first, Alex would quickly reach the summit and begin a shoving and pushing match that would end with Jeremiah or Ethan being thrown off, usually only a few feet to a ledge of shavings recently deposited from the end of the duct. Then, with Alex's status as king settled, the boys would take turns jumping off the top to the soft shavings below.

But this afternoon, the shavings were not soft: a heavy rain had fallen the night before, packing the sawdust down tightly. When Alex finally shoved Jeremiah off, the ten-foot fall to the ledge below bruised Jeremiah badly. Unable to hide tears streaming down his cheeks, Jeremiah yelled: "Alex, you ass-hole! I'm gonna tell yore mama on you. You coulda broke my neck. You dirty asshole!"

"Who you callin' a asshole, you little turd?"

"You. That's who." Jeremiah sobbed.

"Go ahead, crybaby, tell my mama. She thinks you're a sissy. She's gonna know you're one now. 'Sides, I'll whip yore ass if you tell on me."

Jeremiah continued to cry as Ethan came down to check on the injuries. "You gonna be all right, Jeremiah?" Ethan asked.

"I'm gonna be OK," Jeremiah said, rubbing his side. "Alex just makes me mad, that's all, thinkin' he can shove me and you around 'cause he's older'n us."

"Well, you ought not to get Alex stirred up," Ethan whispered, "yellin' like you did about bein' king of the mountain. You know that makes him fightin' mad and he can be a mean rascal when he's mad. You get him pissed off when you talk like that."

Alex came sliding down the pile to the place where Jeremiah lay, still sobbing. Placing a foot on Jeremiah's neck, he said: "Now, who you callin' a asshole, you little turd? You're lettin' yore mouth overload yore butt, you know that?"

"Ouch, you're hurtin' my neck," Jeremiah squealed. "Move yore durn foot, Alex."

Alex pressed his foot down harder. "You know what you are, Jeremiah? You're a tumblebug. You know what a tumblebug does? It pushes little balls of shit—cow shit, dog shit, it don't matter—it pushes balls of turd around on the ground, coating 'em with dirt off the road. That's what you are, Jeremiah, a damn turd-pusher."

A shadowy figure suddenly flashed through an open spot between the sawdust pile and a cluster of chinaberry trees behind it. Alex continued to stand with his foot on Jeremiah's neck, his back to the source of the movement. Ethan alone saw the runner emerge from the shade. With a rush of footsteps, Beagle came up rapidly from Alex's rear. With a flying leap, Beagle tackled Alex, pushing him away from Jeremiah and pinning him down on the sawdust. Alex squirmed, attempting to break Beagle's hold, but it was no use: Beagle held Alex firmly, grinding his head and arms into the shavings, and said: "You give? Say you give, Alex, and I'll let you up."

"You black bastard!" Alex screamed. "You better let go of me. Yore ass is gonna be mincemeat when I'm through with you, you ratty nigger!"

Alex finally managed to squirm loose and break Beagle's grasp. Scrambling to his feet, he locked arms and legs with Beagle, both boys trying to throw the other to the sawdust, but it was a standoff. "You give, Beagle?" Alex yelled, gasping for breath.

"Naw, I ain't givin'," Beagle said. "You gonna give 'fore I do. You oughta be 'shamed, Alex, pickin' on these boys just 'cause they's littler. You needs straight'nin' out."

Beagle Williams lived in the Negro section of Shrewsbury Crossing one mile from the sawmill. Raised by his grandmother, Bootsie Williams, a maid in the home of Dr. Charles Robert Willingham, Beagle had grown up with the three white boys. They had all spent many lazy afternoons playing together. Beagle was eleven years old, the same age as Alex, but he was taller, more muscular, more athletic than any of the boys. A handsome boy with high cheekbones and finely chiseled features, he moved with grace and poise, and with a proud, distinguished bearing. He was every bit a physical match for Alex.

"You damn nigger!" Alex screeched. "Who the hell you think you are—fuckin' with me like this?" They let go of each other and backed away.

"Who you callin' a nigger, you pile of shit?"

His face red with anger, veins standing out on his neck, Alex shouted: "You, you son-of-a-bitch, you're a damn nigger and I'll wipe yore black ass all over this sawmill. If I cain't do it by myself, I know some white boys that'll help me. They don't put up with uppity niggers any more'n I do."

"I might be colored," Beagle said, "but yore daddy kilt hisself—right here on this spot 'cause he couldn't handle the world no more."

"That ain't so, nigger!" Alex's voice broke. "My daddy was kilt by a gang of niggers. Ambushed him without warnin', my mama says. Daddy, he put up a fierce struggle before they held him down and shot him. Black cowards, they was. All niggers is cowards., you ain't nothin' but a bastard. You don't even know where yore mama and daddy is. They run off, left you and yore sister to be raised by yore granny. You ain't nothin' but a sorry, good-for-nothin' nigger, Beagle. You ain't shit!"

Beagle's eyes welled up with tears. Shaking a fist defiantly toward Alex, he said: "You're gonna pay for yore meanness some day, Alex. They'll be a reckonin' some day and you're gonna pay." Beagle then turned and ran up the road toward home.

"Run, nigger, run!" Alex yelled. "I knowed you'd run."

"You oughtn't talk to Beagle like that, Alex," Ethan said. "He's got feelin's too."

"Shit, niggers ain't got no feelin's, that's why they's niggers. And he needs to learn his place." Alex brushed the sawdust from his clothes. "He ain't got no business tryin' to rassle a white boy."

"Beagle's got a good heart," Jeremiah said. "He cain't help it he was born colored, and he's always been our friend—me and Ethan's and yours too. On the pile just then he was just takin' up for me. Didn't mean nothin' 'gainst you."

"You boys ain't old enough yet to know that darkies and whites ain't supposed to mix. They's signs everywhere sayin' 'whites only'—you know, in eatin' places and on water faucets and the like. When niggers try to mingle with whites, they ain't nothin' but trouble, and I ain't shore we oughta let Beagle play with us no more. I been thinkin' 'bout it, and maybe he just oughta play with his own kind. I bet that nigger won't sass me none from now on."

"Durn, Alex," Jeremiah said, shaking his head. "Sometimes you just go way too far. You push folks too much. You gotta learn they's limits. People's got limits, Alex, everybody has. Limits you gotta watch for."

"I don't need no fuckin' sermon from you, Jeremiah, you little turd. You want me to step on yore neck again?"

Jeremiah's lips trembled. Instantly, Alex's scowl disappeared as he smiled and gently touched Jeremiah on the shoulder. "I'm sorry I hurt you while ago, Jeremiah," he said, "and please don't say nothin' to Mama. She's got enough to worry her already. Let's just let it ride, OK?" Alex extended his hand to Jeremiah, who was still trembling from the fight. He paused for a moment, then grinned, and accepted Alex's hand with a shake.

This was not the first occasion when Jeremiah and Ethan had seen an instantaneous transformation of Alex's personality after a display of temper. One such episode had occurred the previous summer when the boys caught a baby squirrel stuck in a wire fence on the edge of a field. Alex had taken a piece of bailing wire from the fence and forced the end of the wire through the animal's neck. Holding the creature with the wire, he had then struck a match, setting the squirrel afire while it screeched and slashed at the air.

Alex had studied the faces of the two younger boys during the torture. As they winced and grimaced, his eyes had narrowed into tight slits. He had then taken his pocket knife and cut out the heart of the squirming animal. Smearing the squirrel's blood on a plank, he told the boys, stunned by their own revulsion, that he had not wanted to kill the animal but that sometimes it was necessary to do such things just to prove that he had what it took to do them.

Then Alex had insisted that they give the squirrel a funeral—'a decent burial,' he had called it. Digging a shallow trench, he had laid the animal lengthwise, covered it with dirt, and placed the blood-stained plank in the ground as a headstone. He then had given a long, rambling prayer, asking that the creature be admitted to heaven, as the boys bowed their heads obediently.

Jeremiah and Ethan had discussed the incident many times during the intervening months, and they confessed to each other their bewilderment over Alex's claim that the killing was necessary. But, they also agreed, Alex had seemed sure of what he was saying, so he must have been right.

❧ ❧ ❧

The sun had moved low over the horizon, filtered now by needles from pine trees and leaves from pecan trees on the rim of the sawmill. A gentle breeze had picked up, the heat and humidity abating as nightfall approached. But gnats still swarmed around the boys' faces intermittently, the boys fighting them off by swiping their hands in the air and directing bursts of wind upward from their mouths by cupping their lower lips outward. The whine of mosquitoes joined the chorus of late afternoon sounds from mockingbirds and crickets, with the occasional barking of dogs in the distance.

The three boys sat on the grass near the sawdust pile. Weary from the afternoon's play, Jeremiah lay back, a twig between his teeth, his eyes gazing into the purple and gold hues of clouds floating lazily overhead. A blue jay's high-pitched squawk pierced the cacophony from the woods. In spite of the fight between Alex and Beagle, the afternoon had become too peaceful for Jeremiah to worry about anything. There was a special security from the familiarity of it all: sharing time with his best friends, savoring the coolness of the late afternoon air, and enjoying the well-known odors from the sawmill and woods. There was also the pleasant aroma of honeysuckle mingling with turpentine and smoke from woodstoves of tenements near the mill where supper was being prepared. A quarter moon hung in the eastern sky.

Jeremiah ended the lull in conversation. "Say, Alex, I can see the moon and it's still daylight. Ain't it strange that you can see the moon sometimes when it's day and sometimes you cain't?"

"I've been told it means you're beatin' yore meat too much. They say you'll go blind if you keep doin' it," Alex said with a grin.

"I don't beat my meat," Jeremiah said. "'Sides, you and Ethan see it too, don't you, and that means y'all beat yore meat too." The illogic of Jeremiah's denial coupled with his allegations about the other boys passed unnoticed.

"I don't need to jack my own dick," Alex said. "I get all the pussy a man could want."

"What's it mean to beat yore meat?" Ethan asked.

"You little turd, you don't even know what a penis is, do you?" Alex said.

"Naw, don't reckon I do," Ethan answered. Jeremiah giggled.

"Well, here, unbutton yore britches," Alex commanded, leaning toward Ethan.

Ethan hesitated, then did as Alex said. Pealing back the folds of the boy's pants, Alex pulled Ethan's penis out, studied it for a moment, then thumped the head vigorously with his middle finger.

"Ouch! Quit, Alex!" Ethan screamed, jerking away from Alex and putting both hands over his crotch. "That hurts!"

"Good," Alex said, "See, I done you a favor. That'll help you remember to keep yore pants buttoned. Might keep you from messin' with some gal someday and makin' a baby."

Jeremiah watched and listened intently to the exchange. "What makes yore peter get hard?" he asked Alex.

It was clear to Jeremiah that he knew more than Ethan about sex, but there were still many things that he didn't understand. Topping the list was masturbation. He had only recently—a few weeks after his eighth birthday—discovered the excruciating pleasure of stroking his penis, and he was already addicted to the habit. Unfortunately, he had also concluded, with a strong degree of certainty, that the act was a mortal sin—a conviction instilled in him through the teachings of his parents and the sermons he heard from the pulpit. He recalled no explicit references to the act, but it seemed that everything joyful, or related to pleasure and the flesh, was to be avoided at all cost. In spite of his strong religious beliefs, however, he didn't seem able to avoid erections, no matter how hard he tried.

Sometimes, late at night, Jeremiah would lie beneath the quilt and promise himself that he would never masturbate again. He became so desperate that he made pacts with God that if he ever did it again, he would voluntarily suffer the eternal hellfire. His theory was that with such an awful punishment hanging over his head, he would surely be dissuaded from repeating the sin, but it was no use: he simply could not keep his end of the bargain. After numerous failed attempts, he had decided to stop offering the deal to God; and sometimes cowering in his bed at night, he prayed with all his might that God was not the kind of deity to hold a foolish, weak-willed eight-year-old boy to such a bad arrangement.

"What makes a dick hard?" Alex repeated Jeremiah's question. "Well, I ain't never told many folks about this, but I got a notion that it's caused by radio waves."

"Radio waves?" Jeremiah asked.

"Yeah, radio waves," Alex said, scratching his ear. "Y'all know radio waves are all mixed up in the air. They's everywhere, all around us, seepin' into our brains and skin. And some of 'em have women's voices in 'em. I believe that the waves with women talkin' gets into our bodies and makes our dicks get hard."

"Durn!" Jeremiah exclaimed, "I doubt that, Alex; you're full of bull!"

"OK, smart ass!" Alex said. "Let's hear somethin' that makes better sense from you."

The challenge stumped Jeremiah. What better explanation could there be? Alex seemed pretty sure of what he was saying, Jeremiah thought, and yes, maybe it was radio waves. Maybe that's why he had erections at all hours, day or night. It wasn't just when he looked at those sunbathing magazines his father hid in the workshop, or when he viewed the sagging breasts of Polynesian women in *National Geographic.* Even when he found the strength to avoid such temptations, erections still occurred and, if Alex had it right, it was no wonder he kept losing the battle against masturbation. How could he keep a bargain with God when he was being incessantly bombarded with women's voices from radio waves?

"Alex, how'd you come up with that notion 'bout radio waves?" Ethan asked.

"Well, boys, I do a lot of thinkin'. Fact is, my mind's workin' all the time," Alex said. "It's always cuttin' through stuff just like that big planer saw cuts through logs. I know y'all ain't gonna believe it, but I'm probably the smartest person alive. Whole world's gonna know it someday, too." The boys listened raptly as Alex spoke.

"You see," he went on, "it really don't matter what folks thinks of you. What matters is yore opinion of yoreself. Folks can snicker and make fun of yore upbringin'—yore clothes, yore family, and all that—but people are really just dumb butts. They whisper, talk about me—my family, my mama, my sister, the way my daddy died—but they don't give a shit about me, and they don't really know nothin'. They's just shit-heads! Clothes and upbringin' don't matter none. What I think 'bout my own self is what counts, and everybody's gonna find out how smart I am someday."

"What're you gonna do? What you gonna be?" Ethan asked, his eyes wide.

"Well, that's the thing," Alex said, "I ain't really decided yet, and it really don't matter. Whatever I decide on, I'm gonna be better at it than anybody can imagine. Who knows! I might even be a preacher. You know Rasty? Owns the sawmill and was my daddy's best friend. Well, Rasty says that Billy Sunday's radio voice makes more gals cream in their britches than Clark Gable does in the picture show."

Ethan and Jeremiah looked at each other, dumbfounded. Then Alex went on: "But then, shit! I might even be a bank robber like ole Dillinger was. Everybody loves big-time bank robbers. You know, it's a shame Dillinger got killed. They say it was a woman turned him in at that picture show in Chicago. You cain't trust a fuckin' woman, y'all know that?"

"Goodness, Alex," Jeremiah said, "they's a world of difference bein' a preacher and a bank robber."

"Not really," Alex replied, "ain't much difference at all. They both take folks' money. Preachers just do it when they's smilin', and they's frownin' and scared when a robber takes it, but the money gets took just the same. Either way, folks get fucked, don't they?"

"Damn, Alex, sounds like you ain't got no respect for religion," Jeremiah said. "You could wind up in hell talkin' that way 'bout men of God. Ain't you skerred of losin' yore soul?"

"Aw, quit worryin', Jeremiah, you always frettin' 'bout stuff too much." Alex stood up to leave. "I'm just as religious as anybody. Y'all know I been saved, washed in the blood of the Lamb and all that. Been baptized too, down in the wash hole with the preacher and everybody lookin' on. Ain't never done nothin' to get me in trouble with the Almighty, and never will! Hell, I was just shittin' you boys about preachers bein' like bank robbers."

Jeremiah and Ethan stared at each other, mouths ajar, and then back at Alex. As he walked away, he said: "And all that mess about radio waves—I made all that up too. God, you boys'll believe *anything*."

CHAPTER 4

Wilma the Wench

"Bernadine: Thou hast committed...
Barabas: Fornication? But that was in
another country; and besides, the
wench is dead."
Christopher Marlowe, *The Jew of Malta*

Pink stood with one leg propped against the front fender on the driver's side of the '39 Chevrolet, her purse dangling from the straps over her left wrist, her right hand holding tightly to the car keys. Melissa opened the passenger-side door and seated herself as Pink barked orders to Ethan and Jeremiah through the wire screen of the back porch. Both women were slightly overweight, Melissa more than Pink, but the extra bulk in the sisters' torsos served only to reinforce their authority, already formidable, in the minds of their two boys. Each mother was fully authorized by the other to mete out any discipline required, and when it came to using a belt or a peach tree switch, the aunt-nephew relationship did not mitigate—even slightly—the severity of the blows. Pink and Melissa consistently assumed that each boy's waywardness struck a perfect balance with the other's, so no protest was ever allowed from either boy as to who got the other into what, and each always received precisely the same beating.

"Now, y'all behave this afternoon," Pink said, almost shouting. "Lissie and me's goin' over to Ludlow a little while, so y'all don't even think about gettin' into any mischief while we're gone. Wilma's gonna be here soon, and y'all mind her, you hear?"

"Yes, ma'am, Aunt Pink," Jeremiah said. Ethan added, "We'll be good, Mama."

From their chairs at the kitchen table, the boys heard the car doors slam and the engine grind slowly until it sputtered to life. Ethan turned back to the conversation: "Now, Jeremiah, what was it you was sayin' about bombin' the Japs?"

"You ain't gonna believe it, Ethan," Jeremiah said. "One bomb was dropped and killed *mill*-yuns of 'em at some place called 'Hero-shimmy' or something like that. I mean, it wiped 'em all out, just one bomb. *Just one bomb*! Can you imagine that?"

"Pshaw! I ain't gonna believe something like that. Ain't no single bomb big enough to wipe out a whole town," Ethan pursed his lips and frowned.

"I swear, it happened," Jeremiah insisted. "I heard the President talkin' about it on the radio last night. He said it was a top secret project, lots of scientists workin' on it out in the desert in Texas or somewhere, made it out of radioactives, he said."

"Well, I ain't sure I believe it, even if the President says it," Ethan said. "You know how people will lie, like Alex admitted he did that time about radio waves."

"This wasn't Alex, Ethan, this was the President of *America*, for gosh sakes, and it was his voice too. I've heard him on the radio before, and he said that brave American pilots flew over that Jap city and dropped the bomb. It was a 'atom' bomb, he said, and it did kill *mill*-yuns of Japs, didn't leave nothin' standin' in that town, tore up everything for miles around."

"Why'd we do it?" Ethan asked, somberly.

"To end the war, stupid," Jeremiah snapped. "One more bombin' like that and they ain't gonna be no Japs left. President Truman said usin' the bomb would save lots of American boys' lives and 'hasten'—yeah, that's the word that he used, '*hasten*'—the end of the war now that we beat the Germans. 'Sides, the Japs deserved it for the dirty stunt they pulled on us—you know, sneakin' up and killin' all them Americans at Pearl Harbor. You ought to be proud for lickin' them Japs, Ethan, *proud* to be American."

"I *am* proud," Ethan protested, "but I get sad thinkin' about killin' all them Japs, and I ain't sure we ought to be droppin' some kind of 'amo-tizer' bomb."

"It's 'atom,' Ethan; it was a '*atom*' bomb," Jeremiah said with disgust.

"Jeremiah, was any kids killed by that bomb, you reckon?"

"Naw, course not," Jeremiah answered. "What I'm figurin' is that the Americans flew over and dropped leaflets tellin' the Japs to get all the kids out of town—that it was gonna rain down fire. That's probably what happened."

It was August 8, 1945. A nuclear device had been delivered to Hiroshima, Japan, two days earlier, vaporizing 80,000 people. Another bomb would fall on Nagasaki the next day, killing 40,000 more. As two eight-year-old boys reflected on world events in Shrewsbury Crossing, Georgia, the hot, sultry dog days of summer were at their peak It would be a good day to go to the wash-hole.

"You reckon them Japs felt anything when that bomb went off, Jeremiah?"

"I doubt it. Them newsreels in the picture show pretty much makes it plain that Japs ain't like us—don't have much feeling. Sorta' like that squirrel Alex killed—when he jammed the wire through the neck and burned it. You know, he says that the squirrel didn't feel nothin'."

Ethan took a final swallow of milk and leaned back in his chair, pulling the front two chair legs off the floor. He nodded, remembering vividly the episode with the squirrel, but added: "Yeah, I heard him say that, but that squirrel was screechin' and hollerin', and ain't nobody gonna make me believe that he didn't feel no pain—not even Alex."

"Ethan, the Japs ain't felt no pain 'cause that bomb blew 'em to smithereens in a split second. They ain't felt nothin', so it was a good thing we done—you know, better than killin' them with guns and flame-throwers. Japs had to be killed and we done it the right way. Like Alex said about the squirrel, he didn't want to do it but it had to be done."

"I never understood that, Jeremiah, what'd he mean?"

"I ain't real sure, but I do know that when it comes to Japs, they had to be killed. Besides, they ain't like us, with them slanty-eyes and yeller skin and such, just like niggers ain't like us."

Wilma walked through the kitchen door just as Jeremiah blurted out the last sentence. "What you mean, boy?" she said, "I ain't got no slanty-eyes and yeller skin like Japs. You callin' me a Jap? What's you…."

"Naw, I didn't mean that," Jeremiah said, embarrassed. "I just meant that everybody's different: white folks, coloreds, Japs, that's all."

Wilma cleared her throat with a "hurrumph," and poured herself a glass of milk. "You two done ate all the cake?" she asked, furrowing her brow.

Wilma, almost fifteen, was Beagle's sister, already showing the swelling breasts, rounding hips and buttocks that sometimes appear with incipient womanhood. Jeremiah's and Ethan's mothers would sometimes ask Wilma to watch over the boys while the mothers were away. They trusted the girl because she had been "raised right" by Bootsie Williams, her grandmother. Bootsie had worked as a maid for many white families in Shrewsbury Crossing, including Melissa's and Pink's. With an impeccable reputation, she was now employed as the chief housekeeper in the home of Dr. Charles Robert Willingham, the town's leading citizen and the founder of the Willingham Clinic.

"Wilma, let's go to the woods and play," Ethan said. "You know, maybe look for scuppernongs. Want to, Jeremiah?"

"Suits me fine," Jeremiah said, "but Aunt Pink said not to leave the house."

"That's what she told me too," Wilma said, shaking her head, "and I ain't about to get no butt-blisterin' from Miss Pink on account of you two, nosiree, I shore ain't."

"Shoot!" Ethan said. "Mama and Aunt Lissie'll be gone all afternoon and we'll be sittin' here with nothin' to do. We can go to the woods and they ain't never gonna know it."

"Ethan's right about that, Wilma," Jeremiah agreed, "and we can be back before they get back. Ain't no harm in that."

"I ain't givin' a hoot about none of that," Wilma shook her finger toward Jeremiah. "We ain't budgin' from this house 'til yore mamas get back."

A relentless debate with Wilma ensued, each boy taking turns pounding home arguments while the other waited in reserve. Like lawyers pleading their cases before a judge, each boy swore that he would never utter a word to the mothers if Wilma would go with them to the woods. They offered bribes: Ethan promised to let Wilma wear his stainless steel bracelet, and Jeremiah offered a dime and two nickels. Eloquently, they pointed out how hot and muggy it was, and how deliciously pleasant it would be to sit on the banks of the washhole with their feet in the water. Having listened in silence to most of the arguments, Wilma fretted and fumed but eventually gave in.

As the three walked down the dirt lane from Pink's house, past the sawmill, and onto a cowpath into the woods, Ethan began running, shouting as he did: "I'm gonna beat y'all to the washhole. Last one there's a rotten egg."

Wilma and the boys found the creek full and running, replenished by late afternoon thundershowers which had been consistently occurring since the first of the month. "Just look at that," Ethan squealed, "I ain't never seen this washhole look so good. Let's go in."

"Ethan, you know our mamas have told us never to go swimmin' down here unless some grownup was with us."

"Well, shoot, Jeremiah," Ethan said, "Wilma's well nigh grown up."

"You forget one thing," Jeremiah said, balking, "we ain't supposed to be here in the first place. And 'sides, we ain't got no swimmin' suits, and we cain't get our clothes wet. Our mamas'll skin us alive if we do."

"Why don't we just shuck off and go in naked?" Ethan asked.

"In front of Wilma? You got to be *loco*," Jeremiah protested.

"Aw, it ain't nothin' she ain't seen before, and you won't look, will you, Wilma?"

"I ain't carin' nothin' about seein' yore little butts," Wilma said, turning her head.

With that, Ethan unbuttoned his short pants and let them fall to the ground, and Jeremiah followed suit by pulling his faded knit shirt over his head. Wilma giggled under her breath as the boys, now totally nude, entered the swimming hole from the shallow side, away from the current, and over a bed of creek sand bleached white by the sun. The mid-afternoon heat made the water feel almost cold by contrast, and the boys squealed as they submerged themselves up to the waist. Watching contemptuously from the bank, Wilma said: "Y'all gonna get in a world of trouble."

"Aw, come on in, Wilma, ain't nobody gonna know," Jeremiah called out.

"Me get in? You done lost yore *mind*, boy," Wilma said. "I ain't gonna get in no creek with two white boys."

"Scaredy cat! Scaredy cat!" Jeremiah and Ethan shouted, almost in unison.

Her resolve weakened by the boys' taunts and the oppressive heat of the August day, Wilma sensed the palpable pleasure the boys felt as they romped in the water. Finally, pulling down her dress and tattered petticoat, she yelled: "Turn yore heads now. I don't want y'all lookin' at my privates before I gets in the water."

The boys obliged, and within an instant Wilma's head jutted just above the water line ten yards from Jeremiah and Ethan. Reserved at first, Wilma watched as the boys splashed water and chased each other, screaming with laughter as they did. Forgetting her modesty, she began to join in the play, and before long, all three were leaving the water to run naked along the bank, jumping feet first, into the washhole. They yelled and squealed at each other with abandon, spending the next fifteen minutes in delirious, unadulterated joy.

Suddenly, there was a loud splash on the far side of the swimming hole, as though a large tree limb had fallen into the water. The three children stared at each other in stunned terror. "What was that?" shrieked Wilma, as a big piece of cypress bobbled to the surface in the area of the splash and began floating downstream. "Where'd that come from?" Jeremiah asked.

Behind a clump of palmettos, Alex and Beagle crouched, holding their hands over their mouths to muffle their giggles. Then Alex stood up, swaggering triumphantly over to the edge of the creek bed.

"Well, well, now don't this just beat all," Alex said. "Jeremiah and Ethan swimmin' in the buff with a nigger gal! You boys havin' fun?"

Neither Jeremiah nor Ethan could muster any kind of response. Wilma quickly turned her back and lowered herself in the water up to her neck.

"I bet yore mamas don't even know where y'all are," Alex said, gloating. "And I'd bet money they ain't got no idea that y'all are takin' a dip in the wash-hole, naked, with this here black gal."

"Alex, please don't tell Mama; she'll whip me for sure," Jeremiah begged.

In the excitement, Wilma temporarily forgot her nakedness, and stood up, full length, out of the water. With his eyes riveted on Wilma's body, Alex mumbled: "You boys just get yore clothes on, and we'll talk about this. Maybe we need a meetin' of the clan. Maybe it's a good time to think about lettin' Wilma into the clan. I been mullin' it over."

Alex had introduced the boys to the game of pretending to be pirates. He had given them a name: the Knights of Captain Blood, and Alex, of course, had made himself the captain. In that role, he had explained, it was his job to decide what rules and rituals the clan should observe, and Alex claimed to know all about pirates from seeing a Douglas Fairbanks movie. With Alex giving orders and commands and threatening horrible punishments if the boys did not obey, the gang took blood oaths of secrecy, and Alex alone had authority to decide who would be a member of the clan. Members so far included only Jeremiah, Ethan, and—only recently, Beagle. Beagle's admission had been the subject of much debate, especially because it would mean breaching the color barrier, but Jeremiah and Ethan had argued persuasively that Beagle's speed and strength would be a great asset if the clan ever had to contest a territorial dispute with another gang. Finally, after intense soul-searching and what seemed to the two younger boys endless procrastination, Alex had allowed Beagle to join the group.

Jeremiah and Ethan crawled from the creek to the spot on the bank where they had discarded their clothes. To their dismay, they found that their garments were wet with water, and covered with sand and mud. Washing the worst off in the creek, they donned their clothes, now soaking wet. As Alex and

Beagle started up the path from the creek, Alex called back: "Come on, boys, let's meet at the sawdust pile. Wilma, you get dressed and come on too."

Soon after the clan meeting convened near the sawdust pile that afternoon, the discussion turned to the issue of whether Wilma should be admitted to the group, and, if so, in what capacity. Alex was seated on a stump, facing the three boys who sat cross-legged on the ground. Jeremiah's and Ethan's clothes were still soaking wet, and Wilma waited at a distance, seated on grass under a shade tree.

"She just cain't be trusted," Alex said, after the three other boys had said they favored her admission. "'Sides," he added, "she's a nigger."

"Heck, Alex," Jeremiah pleaded, "we done let Beagle in, so that argument ain't no count."

"Yeah," Ethan said, nodding his head in support, "and I've heard you say that every pirate clan needs a good wench. Ain't you said that?"

"I meant a white wench, stupid," Alex snapped. "Pirates don't mess with niggers."

"Well, let's just pretend she's white, like we do Beagle sometimes," Jeremiah said. "They ain't no black Indians either, but you done admitted what a good Indian Beagle makes, and we used to let Wilma be a squaw when we played cowboys and Indians, didn't we? Wilma's gonna make a good...."

"It just ain't gonna work, Jeremiah," Alex said. "We'd have to get her to swear on a blood oath that she wouldn't tell nobody about the clan. We'd have to cut her finger and get blood, and ain't no nigger gal gonna go along with that. And there'd be other stuff in her initiation that she wouldn't agree to. Naw, it just ain't gonna work."

"Let me go ask her," Jeremiah begged. "I'll tell her she has to do *anything* the captain says, no matter what. I bet she'll do anything to be a pirate. She wants to be in the clan real bad, and I'll get her to promise to do whatever you say, Alex."

"Well, you can ask her, but I still ain't made my mind up," Alex said.

Jeremiah walked over to Wilma. Placing his hand on her arm, he turned her away from the other boys. Jeremiah whispered in Wilma's ear, cupping his hand over his mouth, and Wilma nodded her head several times. Returning to the group and facing Alex, Jeremiah said: "All right, now, she's gonna do it. She wants to be in the clan. I even told her about the blood oath and all, and she says she'll do *any*thing. She *swears* she will; I believe her, too."

Alex rolled his eyes, pursed his lips, and looked off toward the sawdust pile. The boys waited expectantly for him to speak. Finally, he said: "All right, I'm gonna let 'er in, but we got to initiate 'er real good so there ain't no turnin' back. If she wants to be a member of my crew, she's got to accept my rule completely. Understand, boys?"

"Wait now," Beagle protested, "you ain't gonna hurt my sister, Alex. I ain't gonna stand for no harm to her."

"Naw, I ain't gonna hurt her," Alex said, "but she's got to earn her way into the clan. All my crew has to prove theirselves, cain't be no slackers."

"Yeah, I accepts that," Beagle said, "but you ain't gonna beat her or nothin'?"

"Heck, naw," Alex said, laughing. "She's gonna like the initiation. Ain't gonna be no beatin'. She might whine some, but she'll be proud she done it. Bring 'er on over here," Alex said. Jeremiah returned to Wilma and took her hand, leading her back to the stump where Alex was sitting.

There was a long silence before Alex spoke. "Wilma," he said, "I been told you want to be a pirate—to be in the Order of Captain Blood, is that right?" Alex folded his arms and glared at Wilma.

"Yessir, I does."

"Aw right, then, the secret ritual will now begin," Alex proclaimed, leaning forward and tapping Wilma's head with his hand. "Get on yore knees at my feet," he bellowed, "and raise yore right hand and repeat after me: 'I, Wilma the Wench, swears on the blood oath I'm about to give....'"

Wilma repeated the words.

"'...that I will obey the captain even if it means my death or whatever,'" Alex continued.

"...that I's gonna obey the captain if it means my death or whatever," Wilma responded, gulping as she spoke.

Alex paused, then gazed upward through the tall pines as though waiting on a sign from heaven. Then he looked back at Wilma after peering into the eyes of each of the other boys sitting transfixed in the semicircle before him. Ordering Ethan to produce his pocketknife, Alex opened the blade and gave the instrument to Wilma. "Now, Wench," he commanded, "cut yore finger and draw some blood."

Wilma balked, wincing, and Alex said: "Hell, give it back then, I'll cut yore finger myself if you ain't got the guts."

Wilma screamed, "Naw, wait, I's gonna do it," and she grimaced as she made a small cut in a fingertip. Droplets of blood oozed from the cut. On orders from Alex, she swiped the blood and made a crossing motion with her finger in the palm of his hand. Alex then placed his palm on her forehead. Following Alex's commands, she then repeated the procedure with each of the other boys: Jeremiah first, then Ethan, and finally Beagle. Alex then ordered her to return to her knees before him.

With her eyes gleaming, Wilma asked: "Is I a wench now?"

"Not yet, you ain't," Alex said, the other boys eyed him nervously. "Now crawl on yore knees before me, gal."

"Hey now," Beagle shouted, "ain't she done what you tolt her to?"

"Naw, she ain't finished yet. 'Sides, shut up, nigger, I ain't asked you nothin'."

"Don't be callin' me no nigger," Beagle said. "You ain't gonna mess with my sister no more, either."

"Shit, boy," Alex said, glaring at Beagle, "I'm gonna do anything I want to, and I'll call you a nigger if I take a notion to."

Beagle stood to his feet, facing Alex, his teeth clenched tightly.

"Aw, simmer down, Beagle," Alex smiled abruptly, "don't get so riled up, boy. Just sit down, and let's finish bringin' Wilma into the clan. I ain't gonna ask her to do much more, and I ain't gonna call you 'nigger' no more."

Beagle grunted and sat down, folding his arms. Wilma, now kneeling within reach of Alex, said: "What you wants me to do now?"

"Lean forward and let's see what kind of wench we got here," Alex said, pushing her chin upward and touching her throat and the base of her neck. Wilma trembled, pulling back instinctively. Alex said in stern voice: "Listen now, I'm 'bout tired of this. You wanna' be a wench or not?"

Wilma whimpered, and Beagle rose again to his feet. "Alex," he bristled, "you said you wouldn't hurt her. I'm fixin' to whip yore ass!"

"Shit, this ain't nothin'," Alex said, "I'm just lookin' at the wench, and if she ain't got the stomach for this, she just cain't be in the clan."

"I's fine, Beagle," Wilma said, "I's gonna be all right. Just let him be." Grimacing, Beagle sat down again.

Alex resumed his examination, turning Wilma's face left and right, then looking down at her breasts which were covered by her blouse, still damp from the creek. "You ain't got big titties," Alex said, "but I reckon they'll do. You know, a wench is s'posed to have *big* titties, and a wench's job is to please her captain, ain't that right, Wilma?"

"Yessir, I reckon it is," Wilma answered.

"All right, let's see what you can do with this now," Alex said, abruptly unbuttoning his pants and pulling out his partially erect penis, foreskin covering the tip of the uncircumcised organ.

"What you mean?" Wilma asked, "why you showin' yore privates like that?"

"Well, just put yore hand on it a little. Please yore captain, Wench," Alex said, his voice now soft and pleading. "I bet my thing'll spit somethin' warm and white out at you if you touch it gentle-like with yore hand."

The other three boys were speechless, stunned by the rapid sequence of Alex's actions. Inexplicably, Wilma continued to kneel before Alex, staring at his exposed organ, transfixed by Alex's words. Then, Alex placed his hand over her's, guiding it to his erection, folding her fingers around it. "Is I pleasin' the captain?" Wilma asked, looking directly into Alex's eyes for the first time since the ritual began.

At that instant, Beagle jumped to his feet, shaking his fist toward Alex. "I don't give a damn about the clan," he shouted. "You done shamed me and my sister. I'm gonna bust yore face in, you bastard!

Pushing Wilma away, Alex screamed: "Shut up, Beagle!" Looking again toward Wilma, he yelled: "And you…you ugly bitch! You're uglier than hell! I caint see why I let you touch me."

Crying uncontrollably, Wilma rose to her feet, hesitated a moment, then turned and ran into the woods. As the blood rushed to Beagle's head, he turned to watch his sister flee. Jeremiah and Ethan sat stunned, as Alex regained his composure and said, matter-of-factly: "Well, that's it, boys. Wilma ain't fit to be in the clan. I just ain't gonna let 'er be no wench."

At that instant, Pink's shrill voice pierced the afternoon air, freezing the four boys in their tracks. "*Eeeeee-than! Eeeeee-than*!" she shrieked, the questions falling in torrents. "Are y'all down there around that old mill? Where's Wilma? Did y'all leave the yard after I *told* you not to? If y'all hear me, you better get yourself home *now*, boy, I'm gonna tan yore hide! Is Jeremiah with you?" Pink could not see the boys from her vantage point two hundred yards up the road, but her voice struck terror in Ethan and Jeremiah, as she continued to yell: "You *better* answer me, boy!"

Beagle and Jeremiah skirmished into the woods, leaving Ethan petrified and waiting for the next angry words from his mother. Beagle found Wilma cowering behind a cluster of pines and the two of them made their way to their grandmother's house. Jeremiah fought his way through underbrush to an open field where he took another route to his house, but he fared no better than

Ethan. After they came home and discovered the boys missing, Melissa and Pink had coordinated their plans for punishment. Once the two miscreants were safely home, the mothers, belts in hand, duly administered twenty licks to each child and followed the whipping with a well-worn lecture on the sinfulness of wayward boys and the inevitability of punishment.

The consequences of that day's activities were much less painful for Alex: there would be no discipline from his mother, who neither knew nor cared where he was or what he did. While Ethan was being apprehended by Pink and the other children were disappearing in the woods, Alex crept behind a row of dog fennel to a tin shed beside the sawmill boiler where saws and hatchets were stored. He crawled inside and rested until he caught his breath. Recalling the afternoon's events, he thought of seeing Wilma's breasts outlined beneath her damp blouse, and he could almost feel her hand stroking his penis. His excitement swelled as he thought of the power he had exerted, not only over Wilma but also the other three boys. It was too much for him, and he ejaculated instantly, his eyes rolling back in his head. He then stretched out on the floor of the shed and dozed off.

Pink notified Bootsie of Wilma's breach of trust, and the granddaughter was also whipped with a belt. Afterwards, her role as a baby-sitter for Jeremiah and Ethan was permanently terminated. Aside from the loss of confidence in Wilma for allowing the boys to leave home for the washhole against their mothers' orders, however, Bootsie never quite understood Wilma's abrupt change in behavior from that time forward. She never again seemed interested in girlish things, and showed no desire to socialize with girls her age. A year later, she took up with an elderly carpenter called "Skeeter," and moved with him to a nearby town. Bootsie heard nothing from her for several years. Wilma bore two children, a boy and a girl, and when she was nineteen, Skeeter left her for another woman.

At twenty years of age and destitute, Wilma returned to Shrewsbury Crossing, moving in with Bootsie and Beagle to raise her children. Now gluttonous and atrociously fat, and with no regard for her physical appearance, Wilma found work in the fields, stringing tobacco and picking cotton, and working sporadically as a maid alongside Bootsie.

Regardless of what might lay ahead for her, Wilma's days as a wench were over.

CHAPTER 5

Revival and Hog Heaven

"Indeed the idols I have loved so long
Have done my credit in this world much wrong:
Have drowned my glory in a shallow cup
And sold my reputation for a song."
Edward Fitzgerald, *The Rubaiyat of Omar Khayyam*

"Jeremiah, hurry up! Wash your face. Brush your teeth, and don't forget to clean behind your ears." Melissa was barking orders like a Marine drill sergeant. "Comb your hair. We got to leave here in a few minutes. I promised Pink I'd help her arrange the pulpit flowers, and meetin' starts in twenty minutes. Now, don't make me get no switch after you. You're ten years old and big enough to get yourself ready for church on time."

"Mama," Jeremiah called from the bathroom, "is revival gonna last all week?"

"That's a foolish question. You know it always does."

"Well, have I got to go every night?"

"Of course," Melissa said. "When the doors of the Lord's house are open, we are all supposed to be there."

"But, Mama," Jeremiah pleaded, "this is Hog Heaven week, and the carnival will be settin' up Thursday. Cain't I go to revival the first three nights so I can go to the fair on openin' night?"

"No such thing, and besides, you ain't got no money to throw away like that. All they want is your money—they're just Gypsies roamin' around leechin' off folks who ain't got no better sense than to let 'em." Melissa never failed to seize an opportunity to preach to Jeremiah. "And if you got money to waste, you ought to give it to the Lord."

"Mama, you know I try to tithe, but everybody needs a little fun now and then. Alex says the Lord expects you to have a good time, that it's part of God's plan."

"If you're payin' attention to what that boy says, you *do* need revival, every night too!" Melissa snapped. "Alex's mouth certainly ain't no prayer book."

"Well, cain't I at least go to the carnival on Saturday night?" Jeremiah begged. "Hog Heaven don't come but once a year and this is the first one we've had since the war. I bet everybody's gonna be there—even lots of church folks."

The festival called Hog Heaven had begun for Shrewsbury Crossing in 1935 when someone decided it would be a good idea to have a harvest time celebration. Continued annually until 1942 after the United States had entered the war, the affair was suspended since many local citizens did not think it seemly to sponsor such organized frivolity while the country was involved in a life-and-death struggle. Now, in 1947, the war was over and Jeremiah was thankful that Hog Heaven was back.

The festival was timed for mid-November to coincide with the cooler weather suitable for hog-killing. This year the local paper had carried stories for weeks about all the planned hoopla: arts and crafts, music, dancing, and a variety of hog contests on the final day. There would also be a checker tournament, corn shucking competition, sugar cane grinding, peanut boiling, chitterling cooking, soap making, quilting and rug weaving, and square dancing. The contests included hog-calling, best-dressed pig, and the greased pig chase. At the last festival in 1941 when he was four years old, Jeremiah had watched, wide-eyed, as boys chased and caught the greased pig. He scarcely recalled the other events, but the greased pig contest was firmly fixed in his memory. This year, he had every intention of catching the greased pig himself.

"Well, I guess we can talk about you missin' the Saturday night service if you attend all the others, and pay attention and don't cut up with Ethan or Alex during the…."

"Oh, Mama, I won't. I won't!" Jeremiah promised.

"And don't let Alex get you to gigglin' and whisperin' like he sometimes does," Melissa continued.

"Mama, Alex has changed a lot. He told me he's gonna rededicate his life at the revival tonight, and that he might even be a preacher," Jeremiah said. "Alex can talk rings around a billy goat, you know, so he'd make a good preacher, wouldn't he?" Jeremiah finished combing his hair and walked to the door of the bedroom where his mother was dressing.

"Oh, I don't know," Melissa said, "there's a lot more to preachin' than talkin', and I'm not sure Alex is old enough to understand the high callin' of preachin'. He's only thirteen."

Melissa locked the front door of her house and she and Jeremiah walked the six blocks to the First Baptist Church of Shrewsbury Crossing. As they walked together in the chill of the November afternoon, Jeremiah loved his mother with all his heart, but he knew that the two of them had vastly different attitudes about the upcoming revival.

Melissa was one of the leading workers in the church: she faithfully attended all Sunday services and Wednesday night prayer meetings, and she had held special prayer services in her home each evening the week preceding the revival. She loved the revival meeting, especially the singing which gave her the chance to use her mellow, golden alto voice. Melissa loved the fellowship, the camaraderie she felt with other members of the church, and she enjoyed listening to Pink play the piano. Most of all, she relished the genuine feeling of spiritual renewal that invariably came with a full week of singing, prayer, meditation, and preaching.

For his part, Jeremiah viewed the weeklong revival as an ordeal—a bitter, seemingly endless week of boredom and discomfort. Not that many ten-year-old boys would feel differently. Even his mother's concession to consider allowing him to skip the Saturday night service did little to help him muster a positive outlook on Monday night for the first service, especially when he thought about all the hours of revival that stretched before him during the week.

Jeremiah had many grievances against revivals. For one thing, the services always ran excruciatingly longer than the hour and fifteen minutes they were supposed to last. The preacher was usually a visiting pastor from another church brought in to give the congregation a break from their regular preacher and to rally the troops. During the sermon, he would get caught up in the spirit, and when the invitation was issued, the preacher required the congregation to keep singing "Just As I Am" choruses repeatedly to be sure that any soul even slightly inclined to accept Christ and avoid eternal damnation had an opportunity to do so. On what Jeremiah hoped would be the last chorus, someone invariably would come forward to repent and confess his or her faith, and that would always just add more fuel to the fire so that the door of salvation would be left ajar for what seemed to Jeremiah to be an eternity, and he found himself disliking "Just As I Am" more than any other song.

Other things perplexed Jeremiah about revivals. The sermons were always depressing, concentrating on hellfire and the consequences of a sinful life—things Jeremiah did not want to think about. Revivalists always talked about the evil nature of the flesh and how wretchedly lost human beings are, which did nothing to ameliorate Jeremiah's feelings of inadequacy, feelings he harbored much of the time. Jeremiah guessed that the purpose of these sermons was to make people so sick of their own shortcomings that they would turn their lives over to Jesus and let Him see what He could do with them. The hitch was that at ten years of age, Jeremiah had been through numerous revivals, not to mention innumerable Sunday church meetings and Sunday school, and he had frequently tried to repent and leave his old life behind; but Jesus never seemed to grab hold of his life the way preachers advertised: after a short period of feeling pious, Jeremiah would revert to his fantasies about women's breasts and crotches, and he would resume masturbating to beat the band. Now, at age ten, Jeremiah was becoming increasingly cynical that the ordeal of enduring everlasting sermons and singing "Blessed Assurance" and "Rock of Ages" at the top of his voice would ever accomplish anything.

Maybe tonight will be different, Jeremiah thought, as he and Melissa entered the sanctuary. Walking down the aisle, Melissa continued to the pulpit area where Pink was busy arranging flowers. Alex was seated alone on the second row when Jeremiah sat down beside him. His head bowed and lips moving in low, prayerful tones, Alex was seemingly oblivious to Jeremiah's presence. Jeremiah said nothing, not wanting to interrupt the other boy's worshipful meditation.

After a few moments, Alex lifted his head, looked over at Jeremiah, and winked. "How'd you like that, Jero?" he whispered, glancing back over his shoulder at the congregation, "these grown-ups eat this religious shit up!"

Jeremiah's mouth flew open. "Alex! You shouldn't talk like that in the Lord's house and all."

"Settle down," Alex said. "You know I like to say stuff like that to get you rattled, don't you see?"

Pink took her place at the piano, and the service began with a long opening prayer from the local pastor, followed by a twenty minute song service. As the congregation sang, Ethan, who had deftly avoided the opening prayer by loitering outside the church, eased into the rear of the sanctuary and took a seat on the back row.

The sermon was typically long and depressing. Sweating, snorting, and clapping his hands as he spoke, the visiting evangelist had one habit that especially troubled Jeremiah: he would come to the edge of the pulpit directly in front of the two boys and shower them with droplets of saliva. With each episode, Jeremiah grew increasingly queasy and considered moving to the rear of the church by Ethan, but he discarded the idea when he realized that Melissa would be watching and weighing his disruptive conduct against the bargain she had made to give him Saturday night off to attend the carnival.

Strangely, even as saliva rained down, Alex never moved; he gazed directly at the preacher during the entire sermon in what appeared to Jeremiah to be a state of rapture. As the song of invitation began, Alex began to sing more loudly than anyone in the building—something distinctively conspicuous since Alex was tone-deaf and couldn't carry a tune in a bucket.

After one chorus, Alex stepped into the aisle and marched up to the ministers, standing side by side with them in front of the pulpit. Both men hugged Alex, and the boy responded by grasping both men around their waists. Sobbing audibly, Alex whispered in the two preachers' ears that he needed salvation and that he was determined to live his life for Christ. With tears trickling down his cheek, Alex turned and faced the congregation. The evangelist raised his arms, palms down, to request quiet.

With trembling emotion, Alex addressed the silenced crowd: "Please, y'all, I ain't nothin' but a uneducated boy, but I've found the peace and joy that Jesus brings, and I'm beggin' all of y'all to do the same. It says somewhere in the Bible that a child will lead. Maybe—just maybe—I can be that child. Come on, I beg you, give yore hearts to Christ."

The congregation responded with uproarious applause. Shouts of 'hallelujah,' 'amen,' and 'praise God' reverberated throughout the sanctuary. As he watched the tears streaming down Alex's face, Jeremiah was overcome with emotion. Suddenly feeling guilty that his aversion to the preacher's saliva had kept him from hearing much of the sermon, Jeremiah joined Alex and the smiling preachers at the front of the church. Soon, a half-dozen others came forward to confess their sins and repent.

It was a joyful occasion: Alex was the centerpiece, leading everyone in penitence while Jeremiah was overwhelmed by his own feelings of redemption. As the pastor and the revivalist raised their arms skyward, Jeremiah decided that the scene was clear and convincing proof of the power of the Holy Spirit working through Alex. After a lengthy prayer praising God for delivering the sinners to the fold, the revivalist concluded the service with the converts and preachers clasping hands in a semicircle, while the notes from Pink's piano rang out and all sang:

When we all get to heaven, what a day of rejoicing that will be;
When we all see Jesus, we'll sing and shout the victory.

After the service, the entire congregation was invited to come forward to congratulate Alex and the other converts, alternately hugging, kissing, and crying over each newly saved soul.

Jeremiah and Alex were among the last to walk up the aisle to leave. Melissa had told Jeremiah that she would wait for him in the parking lot, since she had something to discuss with Pink and another member of the Ladies' Missionary Society.

As they neared the door, Alex whispered: "Jero, did you see the *tits* on that visitin' preacher's wife?"

Jeremiah blurted out: "Hush, you idiot! People are still right outside the door. They'll hear you."

"I ain't talkin' too loud," Alex looked around and saw that he and Jeremiah were alone. "But you didn't answer me. Did you notice them *tits*?"

Jeremiah grimaced.

Alex went on, "you wanna know what I told that old gal when she was huggin' my neck and all? I felt them titties on my arm, and I whispered in her ear that I wanted to fuck her."

"You're lyin'," Jeremiah said, "you must take me for a fool! You ain't said no such thing. That woman'd slap the *daylights* out of you if you said something like that."

"Like hell, I didn't!" Alex insisted. "Fact is, she whispered back that she wanted me to come over to Ludlow and see her when her old man's out of town."

Just then, Ethan, who had slinked down in his seat on the back pew and slept through most of the service, walked into the church foyer where Jeremiah and Alex were standing. "What you two talkin' about?" he asked.

"Alex is tellin' me how he's gonna screw the visitin' preacher's wife," Jeremiah said, rolling his eyes upward. "Do you believe that, Ethan? Said he told her when she was huggin' his neck about gettin' saved and all, and he says she said she would, too—you know, screw him. Can you believe that hogwash?"

"Y'all beat all!" Ethan said. "I mean, you two standin' in front of everybody talkin' about how y'all been born again and all, and now here you are—minutes later—in the doorway of the church talkin' about screwin', and screwin' a preacher's wife at that!"

"I ain't talkin' about it, Ethan. I ain't said nothin' to the woman," Jeremiah protested. "'Sides, Alex, why'd you want to mess with that old woman? She's thirty-five if she's a day."

"That's the trouble with inexperienced boys like you and Ethan. You don't know a good piece of tail when you see one. The old gal cain't wait for me to get in her britches. She just looks at me and knows how good it's gonna be. A woman like that loves fresh meat like me."

"But didn't you just give yourself to the Lord?" Ethan asked.

"What's that got to do with it?" Alex snapped. "Yeah, I just gave my life to the Lord, and now He wants me to give my cock to the preacher's wife. He knows how dull and lonely her life is, married to that old spit-throwin' fool, and God just wants me to brighten her life up some. Yeah, I'll be doin' the Lord's work by screwin' 'er. Look at it that way."

Alex did not attend any other revival services that week. Jeremiah and Ethan received no leniency from their mothers, however, and they were present at every meeting except Saturday night, when faithful attendance and good conduct would be rewarded by a night off for the carnival. From the two boys' perspective, the good thing about Alex's absences was the opportunity to study the visiting preacher's wife and debate whether Alex deserved any credibility with his claims about her. Huddling after each night's service in the parking lot, they compared their observations. They agreed that she looked very stern and seemed to take her role seriously as an evangelist's wife. By the end of the week, they had come to doubt that she would be interested in sex with anyone, except perhaps the preacher himself on rare occasions. Using no makeup and wearing her hair pulled tightly in a bun, the woman exhibited no evidence that she would engage in sinful conduct, and the boys concluded that Alex must have been lying. It was not that they disbelieved all of his stories; they had firsthand knowledge of some of his exploits. But by the end of the week's services, they had together arrived at a solid conclusion: A preacher's wife? Never!

✦ ✦ ✦

The greased pig contest was scheduled for eleven o'clock Saturday morning, and Jeremiah was beside himself with excitement and anticipation. Arriving shortly after ten, he and Ethan paid the fifty-cent entry fee, and nervously moved to a place under the grandstand by a cage holding the pig. The winner's prize would be a twenty-dollar bill.

The site for the Hog Heaven festival was a twelve-acre field two miles from the center of Shrewsbury Crossing. The entrance was marked by a ticket booth where admission was ten cents for students and a dollar for everyone else. A side entrance was available for blacks, who were permitted to purchase food and other items but were barred from all of the contests and the carnival's rides.

Arts and crafts were displayed in a row of tents near the entrance. The smell of barbecued pork and fried chitterlings permeated the air. On the far side of the field was the carnival, which included a number of rides, the most prominent of which were a Ferris wheel, a merry-go-round, and a loop-t'-loop. Tickets for each ride were a dime. Twenty or thirty booths formed the periphery for the carnival and featured a variety of ways to lose money in the ethereal hope of winning a stuffed animal or doll. Cotton candy and hot dogs were available at several locations, and at the rear of the fairground were two tent-shows featuring freaks, magic acts, fortune tellers, and music.

An area about seventy-five yards in diameter had been fenced off for the greased pig contest. Age limits for the competition had been set at ten to fourteen years, and Jeremiah and Ethan were among the youngest of the thirty-six contestants. Alex stood by the cage holding the pig as the grease was being applied, and called over to his cousins: "What do you butt-heads think you're doin'?" he asked, "you gonna make complete fools outta yourselves. That hog's bigger than you two put together. You ain't got a prayer in hell of catchin' him."

"We'll see," Jeremiah said, staring straight ahead.

But the pig did seem huge to Jeremiah: it weighed about forty pounds, roughly half his own weight. To win the contest, a boy not only had to catch the pig but also to hold it for a count of ten from the judge. Once in the grasp of one of the contestants, the other boys were prohibited from interfering until the judge pronounced the winner or the pig freed itself.

The spectators sat in a section of bleachers borrowed from the high school gymnasium. Several dozen children and adults were there, many—like Melissa and Pink—parents of the contestants. Their mothers had urged Jeremiah and Ethan not to enter the contest, using such unconvincing arguments as the possibility of injury or ruined clothing.

As time for the release of the pig neared, Jeremiah's heart sank as he surveyed the field of competitors. One boy, obviously near the upper age limit of fourteen, was muscular and stood at least a foot taller than Jeremiah or Ethan.

As the pig was set loose, the crowd howled with laughter as the frightened animal was charged by the horde of boys. The largest boy—the one of such concern to Jeremiah—pounced on the pig almost immediately, but the animal quickly slipped free, running between the boy's long, somewhat bowed legs. Ethan managed to grab one of the pig's ears for an instant, but the pig easily squirmed free.

Jeremiah was winded and on the verge of giving up the chase when the pig reversed its field and circled toward Jeremiah's left. Jeremiah found himself, standing alone, facing the animal, now pinned against the fence. Grabbing both forelegs, Jeremiah turned the pig on its back and was startled at how quickly the judge completed a count of ten.

A loud roar went up from the crowd. Melissa and Pink clapped loudly and screamed with delight. Letting the pig go, Jeremiah stood triumphantly, beaming with a wide smile, his face covered with grease smudges. As the judge presented the twenty-dollar bill and the crowd continued to applaud, Ethan shook Jeremiah's hand.

"I'm gonna split it with you," Jeremiah told Ethan, pointing to the money. "That's ten apiece for us."

"Heck, Jeremiah," Ethan responded. "You ain't gonna do that. You won on your own, fair and square."

Alex walked up, hands on his hips, scowling. "Well, well, Jero," he said, "looks like you done caught yourself a hog. Ain't you something? I ain't never seen anybody so happy over something so silly as catchin' a nasty pig."

Jeremiah turned away, facing Ethan. "Come on," he said, "looks like somebody might be jealous I caught the pig. Let's go home and clean up. We got us some money to spend at the fair tonight, don't we?" Turning back to Alex, Jeremiah said, "'Sides, if catchin' that pig was so easy, why didn't you do it?"

"You little turd," Alex snapped, "I got better things to do with my time than chasin' a hog. And I couldn't get dirty. Y'all remember that preacher's wife in the revival? Well, I'm supposed to meet her behind the nigger school at three o'clock. I'd let you boys come along and get a little piece yourselves if you hadn't got all greased up."

Jeremiah and Ethan stood motionless, staring at each other as Alex strutted away, laughing boisterously.

❧ ❧ ❧

It was after five that afternoon when Jeremiah and Ethan returned to the fairgrounds. As promised, Jeremiah had given his cousin half his winnings, although Ethan continued to protest the act as being unnecessarily generous—perhaps even stupid.

"Shut up, Ethan," Jeremiah stammered with increasing exasperation. "I told you I wouldn't give you no money if I didn't want to, and if you don't quit yappin' about it, I'm gonna take it back."

Ethan made no further protest and changed the subject by suggesting that they should ride the Ferris wheel. And ride they did, first the Ferris wheel and then all the other rides except one with slow-moving swings they decided was suitable only for toddlers. They circled the area, trying to win prizes: throwing hoops over Coca Cola bottles and casting pennies onto plates, all without success until Ethan hit a target with a baseball, netting him a small stuffed bear. As they walked away with the prize, Jeremiah said: "Look, Ethan, you don't wanna be walkin' around this place with that bear. Folks'll think you're a sissy—especially Alex. Nosiree, you don't want Alex to see you with no teddy bear."

"Maybe you're right," Ethan said, spotting a couple approaching with an infant.

"Here, little fellow," he said, holding the bear out to the child, "would you like this teddy bear?"

"How kind of you!" the woman said, as the child reached for the stuffed bear. "Say," the man said, looking at Jeremiah, "Aren't you the kid who caught the greased pig?"

"Yessir," Jeremiah said, pushing out his chest with pride.

"Well, it tickled me to see you win over all those boys that were bigger than you. You got a lot of spunk, young fellow," the man said. "Thanks again for the teddy bear," his wife told Ethan as they walked away.

"Did you hear that, Ethan?" Jeremiah said, "That man knew it was me that won the greased pig contest. I'm sorta famous, ain't I?"

"Yeah, I reckon you are," Ethan said. "It's fun to be famous, ain't it?"

"Ain't nothin' like it. I reckon that was why Alex was so jealous of me. He ain't never been famous or nothin', except maybe when he had them preachers eatin' out of his hands at revival the other night. He enjoyed all that, don't you think?"

"Look, Jeremiah," Ethan changed the subject. "There's that tent show—Punger's Palace—Alex was tellin' us about. Let's go in there."

The largest tent on the carnival lot was owned by an itinerant performer named Punger. The banner over the entrance read: "PUNGER'S PALACE—MAGIC SHOW AND CARAVAN." On Thursday, opening night, Alex had sat on the first row, applauding and whistling loudly with each act Punger performed. Punger was a huge white man, overweight with a massive frame and a shaggy beard. Wearing a black cowboy hat with a red checkered bandanna and overalls, Punger had entertained his audience each night with banjo-picking followed by magic acts and fortune-telling.

After the show ended the first night, he had called to Alex: "Heh, boy, let me talk to you a minute."

"Yessir," Alex had said, moving to the platform where Punger was seated.

"Wanna make a few dollars?"

"What I gotta do?" Alex had asked.

"Not much. Just help me set up each show, take up tickets, and give me dope on the locals so I can use it in my fortune-tellin'. I'll pay you two dollars a night."

Alex had enthusiastically accepted.

As Jeremiah and Ethan approached the tent, Punger stood on a crate selling tickets. A placard read "Admission: Adults—75 cents; Students—50 cents." For several minutes the two boys stood to the side and debated whether the show would be worth the price. Spotting them, Punger yelled out: "You boys gonna miss the time of yore life if'n you don't see this show. Better come on over and get yore tickets. Show's gonna start any minute now."

Punger's admonition ended the debate: Jeremiah and Ethan each gave two quarters to Punger and walked with their tickets to Alex who waited at the entrance to the tent. As he held out his hand to take their tickets, he grinned broadly and said: "Well, look who's here. Hope y'all got all that pig grease off 'cause we don't want nobody smellin' up the place."

"I just hope this show is gonna be worth fifty cents," Jeremiah said. Ethan nodded in agreement.

"Listen, boys, this here's gonna be the best damned show y'all ever saw—I guarantee it!"

Punger's tent seated several dozen people on wooden benches, and Jeremiah and Ethan seated themselves near the front of the tent before a platform made of wooden planks resting on concrete blocks—all of which served as a stage. A phonograph crackled hillbilly music as the audience filed in. More than thirty minutes after the announced show-time, Punger left the ticket booth and came into the tent, tying the entrance curtain behind him. Punger and Alex then huddled on the side of the stage, pausing briefly several times to scan the audience, mumbling to each other. Tex Ritter bellowed from the loudspeakers.

Taking the stage, Punger strummed several songs on his banjo while Alex stood nearby, leading the applause with hooting and whistling at the end of each song. Next came magic tricks, some of which required Alex's assistance. The highlight of this part of the show came with a guillotine act. The device had been standing on the side of the stage draped with a sheet. When unveiled, the blade glistened with splotches of red paint, causing gasps from the audience. The spectators, mostly men and boys, sat spellbound as Punger instructed Alex to place his head in the slot. Locking Alex's head in place, Punger struck a large cymbal repeatedly as he prepared to cut a thin cord that held the blade. Jeremiah and Ethan were terrified, but Alex stared directly at them, his eyes glowing and a smirk on his face.

Punger cut the cord and the blade fell with a loud thud, appearing to slice completely through Alex's neck, but his head did not fall, and he continued to smile at the audience. As Punger restored the blade to its elevated position, he released the clamp holding Alex, who stood and bowed, grinning broadly as the audience gave thunderous applause.

Then came the finale: the fortune-telling. For this, Punger donned a purple turban and a satin cloak, while Alex brought out a green globe with a pedestal. Sitting before the globe and facing the audience, Punger stroked the globe, rolling his eyes upward.

"Let me see now," Punger wailed, "what shameful secret will this mystic ball reveal tonight? Somethin's comin' into view, but it's too cloudy. I cain't make it out."

Alex called out: "They's some unbelievers here. Punger cain't tell fortunes when they's doubters in the crowd."

A hush fell over the audience.

"All right," Punger said, "it's clearin' up some now. I see two little white boys. Looks like they's headed down this cowpath, maybe somewhere in the woods, and they's a nigger gal with 'em. Right pretty nigger gal, but black as the ace of spades."

Jeremiah and Ethan stared at each other, their eyes blinking and mouths wide.

"Now," Punger continued, "looks like they's comin' to a swimmin' hole of some kind—maybe a little widenin' in a creek or something. And now—y'all ain't gonna believe this—them two white boys is sheddin' their clothes and goin' swimmin' in the buff. Not a stitch on, I'm tellin' you, but wait. They's more! That nigger gal has took off her clothes too, and the three of 'em's just rollickin' and playin' in that creek, and ain't none of 'em got a stitch on. Not a stitch! Don't that just beat all?"

"Who was they?" Alex called from the side of the stage, "Punger, tell us who them boys was. We all wanna know. Who was they?" The audience roared and yelled: "Yeah, who was they? Tell us, Punger!" Jeremiah and Ethan sank lower in their seats.

"Heck," Punger continued, "I cain't quite make 'em both out, but I know one. Yeah, I can see 'em pretty good. It's that boy that caught the greased pig this morning."

Jeremiah gasped as several people turned toward him, laughing and pointing. He jumped to his feet and bolted to the rear of the tent, squirming under the curtain, and running pell-mell into the darkness. He ran and ran, the laughter and taunts of the audience ringing in his ears. He felt his life was ruined: at age ten, he had been publicly humiliated and betrayed by someone he had trusted and even admired. As he lay in bed that night sobbing, he wondered how life could be so pernicious—a moment of glory in the contest that morning and absolute disgrace that night. Jeremiah did not see how he could ever show his face in Shrewsbury Crossing again.

CHAPTER 6

A Clockwork Medicine Man

"I do not love thee, Dr. Fell.
The reason why I cannot tell;
But this I know, and know full well,
I do not love thee, Dr. Fell."
Thomas Brown

Near the center of Shrewsbury Crossing stood the home of Dr. Charles Robert Willingham, the town's highly esteemed physician and civic leader. Dr. Willingham and his family had moved to this residence in 1940 following an especially successful year at the clinic.

By local standards, the house was a mansion: sixty-eight hundred feet of living space and two stories of brick accented by front portico columns of white marble taken from North Georgia quarries. The house and grounds conspicuously consumed an entire city block. From the second floor of the house, facing south, one could see the facade of the Willingham Clinic—the second most recognizable landmark in Shrewsbury Crossing.

The grounds of the Willingham estate were immaculately landscaped. Garden paths meandered aimlessly among magnolias and oaks laden with Spanish moss. Mimosas and cunninghamias lined the stone walls segregating the estate from the town. Wisteria vines climbed everywhere, randomly. Just off a balcony at the rear of the house was a swimming pool, an unheard-of private luxury in rural Georgia in the 1940's. Beyond the pool stood a majestic gazebo overlooking a Japanese garden and pond, with a covered rock bridge leading over the pond into a labyrinth of shrubs and flowers, prominently marked by beds of azaleas and camellias. It was early June of 1948, and the sweet smell of honeysuckle, now in full bloom, permeated the air and the senses.

Shortly after 6:00 a.m., the doctor stood before his bathroom mirror, an open window next to the vanity overlooking the garden, a soft breeze ruffling the curtain. His face spotted with patches of lather, he raised the tip of his nose with his left forefinger to accommodate the swipe of the straight razor across his upper lip. He finished shaving but continued to examine himself intently in the mirror to see if he could detect protruding nose hairs, which he detested. Finding one, he picked up tweezers and heard his wife mutter: "Oh my God! I hate to watch you do that."

"Well, don't watch then," the doctor said, "and, Emma, must you insist on smoking so close to me this early in the morning? The odor smothers the fresh air from the garden."

Straddling a stool near the bathroom door, Emma Willingham sat watching her husband, her hair in rollers, a half-burned cigarette dangling from her lower lip.

"What's the matter, your highness?" she asked. "Got a corncob up your butt this morning? Smoking is one of the few pleasures I have, and—besides—what harm does it do?"

"It's an obnoxious habit. It makes you look like the devil—your breath stinks. It probably causes lung cancer and all kinds of respiratory diseases. Do you want me to go on…."

"Don't bother," his wife said, "but if smoking offends you so much, why don't you get on your soapbox and get the farmers to quit growing all that damn tobacco around here?"

"I have to be practical, Emma. You know the local economy depends on tobacco. I might as well urge these folks to give up food and water."

"Well, what *will* you be doing today, Great Physician?" Emma asked, furrowing her eyebrows. "Tell me, what's on the agenda? Speeches? Miracles? Will you be raising the dead?"

"I'm due at the clinic in an hour, Emma, and I'm really not enjoying your harassment this morning…."

"You don't *enjoy* much of anything, do you?" his wife said. She took a long, slow puff, drew smoke deep into her lungs, then exhaled and with her tongue cupped, siphoned the smoke upward into her nostrils. She was proud of the trick, one she had mastered at Vassar. She saw her husband turn and glance toward her, clearly annoyed.

Emma was a bony woman with angular features, her eyes sunken like potholes under a wide, pale forehead. With lips narrow and drawn, her teeth yellowed by years of incessant smoking, she was far different from the vivacious young woman who had married Shrewsbury Crossing's most eligible bachelor in 1932. She was Emma Josephine Epps, a Vassar classmate of a girl from Shrewsbury Crossing whom she was visiting in the summer of 1931. Emma's father was a rich landowner from northern Alabama, where Dr. Willingham had played high school football. Dr. Willingham's name was legend in the area: as an all-star quarterback, he had led the local team to two state championships. When he left for Emory University in Atlanta with a Methodist scholarship in 1921, a parade through the center of Huntsville, Alabama, was held in his honor. That parade, which Emma had watched from the sidelines, remained vivid in her memory years later as her friend introduced her to the doctor that summer night in Shrewsbury Crossing.

Dr. Willingham had graduated from Emory medical school in 1928 and served his residency at Grady Memorial Hospital in Atlanta. At the age of twenty-nine, lured by a committee of citizens who had offered him a rent-free office in the back of the town's largest department store, he had arrived in Shrewsbury Crossing to become the town's only doctor.

During the early years, even after the marriage, the doctor did not earn enough to support the couple, but family money from his wife enabled them to live in reasonable comfort. The social elite of the town showered the Willinghams with attention: they were always at the top of the guest list for parties and weddings, and the doctor was frequently invited to speak at civic clubs and religious services. Indeed, the community was committed to make any sacrifice to keep the Willinghams satisfied with their status because few Georgia towns the size of Shrewsbury Crossing had any kind of doctor in the1930's.

The young Willingham had distinguished himself as a serious, even precocious, scholar and student of medicine during his years at Emory. His natural intelligence and academic excellence were buttressed by an unswerving religious faith entailing a deeply felt dedication to serving his fellow man. Having become a born-again Christian at the age of seventeen, he considered his medical practice in Shrewsbury Crossing to be an adjunct to his real mission in life: to be a living witness for the Gospel. He was determined that all who needed his medical care would have it, regardless of financial status, and he denied help to no one. His medical treatment was always accompanied by strong admonitions to his patients about the merits of clean living and high moral standards. His devotion to medicine and religion endeared him to everyone in the town, but these traits encumbered him with endless hours of work, leaving little time for his young wife and the two children that followed their marriage: C.R., Jr., in 1934, and Gloria Anne, three years later, in 1937.

The doctor quickly won a reputation in Shrewsbury Crossing and surrounding towns for his medical expertise and humanitarian instincts. Concentrating on health problems indigenous to the area, he specialized in respiratory diseases—asthma, in particular—problems severely exacerbated by the pervasive practice of smoking tobacco. Before long, people from all across the region—Tallahassee, Pensacola, Montgomery, Jacksonville, Brunswick—were coming to the small clinic for the treatment of asthmatic conditions.

Dr. Willingham was not only an altruistic care-giver; he was also ambitious. He had a vision of creating a medical facility that would rival the institutions in the big cities. He had begun by recruiting three Emory medical students—all at the top of their class—to do summer work with him for two years in Shrewsbury Crossing before completing their residencies. The three doctors eagerly joined him at the clinic in 1937, having succumbed to the doctor's magnetic personality and discovering firsthand the aura of respect and admiration accorded him by his rapidly growing constituency.

That same year the doctor had persuaded his wife's father and a local banker to help him finance a fifteen-bed hospital. Soon, additional doctors were moving to Shrewsbury Crossing to join the clinic, and the facility's reputation as a first class medical center continued to grow. In 1939 Dr. Willingham had strengthened his reputation by branching out from the respiratory specialties which had first brought him acclaim. He had begun to concentrate on treatment of spinal injuries and limb amputations secondary to trauma.

By the early forties, the clinic had become recognized as one of the finest medical centers in the Southeast. When the United States was pulled into the Second World War in 1941, casualties from the fighting began to fill the clinic beds. Government subsidies had poured in, permitting new construction and the hiring of additional nurses, aides, and doctors. By the end of the war, the little town was the site of a renowned trauma center housing over four-hundred veterans and hundreds of other patients. Moreover, clinic offices had been established in a half dozen cities in Georgia, Alabama, and Florida.

Through it all Dr. Willingham painstakingly developed a staff of dedicated professionals unrivaled for its prestige in the southeastern United States. By 1948 the clinic employed over two-hundred physicians, nurses, and other staff, and the story was frequently passed around town that the doctor knew each individual by first, middle and last names, including nicknames in most instances. The doctor was said to keep up meticulously with names and birth dates of the staff's children, always sending presents and attending the weddings and funerals of employees' family members. Wages and fringe benefits for workers at the Willingham Clinic were far above average for comparable jobs elsewhere, and the doctor followed an unwritten policy of avoiding layoffs and continuing wages of employees who missed work because of illness or other personal problems. Only the grossest misconduct got people fired: wayward personnel were treated more like children to be disciplined—not miscreants to be terminated. As a result all staff members took great pride in their association with the clinic and were accorded great deference by the community for their roles in creating this magnificent medical institution and the economic stimulus it provided. Thus, by 1948, the Willingham Clinic had come to be regarded as a "family" whose existence and continued well-being were matters of first priority in Shrewsbury Crossing, and whose founder, 'Doc Willie,' as he was more and more frequently called, was the town's revered, paternalistic leader.

But there was no deference paid to the doctor this June morning in his own household as he continued to pluck nose hairs before his bathroom mirror. The battle between Charles Robert Willingham and Emma Willingham continued.

"Emma," he said, calmly, "I refuse to allow your carping to ruin what promises to be a productive day. I intend to be a good shepherd of the day the Almighty is giving me, and you would do well to do the same."

"Well said, Herr Doctor," his wife retorted. "Besides ministering to the sick bodies of the downtrodden, unwashed masses—many of whom won't pay you—what *will* you do?"

"I have a staff meeting at seven-thirty," the doctor said, ignoring his wife's hostility. "Then I'm to address the Rotary at noon on this civil rights business. You know, Truman is pushing Congress to pass all kinds of laws for the Negroes—even give them voting rights when they can't read or pay a poll tax. It's insane."

"Yeah, it was bad enough when *females* were allowed to vote, and now they want to let in *niggers*. The world's just going to hell, right?" The sarcasm in Emma's voice was palpable.

"Many of us knew these liberal politicians would wreak havoc when Roosevelt was elected," the doctor went on, ignoring Emma's statement, "and I intend to encourage anyone who'll listen to me to vote the liberals out of office. We need a good states' rights president to rebuild this country and retrieve it from the socialists and communists. Return us to the values that made the country great. Maybe the South can pull together and defeat Truman this November—get some sensible southerner like Thurmond to run the country—that's what we need. We didn't win the war to turn everything over to uneducated, lazy Negroes, did we?"

"So, is that the sum total of your Rotary speech? 'Keep the niggers from getting out of hand'—is that it? Is *that* the message you intend to present to the yokels? Tell them precisely what they *want* to hear, right? Let their high priest confirm all their prejudices and narrow-mindedness. They already *love* you, don't they, and they'll love you even more when you pander to their ignorance."

"Emma, please don't torment me. You know I feel compelled to speak the truth as I see it. I know you belittle my ideas, but I can't believe God wants us to mix the races or He would have never created different races of human beings in the first place."

"Well, well, apparently you don't think God did everything right. He obviously messed up pretty badly when He created disease, because you sure as hell have spent your life trying to change all that, haven't you? Just think: if God hadn't created asthma, you wouldn't have found your way to the top of the damn totem pole. How do you reconcile your tampering with God's creation like that, my dear?"

"That's a ridiculous comment, Emma," the doctor glared at his wife. "You know Jesus healed the sick, and I'm only attempting in my feeble way to follow His example. That's not to say that I can ever be like…."

"Ever be like what? Be another Jesus? Don't be too sure, Sweetie Pie. I kinda' think you're on your way."

"I can't believe your attitude is so profane sometimes," the doctor said.

"I'm just sick of the pompous way you use religion to shore up whatever your views are on any given subject. You quote the scripture on demand to rationalize your racist notions, and it doesn't seem to bother you one iota that you presume to know what was in the Creator's mind when he made the human species. Isn't there a shadow of a doubt in your thinking that your religion is the passport to all wisdom? And doesn't it ever occur to you that the good citizens of this town listen to your views not because you're *right* but because you've risen to the top of the social ladder around here? Doesn't any of that bother you? Don't you ever wonder about…."

"Emma, why must you harass me?" the doctor sounded hurt. "I've never pretended to know the mind of God, and I'm anything but a racist. I pay Bootsie triple the wages most maids earn, and I've spent hundreds of dollars on a tutor for her grandson. Many of my black employees make more than some whites. Is that what you call racism?"

"I think you protest too much, but you're full of bull dookey," Emma said. "Let's get back to the subject: besides the Rotary, what's on your schedule?"

Grateful that his wife's tone suddenly seemed more civil, the doctor replied: "Well, there's another meeting with the architects to review the expansion plans. And—let's see—something else. Oh, yeah. I've agreed to see that young Rumpkin boy late this afternoon to talk about a summer job."

"What's so special about him? I've heard the boy has emotional problems—comes from a bad family—something about his father killing himself when he was a baby."

"Some of that may be so, but I'm told he's very religious and trying to make something out of himself. He may be a deserving boy—someone who'll turn out fine with a little help."

"Always doing good, aren't you, Doc Willie?" Emma said, bringing an abrupt end to the civility. "Always spending time with everyone but your own children? You know how disappointed Doddy was when you missed the father-son banquet at the church. As usual, you were somewhere out-of-town making one of your brilliant speeches."

"That's an especially unkind remark, Emma. You know how badly I hated to miss that banquet, but I have to balance my professional career with the family's needs, and I believe Doddy understands that."

"Like hell, he does, and you never spend a moment with Annie."

"I treasure nothing more than you and the children, Emma," the doctor said, again sounding wounded. "You lack for nothing—the finest home, car, social status. Why aren't you satisfied?"

"Why aren't *you*?" Emma followed the doctor as he went to the closet and took out a suit. "Always pushing everyone to think the way *you* think. Expanding the clinic, building your reputation, making more and more money! If you really believe all your religious crap, why don't you sell everything and—as it says in the Bible—give all you have to the poor? Or, more to the point, just send your children to the Negro school if you're so damn certain that the dilapidated thing is as good as the white's? Why don't you, Doc Willie? You're a pretentious phony, aren't you?"

"I don't understand how I could have caused such bitterness in you," the doctor said, buttoning the collar of his shirt. "I seem to have respect everywhere but in my own home. 'A prophet not without honor,' I guess."

"Oh, my God!" his wife bellowed. "OK, so now you're a prophet, eh?"

Again, the doctor ignored the comment and changed the subject: "Didn't you say you might drive to Tallahassee today to shop for clothes for Annie?"

"Yes, I plan to," his wife said, turning her back toward her husband. "She's eleven and outgrowing everything. Unfortunately, she's inherited your big bones—nothing else, I hope—and the only place to take her is Bernstein's. That's the only store within a hundred miles with anything her size—at least anything her size that's decent to wear for anyone except sharecroppers."

As Dr. Willingham drove to the clinic that morning, he rationalized that the nasty exchanges with his wife were probably just evidence of her early menopause—a nagging role, he guessed, assigned to females by God in the Garden. The remainder of the day would go exceedingly well.

The staff meeting could not have proceeded more smoothly. The executive group had met with two representatives from the Physicians' Advisory Committee, or "PAC," as everyone around the clinic called them. Some doctors had opposed expanding the clinic on the basis that additional beds would bring in new doctors, diluting the revenue pool. But Dr. Willingham had quelled that objection by arguing that additional staff and capacity would bring in new patients; and he had guaranteed that if any doctor's income fell below the 1948 level, he would personally make up the difference. That assurance had placated the PAC representatives, so Doc Willie pushed for a vote and the result was a unanimous decision to double the size of the hospital and begin a new campaign to hire doctors and other staff.

Dr. Willingham's speech to the Rotary had also been a rousing success. Calling Truman a demagogue, the doctor had received a thunderous applause from the assembly, who stopped eating T-bone steaks and French fries long enough to clap and shout support for the doctor's views. He had urged the group to write senators and congressmen to voice opposition to Truman's civil rights initiatives—especially proposals about Negro voting. In a final, tumultuous ovation, the Rotarians had stood and applauded his call for support of the states' rights movement and the election of Senator Strom Thurmond of South Carolina to the Presidency.

About half past six that afternoon, the doctor sat alone in his office, his secretary having departed for the day. Hearing a shuffle in the outer office, he stood behind his desk and called out: "Somebody there?"

In response, a young boy appeared in the doorway. "Yessir, yessir, it's me. Alexander—eh, Alexander Rumpkin."

From the doctor's vantage point across the room, Alex looked frail and frightened, a waif who might turn and run away at any moment. The boy held a cap in one hand, nervously stuffing the other in his pants pocket. With a tear in his britches below the left knee, he wore dirty brogans which were two sizes too large. He managed a weak smile, and the doctor could see that he was a handsome boy with strong facial features, except for a pair of narrow, squinting eyes. Nothing some soap and water and decent clothes won't fix, the doctor thought to himself.

"Well, I had about given up on you," Dr. Willingham said. "You were supposed to be here at six, weren't you? You're late! No way to start an interview for a job, is it?"

"No sir, it ain't, and I'm terrible sorry, Dr. Willingham, but the back wheel on my bike came off and I had to walk the whole way. Then I got mixed up about where your office was. I couldn't help bein' late. Please believe me!"

"If you aspire to work in the clinic, you need to learn right off that I don't accept excuses from anyone," the doctor said, his brow furrowed. "Life's about achievement, not failure, and nobody's going to last long around here with a negative attitude. Never—never again—do I want to hear you make excuses for anything. Won't have it, do you hear?"

"Yessir," Alex said, his hands trembling, "I understand. It won't happen again, I promise."

"All right, then, what do you think you can do for the Willingham Clinic?"

"I can do anything—anything you want, Dr. Willingham. I swear!"

"Never swear, boy, it's against God's law," the doctor thundered, making Alex even more jittery than before. After a long pause, he continued: "Now, Alex, what *specifically* would you do if I gave you a job?"

"I don't know for sure. Maybe run errands when my bike gets fixed? Deliver drugs to shut-ins and old folks, I guess. Stuff like that."

"Where do you live, boy?" the doctor asked.

"Over by the old sawmill. On Elizabeth Street. 187, I think. I ain't sure of the number. We live in one side of the house. They's renters on the other side."

The doctor hid a smile and did not alter his solemn expression. "And what does your family do?"

"They ain't nobody but me and mama—and my sister, Christina. My papa died when I was a baby. Mama takes in washin' and cleans folks' houses, and me and Chris do what we can to help out." As he talked, Alex's hands stopped trembling and his voice grew stronger. "I get in stove wood for mama, take out trash, do stuff like that—and I pick up work here and there where I can, you know, pick cotton and sucker tobacco. But nothin' pays much. That's why I want to work at the clinic so bad. Nothin' in town pays better than the clinic. And I'll take *any* job—any job at all."

"How old are you?"

"Just turned fourteen."

"What about school work? Do you make good grades?"

"Naw, sir, cain't say that I do—at least, not real good. But I don't cut classes and I pass my subjects. Don't have much time to study, though—helpin' mama and all."

"What about religion, Alex? I'm told you attend church."

"Yessir, I was born again when I was eleven, and I ain't missed a Sunday service since." A trace of a smile crossed the doctor's face. "I been baptized in the name of the Father, the Son, and the Holy Ghost, and I read my Bible every day."

"Well then, what would you like to do with your life? Tell me that." the doctor asked.

"Yessir, well, I've give that lots of thought—I mean, *lots* of thought. I've thought about bein' a preacher or missionary in some place like Brazil or Africa or somewhere. But where I finally come out—and you're gonna think this is pretty stupid, I mean, *really* stupid—but where I finally come out is this. I can picture myself bein' in charge of this clinic someday. 'Course, that's way off in the future, after you retire and all. That way, I could continue the work you do—you know, help the sick and all and do good." A wide grin broke across the doctor's face.

"I guess I ought to be ashamed havin' such foolish ideas," Alex said.

"Don't ever apologize for your dreams, boy," the doctor said. "Don't be ashamed to dream. You know, years ago everyone thought I was crazy when I said we were going to build a first class medical facility in this town."

"You showed 'em, didn't you, Dr. Willingham? You showed 'em real good," Alex said. The doctor's eyes sparkled. "I guess this here clinic's just about the biggest thing anybody in these parts ever saw. It's world famous, ain't it?"

The doctor rose from his chair. "Come around to this side of the desk, Alex. Here, sit in my chair."

The boy hesitated, then walked unsteadily around the massive mahogany desk to where the doctor stood. Alex lowered himself tenuously into the rich leather of the chair, resting his hands on its arms and sinking deeply into its softness.

"I ain't never set on nothin' like this," Alex said. "Why you lettin' me do it?"

Tears welled up in the doctor's eyes. "I just want you to realize that you should never lose sight of a dream. Hitch your wagon to the right star, and it'll all work out. This chair and the job of running the clinic can be yours someday if you work hard enough for it and allow God to take charge of your life. Do you see what I'm saying?"

"Yessir, I really do. I'm gonna try real hard."

"Tell you what," the doctor smiled and put his arm around Alex's shoulder. "I won't turn my job over to you just yet, but I am going to take a chance on you. I'll tell the personnel office that you'll be here at eight o'clock Monday morning—don't be one second late, now—and they'll assign some duties for you. If things work out this summer, we'll see about letting you work a few hours each day after school this fall. How's that? We'll pay you seventy-five cents an hour, but I want you to promise that you'll give one-tenth of your pay to the church."

"Yessir, yessir," Alex said, jumping up from the chair. "It ain't gonna be no trouble at all for me to tithe—I been doin' that. I'll be here early on Monday, waitin' for 'em to open the doors. Thanks, Doc Willie, thanks very much." Alex hesitated, then said: "You don't mind me callin' you 'Doc Willie,' do you?"

"Not a bit," the doctor said with a chuckle. "I'm used to it. I think the term is really one of affection, and I've even considered changing the name of the clinic to 'Doc Willie's Clinic,' but Mrs. Willingham won't let me—says it doesn't sound dignified enough."

"Thanks again, Dr. Willingham, you'll never know how much this job means to me."

"Tell you what," the doctor said, "why don't you come to the house on Sunday for lunch—you know, after you get out of church. I'd like for you to get to know my son. C.R. Jr.'s your age, and I think the two of you might be good for each other. Would you like that?"

"Yessir, I'll be there, but I ain't got very good clothes to wear."

"Don't worry about that," the doctor said. You just show up."

"Thanks, thanks again, very much," Alex said as he backed out the door.

Alex turned and walked briskly through the lobby and out to the sidewalk. Twilight was falling and the illuminated street lamps revealed two figures approaching on bicycles. It was Jeremiah and Ethan. "Heh, what's up, Alex?" Ethan asked. "What you doin' here?"

"Aw, nothin' much," Alex replied with a smug grin. "Where you boys been?"

"Picture show," Jeremiah said. "We just got out."

"Well, while y'all been wastin' y'all's time all afternoon, I just got me a job at the clinic," Alex said, pointing his thumb to the building behind him. "How 'bout that?"

"Who said so?" Ethan asked.

"Doc Willie hisself," Alex smirked "I just walked out of his office. Me and him had a long talk, and he told me to follow my dream. Said I might be head of the clinic someday."

"What kinda' job is it?" Jeremiah asked.

"I ain't exactly sure yet, but Dr. Willingham said the personnel office'll be 'assignin' me some duties.' That's just what he said, 'assignin' me some duties.' Sounds pretty important, don't it? I'm guessin', but my job'll probably be orderin' some of the nigger janitors and maids around. You know, makin' sure they clean up good."

"How'd you talk him into hirin' you?" Ethan asked.

"Easy as shit, Ethan, easy as shit," Alex said, "matter of fact, I'll tell you the truth. I was surprised—it was a *whole lot* easier 'n I thought it'd be."

The younger boys looked at each other and then back at Alex. "See y'all later," Alex said as he walked over to the edge of the sidewalk. There, he picked up his bicycle, mounted it, and rode off with a perfectly good wheel on the rear.

CHAPTER 7

Boiled Peanuts and the Dashboard Light

"Though it's cold and lonely
in the deep dark night,
I can see paradise by the
dashboard light."
Jim Steinman and Meatloaf

Rubbing sleep from his eyes, Jeremiah sat up in bed. If he was to accomplish the day's objectives, it was imperative to get up and get started. The proper boiling of peanuts required at least five hours—perhaps six for freshly dug peanuts. It would take thirty minutes to get the fire started and bring the huge washpot of water to a boil.

Jeremiah grabbed his clothes, urinated, threw cold water on his face, and brushed his teeth. Walking to the back porch and down the steps to the yard, he coached a fire to life under the pot, using the small sticks of kindling and dried pine logs he had gathered the day before. Jeremiah watched the sun rise as the water began to boil on this Saturday morning in mid-August of 1950.

The large, black washpot was a treasured possession of the thirteen-year-old boy. Used by his mother for boiling clothes until 1948 when the family moved to a middle-class subdivision two miles from their old house near the sawmill, the pot became superfluous with the move to the new house which featured hot and cold running water, and a state-of-the-art washing machine, complete with ringer. Jeremiah had gleefully claimed the washpot, which was ideal for boiling large quantities of peanuts.

Over the last two summers, Jeremiah had perfected the routine. He would spend Fridays pulling up peanut vines from the farm of a cousin who grew hundreds of acres. He would then push the vines home in his father's wheelbarrow to his backyard where he would perform the laborious task of picking the peanuts from the vines. Picking was the most detestable part of the job to Jeremiah; each pod had to be plucked, one by one, and tossed into a tub. Afterwards, the peanuts had to be washed repeatedly until the water became clear and no trace of grit could be found. For Jeremiah, preparing the peanuts, cleaning the pot, and gathering the firewood always consumed the better part of a Friday.

Timing was critical on Saturdays: the boiling had to start about dawn so that the peanuts would be ready for bagging and selling on the streets by five or six in the afternoon when townspeople and farmers' families did most of the week's shopping for groceries and clothing. Over the last two years, Jeremiah had achieved a reputation for his peanuts that usually made them sell quickly. His peanuts were always fresh and never over-salted. In Jeremiah's estimation, over-salting was a cardinal sin. Others frequently put too much salt in the water, but—more critically—they allowed the peanuts to remain in the brine after the boiling was complete, sometimes for hours. Jeremiah always took his peanuts out of the water immediately when his sampling indicated they were ready. Incredibly, at only thirteen years of age, he had become a master peanut-boiler.

It was nearly two in the afternoon, and Doddy Willingham was just waking up with a violent hangover. On the balcony of the second floor bedroom sat Alex Rumpkin, drinking a Coca Cola and reading the Saturday morning paper. Alex had been up for hours: he had spent most of the morning at the clinic checking the work of the janitorial staff, inspecting the linen supplies, and preparing payroll records. At sixteen, and after only two years at the clinic, Alex had been placed in charge of the seventeen personnel who comprised what was euphemistically called the "Facilities Services" department.

"God, Alex, why'd you get up so early? Ain't you hung over after last night?" Doddy called from his bed.

"Shit, Doddy, I cain't sleep all day like you. I got a livin' to make." Alex had drunk as much as C.R. Willingham, Jr., the night before, but the alcohol never seemed to affect him much the next day. "Come on, get out of bed. Let's see if we cain't stir up somethin' tonight. Ludlow last night was a disaster, wasn't it? I ain't never seen such cold-natured women in my life. Like ice cubes."

"Don't talk so loud, Alex. Mama might hear you, and 'sides, it hurts my head." Doddy got up and walked into the bathroom where he opened the medicine cabinet to rummage for aspirin. "You had anything to eat yet?" he asked.

"Just a sandwich, and a piece of toast this morning." Alex threw the paper on the balcony floor. "Hell, I'm ready to start lookin' for something, though. Come on. Let's go, you lazy shit!"

* * *

This Saturday afternoon, things were going very smoothly for Jeremiah. His peanuts were ready by two o'clock, giving him time to remove them from the brine to let them cool. After bagging them, bathing himself and donning clean clothes, he was on Main Street of Shrewsbury Crossing with forty-four bags of his prize peanuts by five-thirty. Since his cousin never charged for the peanuts, Jeremiah's expenses were limited to fifteen cents for the paper bags and ten cents for two boxes of salt. Selling each bag for ten cents, the operation was virtually all profit for Jeremiah, and this August afternoon he quickly sold all but one bag, netting over four dollars. With dimes and nickels jangling loudly in his pockets, he walked toward the Dixie Cafe and wondered why more people didn't take advantage of this money-making scheme.

The Dixie Cafe was sandwiched between a bank and a jewelry store on Main Street just across from the courthouse square. On the large, plate-glass window of the cafe were the words: "Dixie Cafe, Fine Foods and Friendship." Shaped like an inverted L, with a thirty-foot counter running along the narrow hall from the front entrance, the cafe held fifteen tables, some seating as many as six people in the back where the place ballooned into a wide area behind the jewelry store. In the summer months, houseflies buzzed overhead but were constantly aggravated by four wobbling ceiling fans. A dozen or so customers were in the cafe that Saturday afternoon when Jeremiah sauntered through the screen door and said hello to the waitress, Christina Rumpkin.

"Well, heh, good lookin'," Christina said, brushing back a strand of hair that had fallen in her eyes.

"Guess what, Chris," Jeremiah said, as he seated himself at the counter across from the sink where Christina was washing dishes, "I brought you a bag of my world famous peanuts."

"Well, bless my soul, Jeremiah! Ain't you the sweetest thing?"

"I boiled up a mess of 'em, and sold 'em on the street in just over an hour this afternoon. Cleared over four dollars too," Jeremiah said, beaming with pride.

"Why cain't ever'body be sweet as you?" Christina said. "Fact is, I'd marry you in a heartbeat if you warn't so young and some kind of cousin to me."

The mother of two children, ages four and three, and with nothing more than vague guesses about paternity, Christina Rumpkin was twenty-one years old. She and her offspring lived with her brother Alex, five years her junior, and their widowed mother. Christina had worked as a waitress and sometimes a cook at the Dixie Cafe for four years.

"You gonna eat something, Jeremiah, or you just want a coke?"

"I'm kinda hungry, Chris. Worked up a pretty good appetite with them peanuts. Let's see—tell you what. Let's have a hamburger steak, smothered with onions, medium."

"Anything with that?" Christina asked.

"Fries. Salad with blue cheese dressin'. Large coke, lots of ice. I'm pretty darn thirsty too," Jeremiah tapped his finger lightly on the counter. "Please, mam," he added.

"Let's see," Christina said, jotting numbers on a napkin. "That'll come to eighty-five cents. That dressin's expensive. We ain't been servin' it long, and lots of folks are shocked when we add on a dime for it."

"It's all right," Jeremiah was counting out dimes and nickels. "I don't eat out much and I like that dressin'. Here's an extra ten cents for you."

"You don't hafta tip me, Jeremiah," Christina said, "specially after bringin' me them peanuts like you did."

"Don't worry 'bout it, Chris. You're always nice to me." Jeremiah's eyes sparkled as he impetuously added: "If there was more warmhearted folks like you in this world, it'd be a lot better place."

"All right, now, you smooth-talkin' rascal," Christina smiled broadly, "you gonna make me feel all giddy." She walked to the back of the cafe where Beagle Williams stood by the grill. Sweating profusely and preoccupied with his cooking, Beagle had not noticed that Jeremiah had entered the cafe. As Christina approached to call out the order, Beagle looked toward Jeremiah and waved, grinning broadly. "Comin' right up," he said, loudly enough for Jeremiah to hear.

Beagle was the only black employee of the Dixie Cafe. He cooked, cleaned, and bused tables at night and on Saturdays. It had taken some time for white customers to accept Beagle's presence, but Beagle had worked in the cafe for two years. Starting as a bus boy, he had filled in at the grill one Saturday morning when the white cook failed to show up for work. Beagle had been cooking at home since grade school, routinely preparing meals for his sister Wilma, her two children, and his grandmother Bootsie, who worked as a maid in the Willingham residence. Beagle's cooking at the Dixie Cafe won immediate acclaim from the customers, and Christina and the other waitresses had already come to respect the boy for his good manners and politeness. He was completely reliable, and soon became the regular Saturday cook, filling in as needed during weeknights after school.

Negroes were not allowed to sit and eat meals at the Dixie Cafe in 1950. They were permitted to place carry-out orders at the cash register just inside the front entrance, provided they did not sit down while the food was being prepared.

Just as Jeremiah took the first bite of his meal, Ethan Allday came in and sat on the next stool. Both boys were thirteen and would be entering the eighth grade in the fall; their friendship had strengthened immeasurably over the years. Ethan was nearly six feet tall, while Jeremiah was two inches shorter. They were both handsome youngsters, although plagued with the usual pimples and unruly hair typical of adolescent males. Jeremiah's face was framed by black, straight hair, accented by bushy eyebrows that called attention to his deep, soulful eyes. Ethan's head was slightly rotund, with sandy hair and a broad forehead that gave him the look of an embryonic scholar. Both boys were excellent students, having tied for an academic achievement award given by the Rotary Club at the conclusion of the seventh grade. Ethan excelled in science and math, while Jeremiah's forte was English and History.

"What you been doin'?" Jeremiah asked. Ethan caught Beagle's eye and waved.

"Not much. Saw that Hopalong Cassidy picture at the Pinecrest. Seen it before but I still liked it," Ethan said. "Specially that part where Hopalong shoots them two thieves in the horse stall. You've seen it, ain't you? Remember, he throws hay in their faces and blinds 'em just when they get the drop on him. Boy, that was great! And, boy, it was cool in the picture show. You know, I believe mosts folks go in there just to cool off." In 1950, the Pinecrest Theater, the Willingham Clinic, and the Willingham residence were the only air-conditioned buildings in Shrewsbury Crossing.

"What'll you have, Ethan," asked Christina. "Hamburger?"

"Naw, thanks, Chris," Ethan said. "Had a hot dog at the show. Just a coke, lots of ice, please."

"You can have some of these fries," Jeremiah offered. "I ain't gonna eat 'em all."

"How'd you do with the peanuts today?" Ethan asked.

"Sold out in two hours," Jeremiah boasted, "cleared over four dollars."

"So what are you boys gonna do tonight?" Christina asked, bringing Ethan's coke over with a refill for Jeremiah.

"I gotta be home before too late," Jeremiah said. "Mama's makin' me go to early church in the morning. Gosh, I *hate* early church!"

"Me too," Ethan said. "Mama always knows what Aunt Melissa's makin' you do, and she makes me do it too. Don't you wish they weren't sisters, connivin' with one another the way they do?"

"They're just tryin' to bring you boys up right," Christina leaned on the counter on her elbows and cupped her chin in her hands. "I wish my mama had made me mind better. If I'd been goin' to church more, maybe I wouldn'a got knocked up and had two whinin', snotty-nosed younguns 'fore I was grown."

Jeremiah turned to Ethan, abruptly changing the subject: "Why don't we go over to Frog's Place and skate some, Ethan?"

Christina did not allow Ethan to answer. "Hey, that sounds great. I wanna go with y'all. I get off at eight. Mama's got the younguns, and I ain't skated in two years, I bet. Can I come along too?"

The boys eyed each other and fidgeted during an awkward silence. Finally, Jeremiah spoke: "OK with me, Chris, but you'd have to pay your own way. You know, me and Ethan ain't got no extra money."

A customer in the rear of the cafe called Christina's name and she walked away, leaving the two boys alone. "Jeremiah," Ethan said, "I ain't too sure we ought to be goin' to Frog's with Chris. She's lots older'n us and she's got a pretty rough reputation. I hear she's screwed just about everybody in town. What if our mamas find out?"

"I don't think they'll find out, Jeremiah said, "And 'sides, they ain't heard about her, I'll bet, and she's some kind of kin. At least she's willin' to spend time with us. We don't never see her old big-shot brother anymore since he's so busy with his rich buddy and his fancy job at the clinic."

Christina returned. Pulling a stool to the opposite side of the counter facing the boys, she said: "Lemme ask y'all something." She looked around, wrinkled her brow, and gazed deeply into Jeremiah's eyes. "I know y'all's good in school and all, keepin' up with world events, so I just wonder what y'all think about this Korean mess. Y'all think we shoulda' sent our boys over there?"

Clearing his throat, Jeremiah said: "Well, the President said we had to do it to stop the Communists."

"I shore hope it's the right thing, 'cause one of the Marines I dated from the base in Albany got killed over there last week." Christina's lips trembled as she nervously twisted a paper napkin in her hands.

"Gosh, I'm sorry, Chris," Ethan said. "Was y'all close?"

"Naw," Christina answered. "We just dated a few times, but I kinda liked him. He was from Boston—you know, Massachusetts, up north—and I just loved to hear him talk. He was good in the sack, too, but I reckon you boys are too young to know anything about that."

"I heard on the radio today that the Koreans are about to push our troops into the ocean," Ethan said, raising his eyebrows as he glanced toward Jeremiah. "We cain't let that happen, right, Jeremiah?"

"No doubt about it," Jeremiah said, "and if I was old enough, I'd join up now. We got to stand up to them Communists. President Truman's got General MacArthur runnin' the show now, and you know if he whipped the Japs, he can lick the stupid Koreans."

"Why we so dead set against the Communists,?" Christina asked. "I don't know nothin' about Russians that makes 'em so bad. And, 'sides, these ain't Russians. They's Koreans, right?" She lit a cigarette and blew the smoke toward the ceiling. "What do Communists really believe?"

"Well, I just read some stuff in my daddy's encyclopedia about Karl Marx—you know, the man who started Communism—" Jeremiah said, clearing his throat again. "I can tell you pretty much whatever you want to know about Marx's ideas." Jeremiah went on, "First off, Marx figured it was bad for individuals to own property—you know, farms, real estate, factories, stuff like that—he thought all of that oughta belong to the people."

"Well, they do belong to people, don't they?" Christina asked. "I know a whole bunch of rich farmers that comes in here to eat. And the feller that owns the threadmill, he comes in here a lot. Keeps sayin' he wants to take me out," Christina laughed, "but I tell him I don't date no married men, even if they's rich."

"That ain't what Marx meant," Jeremiah explained. "He meant that property shouldn't belong to *individual* people—just people as a whole, you know, society in general. I ain't sayin' it too good, but he thought no *one* person ought to own nothin'. Get what I mean?"

Christina was called away to refill a customer's tea glass. Returning to the boys, she said: "Well, shoot! That Communist stuff about not owning no property don't bother me none. I ain't got nothin' no way."

"Yeah, but you got the *chance* to work and have something someday," Ethan chimed in. "Ain't that right, Jeremiah?"

"Pshaw! I ain't gonna never have nothin' workin' in this cafe," Christina said. "What else do Communists think, Jeremiah?"

"A classless society," Jeremiah responded. "That's a big part of it. Communists say nobody's any better'n anybody else and everybody's equal. The Russians have done away with czars and kings and such. Everybody's supposed to contribute to the common good. Marx had a sayin': 'from each accordin' to his ability to each accordin' to his need,'—or something like that."

"Well, I say it won't work," Ethan said. "Folks won't ever be satisfied to stay on the same level as everybody else. They all want to get to the top. And what you gonna do about niggers? They cain't never be on the same level with whites."

"Shhhh," Jeremiah said. "Don't talk so loud. Beagle'll hear you."

"Maybe some of that ain't too bad," Christina said. "I get pretty sick and tired of bein' looked down on and treated like trash just 'cause I'm pore. You know, it ain't right for the Willinghams' to live in that fancy mansion—big enough for a dozen families—while younguns in the tenements go hungry."

"Come on, now, Chris," Ethan said. "You picked a bad example. The clinic's the best thing ever happened to this town. And our preacher says Dr. Willingham has done more for the sick and hungry folks than anybody. And he practically paid for the new school library by hisself. He couldn'a done none of that if he hadn't worked hard and made lots of money."

"Ethan's got a point, Chris," Jeremiah agreed, "but I reckon that the worst thing about Communists is that they don't believe in God. Marx says religion is the *opiate* of the people—you know, a drug—and that religion just makes common folks put up with their poverty while the rich run the country. Fact is, the Communists are downright *atheists*. It'd be a terrible thing to let 'em take over the world 'cause they'd tear down all the churches like they already done in Russia."

"Well, hell! We don't want 'em doin' that." Christina exclaimed. "No wonder we got to fight them Koreans. We cain't have 'em tearin' down our churches!"

Everyone turned their heads as the hinges on the screen door squeaked, and Erasmus Bonobo waddled ponderously into the Dixie Cafe.

"Rasty" Bonobo was a gargantuan man. Born with a massive frame and oversized feet and hands, his weight had ballooned during the last decade, and he now weighed over three-hundred pounds. His fortune had been made when he purchased the Shrewsbury Crossing sawmill in the late thirties, just in time to reap the financial bonanza created by the war's demand for lumber. With the war over the mill had been closed in 1947, and Erasmus had bought one of the town's three warehouses where flue-cured tobacco was auctioned off to the giant companies like R. J. Reynolds and Liggett during August and September of each year. During the rest of the year, Rasty's warehouse was used for storing fertilizer, grain, and chemicals.

As teams of auctioneers and buyers arrived in town for the tobacco sales each August, Erasmus made certain that these men had ample recreation—an undertaking for which the gregarious Erasmus was especially well suited. Men contented with generous supplies of liquor and women were likely to reflect that fact in tobacco prices. Erasmus superbly handled the entertainment side of his business, and the above-average prices of tobacco sold in his warehouse attracted farmers throughout the tobacco belt from as far away as Dothan, Alabama, and Havana, Florida.

Erasmus was a legendary figure in Shrewsbury Crossing, having spent virtually all of his adult life there. In particular, he was well known to the customers and staff of the Dixie Cafe, whom he frequently regaled with long-winded tales of his exploits. Womanizing—a special source of pride to him—was a principal ingredient of these tales, and Jeremiah and Ethan had spent many hours listening to him with a demeanor bordering on rapture.

"Hey, fellers," Erasmus said to the boys, as he trudged toward the rear of the cafe. "Ah, my lovely Christina," he whispered, stopping and reaching across the counter for her hand, which he kissed.

"Rasty, you booger," Christina said. "What'll you have?"

"I reckon—let's see—make it three hamburgers, double order of fries, and a big iced tea. And—oh yeah—one more thing."

"What's that?" Christina asked.

"A smile from your lovely face," Erasmus still held Christina's hand.

"Don't give me that crap, Rasty," Christina said, pulling away.

"Come on, boys," Erasmus said, "I'm gonna sit back here at a table where I can rest my back."

Jeremiah had finished his meal, so he and Ethan grabbed their glasses and followed Erasmus to the rear where he positioned himself against the wall with a view of the entire cafe. Beagle continued to fill orders at the grill a few yards away.

"You boys got some hot gals lined up for tonight?" Erasmus asked, as Christina set his tea before him.

"They shore do," Christina answered. "They got me! They gonna take me skatin' over at Frog's." Turning to leave the table, she giggled as Erasmus stuck his tongue out and flicked it back and forth along his upper lip.

"Hell, boys," Erasmus said after she walked away, "y'all cain't handle that hot pussy. She'll fuck both y'all's brains out."

"Shoot, Rasty," Jeremiah protested, "we ain't gonna screw her. 'Sides, we didn't even ask her to go nowhere with us. She invited herself."

"Listen, boys," Erasmus went on. "I've knowed that gal since she was a baby. Used to work with her daddy at the sawmill. And I can tell you, if she makes up her mind to fuck you, they ain't *nothin'* you can do about it." The boys looked at each other and giggled.

"I'll tell y'all somethin' else," Erasmus went on. "If Christina—or any woman, a wife, a concubine, a girl friend—ever gives you a chance to fuck 'em and you don't do it, they gonna hate you for *life*! I mean, you gonna be *shit* in their book. So I say always—and I mean *always*—accept pussy when it's offered. Never turn it down. Don't matter how ugly the gal is neither."

Ethan took a swallow of coke. Resting his chin on his hand, he said: "How can you know it's bein' offered? I ain't never had a gal offer it, I don't think."

"Shit, you can tell," Erasmus responded. "Now, you boys are still a little young, but it'll happen. And one thing you oughta' do: make sure you look at women like you want to fuck 'em. You know, just keep it in your head all the time. They like that, even them that ain't wantin' to fuck. They still want you to *want* to fuck them."

"Rasty, looks like you'd get slapped, lookin' at women like that," Jeremiah said.

"Hell, boy," Erasmus said. "Been doin' it all my life, and ain't never had no woman slap me yet."

Christina arrived with Erasmus' hamburgers. He put his arm around her waist and squeezed her thigh with his big hand; the boys looked at each other and giggled again. Pushing Erasmus away, Christina asked: "What's wrong with you boys? What kind of crap has Rasty been feedin' y'all?"

✤ ✤ ✤

The 1948 Buick Roadmaster convertible eased down the long driveway leading from the Willingham mansion. Painted in a rich, plum color with a white top folded down in the well behind the back seat, the automobile was equipped with the latest technology: a Dynaflow transmission which, although slow in acceleration, was fully automatic. An in-line eight-cylinder engine powered the massive, four-thousand-pound machine. With chrome everywhere and four-inch white sidewall tires, the car was the most awesome vehicle in Shrewsbury Crossing.

Behind the wheel was Alexander Rumpkin. His passenger was "Doddy" Willingham—as shiftless as the Buick. Doddy had received the automobile two months earlier on his sixteenth birthday as a gift from his father. The doctor's son was a complete misfit, frequently skipping school and disrupting classes to the point that teachers jockeyed with each other to avoid having him in their classrooms. Accosted twice by local merchants for shoplifting, he had also been stopped frequently for under-age and drunken driving by the police. As the son of the town's most influential citizen, however, he was never arrested or charged with a crime.

Dr. Willingham was appalled by his son's conduct, but the father had been completely unsuccessful in devising or carrying out effective discipline to change the boy's ways. By contrast, Alex Rumpkin had all the attributes the doctor wanted in a son: he was religious, industrious, and ambitious. Since the doctor gave him his first summer job at the clinic, he had become a fixture in the Willingham household. Although Emma Willingham did not share her husband's admiration for Alex, she was titillated by the numerous compliments he paid her and she admired his gall. He would brush against her shoulder as he reached for a glass in the kitchen, and he would lightly rub a foot against her calf as they sat together with the family for supper. In 1950, Alex had become the constant, inseparable companion of C. R. Willingham, Jr.

"Where you wanna go?" Alex asked as they turned out of the Willingham driveway.

"I don't care, just cruise around some, I reckon." C. R., Jr., lifted a flask containing Jim Beam to his mouth. He was already drunk.

The August sun had dropped below the big oaks and pine trees lining the streets of town, and the air had cooled by several degrees as the automobile lumbered toward the courthouse square.

"Heh, ain't that Rasty's Cadillac?" Alex asked.

"B'lieve it is," Doddy said. "He must be in the cafe."

"Let's pull in," Alex said. "I love to hear that old fart talk. Him and my daddy hung around together before my daddy was killed. Rasty liked my daddy a lot."

Alex pulled the car into the curb and blew the horn loudly three times. Doddy stuck the flask into his pocket as they left the car and entered the café. Alex walked briskly several feet ahead, with Doddy stumbling behind him.

Christina was at the cash register at the front. Alex muttered: "Heh, Sis," and then, seeing Rasty and the boys, proceeded to the rear. Passing the grill, he grinned at Beagle and said: "Well, boy, they still lettin' you burn hamburgers around here?" Beagle did not respond, avoiding Alex's eyes. Alex went on, this time more loudly: "Didn't you hear me, old buddy? I was just tryin' to be friendly."

Beagle hesitated, then said: "Yeah, I'm still here. They cain't find nobody else to work this Saturday shift."

Reaching the table where Erasmus and the boys were seated, Alex gave Jeremiah a pat on the shoulder and said: "Rasty, how y'all doin'? You know Doddy, don't you?"

"That I do, my boy," Erasmus said, a trace of W. C. Fields in his voice. "The offspring of our prominent doctor. Everybody knows this young man." Doddy flinched as he heard his father's name in conjunction with his own. He had heard it often before, as though he had no identity of his own.

"And, Doddy, you know these two half-pints—Jeremiah and Ethan." Alex spoke with the cocky tone he reserved for subordinates. "So what the hell y'all doin'?"

"Just listenin' to Rasty's stories," Jeremiah said.

"Yessir, he tells some wild ones, don't he?" Alex said. "My daddy and you used to tie on some crazy times, didn't you, Rasty?"

"That we did. Never saw many fellers like Jesse. He could drink a gallon of cheap liquor, fuck all night, and put in a twelve-hour day at the mill. Worked harder and drank more'n any man I ever knew."

"See, what'd I tell you, Doddy?" Alex said. "Rasty, tell us about that time you and daddy went to Mobile."

"Shit!" Rasty said. "I bet I told that a hundred times. You don't wanna hear it again."

"Doddy ain't heard it," Alex turned to Jeremiah: "And how about you boys?"

"We wanna hear it too," Ethan said.

"All right," Erasmus cleared his throat, spitting tobacco juice into a cup. "It was one Friday about quittin' time at the sawmill, and Jesse comes up and says he's ready to have some fun for the weekend. Asks why we don't head for Mobile or some place excitin'? I says, 'shit, boy, I reckon we can!' and so we light out for the Alabama line in that old Model-T of Jesse's. Had two flats 'fore we hit the state line, but by then, me and Jesse'd drunk a half-pint of whiskey, and we don't give a damn whether them tires are flat or not."

"Who was drivin'?" Ethan asked.

"We'd take turns, but we had to stop every little while to fix a tire or to get out and pee. Them was the sorriest damn tires I ever seen in my life."

"So, did y'all ever get to Mobile?" Jeremiah asked.

"Yeah, we did. We finally get to Mobile around midnight, and we find this joint on the edge of town that had some of the roughest lookin' rednecks y'all ever seen. They was four or five of 'em, and a little ole shrimp of a bartender pourin' drinks. By then, me and Jesse's goat-screwin' drunk, so we sidles up to the bar and orders triple shots of gin. Drinks was cheap back in the thirties. We had just got paid, but we still didn't have ten dollars between us."

"What'd y'all do," Ethan asked, "get in a fight with them rednecks?"

"Naw, Jesse wanted to, but I told him that fightin' with them boys would be like fartin' in a hurricane—wouldn't do no good." Erasmus paused again to spit. "'Sides, them boys was too drunk to wanna fight. But what did happen was this: they was a juke box blarin' out dance music, and we spotted three old gals sittin' over in a booth—only women in the place. 'Fore you know it, me and Jesse took 'em some drinks, and they'd already had a good bit, like we had, so we start dancin' with two of 'em. I mean, we all so drunk we just standin' around weavin' on the dance floor holdin' each other up."

"What happened to the third gal?" Jeremiah asked.

"Well, that's what I'm comin' to," Erasmus went on. "We danced with them first two for a spell, and then Jesse gets to noticin' the other gal sittin' by herself. The first two weren't no ravin' beauties, but this other gal, she had a harelip and looked madder'n hell. So Jesse decides he's gonna dance with her, and he goes up and asks. Well, she's just sittin' there, her bottom lip pooched up over the top one to hide the harelip, and she tells Jesse she don't want to dance. But Jesse won't take no for an answer, so he grabs the gal's hand and more or less drags her out on the floor. 'Fore you know it, she's dancin' up a storm and havin' the time of her life."

"My daddy was a dirt-road sport, wasn't he, Rasty?" Alex slapped Doddy on the back and laughed loudly.

"That he was, my boy, that he was," Erasmus'eyes narrowed in his bulbous face. "Well, we musta danced like that with them gals for a hour or two when one of 'em says she's ready to go home, and why don't me and Jesse see that they get home all right. Said they lived in a trailer park about three miles down the road, so me and Jesse follows 'em in Jesse's old car. When we get there, we all get naked, and what followed was the most god-awful fuckin' y'all ever seen. Me and Jesse just kept fuckin' them gals, over and over, but what really busted me up was how Jesse fucked that harelipped woman. You talk about likin' it! I cain't believe any gal ever enjoyed fuckin' the way she did. We fucked ourselves silly until we all just passed out."

"What'd y'all do then?" asked Doddy.

"We stayed in bed, sleepin' it off, most of the next day. Then we drug ourselves home to Georgia so's we could get back to work that Monday. But I'm here to tell you: we had a fuckin' good time with them three old redneck gals."

"Didn't I tell you my daddy was something, Doddy?" Alex said just as Christina walked up. "Sis, you oughta heard Rasty talkin' about one of the wild times him and Daddy had over in Alabama—women all over the place."

"Yeah, and I s'pect me and mama was sittin' home hungry while he was off carousin' and spendin' all his money." Christina pulled a pencil from her apron and said: "Rasty, you ready for yore check?"

"Yeah, I gotta go," Erasmus struggled to lift his massive body from the chair.

"Any of you fellers need anything else?" Christina asked. "I'm fixin' to get off." No one responded so she returned with Erasmus's check to the cash register.

"What you gonna do tonight, Rasty?" Alex asked. "You wanna hang around with me and Doddy?"

"Naw, I'm pickin' up a little gal that works in the office at the warehouse. Her old man's off fishin' in Florida this weekend, and we're goin' over to the Legion to meet up with three of the auctioneers. Might play a little strip poker after we get to drinkin'."

"You really know how to have fun, don't you, Rasty? Alex has told me all about you," Doddy said, taking a sip from the flask and returning it to his pocket, oblivious to the stares from Jeremiah and Ethan.

"Rasty, do me a favor," Alex said. "You was real close to my daddy. Tell these boys how he died."

"Ain't no question about it," Erasmus snapped. "Two niggers killed him with his own gun. Don't nobody know how they took it from him, but they got it somehow. County coroner tried to make out like it was suicide, but he was just tryin' to get outta more work. I knowed Jesse like a brother, and he ain't killed hisself. Nosirree! That boy loved life too much, and havin' a good time." Alex beamed. "See you boys later," Erasmus said, waving his hand and shuffling toward the door.

As Erasmus left, Beagle came up with a large basin to clear the table. Placing the dirty dishes and glasses in the basin, Beagle backed away to turn toward the kitchen, but Alex's foot was behind him. Beagle stumbled, sprawling against the wall, as dishes and glasses flew everywhere, breaking with loud crashes. Alex howled with laughter and yelled: "Damn, boy, I heard you was a standout basketball player. I don't see how you can score any baskets stumbling around like that."

Jeremiah scrambled to his feet and helped Beagle stand up. With veins in his neck bulging, Beagle gritted his teeth and said: "Alex, you done that on purpose."

"You crazy as hell, Beagle. Why'd I want to make a mess like this?" Alex said, turning to look at the other boys with a sneer.

Jeremiah was picking up plates and broken glass, but Alex said: "Let it be, Jero. Let the nigger clean up his own mess." Turning to Doddy, he said: "All right, Mr. Willingham, sir, let's get outta here. See if we cain't stir up a little fun somewhere."

"Suits me," Doddy was slurring his words. "Maybe we can pick up some gals." Ethan was helping Jeremiah and Beagle clean up the debris.

"Hell," Alex boasted, "I done knocked me off a little piece this afternoon."

Beagle had taken the tray of broken dishes to the kitchen. Jeremiah returned to his seat at the table and asked: "Who, Alex?"

"Yeah, who?" echoed Ethan.

"Hell, I don't mind tellin' you boys," Alex said. "It was Geraldine Stillwell. I been bangin' that gal over two years now. She's told me she'd kill herself if I quit, so I try to take care of her about twice a month. I picked her up in Doddy's car this afternoon and screwed her behind the farmers' market."

"Gosh, Alex, she ain't no older'n me and Ethan She's sorta ugly too—you know, bony and skinny," Jeremiah said. "Why you wanna mess with her?"

"Two things," Alex replied. "She's a pretty good piece of tail, and she's also old lady Hawthorne's niece."

"What's her aunt got to do with it?" Jeremiah asked.

"Shit," Alex said. "The old bitch flunked me twice in English, and that could keep me out of Georgia Tech. Doc Willie says he'll pay my way to college if I can get in when I get out of high school."

"But what's that got to do with her niece?" Jeremiah asked.

"I ain't sure," Alex replied, "but I just get a kick out of knowin' the old woman's her aunt while I'm screwin' Geraldine."

"Shoot, Alex," Ethan said. "I bet you're just pullin' our chain. You ain't never screwed that gal. You just like to brag about it."

"Shit, Ethan, I can take you boys to the spot where I fucked 'er—just a little over five hours ago, probably. I can show you the rubber. Hell, it might still have cum runnin' out of it."

Christina came back to the table and said: "Jeremiah, you and Ethan ready to go to Frog's? I'm off duty now."

"Sis," Alex interrupted. "I was goin' to take these boys and show 'em where I had some fun with a gal this afternoon, but you can come too. 'Sides, it's a chance for you to ride in Doddy's convertible."

Hesitating for a moment, Christina said: "All right, I reckon so. Then maybe you can drop us off at Frog's. I was countin' on skatin'some."

As they reached the car, Alex directed Jeremiah and Ethan to sit in the back seat, and he told Christina to sit up front between him and Doddy. Seating himself on the passenger side, Doddy pulled a Jim Beam bottle from beneath the seat, took a long gulp, and offered it to Alex, who took a swallow. "Here, Sis," Alex said, "why don't you unwind some too?"

"Ain't sure I oughta," Christina said. "Doddy acts like he's already drunk."

"Aw, come on," Alex said, "let's get a little loose." Turning to the back seat, he said: "Ethan—Jeremiah, y'all want a swig."

"Naw, I better not," Jeremiah shook his head. "If Mama smells that stuff on my breath, she'll shut me up in the house for a month. You ain't gonna drink, are you, Ethan?"

"Uh-uh, not right now, but I could if I wanted to. I just ain't in the mood tonight," Ethan replied.

Alex drove to the farmer's market on the outskirts of Shrewsbury Crossing. He pulled the car to an open spot on the back side of the deserted sheds where farmers sold produce during the spring and early summer. Opening the car door and pointing to a crumpled condom on the ground, he said: "See, there's the rubber." Jeremiah and Ethan stood in the rear seat, craning their necks, and Ethan uttered a soft "wow!" under his breath.

Alex looked at Doddy and winked. As the car pulled away, Doddy and Christina continued to drink from the bottle. Slurring her words now, Christina said: "Aw right, cain't we go to Frog's now? I wanna skate some."

"Shit, Christina," Alex said, "you can skate anytime, but you cain't ride around in Doddy's car just when you please. Tell y'all what? Let's ride up to Pea Ridge Lake. The moon oughta be real pretty on the water tonight."

Alex turned on the car radio. Christina squealed as Doddy, his arms around her shoulders, began nuzzling her neck. They raced along toward the lake under a half-moon. Jeremiah and Ethan watched in awe the scene unfolding in the front seat. Alex pulled the car to an abrupt halt at a deserted marina, turned off the headlights, but left the front seat dimly illuminated by the dashboard light.

They all sat silently for a while, the only sounds coming from the radio and the crickets and frogs along the lakefront. The bottle of Jim Beam was almost empty.

Christina was locked in a deep, passionate kiss with Doddy. "You kinda like Doddy, don't you, Chris?" Alex said, placing his right hand behind his sister's head and playing with her hair.

"Yeah, he's aw right, I reckon," Christina said.

"Why don't you just check out what he's got in his pants then?" Alex said. The two boys in the back seat gasped and covered their mouths with their hands.

"What you sayin', Alex?" Christina responded. "I ain't wantin' to see this boy's doodle-bug."

"You can like a rich boy as good as any other kind, Chris," Alex said. "You know that, don't you?"

"Shit, I reckon you're right," Christina giggled. She then reached down and unbuttoned Doddy's fly as he sat sprawled on the seat, head thrown back. "Hell, this little rock's a—thing's hard as a rock," she garbled her words. "But I seen some a lot bigger."

"Why don't you lean over and take care of that thing?" Alex said.

"Aw, come on, Alex," Christina protested. "I don't wanna."

"Shit, you'll enjoy it, gal," Alex said, grasping her neck firmly. "Here, just lower yore mouth down a little on Doddy and he'll love you forever." Alex pushed his sister's head down. The boys in the back sat wide-eyed on the edge of their seat. Doddy's ejaculation was instantaneous, and he moaned softly as

Christina raised her head. She suddenly turned to the back and said: "Jeremiah, you and Ethan don't think bad of me, y'all hear? Y'all saw it. It was Alex! Alex made me do it."

Alex turned off the radio and for a moment no one said anything. Then Jeremiah whispered in a hoarse voice: "Gosh, Alex, it's after ten-thirty; you gotta drop me off somewhere so's I can get home!"

CHAPTER 8

Fast Break

"But I reckon I got to light out
for the territory ahead of the rest...."
Mark Twain, *The Adventures of
Huckleberry Finn*

During the early months of 1952 in Washington, D. C., lawyers and staff of the National Association for the Advancement of Colored People were collecting and meticulously examining motions, briefs and lower court decisions from various lawsuits around the United States. Two of the attorneys—a man in his mid-forties named Thurgood Marshall and a colleague, Robert Carter—were especially interested in an obscure civil rights case filed in Topeka, Kansas, where a black railroad worker named Oliver Brown was suing the local school board for denying his young daughter permission to attend an all-white school near her home.

All of the litigation in the various states was governed by a central theme: an effort to overturn legally imposed state policies requiring racially segregated public schools—policies sanctioned by the Supreme Court of the United States for many decades. In 1952 legal experts generally agreed that chances for reversing the law of the land upholding the "separate but equal" doctrine were virtually nil.

No one at that time in Shrewsbury Crossing, Georgia, knew about—much less cared about—the lawsuit filed by the black man in Topeka, Kansas. And as

Beagle Williams prepared for the most important basketball game of his life, neither did he. But what would happen two years later in that case would shake the foundations of American society, and it would mean a sea change for Beagle.

⁂

Jeremiah pedaled his bike furiously as he rounded a curve, the streetlights now making it possible to see the white picket fence of Aunt Pink's house two hundred yards away. The slight chill in the early evening air of March had not kept Jeremiah from breaking into a sweat. He had no watch, but he knew it was only a few minutes before tip-off at the Lincoln Memorial High School gymnasium, where the state basketball championship for black schools would imminently be decided.

Pink was beating a rug on the railings of the front porch as Jeremiah slammed on his brakes and screeched to a stop on the walkway not more than five feet from his aunt. "Jeremiah," she said, "what you in such an all-fired hurry for?"

"Ain't Ethan ready yet, Aunt Pink? We got to hurry if we're gonna make Beagle's game. It's for the championship, you know." Jeremiah was breathless.

"Now, listen, boy," Pink said in a stern voice, "I ain't sure you and Ethan have any business going over to that Negro basketball game. Colored folks don't like whites messing around in their affairs."

"Aw, we'll be OK. Mama says it's all right if I go, and you know me and Ethan's been over there to watch Beagle play before."

"I know you two think you're mostly grown, but you're only fourteen, and sometimes act like you're too big for your britches." Pink's eyes twinkled, but her voice was stern. "You just don't forget that me and your mama can still burn y'all's little rear ends when we need to."

It had been several years since Pink had used a belt on her nephew, but Jeremiah said nothing to challenge the threat. Changing the subject instead, he said: "Aunt Pink, you oughta see Beagle play. He's a sight to behold. They ain't another boy on the team that can shoot and run like him. But where *is* Ethan? We gonna be late."

"Eeee-than! *Eeee*-than!" Pink turned and yelled through the door, still partially ajar as she had left it. Ethan appeared, pushing a comb through his hair. "Mama," he said, "you don't hafta yell so loud. Half the neighborhood'll hear."

As Ethan descended the porch steps and mounted his bicycle, Pink said: "Now, y'all be careful at intersections on them bikes and get home right after the game. And for goodness sakes, don't be gettin' in fights with those Negroes."

"You know we got better sense than that, Mama," Ethan said. "We'll keep to ourselves like we always do."

Pink was still lecturing as the two boys rode away. Reaching the Negro school two miles away, they paid their admission and entered the gymnasium just as the names of the home team players were being announced over the loudspeakers. Boisterous cheers erupted as each name was called, but the loudest cries were for Beagle, who was introduced last. As Jeremiah and Ethan climbed to an area in the upper bleachers nearest the entrance, they joined in the chants from the crowd: "*Beee*-gal! *Beee*—gal!"

The crowd continued to stand and yell as the two white boys seated themselves in a sparsely occupied section of the stands. Mostly ignored by the sea of dark faces, the boys saw several black teenagers on the seats below turn back and glare with hostility in their direction. One black kid—bigger than the rest—raised a clenched fist and grabbed his bicep with the other hand. He said something to his companions and they all laughed. Ethan and Jeremiah gazed straight ahead, nervously, as the game started. Distracted by the action on the court, the Negroes turned in their seats and watched the game.

This was Beagle's last game. Jeremiah and Ethan had watched him play throughout his high school career. Beagle was very good. Since his sophomore year, he had been the starting forward for the Lincoln High Panthers. On a team of fine athletes, he was the best. He had a masterful jump shot which he released hanging in midair, as though in suspended animation, defying gravity, effortlessly tossing the ball so that it made the goal without grazing the hoop and seldom ruffling the net.

But, most of all, Jeremiah and Ethan admired Beagle's fast break. Taking a rebound from the opponents' board, or a pass from a teammate, Beagle would lope down the court like a greyhound. With one fluid, seamless motion, his muscles rippling, his body glistening, his feet would kiss rather than strike the hardwood on his way to the goal. Opposing teams frequently found themselves standing flat-footed and paralyzed on the opposite end of the court as Beagle made the basket.

And so it was this night. The game was a total mismatch with Beagle's team winning by twenty-two points. Beagle himself scored twenty-eight in addition to contributing numerous steals and assists. Jeremiah and Ethan stood with the crowd and cheered wildly as the final buzzer sounded. Beagle and the coach were carried on the shoulders of the other team members around the gymnasium floor while the crowd clapped and thundered with a deafening roar. They stomped their feet on the bleacher seats while the cheerleaders turned cartwheels, grabbed Beagle's legs, and screamed his name.

Bursting with pride and smiling broadly as they descended the bleacher steps, Jeremiah and Ethan left the gym. Virtually all of the Negroes were still standing and cheering as the two white boys passed quietly through the exit to the parking lot. They were the first to see the large, crude letters, written in creosote, emblazoned on the white wall of the classroom building facing the gymnasium: "*HOORAY BEAGLE—NIGGER BASTARD.*"

The boys stood frozen, stunned, paralyzed. Jeremiah's first impulse was to rush to the wall and attempt to erase the markings. But the crowd was filing out of the gymnasium, and the teenagers sitting in front of Jeremiah and Ethan were among them. The largest boy who had gestured defiantly at Jeremiah and Ethan yelled in a loud, angry voice: "Look at that shit!"

Then he saw Ethan and Jeremiah. "Did y'all do this, mother fuckers?" he screamed. "I'm gonna wipe up this parkin' lot with yore white asses."

The ringleader, followed by his companions, then ran toward the white boys, who had just reached their bikes. With the Negroes a few yards away, Jeremiah and Ethan ran with their bicycles to the entrance of the parking lot, jumped on and pedaled furiously away. Out of breath, they finally stopped to rest at a streetlight several blocks from the school. "Oh, my Lord, that was scary," Jeremiah said, his head resting on the handlebars. "I think them nigger boys woulda' beat us to death."

"Well, I'm glad we didn't find out. Who you reckon painted that mess on that wall?" Ethan asked.

"Beats me," Jeremiah answered.

At that instant, an automobile engine cranked down the darkened street to their left. As the vehicle rolled forward fifty yards away, its lights suddenly came on, and the distinctive taillights of a Buick Roadmaster receded into the night.

At noon three months later, Beagle stood on the platform of the Shrewsbury Crossing railroad station, waiting on the 12:40 run to Atlanta. Clad in a starched gray shirt with his best pair of khaki pants, he wore polished brown shoes which looked new but were one size too small since they had been bought to wear at a relative's funeral two years earlier. Although his feet ached and the midday June sun brought large drops of sweat to his brow, Beagle smiled and chatted nervously with the two women standing with him.

One was his grandmother, Bootsie Williams, who had permission to take the day off from her maid's job at the Willingham estate. Now in her fifties, a proud woman always impeccably groomed and neatly dressed, Bootsie had worked in the Willingham household almost from the day the doctor came to town in the Twenties. She had moved with the family three times: first, from a small cottage on the edge of town; then to a more spacious home in a middle class subdivision; and then finally to the mansion where they now lived.

Bootsie's home was in one of the nicer black sections, away from the tenements and row shacks near the old, abandoned sawmill. The house would have been quite comfortable, had she lived alone, but it was cramped for five people: herself, Beagle, his sister Wilma, and her two children. Beagle's departure would give them more room, but Bootsie would have given anything to get Beagle to stay at home. She fretted constantly about his leaving; she feared for his safety and morals in Atlanta. Her single-minded objective for the last two months—since Beagle made the decision to leave—had been to persuade him to change his mind. She had talked Dr. Willingham into offering him a job in the clinic coupled with enough time off and financial help to attend a technical school to train to be a brick mason. Nothing could change Beagle's mind.

The other woman on the platform was Beagle's sister, Wilma. Three years older than her brother, she had a six-year-old son, Leeman, and a daughter, Clarisse, age four. The little girl stood by her mother, holding tightly to her hand and leg, while the boy ran up and down the platform begging Beagle to chase him. Since coming to live with Bootsie two years earlier, Wilma had worked as a field-hand during the summer—picking cotton, hoeing weeds, and stringing tobacco—while picking up jobs as a maid and baby-sitter during the remainder of the year.

Bootsie's family was highly respected in Shrewsbury Crossing. Whites viewed them as reliable, hard-working, trustworthy Negroes. Blacks admired Bootsie for her compassion for the sick and elderly, and she was a matriarch in the church, always faithful in attendance and requiring the same of Wilma, her children, and Beagle.

Beagle had just graduated from the black high school, second in his class. Because of Bootsie, Dr. Willingham had provided tutoring for Beagle from one of the best white teachers in town, Miss Ethyl Hawthorne, a spinster who had taught English and Math in the white high school for decades. These were Beagle's hardest subjects, and she had tutored him since he entered high school. She taught him how to diagram sentences, making subjects and verbs agree, spotting the different functions of adverbs and adjectives, and avoiding dangling participles as though they were sinful. She gave him weekly assignments to improve his vocabulary and spelling. She introduced him to Shakespeare and Chaucer, Faulkner and Twain, Sandburg and Hemingway, Fitzgerald and Wolfe, Whitman and Wordsworth. And she drilled the fundamentals of Math into his head. Much of this came hard for Beagle, but Miss Hawthorne had seen his potential and would not let him rest until, near the mid-point of his junior year, he began to read not because she insisted, but because he wanted to.

But now, on the railroad platform, Bootsie was making life miserable for Beagle. She was repeating all the lectures she had given him during the last few months about the evils of the world and the rampant racial hatred he could expect everywhere.

"Listen, baby," she said, "you cain't let up yore guard at all. You know how white folks in this little town feels about colored people, but big city whites is just as bad, only they don't admit it. They'll smile and grin at you, but treat you like dirt. That's even worse than they is here."

Beagle had heard these words many times before, but he listened patiently and respectfully.

"And don't you forget to write," she went on. "That's the least you can do for yore grandma." Tears ran down her cheek. "Just as soon's you gets to Atlanta, and you gets settled, write me 'bout yore train ride, who you meet, things like that."

"Granny, *please*!" Beagle said. "Sometimes I wish I'd just taken off in the middle of the night without you knowin' it. Maybe saved all this fuss."

A faint, distant whistle signaled that the train was nearing the south side of town. It would be briefly delayed as it moved onto side tracks to pick up cars laden with cattle and produce bound for slaughter houses and markets in Atlanta. Bootsie sobbed softly and wiped her cheek with a handkerchief; Beagle breathed a sigh of relief as the train approached. Wilma began to cry, however, and Beagle wondered if he could survive the last-minute hugs and kisses these two women would deliver when he boarded the train.

Just then Beagle saw Jeremiah and Ethan walking rapidly up the steps to the railway station platform.

"Heh, Beagle," Jeremiah shouted, "You tryin' to leave town without sayin' goodbye to anybody?"

"Yeah, Christina told us you quit at the cafe and was goin' to Atlanta today," Ethan added. "What you gonna do up there?"

"Goin' to college," Beagle said with a grin, "but I'll be workin' in a big hotel as a bellboy, too." The appearance of the two boys had briefly distracted Beagle's grandmother and sister from their grieving good-byes. "Got the job through one of my cousins who works at the hotel," he went on. "Pays good money too. Says he'll put me up 'til I can find a place of my own."

"What college you goin' to?" Jeremiah asked.

"Morehouse, a school for colored folks," Beagle responded. "They already accepted me. Classes start in September."

"What kinda hotel is it?" Ethan asked.

"The Henry Grady—just about the biggest one in Atlanta. Granny's cousin says all the white politicians and bigwigs stay there—you know, county commissioners and such, state politicians when the legislature's in session. My cousin says they give big tips. He's even seen the governor there."

"Well, what'll you do? Tote bags and stuff?" Ethan asked.

"Yeah, I'll be totin' bags, but my cousin says they want you to do all sorts of things. Like fetchin' liquor for 'em, stuff like that." Beagle shifted his eyes toward his grandmother.

"I better not catch you messin' around with liquor for them white men," Bootsie warned. "I'll come up there and whip yore rear and bring you home."

"Aw, Granny, I was just teasin'—cuttin' up with Ethan and Jeremiah. You know I ain't gonna be doin' nothin' like that," Beagle touched his grandmother lightly on the arm.

Turning back to Jeremiah, Beagle said: "So you two ain't got nothin' better to do today than come down here and wait for the train?"

"'Course not," Jeremiah joked, "me and Ethan's just killin' time. We love to watch the train roll in, don't we, Ethan? Ain't got nothin' to do with you."

Bootsie broke in: "Well, I shore appreciate you boys comin' to see Beagle off. It means a lot to me—and Beagle too. He's always thought a lot of you boys."

"He ain't too bad hisself," Ethan said, "but he ain't worth nothin' on the basketball court."

Everyone laughed.

The depot was deserted except for the assembly around Beagle and a ticket agent who doubled as a porter on those few days when Shrewsbury Crossing had a passenger taking the train.

After blowing two loud bursts from its whistle as it crossed an intersection just below the terminal, the train screeched to a stop by the depot. Emerging from his office with a mail sack, the agent called to Beagle to board the passenger car. Beagle picked up a tattered suitcase and placed it on the steps of the train. Bootsie hugged Beagle tightly, kissed him, and then squeezed a twenty dollar bill into his hand.

"Granny, you don't need to do that," Beagle protested. "I got money. Just got my pay from the cafe, you know."

"Now you just hush, chile. Don't be tellin' yore grandmama what she cain't do." Tears streamed down Bootsie's cheeks.

After hugging Wilma and her children, Beagle turned to Jeremiah and Ethan. With an awkward movement, Jeremiah threw an arm around Beagle's neck, embraced him for an instant, and said: "Take care of yourself, Beagle. Let us know how you're doin' and where you are." Tears welled up in Jeremiah's eyes.

"I will," Beagle said, his voice breaking. "You ain't seen the last of me. I'll stay in touch."

Then Ethan reticently held out his hand to Beagle, who responded with a strong clasp. Ethan then grabbed him around the shoulders and said: "Don't get in trouble, Beagle, and don't do nothin' I wouldn't do."

"Ain't much chance of that," Beagle said, laughing.

Bootsie again threw her arms around Beagle and kissed him on both cheeks. "Now you take care of my baby," she said.

"I will, Granny, I will," Beagle said. "You take care of yourself and Wilma and the babies."

With those words, Beagle boarded the train through the rear door and took a window seat near the front of the section reserved for Negroes.

Jeremiah and Ethan had left the platform as the train was pulling out of the station. "You reckon anybody saw us huggin' Beagle?" Ethan whispered.

"Don't reckon so, but what does it matter?" Jeremiah said. "He's our friend, ain't he?"

"Yeah, but somebody might call us 'nigger-lovers,' huggin' Beagle in public like that."

"Right now, Ethan," Jeremiah said, "I just don't give a shit!"

Bootsie, Wilma and the children continued to stand on the platform as the train left the station. From his seat in the railroad car, Beagle grinned and waved, his face pressed against the glass.

Then, like a flash on the basketball court, he was gone.

CHAPTER 9

Puppy Love and Loose Lugs

"I knew you were in love with him
when I saw you dancing in the gym."
Don McClain, "American Pie"

Emma Willingham rolled over on her son's bed, stretching as she shifted from her face-down position to her back. She propped her head on two pillows that rested against the headboard and drew a cigarette from a silver-plated case on the nightstand. Wearing nothing beneath a mauve gown of silk, loosely tied around the waist, she fiddled with a strand of hair that curled just beneath her right ear lobe. Lighting the cigarette, she listened to a Perry Como song—one of the hits of 1954—playing softly enough on Doddy's Magnavox to allow her to hear the running shower in the adjoining bathroom, even though the door was almost closed.

The shower stopped, and she heard off-key whistling and the swoosh of a towel as the bather dried off. The sound of the flushing commode and more whistling made her smile as she drew the smoke deeply into her lungs and exhaled, creating smoke rings that lofted lazily toward the ceiling. Suddenly the bathroom door opened wide: a nude Alex appeared, a wet towel draped over one shoulder, his eyes blinking as he peered into the bedroom.

"Oh, my gosh, Miss Emma," he said, dropping both hands to hide his pelvic area. "I didn't know you was here." Hastily retreating to the bathroom, he pulled the door shut behind him. "I'm sorry, Miss Emma, please believe me, I'm real sorry," he yelled through the door.

"Ah, Alex, your modesty amuses me," Emma said, "you do such an excellent job of exploiting conventional values and common decency when it serves your purpose, don't you?"

Reappearing in the door, wearing one of Doddy's robes, Alex said: "I don't know what you mean, Miss Emma. I ain't exploitin' nothin'. I swear, I didn't know you was here. I was just gettin' ready for the prom. Where'd Doddy go?"

"How many times have I heard my loving husband tell you not to swear, Alex? You're not too fast a learner sometimes, are you?"

"Miss Emma, why're you pickin' on me? I ain't done nothin' wrong. I wouldn't have walked in on you—you know, without my clothes and all—if I'd known you was here. I heard somebody but I thought it was Doddy and…."

"Hell, forget it, Alex. You don't have a monopoly on doodles. I've seen quite a few in my time." She winked and added, "Some that might surprise you."

"Miss Emma, you don't need to be talkin' like that. It makes me nervous."

"I have trouble believing anything makes you nervous. You're quite an accomplished actor. I guess you know that though."

"Like I said, Miss Emma, I wish you weren't here talkin' like that. Where *did* Doddy go?"

"Downtown for some cigarettes, he said," Emma answered. "I wouldn't be surprised if my son's tryin' to pick up some booze somewhere too. You two college boys will need a good supply tonight, won't you? I'm confident you'll get loaded and make the Shrewsbury Crossing High School's 1954 senior prom quite memorable. Am I not right?"

"Miss Emma, you know I don't drink, and I try to keep Doddy dry too. Sometimes, I get worried that…."

"Hell, I doubt you worry much about anything," Emma interrupted, "and like a fish, that's how *you* don't drink, Alex. I've watched you and C.R., Jr. stagger in at midnight—holding each other up to climb the stairs. Save your lies for the doctor. I know more about you than you can imagine. I've had you figured from the start and…."

"I cain't see why you feel bad towards me, Miss Emma. I owe everything to you and the doctor, and I wouldn't do nothin' to cause you to get upset with me. Not if I knew it, I wouldn't."

"Don't give me that stuff, Alex. I can read you like a book." Emma shook her head defiantly as she spoke. "I've let you play your games all these years for two reasons: I wanted to see how far my idiot husband would allow you to go. But more importantly, you amuse the hell out of me and provide something colorful around the house."

"Why, Miss Emma, I can't believe you're talkin' like this," Alex said, his voice shaking. "And the way you're dressed! What if Annie or Dr. Willingham walked in like this and found us together? They'd both be upset. What would they think?"

Emma sat up in bed, allowing her gown to slide off one shoulder. "Shit, Alex, quit worrying. Charles is in Tennessee and Annie's having her hair done," she said, placing the burning cigarette in an ashtray. "We've got the house and the bed to ourselves. *All* to ourselves, Alex! Does that excite you?"

Jeremiah sat on the footstool in the den shining his shoes. He couldn't imagine anything worse: here he was, chairman of the prom committee, and he didn't even have a date for the dance. Everyone would know about it, too, and would probably be snickering about him when he made the welcoming address.

What had begun as a momentous episode in his life had turned into a disaster. He remembered squirming nervously, his arms folded across his chest and his hands and underarms perspiring, as the principal of Shrewsbury Crossing High School announced the election results two months earlier. He had worried that someone seated around him might detect body odor from all the sweating; and a large, infected pimple on his right cheek had given him special concern—not just because of its prominence but also because its soreness was a constant reminder of his imperfections, even in a moment of glory.

The words of the principal still reverberated, loudly and clearly, in his ears: "Boys and girls, and fellow faculty members, the ballots have been counted and I'm pleased to say that this year's chairman for the junior-senior prom committee—by a wide margin—is Jeremiah Goodwin."

Jeremiah remembered momentarily sinking lower in his seat, his hands sweating even more profusely, while his schoolmates broke into loud applause, some hooting and whistling. Ethan, seated to his right, slapped him hard on the back. The principal had beckoned Jeremiah to the stage, and he had finally managed to stand, crawling over people to reach the end of the row.

Winning the election had been no surprise to Jeremiah. Many classmates had told him that he was a shoo-in, and he had been sure he would receive most of the faculty votes. Now in his junior year, he had gained a reputation as a superior student, and he was a leader in most school activities: the Beta Club, the debate and drama clubs, school newspaper, choir, band—everything but athletics. He disdained the violence of football and at 130 pounds, he was too small to play. He disliked the arrogance of the basketball coach, so with a natural inquisitiveness and strong intelligence he had concentrated on academics. Now, it had paid off: he had won the role he wanted most—chairman of the prom committee.

Jeremiah had taken his place at the podium and delivered an appropriately short and humble acceptance speech.

"First," he had said, nervously shuffling his feet, "I want to thank all of you for allowing me to head up the 1954 junior-senior prom committee. This event has special meaning to everyone—particularly the senior class, and we juniors will do everything we can to make this year's prom the best ever. I know I can count on everyone for support. Y'all know me," he had added with a grin, "I'm good at gettin' other people to do all the work."

Laughter and enthusiastic applause had rung out as someone yelled: "Yeah, old slavedriver Jeremiah, we all know you." Jeremiah had paused and cleared his throat. As he had waited for silence, he remembered thinking how his public speaking seemed to stir audiences and yet he didn't understand why. He did not consider himself a good orator, but something—maybe the note of sincerity, the deep sense of purpose in his voice—appeared to win his listeners' response. Although he always had to battle a bad case of butterflies, public speaking invigorated him and imbued him with a feeling of status and importance. The power to move people with the spoken word was an awesome responsibility, in his view. Jeremiah knew that all great leaders—Churchill, FDR, Ghandi—had a mystic power to persuade, some for good, some for evil:. He had watched, awestruck, newsreels of Hitler extolling frenzied Germans to fight on hopelessly and face almost certain death in the last days of the war when Allied soldiers were closing in on Berlin. He had not understood Hitler's words, but he had sensed their magical power to control people's minds.

Jeremiah had concluded his acceptance speech with a call to arms: "I sincerely seek your suggestions and ideas. This prom can be our finest ever. And it is only fitting that we send our fellow students in the senior class forth after graduation with an unforgettable dance. With your help, this prom can measure up to the superb accomplishments of our school in all its activities: on the athletic fields, in the classrooms and in academic, literary, and artistic pursuits. So, let's get together and produce a prom that will do honor to SCHS—the best high school in Georgia."

Thunderous applause had followed Jeremiah as he stepped off the stage and started toward his seat. As he brushed past Annie Willingham, she had smiled warmly and taken him by the arm. Their eyes had met as she whispered: "Congratulations, Jeremiah, that was *great*!"

Ethan had been smiling broadly as Jeremiah returned to his seat. "Well, old boy," Jeremiah had said, "you'd be wiping that grin off your face if you knew how much work you're gonna have to do. I'm makin' you vice-chairman and treasurer of this committee."

"Like the dickens, you say. You ain't gonna stick me with that."

"No question about it," Jeremiah had said, "I gotta have some dumb butt to do all the work."

Although Ethan had grumbled throughout the process, Jeremiah had known from the beginning that he could count on his cousin. Ethan was meticulously careful with money; he would count every penny and spare no efforts to get the best prices for the prom's supplies. Ethan had the patience of Job, even to the point that at times Jeremiah berated him for being painstakingly slow. But Jeremiah knew that the prom's resources—funds raised over the last two years by his class with projects such as magazine sales, cake raffles, and car washes—would be in good hands with Ethan. Conscientious to a fault, Ethan took his assignments as treasurer and vice-chairman as though they were sacred missions.

As the two cousins walked from the auditorium, Jeremiah had stopped periodically to accept a congratulatory handshake. "So who all's gonna be on the committee?" Ethan had asked.

Jeremiah had given the task of selecting the committee a great deal of thought, even before he heard his name called as chairman. Selection of committee members would be a tricky job. Choosing vocal, influential classmates would be smart, he knew, since their appointment would silence their tendency to second-guess everything. At the same time, real workhorses would be needed, and Ethan was clearly the best choice for one of those.

Another workhorse was Annie Willingham, whom Jeremiah had placed in charge of the planning subcommittee. Although the daughter of the richest and most influential citizen in town, Annie was no snob. She and Jeremiah had worked together on many school projects, and he had always found her to be sensible, hardworking and cooperative. She was co-captain of his debate team and co-editor with him for the school newspaper. She had played the female lead in the last school play, a play he had directed.

Annie Willingham was no beauty queen, but in Jeremiah's eyes she had all of the attributes of the perfect female. She was incredibly smart, and had a bright, sparkling personality. Taller than Jeremiah by two inches, she had inherited Dr. Willingham's stature as well as the sharp, angular features and high cheekbones of his face. A good athlete, she had been the starting center on the girls' basketball team since her sophomore year. No one in school understood why Annie had not left Shrewsbury Crossing for one of the exclusive girls' finishing schools in Virginia or the Northeast. But Annie did not fit the pattern of debutantes that Jeremiah imagined would attend such schools. She was down-to-earth, full of laughter and good humor, all of which made Jeremiah enjoy working with her. At the same time, he never had been able to lose sight of her family's status and wealth and the Willinghams' position at the apex of the town's social register. While Annie appeared to be comfortable with Jeremiah—even liked him, he felt—she carried herself with poise and dignity that Jeremiah attributed to her family's prominence. Something about the rich, as he recalled in *The Great Gatsby*, made her different from him, something that would separate the two of them forever.

So Annie and Ethan had been chosen as his workhorses; two others had been picked to cover the political angles. John Weaver and Eloise Haynes were perfect choices. Haynes was the daughter of the chief surgeon of the Willingham Clinic, and Jeremiah had appointed her to be deputy chairman for liaison between the committee and the faculty. The position had given her the visibility and status she craved, but was a rather innocuous role that would not interfere with the real work of planning for the prom.

Weaver was the son of the chairman of the county commissioners, a close friend of C. R., Jr., and Alex. He had been their constant companion before their graduation from high school two years earlier and their departure for Georgia Tech. Jeremiah had named Weaver to chair the band selection subcommittee, a role that would be primarily confined to information gathering while the final choice of a band would be reserved for Jeremiah himself, with advice from Ethan and Annie.

For the next two months, Jeremiah had relished his role as prom chairman. Meeting almost daily with Annie and Ethan, the three of them had been dubbed the "Musketeers" by their fellow classmates and a few of the teachers. Jeremiah's infatuation with Annie had grown as he observed her shrewd organizational skills and her clever handling of classmates' idiosyncrasies as she put the prom's infrastructure in place. But his growing emotional attachment to Annie made him flustered even more after each encounter with her, since he constantly reflected on the barriers between them, insurmountable barriers, he figured, because of their disparate family backgrounds. She was simply beyond his reach, he had thought.

Three nights before the prom, Jeremiah had sat alone in his bedroom studying for an English test. As the telephone rang in the den, Jeremiah scrambled to answer

It had been Beagle. "Jeremiah, how you doin'? Know who this is?"

"Well, for Pete's sake, Beagle," Jeremiah had exclaimed, "it's good to hear from you. Where are you? Still in Atlanta?"

"Yeah, I'm still here, but I won't be for long. I got some news today that I just gotta share with you."

"Sure," Jeremiah had said, "shoot!"

"Just listen to what I'm about to read, a telegram I got this morning. Just listen," Beagle had said, the excitement ringing in his voice. "It's addressed to *Mr.* Beagle Williams—imagine that, Jeremiah, somebody calling this darky from Shrewsbury Crossing 'mister.' And in a telegram too."

"What's it say?" Jeremiah had asked.

"It says—I'm readin' from it now—listen, Jeremiah: 'Dear Mr. Williams: Am pleased to advise that I am now able to offer you a principal appointment to the Naval Academy for entrance in July 1954. Please inform me immediately if you desire to accept this appointment in order that I may make the proper arrangements with the Navy Department.' And get this, Jeremiah: it's signed 'Richard B. Eastman, U. S. Senator.'"

"Wow," Jeremiah had muttered, "Holy cow! You gotta be lyin', Beagle. You can't be serious."

"It's a fact. I'm holdin' the telegram right here in my hand."

"You gonna accept?" Jeremiah had asked.

"Man, I gotta take it," Beagle had answered. "It's a free education at a military academy. You know I'm gonna take it."

"How'd you get the senator to pick you?" Jeremiah had asked.

"It's a long story, but basically I just took a statewide civil service exam the senator uses to select military academy appointments—you know, a basic skills test, aptitude, all that kind of stuff—and I came in third in the state. He probably never figured he'd be faced with appointing a Negro, but the first and second place finishers flunked their physicals, so here I am—going to the *United States Naval Academy*! Ain't that something?"

"It sure is," Jeremiah had answered. "Who else have you told?"

"I called Granny right off, of course, and she's gonna tell Doc Willie. You know, I would have never scored so high on that test if Dr. Willingham hadn't paid for my tutor all those years. And now, I'm callin' you. I want you to tell Ethan."

"So you begin in July? That's amazin'," Jeremiah had said. "Hope we can see you before you go."

"Guess I better hang up now," Beagle had said. "You know, these long-distance calls are beginnin' to add up."

Jeremiah had first called Ethan to relay Beagle's news and then he had attempted to get back to studying, but he could not concentrate. Overwhelmed by the news from Beagle, Jeremiah had reminisced about his youth with Beagle—the sawdust pile, the fights with Alex, all the games, the joy of watching Beagle play basketball. Recalling how hard it had been for him and Ethan as they grew older to understand why Beagle's color branded him an outcast from their town's white world, isolating him from everything decent and hopeful, tears came to Jeremiah's eyes. Then a lump had risen in his throat as it dawned on him that Beagle was finally overcoming the obstacles of race—succeeding against overwhelming odds. If Beagle could do that, Jeremiah had reasoned, then he certainly should have the nerve to ask Annie to the prom. Wasn't he president of the Beta Club and captain of the debating team? Hadn't he won second and third place for boy's solo the last two years in the state literary events? And wasn't he one of the fastest sprinters on the track club. He knew Annie admired him, or seemed to. He could spot her easily in the congregation when he sang a special on Sunday night at church services: she would smile and compliment him warmly afterwards.

Jeremiah had made the telephone call on the pretense that he needed to discuss last-minute items concerning the prom. Then, spitting the words out, he had said: "Oh, by the way, I still—and it's terrible waitin' 'til the last minute like this—but I was wonderin'…."

"Wondering what?" Annie had asked.

"Well, you know," Jeremiah had stammered, "Ethan said this afternoon that he didn't think you had a date yet, and I thought—" Jeremiah had cleared his throat, "that you might go with me."

"Oh, Jeremiah, I wish you had asked earlier," Annie had responded, "but I called Alex two weeks ago and asked him to go with me. You know, Doddy is takin' Eloise Haynes, and he and Alex will be comin' in from Tech Friday night."

Jeremiah's heart had sunk. "Just thought I'd ask," he had mumbled, "I'll see you at school tomorrow." Quickly hanging up the phone, the rejection had been even more bitter than he had feared: not only had Annie turned him down, but she had made it worse by saying that she had invited Alex to be her date. Jeremiah did not see how he could ever face Annie again.

⁂

"Well," Emma said, reaching over and pinching Alex's nipple, "have you ever taken a girl to a dance right after you've fucked her mother?"

"That's an awful thing to say, Miss Emma," Alex said, rolling over to the other side of the bed and sitting up. "I feel ashamed of myself, and you oughta be too."

"Well, this is a first for me too. I haven't fucked a twenty-year old since I was a teenager. I am feeling a little guilty, but it's not because I've slept with you." Emma reached for a cigarette. "I should be ashamed of myself for letting you take Annie to the prom in the first place." Lighting the cigarette, she added: "And cut out that 'Miss Emma' shit! It's not exactly what I want to hear right after you've screwed me."

Alex stood up and pulled on his shorts and pants. Retreating to the bathroom, he said: "Look, Miss Emma, I got to get dressed. Doddy'll be back any time now, and looks like you need to get on some clothes too and get downstairs." Before she could respond, he turned and closed the bathroom door.

Standing a foot from the door, Emma said: "Yeah, I guess you're right, there's no use to upset the family with any of this, but you need to get one thing straight, Alex. This dance with Annie tonight, this is it! I don't want you having anything else to do with her, and if you lay one fucking hand on her tonight, I'm going to bring your little dreamworld crashing to earth. If you don't stay away from her, I'll tell the doctor you tried to rape me, that I had to fight you off, and you might even wind up in jail. One thing's for sure, I'll open the doctor's eyes to what a conniving little bastard you really are. Do you understand?"

"Miss Emma, I didn't want any of this to happen," Alex whispered meekly as he opened the door. "You can't tell Dr. Willingham stuff like that. I didn't try anything with you. You started it, and you know it."

"Sure I did, but that won't make a damn," Emma said, her nostrils flaring. You know who they'll believe, don't you? Sure you do, Alex, you're no fool.

And you'll stay away from Annie, won't you? You're a shitass, but you're no fool."

Things were moving remarkably well in spite of Jeremiah's anxieties. The flurry of work through the day on Saturday had made him temporarily forget the embarrassment of Annie's rejection, and she had made no mention of it.

The gymnasium was full of people: chattering, giggling teenage girls in pastel gowns of many colors with crinoline petticoats; uncomfortable, stiff-necked boys in white tuxedo jackets; teachers and their spouses sitting together like wagons circled against Indians; and parents sprinkled as chaperones in small groups of two or three couples in the bleachers. As prom committee chairman, Jeremiah had the responsibility of making welcoming remarks. Standing on the bandstand and clearing his throat, he tapped three times on the microphone to get the crowd's attention.

"Parents, faculty, guests, and seniors of the class of 1954," Jeremiah said, "it is my privilege, on behalf of the junior class, to welcome you to this year's prom. This group of seniors—all friends of mine—are among the finest graduates ever from Shrewsbury Crossing High School. we will feel great pride as you make your contributions to society and the betterment of this nation."

"Before the promenade begins," Jeremiah went on, "I must give recognition to some of the many individuals who made this night possible." He then called the obligatory names of Eloise Haynes and John Weaver, and perfunctory applause followed. He then thanked the faculty advisors for their support, calling two by name.

"Finally," he said, "I must single out two people who have worked untiringly with me each step of the way. They are the cement that held everything together and their contributions were invaluable. Annie Willingham and Ethan Allday, please stand and take a bow." Enthusiastic applause followed as Annie and Ethan stood and waved to the crowd from opposite sides of the gym. Annie sat down and Jeremiah watched as Alex put his arm around her shoulder and kissed her cheek. Tears welled up in Jeremiah's eyes, but he quickly recovered and said: "Now, it is my pleasure to ask the band to play our school song—'Glory, glory to old SCHS'—as the 1954 Junior-Senior Prom gets underway."

Spotlights from the upper stands skipped around the gym floor as the first dance began. One spotlight found and stayed on Annie and Alex, who swayed softly to the music, and gazed deeply into each other's eyes. Annie was more radiant than Jeremiah had ever seen her. Dressed in a soft pink, strapless chiffon gown tiered from the waist to the floor, Annie wore a diamond tiara in her hair that had cost many times the price of all the other girls' gowns and accessories combined.

The evening wore on, and the gym became sticky and hot. Jeremiah asked Ethan if he wanted some fresh air, so Ethan excused himself from his date and followed Jeremiah through a side door leading to the parking lot. Under a streetlight on the edge of the school grounds were six or seven male figures standing around a central figure. As Jeremiah and his cousin drew closer, they could see that the central figure was Alex, holding a lit cigarette. When he recognized Jeremiah, Alex said: "Well, look here, boys. Here comes old Jero, Mr. Big Shot Chairman of the prom committee! Ain't we lucky to have him join us?"

Jonah Futch spoke up: "Get yore butt on over here, Jeremiah, if you're through brownnosin' all the shitty teachers." Jonah had the personality of a scorpion. Regularly suspended from school for fighting, his graduation was still very much in doubt. Speaking to Jeremiah, the sneer and arrogance in his voice was palpable. "Come on over here, you little shitass, and listen to Alex. He's tellin' us about the college girls he's been fuckin' in Atlanta."

Alex chuckled. "Now, now, there, Jonah: it ain't that many—probably not more than two dozen. 'Course, keep in mind that I ain't been up there but two years. There's several dozen more on my list."

The group howled with laughter. Jonah slapped Alex on the back, adding: "But hadn't you better watch out, Alex? Ole' man Willingham would pull yore plug if he found out that you and Doddy's carousin' all over Atlanta ever' night."

"Hell, he ain't gonna find out nothin'," Alex said. "If it wasn't for me, Doddy would'a wound up in jail before the dust settled up there. Me and Doddy's buddies. We do everything together." Turning to Jeremiah, Alex held out a silver-plated flask and said: "Here, Jero, have a drink."

"No thanks," Jeremiah said, backing away from the group. "Guess I better get back inside. Ready, Ethan?"

"What's the matter?" Jonah asked. "'Fraid some of them strait-laced turds'll find out you're here with some real men?"

"Aw, cut it out, Jonah, I gotta go," Jeremiah said, turning toward the gymnasium.

"Don't turn yore back on me," Jonah said, grabbing Jeremiah by the arm. "I'll beat the shit out of you, you little cocksucker. I think you probably need a good piece of tail, ain't that right, boys? We oughta take him out and find him a little piece of nigger pussy."

Alex took Jonah by the collar and snapped: "Cut it out, Jonah, lay off Jeremiah. Ain't nobody gonna mess with him. He's my kin, and blood's thicker than water, everybody's knows that."

"Aw, I was just shittin' him, Alex," Jonah said, brushing Jeremiah's sleeve lightly with an apologetic flurry. "I ain't mad at the boy."

"Come on, Jeremiah," Alex said, "You too, Ethan. Let's get back to the gym. I cain't keep Annie waitin' too long, can I?" Alex tossed the flask to Jonah and said: "Here, fellers, y'all can keep the likker." As they left the group, Alex walked between his two cousins, his arms draped around their shoulders. He spoke softly so only they could hear: "See there, we gonna stick together, ain't we, boys? We always have, ain't we?"

❧ ❧ ❧

Three months later on a Saturday morning Emma Willingham poured her second cup of coffee as Alex entered the kitchen. "I finally got Doddy up, Miss Emma, and he's packing now. OK if I get some coffee?"

"You usually don't ask," Emma said, "you normally just help yourself. And I've told you repeatedly to cut out that 'Miss Emma' shit when we're alone."

"I'm sorry, I just cain't get used to anything else," Alex said, pouring the coffee.

"Are you all packed?"

"Yeah, I got my stuff in the trunk already, and we probably oughta be shovin' off before long. There's a rush party at the fraternity beginnin' at four."

"Alex, I need to say something," Emma said, reaching for his hand, "I've really enjoyed the sex with you this summer, but you must understand—none of that has changed my attitude toward you and Annie."

"What are you sayin'?"

"I just mean that you're spendin' more time with her than I want, and I can sense that she's become infatuated with you. But I won't have you messing up her life. As good as you are in bed, she deserves someone better, and I'll carry out the threats I've made if you don't leave her alone. Now that you'll be in college for the fall, I think she's going to get her mind off you. In fact, that's why I sent her over to Huntsville yesterday to visit her cousins. I didn't want her here to see you off."

"Miss Emma, I ain't tryin' to mess up Annie's life, but I am crazy about her and I believe she's fallin' for me."

"Well, you better get over it, Alex," Emma snapped, "because it just ain't going to happen. You two have no future together. I'll fight you every step of the way and I'll ruin you with Dr. Willingham."

Doddy walked into the kitchen, rubbing his eyes and stretching. "What y'all talkin' about? Where's Daddy?" he asked.

"Had to go to Albany for a conference today," Emma answered. "Left early this morning. Said to tell you both 'bye' and for you, Doddy, to get your grades up this quarter. You're going to flunk out if you don't get yourself together. Have you finished packing yet?"

"No ma'am," Doddy said.

"Well, let me come upstairs. Maybe I can help you. Alex says you need to get on the road."

Emma and her son left Alex in the kitchen. He finished his coffee, put the cup in the sink, and walked outside to the garage where Doddy's Buick waited with its trunk lid up. Next to it was the glistening new Cadillac Dr. Willingham had bought his wife four months earlier for her forty-eighth birthday. Minutes later Alex walked into the upstairs bedroom where Emma and her son sat talking. "Is your bag ready to go in the trunk?" he asked Doddy.

"Yeah, he's all packed," Emma answered.

"I'll take it to the car then," Alex said.

Emma and Doddy followed Alex down the stairs, through the den and into the garage. "You boys be careful with the driving," she said, "and, Doddy, study hard. You need to leave off some of the partying this quarter." She then pulled her son to her in a long embrace, kissing him several times on the cheek. Her farewell to Alex was cool, even though he attempted to brush her cheek with his lips. Alex backed the Buick out of the garage and the boys waved to Emma from the open convertible as the car disappeared behind the shrubbery of the drive. She returned to her kitchen, a tear running down her cheek.

Alone in the house, she spent much of the remainder of the morning on the telephone—first a long call to Annie in Huntsville and then with several of the clinic doctors' wives. She wanted to go to Tallahassee for an afternoon of shopping and maybe dinner, she told the wives, but none could join her; they were all busy with previous commitments. Shortly after 1:00 p.m., she decided to go by herself.

She went to her car, turned the ignition key, and drove slowly down the long drive leading from the Willingham estate. She stopped at a convenience store for cigarettes before turning onto the heavily traveled road to Tallahassee. As the automobile accelerated and the speedometer needle approached fifty, the car suddenly lurched to the right, slamming violently into a giant pecan tree forty feet off the road. Emma Willingham was impaled on the steering wheel and died instantly.

The city police investigated the wreck and found that the right front wheel on the Cadillac had separated from the hub before the crash. The speculation was that lugs were probably not tightened properly during the manufacturing process. Several lawyers urged Dr. Willingham to sue General Motors and the Thomasville dealership where he bought the car; but he refused, saying that he was too grief-stricken and that he abhorred litigation.

So nothing ever came of it.

CHAPTER 10

Marrying Fools

"...when reason falls to reasons,
cause is true.
Men marry what they need.
I marry you."
John Ciardi

A warm September breeze whistled through the trees outside the open window of Jeremiah's efficiency apartment where he was studying. The year was 1960, and Jeremiah and his wife lived in a unit on the third floor of a five-story stucco building containing seventy-one apartments used by Emory University to house married students in graduate programs, including Law and Medicine. Jeremiah's matriculation in the School of Law four weeks earlier had gotten him in his current fix: studying for his first major examination in Contracts—a required course for all freshmen. During his orientation program, a counselor had recommended that students use several markers to color-code each case as to facts, holdings, and dicta, and Jeremiah had dutifully followed the procedure. He now sat with his casebook open, each page variegated like a rainbow.

Some graduate students on the third floor of the apartment building were Pakistanis whom Jeremiah had met on the stairs and in the parking lot. They were friendly enough, although their broken English had hardly enabled Jeremiah to get to know much about them. On this September afternoon all he knew for sure was that some were cooking native dishes and unfamiliar aromas permeated the air and his nostrils. Sarah was still at work. She and Jeremiah had married one year earlier—in September of 1959—on the eve of his undergraduate senior year. They had met six months before the wedding at a party near Agnes Scott, and Jeremiah had fallen instantly in love. Sarah Mitchell was the only child of an Episcopalian minister from Chattanooga. She was a year older than Jeremiah, an age difference that concerned her much more than it bothered him. In fact, he treasured her maturity and sophistication—qualities he felt he sometimes lacked. While a teenager she had traveled to Europe and the Holy Land with her parents, and she had spent a summer on her own studying French at a small girls' school near Lyon. Unlike the rigidities of Jeremiah's Baptist upbringing, Sarah's indoctrination as an Episcopalian had not stifled her mind or placed undue restraints on her conduct: she enjoyed alcohol, talked openly about her religious doubts and inconsistencies she saw in the Bible, and brazenly endorsed evolutionary theory. Jeremiah had fallen in love with her mind and her independent spirit.

But she was also beautiful. With a voluptuous figure and blond hair falling to her waistline, Sarah was for Jeremiah the epitome of womanhood, a perfect answer to his search for a mate. Their courtship had been a whirlwind affair; for months they had spent every waking hour together, walking aimlessly through parks holding hands, rolling playfully on the grass outside the college library, and playing tennis on the public courts in Avondale. Many Saturday afternoons had been spent at a pub on Highland Avenue near Emory with dozens of other students, drinking cheap beer and planning their future. Since Sarah would graduate one year ahead of Jeremiah, their strategy was that she would get a job and put him through law school, after which she would quit working, have their children, and become an elegant hostess for their friends and his clients.

The Goodwins had urged their son to wait to get married until he completed his education and had a job, but he and Sarah did not want to wait. Their passion was too intense, but there were also financial considerations. Although Jeremiah had received scholarship aid and worked part-time to help with his college expenses, his parents had contributed all they could and had nearly depleted their savings as he entered his senior year. Soon after her graduation, Sarah had landed a secretarial job with a downtown law firm earning over five-hundred dollars a month, and she picked up extra money—forty to fifty dollars some weeks—typing student papers. So their first year of marriage had been marked with a steady improvement in their finances, and as he entered law school, they had been able occasionally to buy a pizza or see a movie without serious damage to their budget.

Jeremiah was terribly anxious about the Contracts exam. Even though he had finished college with a 3.8 GPA and scored in the ninety-eighth percentile on the LSAT, his first few days of law school had convinced him that academic success here would be infinitely more difficult than ever before. The professors were unmerciful, sadistically scolding students for the slightest foible in briefing a case. Having labored with severe self-doubt and a lack of confidence all his life, Jeremiah had quickly become persuaded that he would not survive the first quarter of law school.

But Sarah had kept encouraging him, stressing that she had heard other law students admit to the same qualms, and emphasizing her belief that his writing skills were superior to anyone's and would place him in good stead on written exams. Sarah worked hard to build Jeremiah's self-confidence, and—most importantly—she repeatedly told Jeremiah that even if he flunked out of law school, she would still love him and support him in anything he chose to do.

The telephone rang. Jeremiah doubted that it would be Sarah, since she knew he was studying and she always made a special effort to avoid telephone calls that would distract him.

"Hello," the female voice said.

"Yes, who is it?" Jeremiah asked.

"Jeremiah, this is Annie—Annie Willingham."

"My gosh, Annie," Jeremiah moved from his desk to a couch. "I didn't recognize your voice. Where are you?"

"Home. Shrewsbury Crossing. I hope I'm not calling at a bad time. Am I interrupting anything there?"

"Oh, no. No, it's fine," Jeremiah said, "Sarah's at work. I'm studying for my first big exam, and frankly, I'm terrified, Annie. I'm not sure I'll make it in law school."

"Oh, come on, Jeremiah. You'll do just fine," Annie said. "You always fretted about tests in high school and wound up acing them all. But if you're studying, maybe I should call back later…."

"No, no." Jeremiah protested. "I'm just glad to hear from you. What have you been doing since you graduated from Vanderbuilt last spring?"

"Well, I've been doing volunteer work for the Kennedy campaign for the last few weeks, but it's about to drive Daddy mad. Can't believe his daughter isn't supporting Nixon. He says Jack Kennedy will ruin the country."

"I kinda like Kennedy myself," Jeremiah responded, "but I haven't registered to vote. I'm ashamed of myself. I need to…."

"Listen, Jeremiah, I didn't call to chitchat about politics." Annie coughed into the phone. "I'm just beside myself with excitement. I have the most wonderful news, and after I tell you, I want to ask you for a special—I mean, *really special*—favor."

"Like what—what's going on, for goodness sake?" Jeremiah stuttered. "Don't keep me in suspense, Annie."

Annie was silent for a moment, and Jeremiah said: "Come on, Annie, now what?"

"Alex and I are going to be married. First Saturday in December, can you believe that?"

Jeremiah took a deep breath. Annie repeated: "Jeremiah, can you believe it? Did you hear me? Are you there?"

"Yes, I'm still here," Jeremiah finally responded. "I'm just stunned. What a bombshell, Annie! When did y'all decide?"

"Last week, and guess what? We both want *you* to sing at the wedding." Annie's voice rose with excitement. "I've got the song picked out: the Theme from Tara, you know, *Gone with the Wind*. I've heard you sing it. You do it beautifully."

"Well, sure, Annie, sure." Jeremiah struggled to speak. "But I can't believe you want *me*. I'm flabbergasted. You could have anybody—a real professional, and a fifty piece orchestra thrown in. Are you sure you want *me*?"

"Absolutely," Annie said, "and Alex too. He says he's always envied your voice."

Jeremiah paused. "Good gracious, this still hasn't sunk in yet. So you and Alex are tying the knot. How's he doin'?"

"Great. He gets more charming and considerate every day. The most wonderful man I know—except for you, of course, and you're already taken," Annie said, laughing.

"Is Alex doing well at the clinic?"

"*Heavens* yes," Annie said. "The clinic's my only rival for Alex's attention. You know how Daddy thinks he hung the moon. Alex is now director of personnel, in charge of everyone except the doctors. And he works like a Turk. In the office at six each morning, the last one to leave for the day. Works most weekends too. Daddy would be lost without him."

"And he's good to you?" Jeremiah knew the question wasn't diplomatic.

"Of course," Annie said, somewhat startled. "He's always been good to me, and, Jeremiah, you can't imagine what a source of strength and emotional support he's been since Mama was killed. Her death almost tore the whole family apart, but Alex was always there when we needed him. He's been a saint."

"It's good to hear that, Annie." Jeremiah hesitated, his voice breaking slightly as he went on. "I don't want to rain on your parade, but I wonder—I guess, I should say—it bothers me that you may not know Alex as well as you think sometimes. Everything about his personality and all."

"Rain on my parade?" Annie asked. "What do you mean?"

"Yeah, you know, say something to spoil your—how should I put it? Your dreams? Your excitement."

"Jeremiah, you're not about to say something petty, are you?"

"No, no, that's not my intention, but I've never said this to you. You know, Alex seemed to have a dark side I never could understand while we were growing up. You know, he had to fight to survive, with his family torn up like it was, and maybe that's why I had trouble understanding him…."

Annie interrupted: "A dark side?"

"Well, yes," Jeremiah regretted that he had created this mess for himself. "I found—er, he seemed to be rather cruel at times, Annie. You know, he seemed that way to me, to Ethan, Beagle—even his own sister, and he wasn't always sweet-natured and considerate—you know, like you seem to think. Don't forget that he and I grew up together."

"And you shouldn't forget, Jeremiah, that Alex has practically been a member of our family since he was fifteen and started working at the clinic. He and Doddy are like brothers, and Alex has probably eaten more meals at our house than I have." Annie's voice had become tense, with a tinge of hostility. "How can you say that I don't know him well?"

"I didn't mean it that way, Annie, and I guess I really am off base." Jeremiah struggled for a way out. "That was years ago, when we were just kids, and I haven't seen Alex much for the last few years. I shouldn't have said any of this. I didn't mean to say anything negative."

"You always worried too much, but believe me, Jeremiah, I know what I'm doing, and I'm happier than I've ever been in my life."

Clearing his throat, Jeremiah asked: "And you really want me to sing?"

"Yes, I do," Annie said, "very much."

"All right, then, I'll do my best, which probably won't be too good," Jeremiah said, laughing, "but it's your wedding and you've got a right to ruin it with tacky singing if you want to." He hesitated and asked: "By the way, how's Ethan? How's he enjoying his job at the clinic?"

"He's reached nirvana, I think. You know how Ethan is. He's always been blissfully happy when he has numbers to play with and now he has all of Daddy's books to keep straight. Oh, and get this: he and Irene just announced that she's pregnant again. Number two on the way. What about you and Sarah?"

"Don't even mention the word," Jeremiah laughed. "Not while I'm in school. Sarah's the bread-winner. She gets pregnant and we both starve."

"What about Beagle?" Annie asked. "Have you heard from him lately?"

"Matter of fact, he called from the airport a couple of weeks ago on his way to see Bootsie."

"I heard someone say he's in the Pentagon now," Annie said.

"That's right. Went there directly from Annapolis, I understand. Some kind of hush-hush work. Said he couldn't tell me much about it."

"Isn't it amazing how far he's come since he left Shrewsbury Crossing," Annie said.

"You can say that again," Jeremiah agreed, "and he owes a lot of his success to Doc Willie—you know, getting him a tutor and helping with the tuition at Morehouse."

"Daddy wanted to do it. You know how he loves to help young people. That's why Alex turned out the way he did. But back to Beagle: Is he married, or does he date anybody seriously?" Answering her own questions, Annie went on: "Probably not, huh? Probably too busy with his career to think about marriage?"

"Gracious," Jeremiah exclaimed. "I'm glad you mentioned that. I was about to forget. Fact is, he's getting married in early December."

"Who's the bride?"

"Someone he met in Washington. She comes from a rich Negro family in New Jersey and works as an aide to Thurgood Marshall—you know, the NAACP lawyer who won the school desegregation decision."

"Sounds like Beagle's in high cotton," Annie said.

"He certainly is," Jeremiah said. "He'll have some pretty major contacts when he leaves the Navy, and he says he'd like to go to law school. Being married to one of Marshall's aides won't hurt his chances, will it? I hope he won't get all tied up with a lot of this civil rights stuff, though. I'm afraid there could be a lot of violence before all this integration business is over. It's a very explosive issue around the law school. I've learned not to say too much about Thurgood Marshall because some people here think the desegregation decision was a constitutional travesty, and that Earl Warren is trying to destroy civilization as we know it."

"Well, I'm delighted for Beagle, and I can't wait to tell Daddy about him," Annie said. "I know you're trying to study, Jeremiah, so I'll let you go now. I'll send you more details about the wedding soon. Incidentally, and I hope you won't be offended by this, but you don't need to rent a tux if you don't want to: Doddy's got several and I think you two are about the same size."

"Thanks, Annie," Jeremiah said. "Believe me, I'm not offended at all. I may take you up on that since funds are a little tight for us right now."

"Give my best to Sarah," Annie said.

"I certainly will," Jeremiah assured her, "and our best wishes to you and Alex. I'm honored that you've asked me to sing, and I'm really glad you called."

Hanging up, Jeremiah felt a numb, inexplicable foreboding in the pit of his stomach. Somehow it had just never occurred to him that Annie would *marry* Alex. The two of them didn't seem to belong in the same universe—much less married to each other for life. Then the memories from the past came flooding in—the torturing of the squirrel, the grimace on Alex's face as he set fire to the animal, the humiliation of Beagle, the episode with Wilma, Christina and C.R., Jr. in the Buick. Jeremiah could still feel the sting of embarrassment—the trauma—of being publicly identified as the naked boy in a washhole with a black girl, although he wondered why it had been such a big deal to him then.

Annie doesn't know any of those things about Alex, Jeremiah thought, and he wondered if she would even consider going through with the marriage if she did. And should he tell her? Maybe just a short telephone call and he could unload all this on Annie, then let her decide things for herself. But then Sarah didn't know some things about him, he realized, and there was some history he would like to keep buried.

Besides, all kids do foolish things, Jeremiah thought, and Alex had also displayed warmth and gentleness many times. He had come to Jeremiah's rescue—protected him on many occasions. Boyhood was a long time ago, and time changes people. It had certainly changed Jeremiah.

Of course, marrying the doctor's daughter would never hurt Alex's career with the Willingham Clinic, and the thought that Alex was just using Annie nagged at Jeremiah. But then, some might say that he was just using Sarah—or Beagle, his fiancee, for that matter. Each marriage, in its own way, would allow them to get where they wanted to go. It's human nature, he decided, to use other people to get things we want, and everything is just too complicated to understand.

"It's all a mystery—life's just a mystery," Jeremiah mumbled under his breath as he returned to his lawbook.

CHAPTER 11

A Little More Detail

"We will now discuss in a little more detail
the struggle for existence."
Charles Darwin, *The Origin of Species*

Sitting alone on a wooden bench with the word "COLORED" stamped in fading block letters on the back, Leeman Williams thumbed through the pages of a *Time* magazine. It was a few minutes after 1:00 p.m. in mid-December, 1964, and Leeman was waiting in the Trailways station in Shrewsbury Crossing for a bus that would carry him to Tallahassee, Florida, where he would board an airplane to Atlanta. His mother, Wilma, and his great-grandmother, Bootsie Williams, had both been frantic with worry when they dropped the boy off at the station twenty minutes earlier. Leeman was eighteen, a senior at the all-black Lincoln Memorial High School, but he had never been north of Macon and had never crossed the Georgia line to any other state.

Had they been allowed to choose, Wilma and Bootsie would not have left Leeman to catch the bus alone, but choices had been denied. The two women were being required to spend all afternoon and much of the evening at the Willingham mansion—cooking, cleaning, decorating and serving guests for Dr. Willingham's annual Christmas party. The affair was a major social event each year for Shrewsbury Crossing: in attendance would be all of the clinic doctors and staff, their families, and every elite citizen of the town as well as notable guests from Florida, Alabama and other towns in Georgia. Bootsie had begged for permission to be late enough that afternoon to see Leeman safely on the bus, but Annie Willingham Rumpkin, hostess for the party, had declared firmly that she could not even spare Wilma, Bootsie's granddaughter, much less Bootsie herself—the family's dependable, highly respected maid for the last three decades.

"You know how I count on you, Bootsie," Annie had said the day before. "Why, you're just my strong, right arm. You know where everything is, how to do it all just right, and you are perfect with the other servants. They'll mind you when they won't pay one *dab* of attention to me."

"But, Miss Annie," Bootsie had pleaded, "Leeman gets real nervous, and that boy ain't never been nowhere. Just let me make shore he gets on the right bus, and I'll be on here as quick as I can."

"I'm sorry, Bootsie, I really am, but I just can't get along without you. Wilma either. We need both of you here. Daddy and Alex want everything to be perfect for this party, and Leeman's going to be just fine. Pshaw! That boy is almost grown. He'll be going off to school next year. It's time he started doing things for himself." With those words, Annie had turned and walked away.

The waiting room of the bus terminal was deserted except for Leeman and an elderly white couple seated several yards away. They paid no attention to the boy, who was dressed neatly in a starched white shirt and navy blue pants, a light-weight beige jacket over his back with the garment's sleeves tied loosely around his neck. He was a handsome, slender boy, about 130 pounds, almost effeminate, and he wore glasses which gave him a studious, scholarly look. In no sense an athlete, he had never played high school basketball or football. By contrast, his uncle was the most legendary athlete Lincoln Memorial had ever produced: his uncle was Beagle Williams who had been chiefly responsible for winning the state Negro high school championship in basketball a dozen years earlier.

But Leeman was uniquely gifted himself. With his great-grandmother's encouragement, he had started taking piano lessons at age seven from the pianist at Bootsie's church. With a natural ear for music, he was highly intelligent, well-coordinated, and he had long, limber fingers; he had quickly mastered songs in the church hymnal and by the time he was ten years old, he was playing for some of the services. Soon after Leeman turned twelve, Dr. Willingham had arranged for the boy to take lessons from an accomplished white teacher, a woman who had taught briefly at Juilliard before retiring with her husband to south Georgia. By the time he entered high school, Leeman was widely acclaimed as a prodigy. For most of 1964, he had been entertaining audiences, black and white, in Shrewsbury Crossing and surrounding towns with classical piano renditions.

The trip he was taking today was something he had eagerly anticipated for weeks. He was going to visit his uncle, a naval officer, in Washington, D.C., who had sent money for the bus ticket and airfare. With school out for the Christmas holidays, Leeman would be spending the next four days with Beagle and his wife, Talisha. Since the itinerary involved a change of planes, Bootsie had ensured that Leeman would be met by an adult relative in Atlanta, who would assist the young boy in making the connecting Delta flight to Washington. Then Beagle was to pick him up at Washington National Airport at 10:15 that night.

As Leeman turned the pages of the magazine, he glanced up occasionally at the clock above the door of the terminal leading to the parking slots for buses. His bus was already twenty minutes late, which was eating into the time cushion he had planned for the taxi transfer in Tallahassee. Fidgeting and twisting from the discomfort of the wooden bench on his backside, he stretched out lengthwise on the bench, resting his head on the satchel containing his toothbrush and clothes, and he continued to read.

The December issue of *Time* was brimming with articles about civil rights. Segregation and integration had been the dominant social issues of Leeman's life for as long as he could remember. He had been eight years old when the *Brown* decision was announced, and here he was a senior in high school, but there was still no integration of the public schools in Shrewsbury Crossing. Some neighboring towns had placed carefully selected Negro students in a few white schools, but all-black facilities were still common throughout Georgia.

Leeman came across an article about Malcolm X and his escalating feud with the Black Muslims. Leeman had little sympathy with the radical, separatist views of either faction. Martin Luther King had made a speech in the summer of 1963 during a massive demonstration in Washington. That address—the "I have a dream" speech—had solidified Leeman's feeling that future progress for Negroes would be best achieved with new laws insuring civil rights, integration and equality between the races. In discussions with high school classmates or in chuch meetings, Leeman had been a staunch advocate of non-violence. He had argued in heated debates against participation in sit-in's and street demonstrations—especially in Shrewsbury Crossing, where Leeman feared such confrontations would destroy what he viewed as generally harmonious racial relations.

The Trailways terminal was a drab gray, poorly heated building constructed of cement blocks. A small cubicle served as a ticket booth just outside the building near the entrance to the bus loading and unloading area. Inside the building and adjoining the passenger lounge was an enclosure housing a snack bar. Twenty feet long and twelve feet wide, the area was large enough to contain a small cooking area, several tables, a magazine and newspaper rack, and two pinball machines. A wall of thick plate glass separated the snack bar from the passenger waiting area and provided a measure of noise insulation from the clattering and bell-ringing of the pinball machines, which sat side-by-side with the upright score boards against the glass partition. The position of the machines allowed their operators an almost unobstructed view of the passenger waiting area.

Today, for more than an hour, well before Leeman's arrival, the two machines were being played by two lanky white males, one in his late twenties and the other no older than fifteen. Both wore overalls and denim shirts smudged with grease and dirt. Hand-rolled cigarettes dangled from their lips as they concentrated on the machines, furrowing their eyebrows, laughing boisterously and cursing occasionally. The older man was Jonah Futch, who had barely managed to graduate with the1954 class of Shrewsbury Crossing's white high school. Futch had drifted from job to job in the intervening years. Currently out of work, his most recent job had been driving a pulpwood truck. He had been fired a week earlier when half-drunk, he had slammed the truck into the rear of a school bus, injuring two children.

The other pinball machine was being played by Jonah's nephew, Thomas Futch, a grade school dropout. A thin, bony-faced boy, his hair dingy and disheveled, his cheeks riddled with pock-marks, Thomas worshipped his uncle, hanging on his every word. When Jonah allowed it, the two were inseparable. Carousing together, they had been arrested for public indecency a month earlier when they were caught urinating in the parking lot of a grocery store.

Engrossed with his reading, Leeman paid no attention to the muffled noises and sporadic cursing that escaped from the snack bar to the terminal waiting room. Sitting up again, he checked the terminal clock and frowned when he realized that the bus was now forty minutes overdue. It was nearly two o'clock, and the trip to Tallahassee would take over an hour. Pulling an envelope from his pocket, he reviewed the ticket coupons: the flight to Atlanta would depart at 5:20, so he had just over three hours to get to Tallahassee and make the taxi ride to the airport. Pursing his lips, his palms were sweating as he studied the clock once more. Maybe, he wondered, he should use the public telephone to call Dr. Willingham's residence and ask Bootsie or his mother for their advice—perhaps postpone the trip until the next day? But he quickly dismissed the thought: they wouldn't know what to tell him, he reasoned, and the call would only upset them. They were already worried enough thinking he couldn't take care of himself. He would wait a little longer, he told himself; the bus would probably arrive any minute.

Leeman stood up, thinking that moving around would relieve his anxiety. Except for the white couple, he was still alone in the passenger lounge. He tried to whistle, but his throat felt dry, so he walked to the water fountain hooked to the cement block wall in the colored section of the terminal. He bent down and turned the handle. At first, nothing happened, but then a rusty, brownish ooze seeped from the faucet. He stood erect, releasing the handle. He grimaced in frustration and began walking back to his seat when he spotted the "white only" fountain on the opposite wall near the snack bar door.

Leeman stopped, folded his arms, and hesitated. He shifted his eyes toward the white couple. The woman had a large map spread open in her lap, and the old man was dozing, his eyes closed and mouth open, his head tilted back awkwardly on the top of the bench. Leeman took three halting steps toward his seat, but then turned abruptly and walked with a brisk pace toward the "white only" fountain thirty-five feet away. Reaching the fountain, he turned, scanning the room once more, reassuring himself that the white couple was paying no attention. He turned the handle and a stream of sparkling, clear water came from the faucet. As he leaned forward to drink, two loud thumps jarred the window of the snack bar. Leeman stood erect, turning his head toward the window. Inside, a scowling Jonah Futch was shaking his fist and shouting loudly enough to be heard through the plate glass: "Get away from there, nigger!" Thomas Futch, a bemused grin on his face, stood next to his uncle.

Instinctively, Leeman glared back at the two white faces. His first impulse was to yell, scream that he was thirsty, that he had tried the other fountain. But he bit his lower lip and said nothing, instantly realizing that any attempt to explain his presence at the "white only" fountain would provoke only ridicule from the leering heads defying him through the glass. So he did something he had never done before in his life—never to anyone, black or white: he extended his right arm, the palm of his hand turned up, and he gestured toward them with his middle finger. The mouths of his two stupefied antagonists flew open, their eyes wide, and they seemed for an instant like lifeless mannequins beyond the glass. A faint, sneering smile crossed Leeman's lips, and he felt a rush of satisfaction as he savored the look of disbelief he saw on their faces.

Then he slowly but confidently turned back to the fountain and leaned down, pushing the handle and beginning to drink. In a split second, the snack bar door flew open, and Jonah Futch dashed to the fountain, grabbing Leeman's belt and the seat of his pants as he bent forward, driving his face and head violently into the fountain's faucet and against the block wall. His lower lip and chin were ripped open by the water tap, tearing through teeth and the jawbone, raining blood over the fountain and the wall, and the collision split Leeman's skull.

"That'll learn you what happens when a nigger shoots me a bird," Jonah shouted, shaking his fist, as Leeman collapsed beneath the fountain, unconscious in the pool of blood.

"Hell, I reckon you done took care of this fucker, ain't you?" Thomas yelled, having followed his uncle through the door. He grinned broadly and slapped Jonah on the back.

"Shit, I ain't through with 'im yet!" Jonah threw the stub of his cigarette to the floor. Turning to face his nephew and holding out his hand, he said: "Gimme that damn switchblade you tote."

"What you gonna do?" Thomas pulled the knife from his pocket.

"I'm gonna fix this black piece of shit where he won't never throw no finger at a white man again."

Beagle Williams, Lieutenant Commander in the United States Navy, stood proudly before a full-length mirror, admiring himself. He had just been promoted, and he was wearing his full-dress blue uniform for the first time, his white hat squared precisely on his head, the brim fixed two fingers above the bridge of the eyes. The golden oakleaf clusters shone brightly on the collar, reflecting light in the mirror. He stood erect, his chest pushed forward, chin down.

"How do I look?" he asked his wife, Talisha, sitting eight feet away at her dresser, combing her hair.

"Wonderful, Lieutenant Commander, just wonderful," she responded. "If you looked any better, I might come over and ravish you right now. By the way, I love your hat with all the gold braid and everything."

Beagle and Talisha Williams lived in a two-story townhouse just off Wisconsin Avenue in Georgetown, one of Washington's trendier neighborhoods. They had been attempting to purchase a home in the area for over four years, but high prices and color barriers had kept them in an apartment on the southwest of the District until a year earlier, when they finally succeeded in buying the townhouse. The building was of modest size, only sixteen-hundred square feet, and its age—over forty years—had left the couple with severe plumbing problems; but the Williams felt fortunate that they had finally succeeded in moving into Georgetown. Few young black couples were so lucky.

"What time is what's-his-name picking us up?" Talisha asked.

"Paul Neeley—*Commander* Paul Neeley, Talisha. My gosh, you need to remember the man's name and rank. He's *very* important to our future." Beagle's voice carried a trace of agitation. "And his wife's name is Susan."

"Yes, I think I remember her," Talisha said. "I met her at an officers' wives' luncheon in Arlington this fall, but she probably won't remember me. To tell you the truth, she seemed a little stand-offish. I got the feeling she didn't want the other white women to see her talking to me."

"Probably just your imagination." Beagle shrugged, pulling his hat off and placing it gingerly on the bed. "Sweetheart, you're going to have to learn the lingo. Navy men never call this a hat. We call it a 'cover.' And the braid on the brim, that's 'scrambled eggs.' My 'cover' is a beauty, isn't it?"

"It looks great, whatever you call it. The whiteness matches your teeth." Talisha chuckled. "And you never answered my question: what time must we be ready?"

"Paul said he'd pick us up at 3:15. The reception at the Pentagon begins at four."

Beagle's promotion to the rank of Lieutenant Commander had been announced the previous day. Beagle had just turned thirty, and he was on a fast track in the Navy. He had graduated from Annapolis six years earlier and had married Talisha in 1960. Assigned to naval intelligence in the Pentagon, partly with the help of Talisha's father—a wealthy Negro executive in New Jersey with highly placed friends in the federal government—Beagle had impressed higher-ups in the Pentagon with his intelligence, even-headed disposition and winning personality.

Commander Paul Neeley was Beagle's immediate superior. A 1956 graduate of the Naval Academy, Neeley had befriended Beagle immediately upon his arrival in Washington. The last two years, Neeley had worked tirelessly for Beagle's promotion, pulling strings and politicking aggressively. It had paid off, and Beagle and his wife would now be escorted by Neeley and his wife to a Pentagon reception to celebrate the promotion. And afterwards, the Neeleys' would treat Lieutenant Commander and Mrs. Beagle Williams to dinner at Duke Zeibert's, a popular restaurant in the heart of downtown Washington on L Street specializing in prime ribs, red snapper, and banana cream pie.

Leeman Williams was unconscious, but his vital signs were stable. After Jonah Futch and his nephew had left the bus station, the horrified elderly couple had alerted the Trailways attendant, who had called the police. An ambulance had been dispatched immediately and the boy had been delivered within minutes to the emergency room of the Willingham Clinic. Leeman was now in a holding area, surrounded by two doctors and several nurses. In a nearby waiting room, Dr. Willingham and his daughter Annie were attempting to calm Wilma and Bootsie, who were both sobbing uncontrollably.

"They tell me he lost a lot of blood, so they're trying to get him stabilized," Dr. Willingham said, mostly to Bootsie, who was unable to stop shaking. Her lips trembled as she struggled for breath. The doctor touched Bootsie's arm and said: "Look, you and Wilma need to sit down and rest. It may be awhile before we know more about the boy's condition." Bootsie clasped her hands and raised her eyes upward. "Lord Jesus, sweet Jesus!" she cried. "Please, Lord. Let my precious baby live!"

The restaurant was filled to overflowing as the maitre d' showed the two naval officers and their wives to their table. Beagle and Talisha had dined at Duke Zeibert's on several occasions before, always alone. In 1964, the restaurant had become a favorite hangout for the Washington Redskins, who had integrated the team two years earlier and had several black players now. This evening, Beagle recognized one of the defensive backs at a nearby table. Scanning the room, he spotted a sprinkling of other Negro patrons. He breathed a sigh of relief because it meant that at least for tonight, he and Talisha would not stand out as the only blacks in a sea of white faces.

"What'll y'all have to drink?" Paul Neeley smiled broadly. "Better drink up. You ain't gonna catch me payin' the bill very often."

Neeley was a large, heavy-set individual with an outspoken, homespun personality—born and bred in Texas and the kind of man Beagle would have expected Texas to produce. He had played offensive tackle at the Naval Academy and had been named an All-American during his senior year. His uncle was a congressman from Oklahoma, who had used his connections to get Neeley assigned to the Pentagon immediately after graduation from Annapolis. His wife was a debutante from Houston, the daughter of an oil company executive, but educated at Stanford University. She had met Paul Neeley on a trip to Baltimore, and they had married a month after his graduation from the Academy.

When the drinks came, Neeley raised his glass and offered a toast: "Here's to Lieutenant Commander Beagle Williams—a colored boy from Georgia who's goin' places with Uncle Sam's navy!"

Beagle smiled weakly, then awkwardly craned his neck to see who might have heard the word "colored" in the toast. Regaining his composure, he clicked his glass against Neeley's, and then the glasses of the two women. Talisha felt the tension in the air: she took a sip of wine and coughed as it went down the wrong way. She held her hand over her mouth and cleared her throat nervously.

"Thanks very much, Paul," Beagle said, "I really appreciate your confidence in me and all you've done to bring about this promotion and advance my career."

"Well, hell then," Neeley bellowed with a flourish. "When do I get the money?"

Beagle laughed. "Be serious, Paul," Beagle said. "I'm trying to be. I want you to know I really do appreciate what you've done."

"Heck, fellow, you ain't seen nothing yet. I've been bouncing around the Navy a little longer than you have, and I've caught on to a few things. My theory is that the top brass are just itchin' to find half-way intelligent Negroes to move up in the ranks. And ole' Lyndon Johnson—he may come from Texas and all—but he's determined to pass all this civil rights stuff. He's liberal to the core. Don't get me wrong," Neeley added, eyeing his wife, "I'm not too wild about the way thing's are going, but I can read handwriting on the wall. Now, Susan, she's the one in our family that's clamoring for integration."

Susan Neeley smiled politely but disdainfully at her husband, who continued talking.

"Johnson wants to set a record for bringing blacks into the mainstream, and you've got all the credentials, Beagle. For you, the sky's the limit. Shoot, it wouldn't surprise me if you go right to the top. Who knows? You might even make it to the joint chiefs someday. I just hope you'll remember your buddy Paul Neeley when you get so high and mighty."

Neeley's wife stared aimlessly into space, aloof, bored by the conversation. She made no effort to talk with Talisha. She pulled a cigarette from a gold-plated case, put it between her lips, and leaned forward toward her husband, who lit it from a book of restaurant matches.

"I'm not sure about my future," Beagle responded. "I've thought about leaving the Navy and going to law school. There's a lot of work to be done in the court system to enforce the new laws and bring about integration." Seeing Talisha's discomfort with the turn of the conversation, Beagle smiled and said: "But I'll tell you what: if I stay in the Navy and zoom up the ranks like you're fantasizing, you can count on me remembering *all* my friends—*especially* Paul Neeley from Texas."

"Of course, he's going to make a career in the Navy," Talisha said firmly. "He's worked very hard against major odds to get where he is, and I would be horrified if he changed careers now."

"But, sweetheart," Beagle countered, "You believe in the cause as much as I do, and as a lawyer, I feel I could do more for civil rights. You worked with Thurgood Marshall. You know what an enormous impact he's had."

"Marshall? Thurgood Marshall?" Susan Neeley asked, her voice warming as she showed sudden interest in the conversation. "When were you with him?"

"Fifty-nine through sixty-two," Talisha said. "I was an aide working as liaison with Congress."

"How interesting!" Neeley's wife turned in her chair to face Talisha. "Why on earth did you leave?"

"Frankly, I wasn't sure my work was good for Beagle's career," Talisha responded. "You know, a lot of higher-ups in the Navy are uncomfortable with civil rights and Marshall's role in the integration movement. I just felt it would be best if I dissociated myself from that activity."

"I see your point," Neeley said, "and if I might say so, I like to see a woman subordinate her ambitions to help her husband."

"Well, I didn't look at it exactly that way," Talisha glanced uneasily toward Beagle.

"Tell you what," Neeley said, "after dinner, why don't we take a drive over toward Alexandria. They have beautiful Christmas decorations and lights. You ladies will like that, I know."

"Well, I don't know if we can be out that late," Neeley's wife said, "I think the baby-sitter has to be home by ten."

"We can't go, I'm afraid," Talisha said. "Beagle's meeting his nephew at the airport about ten. The boy's coming from Georgia to spend a few days with us."

"That's nice," Susan Neeley said, "how old is he?"

"Eighteen," Beagle answered. "Never been out of Georgia. Talisha and I are really looking forward to showing him around—you know, the monuments, the Smithsonian, the White House, all the usual tourist things."

"Too bad the season's over and you can't take him to a Navy game," Neeley said.

"Yeah, he would probably get a kick out of that." Beagle grinned apologetically. "Not much of a pun, was it?" Then he went on: "He's not too interested in sports. He's a tremendously talented musician, though. Plays piano better than anyone I've ever heard—all the classics, Bach, Mozart, Brahms, Chopin, Rachmaninoff…."

"Rachma—what?" Neeley interrupted.

"Rachmaninoff," Beagle repeated with a chuckle. "A great Russian composer, but some of his works are extremely complex—very difficult to play. My nephew just breezes through them."

"Sounds too highbrow for me," Neeley snorted.

"Well, I'd like to hear him sometimes," Neeley's wife broke in. "I play the piano myself—not too well, of course—but I would certainly enjoy hearing your nephew play. If he has that kind of repertoire, he must be a real prodigy."

"He really is phenomenal, a very gifted young man," Beagle said. "I'm very proud of him and I'm going to do my best to get him into a first class conservatory after he graduates from high school next year. And while he's in town, perhaps we can have you and Paul over to our place so Leeman can play for you. I'm sure he'd enjoy meeting you."

"That sounds wonderful," Susan Neeley said, more enthusiastically than anything she'd said that evening, "and if Paul thinks the performance would be too 'highbrow' for him, I'll come by myself."

* * *

Shortly after nine o'clock, Paul Neeley dropped the Williams' off on Wisconsin Avenue in front of their home. Unlocking the townhouse door, Beagle heard the telephone ringing. "Get that, sweetheart," Beagle said, "Tell whoever it is I had to leave for the airport. I don't want to be late for Leeman's flight."

Beagle walked into the kitchen to pick up his car keys as Talisha lifted the receiver. After a moment Beagle heard her scream: "Oh, no! No! Granny!"

Beagle rushed to her side. "What is it, Talisha? Is that Granny?"

Talisha placed her hand over the mouthpiece. "She's just squalling her head off, Beagle. Screaming something about Leeman. That he's been hurt—badly hurt. Attacked by someone in the bus station. Here, you talk to her."

Beagle took the telephone. "Granny, listen, it's me. Please calm down so you can talk. What is it about Leeman? Is he all right?"

Beagle listened silently as his grandmother's garbled, frantic words poured from the telephone. He swallowed hard and his hand began to shiver as a tear rolled down his cheek. At last, his voice breaking, he said: "Granny, please listen to me. *Please* get hold of yourself. Listen—listen to what I'm saying. Talisha and I'll catch the first airplane in the morning and we'll be with you as soon as we can tomorrow afternoon." Then he paused again, his hand quivering, as he said, "Granny, you and Wilma be strong for each other. Just trust in God. He's not going to let Leeman die."

As he said goodbye, Beagle collapsed in a chair and turned to face Talisha. He reached out for her, pulling her close and holding her tightly. With his face pressed against her cheek, he trembled and said: "Talisha, I had trouble understanding Granny through her blubbering, but it appears that Leeman got in a fight with two white punks. He was knocked unconscious for a while, but he's come to now. He's being treated at Dr. Willingham's clinic. The doctor and Annie's been with her and Wilma. She says the doctors are worried about brain damage."

Tears filled his eyes as Beagle paused, closing his eyes and burying his face in Talisha's chest. "And you can't imagine what else—you just can't *imagine*!" he blurted out. "Those punks—those pieces of white scum—they cut off one of Leeman's fingers! One of his fingers, for God's sake! What kind of worthless animal would do something like that?"

Beagle found a parking space a few yards away from the entrance to the Willingham Clinic and his wife and he hurriedly made their way to the information desk in the lobby. They were an attractive young couple: Talisha dressed in a light tan suit and Beagle in his uniform, but their clothes were creased and wrinkled from the long day's trip. They had caught an early morning flight from Washington to Atlanta, where Beagle had rented a car. The drive to Shrewsbury Crossing had taken four hours, and it was now after three in the afternoon.

A receptionist directed them to a waiting room on the second floor, where they found Bootsie and Wilma sprawled on sofas. As Beagle and Talisha walked through the door, Wilma was dozing, but Bootsie was awake and rose quickly to her feet to embrace her grandson. Now in her mid-sixties, a small-framed woman just over five feet tall, Bootsie wore her hair in a bun—the same way she had worn it when Beagle was a toddler—except it was now a silvery white, framing like a halo the proud contours of her face. She barely came to Beagle's chest as she stretched to reach his neck.

"Baby, baby!" she said, kissing his cheek. "I'm so glad you're here."

"What about Leeman, Granny?" Beagle whispered hoarsely.

"The doctors say Leeman's gonna get well, but he was hurt awful bad. He's gotta have operations, operations to fix his…." Bootsie's voice broke, and her eyes, already reddened from hours of crying, filled again with tears. Wilma stirred; recognizing her brother and his wife, she sat up, struggling to rise from the sofa. She was in her mid-thirties but looked middle-aged, weighing more than 250 pounds. She finally managed to stand, unsteadily, and Beagle and Talisha went over and hugged her.

"Can we see Leeman now?" Beagle turned and asked Bootsie.

"He's down the hall in a room, but he's sleepin' right now. The nurses made me and Wilma get out a little while ago."

"Well, let's go see if they'll let us in now." Beagle put his arms around Bootsie's shoulders as they left the waiting room and walked toward the nurses' station.

The nurse was seated at a desk and looked up as Beagle spoke. "Would it be all right if we visited Leeman Williams? I'm Beagle Williams, his uncle, and this is my wife. We just drove down from Atlanta."

"No more than two at a time," the nurse said, curtly, "and please don't wake him if he's sleeping. We've given him a sedative."

"Granny, let Talisha and me see him," Beagle said, "and then we'll come out so you and Wilma can go in."

As they entered the hospital room, Beagle and his wife found Leeman asleep. His head was wrapped in bandages like an Egyptian mummy. Narrow slits were left for the nose and eyes, but the mouth was fully covered. His right arm and hand lay limp on top of the sheet—the hand also wrapped in heavy tape. Beagle stood by the bed and wept softly, holding Talisha's hand by his side. Leeman did not stir.

"How could they have done this?" Beagle asked, raising his eyes toward the ceiling, his voice breaking again. "How could anyone—*why* would anyone have done this?"

As Beagle squeezed Talisha's hand, the door opened from the rear, and Beagle turned to see Dr. Willingham walking toward him. Nearly six years had passed since Beagle had seen the doctor. Weeks after his graduation from Annapolis, Beagle had returned to Shrewsbury Crossing and, at Bootsie's request, he had visited Dr. Willingham to thank him for his many kind and generous acts. The doctor was now sixty-four, wrinkles creased his face and his hair was a silky white, but he was still an imposing figure of a man: tall, stocky, broad shoulders, and those extraordinary, massive hands, which he now held out in a warm greeting to Beagle and Talisha.

"I'm glad to see you again, Beagle, and to meet you, Mrs. Williams, but I'm so sorry it had to be under circumstances like this," the doctor said, grimacing and shaking his head. "It's all so tragic. Leeman was too fine a young man—too much goodness and too much talent—to have something like this happen to him."

"It's beyond my comprehension—just unreal, like a nightmare, doctor," Beagle said, brushing a tear running from his cheek. "Did you know he was waiting to catch a bus to visit Talisha and me in Washington?"

"Yes, that's what Bootsie told me. What a tragedy! I know how devastated you must be. This all brings back memories of how distraught I felt when Mrs. Willingham was killed. The pain seems unbearable, doesn't it?"

"I remember when you lost your wife. I admired your strength and the way you went on with your life," Beagle said. "Besides, I guess we should give thanks since it appears that Leeman is going to survive."

"Yes, I really think he's going to come through this." The doctor looked deeply into Beagle's eyes and placed his hand on Beagle's shoulder. "We were worried initially about the head injury—that there might be some permanent damage—but he's regained consciousness enough to relieve our worries somewhat. Of course, we're going to be watching him closely for the next several days, and we'll have to do some surgery on his face—his mouth and jaw—when he's a little stronger. I want you to know that I've assigned my best surgeon to the case, and I'm confident he'll restore the boy's face as well as anyone could. But the finger—of course, there's nothing we can do about that."

"Which finger was it?" Talisha asked.

"The middle one. As you can see from the bandage, it was his right hand."

Leeman stirred restlessly for a moment but did not waken.

"Dr. Willingham, I know Bootsie and Wilma can't afford these medical expenses," Beagle said, "so please just send me the bills."

"There'll be no bills, Beagle," the doctor replied, firmly. "That's the least of my worries. Bootsie, you—all of your family—are dear to me. I only wish this meaningless tragedy could have been avoided."

"Have they found out who attacked my nephew?" Beagle asked.

"Yes, it was a couple of boys from the Futch family, two low-life individuals if I ever saw any. They're locked up now."

"Well, I know it's supposed to be divine to forgive, but I want those two to pay for this insane act. What should I do? Should I talk with the prosecutor or the police?"

"Alex has been on the telephone today about that. You might want to go upstairs to the fifth floor and see him. He's still in the office, and I know he'd like to see you."

"Thanks, Dr. Willingham," Beagle said, as the doctor turned to leave. "Thanks for everything. You have no idea how much you've meant to everyone in my family. We all appreciate you." Hesitating a moment, he added: "Now, I hate to bother you with this, but please do me one more favor. Granny and Wilma are in the waiting room, and they've been here since yesterday. They'll listen to you. Please order them to go home and get some rest tonight. If you can, assure them that Leeman's going to be all right."

"I can certainly do that," the doctor said, smiling. "Now, everything's being done for Leeman here, so you and your wife get some rest too. I'm sure you're both exhausted."

After the doctor shook Beagle's and Talisha's hands and left, Beagle turned to his wife: "Sweetheart, please take Granny's car and see that she and Wilma get home. I want to talk with Alex Rumpkin before I leave. I'll be home a little later."

Beagle took the elevator to the fifth floor which housed the administrative officers for the Willingham Clinic. Leaving the elevator, he turned down the hall to his right until he saw a placard reading: "Alexander W. Rumpkin, Vice President-Personnel." The hall door was open, revealing an outer office and a mahogany-lined room beyond. Alex was sitting at his desk on the far side of the room, absorbed in paperwork. Beagle stepped to the inner door and rapped gently on the facing.

Alex looked up. "Beagle!" he said, loudly. "Come on in, fellow. I heard you were in town to see about your sister's son."

Alex stood and reached across his desk, extending his hand. Beagle hesitated for an instant but then stepped forward, clasping Alex's outstretched hand. As they shook, it dawned on Beagle that he had known Alex for nearly thirty years, and this was the first time they had ever shaken hands. In fact, it had been many years since the two men had seen each other. Through Jeremiah, Beagle had kept up with Alex and Annie, along with Ethan Allday and his family, but today was the first time he had seen Alex face-to-face since leaving Shrewsbury Crossing in 1952. Alex had become a mature, filled-out man in the intervening years: he had gained weight, but he couldn't be called fat. Alex's voice still carried the nasal twang Beagle remembered from childhood, and there was a slight twitch in his left eye as he spoke.

"I'm so sorry this damn thing has happened to your nephew, Beagle," Alex sat down behind his desk, and motioned Beagle to take the chair facing him. "I know you and Bootsie and everyone's all broken up about it."

"We certainly are," Beagle said. "It was such an insane act. Impossible to believe that human beings could be so callous, so utterly without conscience."

"I couldn't agree with you more." Alex sniffed and shook his head.

"What about those Futch boys?" Beagle asked. "How on earth did this happen?"

"Yeah, they pretty much spilled their guts when the sheriff picked 'em up. Their story is that Leeman was drinking from the 'white only' water fountain at the bus station, and he shot them a bird when they told him to stop. They say they got mad and slammed him into the wall."

"That's ridiculous," Beagle grimaced. "I want them locked up for life."

"I've already taken care of that. Talked to the D.A. several times today—he's a personal friend of mine—a young lawyer named Randall Murphy. I told him I want to throw the book at the boys. He assures me that he will." Alex rolled a metal paperweight between his hands.

"Good!" Beagle said, "I really appreciate your involvement. Punishing those two won't make up for what they've done to Leeman, but it's the only way any kind of justice will be done. This whole thing's unbelievable, just an outrageous tragedy, Alex. Leeman could have permanent brain damage, his face will probably be scarred for life, and his mangled finger—well, he'll never play the piano again. You're aware that he was a musical prodigy, weren't you? He could have been a professional concert pianist."

"Oh, yeah, I've heard Doc Willie talk about what a whiz he was at the piano. It's all such a damn shame, Beagle. I know it is, but…." Alex hesitated, peering off toward a portrait of Dr. Willingham hanging to his right.

"But what?" Beagle asked.

"Well, you probably don't want to hear this, but if the Futch boys are tellin' the truth, you should realize that your nephew was pushing his luck, antagonizing those white boys the way he did."

"That's preposterous! What are you saying?" Beagle rose from his seat, facing Alex squarely across the desk.

"Well, you know," Alex vacillated. "I mean, Beagle, if the boys' story is true—the boy drinking from the white fountain like that, and then throwing them a bird. That kind of reckless provocation goaded those white boys to do what they did."

"My God, Alex!" Beagle slapped the desk. "Haven't you heard of the Civil Rights Act of 1964? When that law was passed this summer, segregated public facilities were outlawed *everywhere* in this country. Last thing I heard, this little town is still part of the United States. There shouldn't have been any damn 'white only' fountain in the bus station. Don't you realize…."

"Simmer down, simmer down," Alex said, almost in a mocking voice, a weak smile crossing his face. "I didn't mean to get you all riled up. My gosh! Beagle, I wasn't suggesting that the attack on your nephew was in any way justified."

"Well, what were you suggesting then?"

"I was just trying to help you face up to the troubles we're dealing with down here, here in the South—trying to get people to change their thinking about the races. It's not going to come easily or quickly."

"When will it come?" Beagle gestured with his hands, palms up. "Tell me that. It's been ten years since the *Brown* decision, and the schools of Shrewsbury Crossing are as segregated as ever."

"It's coming. Me and a lot of other people down here are trying to change things, but we want to do it peacefully. That's what you need to understand: confrontation and demands won't help. You've got to allow people of good will to handle things."

"All your good intentions didn't help much with the boy in that bed downstairs. The pace of change in this town didn't do him much good, did it?"

Alex rose from his chair and turned his back to Beagle. He peered from his office window for a moment, then turned again to face Beagle. "Tell me this,

Mr. Williams, sir, what would you suggest we do down here? Just burn this town down and start over? Let the Negroes run everything?"

"That's my point, Alex. If things don't change soon, this whole society may go up in flames. Some of us are about to explode. In fact, that's what James Baldwin predicts in *The Fire Next Time*—a catastrophic inferno in America if racial injustice isn't stamped out."

"Who's he? Probably some Negro radical, eh?" Alex ground his teeth, then went on. "That's *my* point, Beagle. When a bunch of shitheads in Washington pass some civil rights law, or a black-robed judge orders races to mix, it just makes things worse down here. Hell, I'm doing all I can to be fair to Negroes. I'm hiring them every week at the clinic, but most of 'em that come in here lookin' for jobs ain't got enough sense to stack peanuts. And to top it off, they've seen so much of this shit on television, they come in here actin' like they own the damn clinic—like we *owe* them a job. Hell, I'm half-way expectin' one to walk in any day now with a grade-school education and demand to be a fuckin' brain surgeon."

"I don't think you've ever been able to relate to the problems of being a Negro in this unjust society." Beagle shook his finger in Alex's direction. "When we were boys, you treated me like shit when it suited you. At times, you acted like we were friends, and then before I could understand what happened, you'd turn on me like a viper."

"Hell, Beagle, we were just kids and I did some dumb things just like you and everyone else. But I had nothin' to do with you bein' born black, and I couldn't help what kind of world we found ourselves in. You never wanted to accept your place as a colored person, and that created a lot of problems for you and everybody else. 'Sides, nobody started life with a worse hand of cards than me, and look where I am today." Alex paused and grinned; then went on: "you ain't done too bad yourself, Beagle. Look at you in that fine uniform furnished to you by the U. S. Government, and shoot, what are you now? Some kind of ensign or something?"

"Not quite, Alex, I'm a *Lieutenant Commander*, if you really want to know."

"Well, I stand corrected and I'm impressed," Alex said, sarcastically. "Yessir, pretty fancy title, ain't it?" Alex took a toothpick from his desk and placed it between his teeth. "I suspect that handle carries some real weight in Washington, doesn't it? You and the missus are in pretty high cotton up there, I bet. With that title and your government money, you can go into all the ritzy bars and restaurants in the District of Columbia and buy anything you want, am I right?"

"Alex, that's not important to me."

"Like hell, it ain't. Shit, Beagle, don't give me that! You're just like the rest of us. You want a good life with money and status, so you can lord it over other people. And there's nothing wrong with that. I can't see why…."

"This discussion's going nowhere," Beagle cut him off, then added: "I'm not sure we'll ever see eye-to-eye about anything but I've got to run. My folks are expecting me home and my main reason for dropping by was to ensure that those two white boys will be punished."

"Well, I've already told you that I'm taking care of that," Alex said. "But don't go away mad. I really like you—I always have—and I admire what you've made of yourself. I think you're a great example for other members of your race."

"I'm not upset, Alex, and I really appreciate what you've done with the prosecutor today. But I've got to go now. Please give my best to Annie."

"I will," Alex said, "and you take care, you hear?"

Beagle left Alex's office hurriedly and walked through an exit, taking the stairway down to the ground floor. He thought the exercise would allow him to let off steam, but it didn't help much. Reaching the lobby, he stopped at a public telephone and called Bootsie's house. Talisha answered.

"How's Granny and Wilma?" Beagle asked.

"They're exhausted. I helped them fix scrambled eggs and grits and then insisted that they go on to bed. I think they're sleeping now. How are you?"

"OK, I guess." Beagle paused, then blurted out: "No, Talisha, I'm not really OK at all. I need to do some thinking, maybe have an hour or so by myself."

"What is it?" Talisha asked. "This thing with Leeman?"

"That's part of it, but it's more than that. Listen, darling, I'm going to just drive around a little by myself. I'll be home in an hour or two."

The clock above the lobby door read 5:43 as Beagle left the clinic and walked to the car he had rented that morning in Atlanta. Cranking the engine, he drove slowly out of the lot and toward the center of town, passing the Dixie Cafe, where he had worked as a boy. He circled the block and drove again past the Willingham Clinic, his pulse still racing as he recalled his words with Alex. Maybe Alex was right, Beagle thought. Maybe he had allowed his status as a rising naval officer to blind him to the pain and suffering he had left behind in this town. Maybe his life was a farce. Maybe he hadn't made it count.

At that moment he came to the intersection of U.S. 19, which led northward toward Albany. He turned left and picked up speed as he passed the city limit sign of Shrewsbury Crossing. A half mile further, a highway sign read

"Albany—39 miles." Albany was a military town, the location of a massive marine supply depot and a SAC squadron of B-52's. Beagle figured he would be able to find a bar admitting blacks—especially blacks in military uniform—somewhere on the south side of Albany, and he figured right.

Talisha sat by a lamp reading as the headlights from Beagle's car flooded the living room of Bootsie's house. Talisha glanced at her watch: it was nearly 10:30 p.m. and she had been been growing increasingly worried about Beagle. She waited by the door as she heard him fumble with the handle, watched as the door slowly opened, and took a deep breath as Beagle stumbled in. He reached for her, holding her tightly, almost roughly, against his chest. She pulled away and held his arm to balance him, leading him to the sofa where they both sat down.

"Sweetheart," she said, "where have you been? You've been drinking, haven't you? I was worried when you were so late."

"I'm sorry, Talisha," Beagle slurred his words. "I didn't mean to worry you, I really didn't." Beagle's uniform coat was badly wrinkled, a button was missing and he had loosened his tie. He looked completely different from the immaculately dressed man who had left Washington that morning.

"Where were you, baby?" she asked.

"Albany—a juke joint in Albany. I been thinkin'." Beagle sat on the couch, staring aimlessly ahead.

"Thinking about what?"

"My life—*our* life, I guess."

"What about our life?"

"I don't know. I've gotta do something. I'm just not makin' my life count. I've gotta leave the service and try to fix things."

"You can't be serious, Beagle. Fix what things? Give up your career? You've just been promoted. You're not thinking straight now. You're feeling the effects of alcohol. You'll be able to think better in the morning."

"Sometimes liquor helps me clear things up, Talisha, and that's what's happened tonight."

"What do you mean?"

"Maybe it was somethin' that damn Alex Rumpkin said. Said I was just like everybody else—wantin' money and status and all that. And maybe he's right. But I know what I've got to do now. It's all clear."

"What's that, baby?" Talisha rubbed a tear from his cheek.

"When we get back to D.C., I'm gonna resign my commission and enroll in law school at George Washington. And I'm goin' to work for the Movement. My brothers and sisters have been carryin' the load, and I've been standin' on the sidelines enjoyin' the parade. My place is with them—in the courtroom and on the streets."

"Beagle, you're doing your part," Talisha insisted. "Think how it inspires other Negroes to succeed when they see someone like you, a distinguished officer in the navy, respected and successful."

"I've been foolin' myself with that kind of thinkin'," Beagle replied. "Talisha, you know this world's got to change, and it's gotta change quickly. Look at Leeman, he never had a chance. All of that talent destroyed for no reason at all! And how many others never get a chance? How many black athletes never get to play the game? How many Negro writers, sculptors, artists, musicians—how many are being destroyed every day in a quagmire of racial injustice and poverty? It's gotta stop! It's *all* got to stop!"

"So that's your decision, huh? You're going to join the fight, and maybe lead it?"

"Yeah, I am. Damnit all, I am! I doubt you really agree with my decision, but I need your love and support to do this. I can't make it without you."

"You're right, I don't agree," Talisha said, putting her arm around her husband's shoulder, "but I'll always love you and try to be a part of whatever life you choose."

"Somehow, I knew that," Beagle said, a tear trickling down his cheek. "I don't imagine I'll be able to start law school until spring, so in the morning I'm going to call Dr. King's people in Atlanta. I understand he's beginning a voter registration campaign over in Alabama—in a little town called Selma. I intend to be with him in January, Talisha. You can come, too, if you want."

Part II

1990

CHAPTER 12

Sterling Lads

"Oh I have been to Ludlow fair
And left my necktie God knows where,
And carried half-way home, or near,
Pints and quarts of Ludlow beer:
Then the world seemed none so bad,
And I myself a sterling lad;...."
A. E. Housman, *A Shropshire Lad*

Jeremiah Goodwin stood by his office window, his eyes fixed on the horizon. It was a brilliantly clear morning—a crisp and cool February day—as Jeremiah sipped his second cup of coffee. From his vantage point facing south from the 32nd floor of what had been called the IBM building, now sold off to Japanese investors, he had a perfect view of the central city where gleaming towers of steel and glass rose like giant exclamation marks against the sky. His vista was of the heart of Atlanta, a panorama fanning out from Five Points where Peachtree Street begins its meandering journey northward.

A beautiful city, Atlanta, thought Jeremiah. Risen from ashes of insane civil war and propelled to the American center stage by engines of commerce and transportation, Atlanta in 1990 had become Mecca to thousands of Yankees swarming south each month, drawn like moths to the flames of the booming economy, but avoiding the central city like a plague. High rises of Buckhead and mid-town, plush subdivisions of Roswell, Dunwoody, Cobb and Gwinnett: these were the settlements of the new upscale arrivals. Downtown Atlanta was for the overnight hotel crowds, the harried business people, the conventioneers, commuting lawyers and bankers, all wanting a short stay and a quick ride to the airport. The central city Jeremiah saw from his office window this morning was a place to conduct business, not to carry on a life.

Spotless, shiny and serene from Jeremiah's viewpoint, the magnificent hotels and towering office buildings belied the deep sickness that permeated the city and its suburbs. Jeremiah knew that most of the pimps and whores who had worked Stewart Avenue the night before were now sleeping or passed out. Marauding gangs had temporarily split up, gone separate ways, giving a few hours respite to the old people and children who spent much of their lives behind the barred windows of housing projects watching the cocaine trading and territorial brawls along the streets and curbs. What a stark contrast, he thought, the reality in the streets compared to the peaceful facade of the Atlanta skyline that greeted him this morning. Where was the real soul of this town—in the upscale townhouses of Buckhead or the west-side tenements? He knew that within a mile of his safe glass enclosure, his plush office high above the streets—literally in the clouds—hundreds of nameless streets slinking like snakes all over Atlanta were twisting, elongated thoroughfares of hatred and violence.

But Jeremiah could do nothing to change all that, he realized, and besides, he faced his own nest of vipers this morning.

Alexander Rumpkin sat in his study reading the morning paper as the maid readied his suitcase upstairs. "Mr. Rumpkin, do you want your suits in a hang-up bag?" she asked from the top of the staircase.

"Judith, what in hell do you mean asking me that?" he shouted. "How many times have I told you that I always want my suits hung up so I won't be walkin' around lookin' like crap."

"I'm sorry, Mr. Rumpkin," she said, her voice trembling. "I just wondered if you were planning to carry everything on the plane instead of checkin' it."

"Hell, I never carry bags. Who do you think I am, Judith, some damn janitor at MedAmerica?"

"Alex," Annie said, walking in from the kitchen, "please don't talk to Judith like that. You'll hurt her feelings."

"Well, she ought to use a little common sense. For God's sake, how long has she been here? Six, seven years?"

"Not long enough to get used to your temper tantrums, and, for that matter, neither have I."

"I'm sorry, Annie," Alex said, putting the paper down. "I'm on edge today. Got to get on the airplane with your fuckin' brother and spend the next two days tryin' to keep him sober. It's enough to keep anybody on edge."

Annie sat down next to him, still dressed in a robe. The couple had been married for twenty-nine years and lived in a three story home abutting the sixteenth green in a golf community two miles from the center of Shrewsbury Crossing. Annie's family home, the mansion covering a downtown city block, was occupied by her father, Dr. Charles Robert Willingham, and her brother, C. R., Jr. Her brother had been married and divorced twice, the last time to a showgirl in her twenties and eighteen years his junior.

"Well, don't take Doddy," Annie said, shrugging her shoulders.

"Don't have a choice," Alex answered. "Doc Willie has this crazy notion that I've got to introduce him to the lobbyists and bureaucrats I deal with in Washington. Wants 'em to get to know Doddy, he says. I've told him that having them meet Doddy could do the company more harm than good—particularly if he goes on one of his binges while we're up there."

"When will you be back?"

"Hopefully, day after tomorrow, if we don't run into something unexpected. Also, I'm planning to have lunch with some folks from the Panacea Company while we're in town. I still get sick on my stomach thinking how that outfit is just sittin' there, ripe for a takeover, but your old man doesn't even want to consider it."

"Well, if Daddy's so dead set against it, why are you meeting with them?" Annie asked.

"You never know when things might change. I just want to keep the doors open. Just don't mention this to your daddy. By the way, while I'm dressing, how about callin' Doddy and tellin' him to get his butt to the airport."

Jeremiah was a creature of habit, compulsively so, his wife Sarah said. He routinely arose at five a.m., showered and dressed, leaving his Roswell home by six-forty-five. He and his wife lived in a five-thousand square-foot house on a two-acre lot abutting the western bank of the Chattahoochee River, prime real estate he had bought for a song in the late sixties.

Sarah rarely got up before he left for work, but the night before she had set her alarm clock and now sat across the breakfast table from Jeremiah as he ate his cereal. At fifty-four, Sarah had aged rapidly over the last two years. Her eyes had lost much of their luster and wrinkles and cellulite had long since replaced the smooth, unbroken beauty of her skin. Her decline had accelerated when their son left home after his graduation from college. While Richard had been at Emory and lived at home, he had spent much of his time with his mother, frequently taking her to dinner, sometimes with his date. He often had young friends around the house, and Sarah would join them as they swam in the pool or played tennis on the courts between the house and river. After Richard left, Sarah had increasingly frequent bouts of melancholia and depression, which medication hadn't seemed to help.

"Did you sleep OK?" Jeremiah had asked.

"So so," Sarah had said, "and you?"

"Not too good, I guess. I woke up about three-thirty and couldn't get back to sleep. I kept turning over that damn Edgewood deal in my mind. Why'd you get up so early?"

"Jeremiah, I wanted to remind you that Mama and Daddy are driving down from Chattanooga this afternoon, and I *really* want you to arrive here early enough for a pleasant evening at home. I'll have dinner ready at seven. You know, you haven't gotten in before ten or eleven for several weeks—always working late or entertaining clients—and it's just very important to me that you be here tonight with my parents." She pursed her lips, struggling to keep her feelings inside. Maybe if he came home to be with her parents, she thought, it would mean he still cared for her, too. She found herself searching constantly for signs of his affection these days.

"Sure, Sarah," Jeremiah had responded, "but I hope you don't think I practice this lifestyle for the fun of it. Somebody has to pay for this house—for your diamonds and evening dresses, and Richard's college—not to mention Rachelle's wedding. You don't have to worry about it, but that wedding in particular took one hell of a bite out of our savings."

"I know you work hard, Jeremiah, but tonight is special for me. Please be here."

"Don't worry," he had said, as he left the room to brush his teeth, "I'll be on time."

As usual on his drive to the office, Jeremiah had beaten the morning rush, encountering very little traffic. Arriving in the parking garage shortly after seven, he had seen no other cars in the cluster of spaces reserved for the firm. He had followed his customary practice of picking up copies of the *Atlanta Constitution* and the *Wall Street Journal* just before boarding the express elevator to the 32nd floor. His suite of offices was always deserted when he arrived so this morning there had been time—undisturbed time—to organize his work and psyche himself up for what lay ahead.

On his desk he had found a three-inch thick document innocently titled: "The Edgewood/Deering Acquisition Agreement," and in huge red letters across the cover page was stamped the words, "DRAFT FIVE." The 300-plus pages had been FedEx'ed overnight and placed on his desk by a security guard. Jeremiah's job today was to review the document for what seemed to him the hundredth time, marking his comments, so that he could fax them to the battery of New York lawyers who had each been paid $500 an hour over the last three months to create this monstrosity. Jeremiah had begged his client, Robert Edgewood, to leave the New Yorkers out of the picture, but Edgewood had said that his investment banker had insisted that they retain Shaw and Bickworth, a massive Wall Street firm of over 800 lawyers. Edgewood wanted to acquire Deering Engineering Associates, a medium-sized engineering and architectural firm, and Edgewood had given Jeremiah the task of "keeping the damn legal costs down," an impossible assignment, Jeremiah knew.

So after giving the morning papers a hasty glance, Jeremiah plunged ahead with his review of the acquisition agreement. By the thirty-fifth page, he was nauseated by the hodgepodge he had found, sickened even more by the $500 an hour these incompetents were being paid. He had discovered numerous typographical errors, sentences hopelessly convoluted, cross-references to nowhere. As noontime approached, he shook his head in disbelief at what he was finding: twenty-two pages of definitions, jumbled paragraphs, misplaced modifiers, plain English eradicated anywhere it might have survived the fourth draft. As he took a break to the men's room, he reflected on how working with such trash had become his stock in trade, the rather useless thing he did to afford the sumptuous residence on the Chattahoochee. He had a good life, he had joined in the dance and he had gained status and prestige, but he felt he had traded off a part of his soul.

Returning to his office, Jeremiah stopped at his secretary's desk. "Michelle, I'm having lunch with Mr. Ansley in a few minutes. I've gotten through the first eighty-seven pages of the Edgewood agreement. Let's fax my mark-up to

Shaw and Bickworth—maybe that'll give them enough to chew on until I can finish this thing up this afternoon."

"Are you going to discuss Stripling with Mr. Ansley?" Michelle asked.

"I have to," Jeremiah said. "This thing's gone as far as I can let it."

The reference was to Kenneth Stripling, one of the four associates assigned to Jeremiah's area of responsibility—mergers and acquisitions. His firm—Proctor, Bennett, and Goodwin—had thirty-seven partners and 112 associates—a medium-sized law firm for Atlanta. Each partner was responsible for the supervision of three or four of the associates, and Stripling had been the most recent addition to Jeremiah's group. Stripling was a mousy-looking, heavy set boy with beady eyes. He was no more than five-foot seven inches in height and frequently called 'shrimp' behind his back by several of the secretaries.

Simply put, Jeremiah had caught Stripling stealing and lying. While the boy's legal work was mediocre, he was affable and popular with the other associates and some of the partners. No serious problems had surfaced until six months after Stripling had entered the firm and a secretary from the office pool had approached Jeremiah in private about her misgivings. Stripling had asked her to perform an inordinate number of *personal* tasks, including a number of trips about town to buy gifts for his girlfriend and extensive work typing letters and other documents relating to his pending divorce. The secretary's concern had been that her other work with the firm was being neglected to meet Stripling's demands, and she didn't want to be criticized for getting behind with office work. Jeremiah had assured her that she wouldn't be penalized for carrying out Stripling's instructions, and that her confidence in discussing the matter with him would be protected.

Tipped off by the secretary's warning, Jeremiah began to watch Stripling closely, sometimes feeling like Captain Queeg with the strawberries. But the scrutiny produced results: he had discovered that Stripling was falsifying expense reports, inexplicably absent from the office during business hours, and padding his billable hours to the point where several clients had complained. Worst of all, Stripling had told bald-faced lies about his conduct when questioned by Jeremiah, even when there was hard evidence to the contrary. Jeremiah had become so exasperated with Stripling's stonewalling that he had concluded the boy had mental problems and had to be fired.

Jeremiah had requested a meeting to discuss the situation with Ben Ansley, the firm's managing partner, who had agreed to meet over lunch today.

"Well, you know it's going to be tough to get Mr. Ansley to do something," Michelle said. "He has an aversion to any kind of conflict, doesn't he?"

Jeremiah seldom talked about office politics or personnel matters with his secretary, but he had become perplexed enough with Stripling to discuss some things with her. She had listened sympathetically to Jeremiah and confirmed some of his suspicions with scuttlebutt she had heard around the office. Jeremiah treasured Michelle: she had been with the firm for nearly ten years and his personal secretary for the last six. She was far and away the best secretary he had ever had: excellent skills, good instincts, an uncanny ability to protect him when he needed it. Although his relationship with her had been strictly professional, he considered her to be one of the most gorgeous and intelligent women he knew: completely feminine, a graceful, dark-haired beauty.

By the same token, Michelle admired and respected Jeremiah. And she was pleased that he had confided in her about Stripling: in her mind, it meant the possibility of an embryonic attachment between the two, some emotional connection she badly needed. Although she fulfilled her marital responsibilities faithfully and was a good mother, the romance she craved in her life had disappeared years ago.

Lunch for Jeremiah did not go well. Ben Ansley seemed preoccupied and showed little interest in the conversation. To make matters worse, the bistro they had selected was unusually noisy and crowded. Service was abominable, the food cold when it finally arrived.

"Ben, I hate to bother you with this," Jeremiah said after the waiter took their dirty plates away, "but I think we've got to do something about Kenneth Stripling. I've got major problems with him."

"Yeah? Like what?" Ansley asked, turning his head to stare at a leggy blonde leaving the next table.

Jeremiah went over his findings—the lying, unexplained office absences, the fraud, the stonewalling denials.

"So what do you propose doing with him?"

"I think we have to fire the bastard," Jeremiah said. "I've got all the evidence we need. It's that simple."

"Aw, hell, Jeremiah," Ansley looked in Jeremiah's eyes. "You know we can't do that. His old man's in tight with the damn governor of Florida and probably one-third of the state's legislature. We'd lose half our clients down there. Besides, it looks to me like maybe you're over-reacting a little."

"No, I'm not, Ben," Jeremiah snapped, slapping his palm on the table. "We simply have to confront reality here, and this boy's going to do a lot of damage to the firm if we don't get rid of him. We're dealing with a psychopath, and I don't care how rich and influential his father is."

"Maybe you can forget about his father, Jeremiah, but I can't. We simply can't afford to piss his old man off." Ansley touched Jeremiah lightly on the arm. "Tell you what, I'll talk to Stripling about how he's letting you down—tell him to shape up and keep you happy. Won't that solve your problems?"

"I think you're putting your head in the sand."

"Naw, you worry too much." Ansley was giving the waiter a credit card for the check. "Just leave everything to me, it's gonna work out, you'll see."

It was nearly two o'clock when Jeremiah returned to the office and brushed past Michelle's desk without speaking. She got up and followed him into the office. "What's the matter?" she asked. "It didn't go well?"

"It was awful," Jeremiah walked over to his window and stared straight ahead. "That Ansley's a turd! It's always been useless to ask him to do anything that takes any backbone. Always looking out for the political angle. Never sees any bold type or black and white anywhere."

"Boy, he really got you stirred up, didn't he? What's he going to do about Stripling?"

"Talk to the boy! Can you believe that?"

"Well, maybe it'll help," Michelle said, turning to go back to her desk.

Jeremiah sat down behind the desk. "The *last* thing I want to do this afternoon is finish the damn Edgewood agreement, but that Bickworth bunch are having conniptions to get this thing back. So take my calls the rest of the afternoon—say I'm in conference or something, can't be disturbed, OK?"

"Sure, Jeremiah," Michelle answered, closing his door.

❖ ❖ ❖

Two hours later the telephone rang.

"Hello, Mr. Goodwin's office," Michelle said, intercepting the call.

"Well, *hellooo*, beautiful," the voice on the other end said. "Know who this is?"

"I'm sorry, sir. I don't recognize your voice," Michelle said, "may I help you?"

"Oh, I'm certain you could help *me* any time," the caller said, "but we can talk about that later. Lemme talk to Jero. Is he there?"

"Mr. Goodwin's in conference, sir, and can't be disturbed right now. May I take a message?"

"Aw come on, don't give me that 'conference' crap," the voice snapped. "Tell him his old cousin from the sticks is on the phone—Alex Rumpkin. Tell him he better damn well speak to me."

"Oh, Mr. Rumpkin, I do apologize for this, but Mr. Goodwin has given me strict instructions that he's not to be disturbed."

"Goodness, baby doll, I don't mean to be a nuisance, but I know Jero'll wanna talk to me if he knows I'm callin'." Alex spoke slowly and softly now, an almost begging tenor in his voice.

"I just can't bother him right now, Mr. Rumpkin," Michelle insisted.

"What's your name? 'Michelle,' isn't that it?" Alex asked.

"Yes, sir. How did you know?"

"I recall meeting you at Jeremiah's house. A Christmas party several years ago, I believe it was. I remember you wore a beautiful green dress with sequins—you were stunning."

"What an incredible memory!" Michelle exclaimed, her voice warming. "You must forgive me for not catching your voice. I know who you are now. From Shrewsbury Crossing, aren't you? You and Jeremiah grew up together."

"You're absolutely right," Alex said, "Old Alexander Rumpkin, that's me, Executive Vice President of a little outfit called the MedAmerica Corporation."

"Oh, yes," Michelle said, clearing her throat, "I'm really sorry I didn't recognize you. Tell you what, I'll slip a note to Mr. Goodwin and see if he can break away for a minute."

Jeremiah scowled at Michelle as she entered the office, but he smiled broadly when she said: "I know you said not to bother you, but Mr. Rumpkin is holding on line two."

"Hello, that you, Alex?" Jeremiah said, picking up the phone.

"Hey, you little peckerhead, what the hell you doin'?" The voice was from Jeremiah's past, the same nasal, whiny tone he recalled from his boyhood, but now imbued with an electricity and energy that reflected Alex's status and power in the world.

"Alex, you rascal," Jeremiah said, rising to his feet behind his desk, "where are you?"

"I'm at the airport in Delta's VIP lounge—you know, the Crown Room. Got this gorgeous chick—I mean, a full-bloodied *winner*, juggernaut tits and all—fixin' me Manhattans as fast as I can drink 'em. Come on out and join me."

"I don't see how I can," Jeremiah said. "You can't imagine how high the paperwork is stacked on my desk, and everybody's chewin' my tail to get some things done."

"Well, I'll understand if *you* can't make it," Alex said. "I know how valuable *your time* is. It just ain't gonna happen often that a hot-shot city lawyer's gonna make time for one of his red-neck relatives from the backwoods." The whining tone of the voice dripped with sarcasm.

"Come off that 'country boy' routine, Alex, for God's sake." Jeremiah sat down and twisted the telephone cord as he propped his feet on the desk. "This is *me* you're talkin' to. What are you doin' at the airport?"

"What does anybody do at a fuckin' airport, Jero? I'm waitin' on the next flight to Washington. Delta canceled the one I was supposed to take—the one connecting to my little puddle-hopper ASA flight from home. I run into this shit all the time. Wouldn't have to put up with this if I could talk the old man into buyin' one of them little Lear jets. Been beggin' him for years."

"So when's the next flight?" Jeremiah asked.

"Six-thirty or so, hell, I don't know."

"So you're making the best of things by living it up in the Crown Room?"

"Hell, yeah, you know *me*—I always make the best of things, Jero, and the best thing I can do right now is let this lovely woman fix me drinks—what was your name again, sweetheart?" Alex lowered the receiver to talk to the attendant, then came back on the line. "*Jennifer*, yeah, that's it, Jero, that's the name of this exceptional female, and you need to get your butt over here and let her mix up a few cocktails for you."

"Are you traveling alone?"

"Not entirely, I've got this damn Doddy with me, but he's passed out over on the other sofa. Didn't want to bring the drunk with me, but Doc Willie insisted. Say, Jeremiah, you coming out here or not?"

The Edgewood agreement lay before Jeremiah, sprawled in several stacks across his desk. The New York lawyers had called Michelle several times since lunch, inquiring about the status of Jeremiah's review, and Edgewood himself had left messages that the paperwork simply had to be finalized before the weekend. It was now Wednesday, no time to spare, Jeremiah thought, but this was also a rare opportunity to visit with a childhood friend. And there was tonight's dinner with Sarah's parents, but maybe he could get up early enough tomorrow to finish everything before noon.

"Yeah, maybe I'll come out," Jeremiah said, standing again to sort the papers. "But it's going to take a few minutes to wind up things here."

"Great, get your butt on over here, and say, Jero?"

"What?"

"That Michelle, that's the good-lookin' Jewish bitch I met at your Christmas party, isn't it?"

"Yeah, she's not only beautiful but a wonderful secretary. Why?"

"Well, why don't you bring her with you? I wouldn't mind fuckin' her right here on this couch."

"You're living in some kind of fantasy world. How many drinks have you had, Alex?"

"Aw, I'm just kiddin' about the screwin', Jero, but do think about bringing her with you. You know, a little female companionship is always good for the soul."

"I was under the impression that the juggernaut titties were taking care of your soul, but I will invite Michelle if you promise to be a gentleman. I know that's a stretch for you, but do we have a deal?"

"Jero, you wound me greatly! I'm always a gentleman," Alex said, laughing.

"OK, but she won't come. Always goes straight home after work to her family. I'll see you in about thirty minutes."

Alex was now fifty-five and Jeremiah was almost three years younger. Jeremiah's fascination with Alex had begun in childhood. Alex had been the tutor, the mentor, the wizened seer who knew all about life and sex. But something beyond that had kept Jeremiah and his cousin Ethan enthralled during their growing up years: Alex had exuded some kind of confidence, a self-assurance and certainty about life that his younger cousins simply couldn't fathom. And now, in his middle-age, Jeremiah had finally realized that there was no reason on earth that Alex should have such an inner compass; he had no talents, no artistic bent, no useful skills whatsoever. He had made it through Georgia Tech by only the barest margin. And while he was a charmer, he was also frequently obnoxious—a braggart and a bore. Yet here he was at the apex of business success—heir apparent to one of the largest, most prestigious health care companies in the world.

As the light on the telephone line went out, Michelle called from her desk: "Jeremiah, you still want me to take your calls?"

Jeremiah walked to his secretary's desk. "You're going to think I've lost my mind—all this work here and everything—but I think I'm going out to the airport for a drink with Alex Rumpkin. As a matter of fact, he told me to invite you along too."

"That was an awfully nice thing to do," Michelle smiled broadly. "He said he remembered me from one of your parties—even recalled the dress I wore."

"Yeah, he's smooth, all right, and he does have a phenomenal memory for names, personal backgrounds and the like. He uses it to flatter people, you know, win them over to his way of thinking."

"I guess he might be offended if I *didn't* come," Michelle said.

"Oh, no, Michelle," Jeremiah waved his hand back and forth. "You needn't feel any pressure to go. To be honest, I told Alex you probably wouldn't come—that you always go home right after work."

"Maybe that's the damn trouble." Michelle said, raising her eyebrows. "I've always been too predictable."

"I'm sorry, I didn't mean it that way," Jeremiah said, shifting his feet. The expletive—coming from Michelle—had shocked him.

"Well, if it's all the same to you, I think I'd *like* to come along. I feel like I'm in a rut. I need a little change of pace."

"I—I guess it'll be OK," Jeremiah stuttered. "But maybe you should first call Arnold? Weren't you meeting for dinner?"

"Look, Jeremiah," Michelle stormed, "nobody appointed you my guardian. I'll call my damn husband if and when I feel like it. Come on, let's go!"

Michelle's outburst made it clear that Jeremiah had stirred up a hornet's nest. Even though he had worked closely with her for years, Jeremiah was shocked to learn that she was capable of such an angry display.

Jeremiah left word with the firm's receptionist that he would be gone for the rest of the day, and he and Michelle took the elevator and walked to the parking lot without speaking. He did not want to provoke her further, but he was also slightly miffed that she was barging in on his meeting with Alex.

As they pulled out of the parking garage in his car, she looked over and said: "Don't pout now. Please don't get riled up thinking I'm going to *spoil* your *bonding* session with your friend. I'll keep quiet and let you two talk. I just need a chance to get out a little."

"No problem," Jeremiah said, as he pulled to a stop at the 14th Street red light. "I guess the main thing was that it just shocked me that you wanted to come. You know, we've never even had a drink together—you and me, alone, I mean."

"Well, maybe you never asked me, did you think of that?"

Michelle's skirt had inched up well above her knees, and Jeremiah gave a quick, sidelong glance at her shapely legs as he waited for the light to change. Funny thing about working with someone all the time, it dawned on him: the person becomes a fixture, part of the office furniture, a piece of the environment you hardly notice. He had never fully appreciated Michelle's physical beauty, he thought, and maybe he hadn't even understood what made her tick, either. But it troubled him that maybe today he was finding out more about his secretary than he wanted to know.

The light turned green and they drove onto the entrance ramp of the interstate leading south to the massive airport serving Atlanta. Hartsfield International, the second or third busiest in the country, Jeremiah couldn't remember the exact standing, but it always impressed out-of-town visitors when he mentioned it. Tossing out statistics like that to impress people was required in Jeremiah's profession.

"What's Alex Rumpkin really like?" Michelle asked, tinkering with the radio.

"That's some question, Michelle," Jeremiah turned his head and smiled. "Gosh, how would I describe him? You need a whole list of adjectives, I think. Let's see—irresistible, charming, arrogant, despicable, deplorable, obnoxious? Maybe all of those and quite a few more."

"Not sure that's much help, Jeremiah." Michelle examined her lipstick in the visor mirror. "What was he like as a boy? You grew up with him, right?"

"Yeah, I did, but it was always hard to figure him out. He grew up dirt-poor on the wrong side of the tracks. Of course, my family wasn't rich either, but we were middle class compared to Alex's folks. I remember how threadbare his clothes were. And he would sometimes be hungry—*really* hungry, I mean. I can recall him coming in my mother's kitchen, and when I opened a jar of peanut butter, Alex would get a spoon and eat the *whole* thing—just peanut butter, no bread or *anything*—and then he'd drink three or four glasses of milk. Or he'd take an onion from our pantry and just eat it *raw.* I sometimes got the feeling he hadn't eaten in weeks."

"How on earth could he get where he is today with that kind of upbringing?" Michelle asked.

"I often wonder myself, and I really don't know how to explain it." Jeremiah paused to adjust his rear-view mirror. "I guess it all boiled down to some knack Alex had for getting to people—for making them like him. It was uncanny, but I was subject to it myself, even though he sometimes treated me awful when we were boys. He could sell himself to anyone, and one of the people who liked him right off was Dr. Willingham, you know, the founder of the Willingham Clinic—later, MedAmerica."

"Oh yeah," Michelle said, "that's where your middle name came from, wasn't it? I never made the connection until now."

"That's right, he was the doctor who birthed me," Jeremiah said, smiling, "and he took Alex in like a son. Gave him a job at the clinic, put him through high school and Georgia Tech, and let him work his way up through the organization to his present position. Topping it off, Alex married the doctor's daughter, Annie, one of my high school classmates. Alex's story is unbelievable, isn't it? A real Horatio Alger story, if there ever was one."

"That's exciting," Michelle said, "things like that just don't happen to many people. I guess that's what makes him unique. I can remember that night at your Christmas party: when he looked at me, it seemed his eyes pierced through to my soul. Does he affect you like that?"

"No, not a bit. And I'm not about to let his little riveting eyes get a peek at *my* soul," Jeremiah said, as they both laughed.

❦ ❦ ❦

Delta had three VIP rooms at the Atlanta airport and Alex had said he was in the Crown Room on Concourse A. The attendant at the door eyed Jeremiah and Michelle suspiciously when she learned that Jeremiah had no Crown Room membership. The couple were about to be turned away when Alex spotted them from across the room. He came bounding toward them, and said in a booming voice: "My lovely, these are my friends; please let them in." Then Alex laughed loudly and added: "Don't worry, I won't let them steal anything."

The attendant smiled nervously and apologized: "Oh, I'm very sorry, you didn't say you knew Mr. Rumpkin."

Alex gave Jeremiah a hard slap on the back and shook his hand. "Jero, you old rascal, it's good to see you." Then turning toward Michelle, he said: "And this is Michelle, as beautiful as I remember." He took her extended hand, cupped it between his hands, and gazed deeply into her eyes. "Lovely, yes, lovely," he murmured, "Come, let's go where we can be comfortable."

As they walked across the spacious room, lined with mahogany, marble and expensive-looking pictures and mirrors, they seated themselves and were immediately joined by an attractive woman wearing a Delta uniform, similar to those worn by flight attendants. "Oh, how rude of me," Alex said, turning to the girl. "Jennifer, this is my long-lost cousin, Jeremiah Goodwin—the one from the sticks I was telling you about. He's now a big-shot city lawyer, and this lovely woman with him is his secretary, Michelle."

"I'm pleased to meet you," the girl said. "Mr. Rumpkin said some nice things about you, Mr. Goodwin. Said you were the smartest man he knows."

"Well, he's obviously wanting something, if he said that."

"What I didn't tell you, Jennifer," Alex broke in, "is that without Michelle to make him look good, Jero here wouldn't know his ass from a hole in the ground." Laughing boisterously, Alex grabbed Jeremiah with an arm lock around the neck as he spoke. The two women looked at each other and blushed.

"Just kidding, girls," Alex said. "Look, I love this little bastard. Taught him everything he knows. Just a few rough edges left, and I'll get those yet." Jeremiah grinned broadly as Alex said: "Tell you what, Jennifer, you can bring me another Manhattan, please, and something for these beautiful people."

"A Margarita, no salt," Michelle said.

"Jack Daniels, on the rocks, with a twist of lemon, please," Jeremiah added, loosening his tie. "How are things in Shrewsbury Crossing, Alex?"

"Boring as hell, but otherwise great, just great," Alex replied, "and how's Sarah and the family?"

"Fine, just fine. Stays busy all the time with charity work, the historical society, and all that. It seems we just meet each other going and coming. Don't spend much time together, since my workload has become so hectic the last few years. Fact is, I really ought to be in the office right now. But let's don't discuss that. What about Annie? How's she doing, and the girls?"

"Annie's doing well, and the girls are fine, except Annie's lost more weight than I would like. Thin as a rail, I tell her, almost anemic."

"And Dr. Willingham? Is his health still good? I guess he's in his eighties now." Jeremiah turned toward Michelle. "I hope we aren't boring you too much with all this home town stuff."

"Not at all," Michelle said. "You just go ahead and catch up."

"Doc Willie's eighty-three," Alex said, "and he's still going strong. Beats all, I tell you! Makes two or three speeches a week, attends medical conferences all over the world. But that suits me fine, 'cause I can get more done when he's not around second-guessing all I do. I really wish he'd just turn MedAmerica over to me so I could turn it into the competitive Goliath it ought to be. Jero, we're just sitting on a cash horde that could be used to make the company the biggest health-care organization in the whole country, but the old man has a hemorrhage each time I spend a dollar. Like I said, we need a company airplane so I wouldn't have to spend half my time waiting around in airports like this."

"Well, whatever you're doing at MedAmerica, it must be pretty good, because the company's reputation is hard to beat. Any time someone finds out that Shrewsbury Crossing is my home town, the first thing they want to talk about is Dr.Willingham and MedAmerica. Most of the time, they even remember when it was the Willingham Clinic. I had a fellow tell me recently in New York that if he had a serious illness—you know, life threatening—he would check into a MedAmerica facility. Whatever happens, you need to preserve that kind of reputation."

"Oh hell yeah, Jero, we will. You know that." Alex said. Jennifer had returned with their drinks. "It's just that the company is being held back by a lot of outdated thinking."

"By the way, where's Doddy?" Jeremiah asked. "I thought you said he was with you."

"I told you on the phone: son-of-a-bitch passed out," Alex looked at Michelle. "Pardon my language, Michelle, but Doddy's Dr. Willingham's son and has a serious drinking problem. He turned back to Jeremiah. "I gave a taxi driver fifty bucks to take him over to the Marriott and check him in."

"What'll you do—just go on to Washington alone and leave him here?" Jeremiah asked.

"I don't know, Jero," Alex raised his eyebrows. "May just stay here tonight and leave in the morning. Besides, this is my third Manhattan and I'm not too thrilled with the idea of leaving such good company." Looking at Michelle, he said: "I can't imagine getting on an airplane as long as my old red-neck cousin and this beautiful woman are able to stay and visit with me. By the way, how long *can* you stay, Michelle?"

Michelle had finished her first drink. She glanced at her watch. "Oh, I don't know, Mr. Rumpkin, maybe I have time for one more drink."

"Call me Alex, for goodness sake, Michelle. Call me *Alex*!"

Michelle Silverman had never looked more radiant to Jeremiah. Watching her respond to Alex's invitation for another drink, he was stunned by the warmth of her smile and the glow of her eyes. As Alex ordered another round of drinks for everyone, Jeremiah knew the alcohol was beginning to take hold. He adored this stage of inebriation: no slurred words, no silliness, no foolish grimaces, just a happy state of well-being. Andrew Lloyd Weber themes played softly in the background, and he took his tie off and stuffed it in his coat pocket.

Jeremiah had not touched alcohol at all until his early twenties, shortly before his marriage to Sarah. A blurred sense of morality and rigid religious upbringing had colored his attitude toward the drug. Barriers to drinking had been erected by the virtually total abstinence of his parents: his mother never drank and his father treated himself only to one or two eggnogs at Christmas. As he grew up in Shrewsbury Crossing, everyone knew who the drinkers were, at least those who went public, and they were shunned and pitied. Something deep in Jeremiah's psyche said he did not want to be—would *not* be—one of *them.* The barriers had withstood the temptation to drink all those years.

But marriage to Sarah and law school had changed all that. Before the couple met, Sarah had drunk socially, but never too much. As Jeremiah entered his final year of law school, with a superb academic record behind him and a growing sense of self-importance (after all, he was editor of the law review), he and Sarah had become frequent visitors to taverns and bars around Virginia and Highland Avenues where students gathered to drink beer and discuss politics and cases. Most law students drank, Jeremiah had learned, and to him it seemed sophisticated. Out of law school, he had soon progressed with his drinking habits from beer to vodka tonic and later Jack Daniels, and now that he could afford it, he and Sarah had begun keeping large quantities of liquor at home for themselves and guests.

Sitting in the Crown Room with Alex and Michelle, Jeremiah wondered how he could have spent the first twenty-odd years of his life *without* drinking. Happy hours had opened many doors for him. The wheels of business were lubricated with alcohol. At fifty-three, Jeremiah felt that Jack Daniels was indispensable to his lifestyle although Sarah had become increasingly concerned about his drinking. Jeremiah felt most of the time that it was just another way for her to vent her hostility toward him, but she had recently stepped up the campaign by attending Al Anon meetings and urging him to seek counseling. She had even threatened divorce at times, which caused him to make promises of moderation and he would cut back or even go on the wagon. But there were still occasional binges, especially on out-of-town trips, and the whole thing had settled into an uneasy truce, a stalemate, between him and Sarah. She loved the trappings of success his career had brought them, and they had raised two beautiful, successful children. In the end, what had been unacceptable became acceptable and was a way of life for them.

Alex laughed loudly and slapped his knee. Seated next to Michelle on the sofa, Alex was slurring his words and talking more loudly as the attendant arrived with the next round of drinks. Four feet away, Jeremiah faced the two of them from a recliner. By Jeremiah's count, he and Michelle were into their third drinks, and Alex was well ahead of both of them. Michelle listened with rapture to each word Alex uttered, and Jeremiah could see why. At fifty-five, Alex still had boyish good looks. His charm and knack for conversation were not only unabated but had actually been enhanced by his rise to power at the top of a major American corporation. Michelle giggled frequently as he spoke, gazing deeply and intently into her eyes, asking questions about her family, her interests, her background. Jeremiah had seen him operate this way over the years. Alex always exuded a deep sense of concern about people's feelings, their personal lives; and the uncanny thing was that he always remembered what he learned: children's names, even birthdates, the kind of car driven. All of it served to make everyone think that Alex was genuinely interested in the welfare of others—a masterful device for manipulating people.

"What's so funny, Alex?" Jeremiah mumbled. His tongue had thickened.

"Hell, I don't know, Jero. Something this beautiful woman said, I guess. Say, why have you kept this gorgeous creature away from me all these years?"

Michelle was smiling broadly as Alex reached behind her head and slowly massaged her neck. Jeremiah's eyes fell to the perfect legs and ankles facing him. Michelle had crossed her legs, revealing the inner softness of her thighs. Jeremiah stared for a moment, looked quickly away, and then stared again when he saw that Michelle was oblivious to his gaze. She rested the toe of her shoe lightly against Alex's trousers.

"By the way, Alex," Jeremiah said nervously, "how's Ethan doing?"

"Mr. Allday? Hell, you know Ethan'll never change," Alex said, turning to face Jeremiah. "So damn straitlaced and serious he hurts. Since we made him Chief Financial Officer, he's gone on a crusade to prevent us from spending money anywhere, even when we have to. Follows me around like a watchdog. Shows up at staff meetings with charts and graphs and lectures us about how unit costs are going sky-high and total disaster awaits. I call him 'Mr. Doom and Gloom.'"

"What about Irene and the family?" Jeremiah asked.

"Doing fine. All but one daughter is out of college. You know, they had six, including the set of twins. I don't think they did anything but screw—pardon my language, Michelle—during their first ten years of marriage. His wife was a breeding machine."

Alex cupped the fingers of his right hand under Michelle's chin, pressing her face upward. "Speaking of breeding machines, Jero, have you ever seen such a delicious profile? I swear, I could spend the rest of my days making love to this luscious woman."

Michelle giggled and said: "Alex, Jeremiah doesn't even know I'm female. All he does is worry about his clients and getting his damn pleadings and briefs done. I'm just part of the office equipment."

"Well, that's just a crying shame, my angel," Alex said, "I'll have to straighten him out." A black man and two white women came into the Crown Room and took seats several yards away. Alex turned to Jeremiah. "Jero, y'all just turned Atlanta over to the niggers, didn't you?"

"Shhhhh," Jeremiah scanned the room hastily. "Alex, don't get us mixed up in a fight."

"Hell, I ain't gonna offend nobody, but it's a fact, ain't it? Y'all simply left this city for the blacks, ain't that true?"

"I don't think that's so at all," Jeremiah said in a low voice. "There's a powerful group of white leadership in Atlanta—you know, bankers, lawyers, business people."

"Bullshit!" Alex said, his voice rising. "You got a black mayor, a black police chief, mostly black city council, and blacks outnumber whites two to one. It was bad enough to surrender Atlanta to the Yankees, and now you've given it to the niggers."

"There's no question that blacks have a big voice in the city's affairs, but don't forget, Martin Luther King forged the civil rights movement here. Plus, there are some fine leaders in the Negro community—entrepreneurs and professionals who helped build this city."

"Then why in hell do you live in Roswell, like most big-shot whites? Shit, even rich blacks don't live in the city limits. They've migrated to the suburbs just like the whites." Jeremiah looked at Michelle, who seemed hypnotized by the conversation. "I'm telling you, Jero," Alex went on, "we've about let the niggers and other minorities ruin this country. Y'all even have a black female judge on the federal bench here."

"Yes, Judge Elizabeth Stratford-Hanes," Jeremiah said, "one of the best-qualified, most respected jurists anywhere."

"Hell, she's just one of these liberal judges who turn criminals loose on the streets. That's why you can't walk safely anywhere downtown anymore. And what gets me, she was appointed by that damn Carter. He ought to have known better, being raised in south Georgia like he was."

"Remember, Alex," Jeremiah said, "Beagle was also appointed by President Carter, and we both know what a fine man he is."

"*Was* a good man, maybe, until he went off and got educated and brainwashed." Alex waved his finger toward Jeremiah. "Came back home and led all those damn sit-in's, tearing up the community, suing everybody in sight. Of course, I'm happy to say he's settled down some in recent years now that he's accepted in the white community."

"Is he accepted?" Jeremiah asked.

"Hell, yeah. I helped him a lot myself. Persuaded the membership committee of the country club to invite him in. I'll tell you a fact: it took a lot of pushing on my part to get some of those rednecks to see the light. But I told 'em, I said, look, he may be colored, but he is a damn federal judge, and you never know when you gonna need a little help from a judge. So the committee voted him in unanimously."

"Why don't we change the subject, Alex?" Jeremiah squirmed uncomfortably. "I feel sure that Michelle has heard enough of your racist views."

"Hell, Jero, I ain't no racist. I've been in charge of Affirmative Action at MedAmerica all these years, and we've been cited for outstanding achievement in the hiring and promotion of minorities. But I'm just saying there has to be a limit to everything! Now, the blacks are trying to change the state flag—remove the stars and bars. Stuff like that makes me sick. What are they gonna do? Re-write history? Say there was no Civil War?"

"Michelle, please step in here," Jeremiah said. "Tell Alex you want to change the subject. Tell about your kids—how Ellison made the all-star soccer team."

"Yeah, I want to hear about your boy, Michelle, but just one more thing, Jero. Do you ever think about how good this country's been to blacks, taken 'em into the national culture, paid 'em millions of dollars to play professional sports, let 'em sing, do that rap shit. We've given them food stamps, welfare, Medicare, whatever!"

"I don't think the Africans were wildly enthusiastic about coming to this country as slaves," Jeremiah said, frowning. "The whites have a responsibility for that, don't they?"

"Hell, Jero, we didn't bring 'em over here. It was the English, Spanish and Yankee slave traders. Nobody from Georgia went over there and forced 'em to come here, and it was their own black kings that sold 'em off."

"Well, Alex, you've still got to admire someone like Beagle who's overcome the stigma of race and pulled himself up by his own bootstraps."

"Like *shit*, he did!" Alex shook his head vigorously. "It was Doc Willie helping him, paying for his tutor, things like that. And what the doctor didn't provide, the federal government did."

"You're incorrigible—hopeless, Alex, I give up," Jeremiah said, standing.

"Jero, you take everything too seriously." A wide grin broke on Alex's face as he nudged Michelle and winked. "See there, Michelle, how easy it is for me to get Jeremiah riled up. This Beagle fellow is a black guy we grew up with, and anytime I want to get Jero's goat, all I have to do is bring up his name."

It was almost seven-thirty as Jeremiah stood unsteadily and put on his coat. "I've got to get home, folks," he slurred his words. Michelle had moved closer to Alex, her hand resting casually on his leg. "Shouldn't you call Arnold and let him know where you are, Michelle?" Jeremiah asked.

"Damn it all, Jeremiah," Michelle stormed back. "You just leave my husband for me to handle. You just take care of your own marriage."

"Aw right, Jero," Alex grinned broadly, nuzzling Michelle's hair, "you just run along, now. I'll take good care of Michelle. We two are going to enjoy ourselves and have fun."

"Yeah, I can see that," Jeremiah said, turning and leaving the room, stumbling over a step in the foyer. He took the train back to the main terminal, and walked through an atrium lobby until he came to a bar. He stopped and stood weaving at the open entrance where a mini-skirted waitress in her late twenties, her breasts bulging, smiled and beckoned him to come in.

CHAPTER 13

Wet Things

"And down in lovely muck I've lain,
Happy till I woke again.
Then I saw the morning sky:
Heigho, the tale was all a lie;
The world, it was the old world yet,
I was I, my things were wet...."
A.E. Housman, *A Shropshire Lad*

"This simply has to stop," Sarah called to Jeremiah just as he was going through the kitchen door into the garage. She wore a yellow terrycloth robe and twisted a handkerchief with her fingers, a handkerchief wet with tears.

"I'm sorry, I didn't know you were awake," Jeremiah said, turning back to face her.

"Awake? I've been awake all night, Jeremiah. For God's sake, how could I sleep?"

"Look, I know you're upset with me, and you have every right to be, but I can't talk about it right now. I should've been at the office an hour...."

"You never have time to talk, to face the terrible reality of where we are. Each time for you is just more of the same."

Sarah was right, Jeremiah knew. Last night was just another of many nights when he had staggered home, drunk beyond belief, unaware of the route he had taken home. Like most of the other mornings that followed such nights, this morning he had overslept; and when he had awakened, he found himself in the guest bedroom, his clothes strewn aimlessly over a chair and the floor. His head had throbbed, his eyes were swollen and bloodshot, and his hands had shaken while he tried to shave.

"You're right, Sarah. Absolutely right," he said, straining to see if his words were softening the grim lines of her face. Sarah was an elegant, gentle woman, but when she became angry, she was like a wet hornet. He had learned over the years that at times like this, he should cut his losses, say as little as possible, and retreat to his office. Besides, he was smart enough to know that she held the high ground. "Let me promise you this," he continued, "as soon as I get this Edgewood contract wrapped up—hopefully, by the end of the day tomorrow—we'll talk about things for as long as it takes. I promise that I'll make time for that."

"I've heard too many of your promises before. Like promising me you'd be here for dinner with my folks last night. Can you fathom how painful it was for me to tell them repeatedly that you'd soon be here, that I was certain you had some kind of business delay, that I couldn't imagine why you didn't call? They could see the pain and agony in my face, and they begged me to discuss things with them. When you didn't show up by ten-thirty, they said they just wanted to drive back home last night, and they left."

"I am sorry, I swear I am, and things will be different from now on," Jeremiah said, shaking his head and looking down at the floor. "You don't deserve that kind of treatment, and I wish to heavens I hadn't let the alcohol get the best of me last night. I just forgot all about the time and my obligations."

"Then why don't you quit, Jeremiah? You can see what it's done to us. I just can't go on like this."

Jeremiah walked over to where she stood, her lips quivering. He put his arms around her and stroked the back of her neck. "Please, Sarah, let me just get through this day at work, and I'll sit with you and we'll work this thing out. OK?"

"I'm too tired to argue," she said, "I'm totally worn out, emotionally and physically, just too tired to deal with you anymore."

"It'll be better tonight," he said, kissing her cheek lightly. "You'll see."

Even with frantic haste, Jeremiah arrived at the office after nine, an hour and a half later than normal. As he approached his office door, there was no sign that Michelle had been at her desk, but Kenneth Stripling waited in a chair, his legs crossed and arms folded belligerently across his chest. "Good morning, Jeremiah," he said, "You're a little late, aren't you? Looks like you might have tied one on last night."

"You here to see me?" Jeremiah grumbled.

"Just for a moment," the boy responded. Stripling followed Jeremiah into his office. Jeremiah suddenly remembered that he had not picked up his usual cup of coffee from the shop in the lobby, a serious oversight since he had not taken time to fix coffee at home. Another thing gone wrong.

"OK, Kenneth, what's on your mind?"

"I understand you've talked to Mr. Ansley about me."

"That's right. Did he tell you?"

"Yeah, he told me! What'd you think he'd do after you complained about your so-called problems with me? He said I have to keep *you* happy." Stripling's eyelids blinked erratically and sweat drops appeared on his upper lip.

"I suspect there was more to the conversation than that, but listen, I just don't have time to discuss this with you right now," Jeremiah said, eyeing the remainder of the acquisition document which now seemed an inch thicker than it had the afternoon before. "Look, I'm sorry," he said, realizing that this was the second time this morning he had said those words, "but I've got to finish this Edgewood contract. Let's schedule a time when we can discuss this at length."

"You know something, Jeremiah," the boy countered, "that's part of the problem: you really don't know very much about me or my work You're always too busy with *your* projects, always farming me out to one of the senior associates. I get very little of your time." Stripling's tone was strident. "Which is *fine* with me, but just don't set yourself up to judge me when you don't have any basis for it."

"I've got all the basis I need, you little shitass! If it were up to me, I'd fire your butt." Jeremiah spoke without thinking.

"Yeah, and you'd regret it the rest of your damn life," Stripling said, scowling.

"Is that a threat?"

"Take it any way you want to," the boy said between clinched teeth. "It's just that I place a high value on my good name in the firm, and the stuff you say to other partners can affect my reputation. My *whole* family is pleased that I've joined the Proctor, Bennett firm—especially my *father*. They would hate to see my career end here!"

The not-so-veiled threat irritated Jeremiah, and he felt certain that the boy had dropped his name from the firm name deliberately. But the argument was going nowhere, and Jeremiah knew he had more important things to do, so he said: "Look, Kenneth, I've told you I can't deal with this right now. Come in tomorrow afternoon at five. Hopefully, I'll have this Edgewood business out of the way by then."

"By the way," Stripling said, "Mr. Edgewood was in here at four-thirty yesterday afternoon, and he was pretty upset that he couldn't locate you or your secretary. I wouldn't be surprised if there is hell to pay with him this morning." With a grin, Stripling turned and walked out the door.

After the boy had disappeared, Jeremiah went to the water cooler just outside his office, filled a cup, and returned to his office. Reaching into his desk drawer, he found two extra strength Tylenol capsules and swallowed them. His head still throbbed and his eyesockets ached. He had just picked up the next section of the acquisition agreement when the telephone rang. "Have you heard from Michelle this morning?" Arnold Silverman asked. "She didn't come home last night, Jeremiah, and I'm worried sick."

Scrambling for time to think, Jeremiah asked: "Didn't she call you? Haven't you heard from her at all?"

"She called from the airport about eight. Said she was having a drink with you and a client. She sounded drunk and we got in a shouting match. We were supposed to meet for dinner, had a baby-sitter lined up. I was mad as hell when we hung up, but she said she'd be home soon."

"But she never showed up?"

"No, not all night. That's why I'm calling you. Did she leave with you—have you heard from her?" Michelle's husband sounded frantic. "It's totally unlike her to do this."

Michelle suddenly appeared at Jeremiah's door, her lipstick smudged badly and her hair in distress. As she walked close to his desk, Jeremiah could smell tequila on her even though traces of Jack Daniels lingered on his own breath. Her eyes were vividly blood-stained, and rivulets of mascara were smeared on her cheek. Jeremiah placed his hand over the receiver and whispered Arnold's name, then said: "Well, here she is now, Arnold; guess she was in the ladies' room. I just got here myself."

Michelle motioned that she would pick up the phone at her desk, which she did after closing the door.

Several minutes later, she returned. "What did you tell him?" Jeremiah asked.

"I just said I met one of the secretaries in a bar after you left the airport, had too much to drink, and decided to go home with her for the night."

"Did he ask you her name?"

"No, he trusts me completely. He'll be all right. It would never dawn on him that I would lie."

"Is that the real story?"

"Jeremiah, hell, don't be *naive*! I spent the night with Alex at the Airport Marriott." Michelle turned to leave the room.

"*Jesus*, Michelle, I hope you realize that it was just a one-night stand," Jeremiah said, shaking his head.

"Look, I'm a grown woman, and I knew what I was getting into, even if I was drunk. But, I *needed* a night like that—at least *one* night. My life has become such a boring mess, and, *God*, Alex is exciting! What a dynamo!"

Before Jeremiah could respond, Robert Edgewood appeared at the door. "Am I interrupting anything?" he asked.

"Of course not, Bob, come in," Jeremiah said. Michelle left the room, closing the door behind her.

"Jeremiah, I'll come right to the point. What the hell is holding up the Deering deal?" Edgewood sat frowning in the chair facing the desk. "The Bickworth lawyers say they can't do anything until you sign off on the paperwork. They didn't come right out and say it, but I can sense they think you're dragging your feet."

"My gosh, Robert, I just got the damn thing yesterday, and it's over three-hundred pages. I've given them comments on about half of it, and I'm trying to finish it today. There's some lousy drafting in it—unbelievably bad work when I think about their fees. You told me to protect your interest, didn't you?"

"Yeah, hell yeah, I did, but I know for a fact that you weren't here yesterday afternoon. That boy Stripling that works for you said he saw you leaving with your secretary."

"I do have other clients, you know, and I had to meet one of them."

"Do you always take your secretary to meet your clients?"

"Look, Bob, I'm not going to stand for cross-examination on this. If you want me to finish this acquisition agreement, you've got to get out and let me get to it." Jeremiah's tone was more belligerent than he had intended.

"Well, get on it, for heaven's sake," Edgewood stuttered. "I can't let this Deering deal get away from me. Damn it all, Jeremiah, give it the priority it deserves!" He stood up, gave Jeremiah a last agitated glance and left the office. Jeremiah followed him out past Michelle's desk. The telephone began to ring as

Edgewood left. "Get that, Michelle," Jeremiah said, "and unless it's the Pope or the President, tell whoever it is that I'm in conference."

Michelle said hello, put the line on hold, and called to Jeremiah as he was closing the door: "Jeremiah, it's Alex's wife. She sounds upset."

"I'll take it," Jeremiah said, walking quickly back to his desk. "Hello, Annie, it's good to hear from you. You all right?"

"Jeremiah, Daddy's *dead*!" Annie was sobbing loudly. "He died early this morning."

"I'm so sorry, Annie. So sorry!" Jeremiah paused a moment, then asked: "What happened?"

"A heart attack, we think," Annie continued to sob. "I never dreamed it could hurt me like this, Jeremiah."

"What can I do or say to help you?" Jeremiah stammered. "You know I'll do *anything*."

"I know you would," Annie's voice quivered, "and I do need a favor. I can't find Alex. He and Doddy left yesterday to go to Washington, but he never registered last night at the Georgetown Inn. He said he might call you passing through Atlanta. Did he?"

"He did call me, Annie, he did, and I met him for a drink at the airport. He said Doddy had gotten sick on the way to Atlanta and had checked into a hotel at the airport. Said he was probably going to wait until this morning to go on to D.C. if Doddy felt better."

"Did he say which hotel?"

"No, he didn't," Jeremiah said. "Let me call around and see if I can find him. Either I'll call back, or I'll have him call you immediately. And Annie, please accept my deepest sympathy. Everyone always thought the world of Dr. Willingham. My mother, especially—she thinks he's a saint."

"Thanks so much, Jeremiah," Annie continued to sob, "You've always seemed to be right there when I need you. Will you come down for the services?"

"Of course, I'll be there. Now let me see if I can locate Alex. You take care of yourself."

Jeremiah asked Michelle for the room number, dialed the Airport Marriott, and Alex answered the phone. "Alex, this is Jeremiah."

"Jero, how'd you find me? Oh, I guess Michelle, huh? Listen, that is some *fine* piece of tail you got workin' for you. I'm amazed that you ain't been tappin' that yourself, but she swears you ain't."

"Alex, cut out the crap!" Jeremiah thundered into the phone. "I've got some really bad news. Dr. Willingham is *dead*, and Annie doesn't know how to find you."

After a short pause, Alex said: "Well, I'll be damn. So the old man's gone."

"Annie says he died in his sleep early this morning. I didn't get many details but they think it was a coronary."

"Where did you tell Annie I am?"

"I said I didn't know for sure. That I met you for drinks, Doddy got sick, and that you probably stayed at an airport hotel last night. I said I'd try to find you."

"Good job, old buddy, I guess I owe you one. I'll call home right away."

"One more thing, Alex, do me a favor and take it easy on Michelle. She's a fine woman and doesn't need any grief from you, OK?"

"Hell, Jero, I'd never do anything to hurt that gal. I'm just sweet and lovable. Yeah, all the women say that," Alex laughed.

"You don't sound too upset to hear about Doc Willie," Jeremiah said.

"Hell, Jero, he was an old man, and we all have to die sometime. But you know me, I roll with the punches. Always. Life goes on, and I make the best of any situation."

"Yes, I know you do," Jeremiah said, as he hung up. Then he mumbled to himself: "you bet! I know you do."

CHAPTER 14

Doc Willie's Funeral

"Haul up the flag, you mourners,
Not half-mast but all the way;
The funeral is done and disbanded;
The devil's had the final say."
Karl Shapiro, "Elegy for Two Banjos."

Alexander Rumpkin swept into Shrewsbury Crossing like Caesar entering Rome. News of the doctor's death had spread rapidly. By the time the airplane landed at Willingham Field, Alex was hailed by airport personnel as the heir apparent he was presumed by everyone to be. As he strode into the terminal, Doddy walking unsteadily a few steps behind him, several gate agents and skycaps approached with sympathetic pats on Alex's arm or back and pledges of prayerful support.

After hanging up the telephone with Annie that morning, Alex had jerked C.R. Jr. half-asleep from the hotel room, loaded him into a taxi, and taken the first flight home. Although Alex had long anticipated the doctor's death, the precise timing was not to his liking. It had meant the cancellation of the Washington trip after he had lined up meetings with several bureaucrats and the Panacea people. And there were embarrassments he might have to explain: Annie calling Jeremiah to locate him, spending the impetuous night with Michelle, Doddy passing out in the Crown Room, but he told himself there were some things you just couldn't control. He would work everything out. He had laid elaborate and thorough plans for the old man's death, and nothing would spoil it for him now.

After taking the groggy C.R. Jr. home, Alex went directly to the office. There was no time to call Annie. Greeted by hugs and tears from office workers meeting him in the lobby and halls, his eyes welling up with tears, Alex reciprocated in kind, agreeing with everyone what a wonderful man the doctor had been, what greatness, how much he would be missed, how difficult to carry on.

Closing the door behind him, Alex walked into his office and seated himself at the mahogany desk he had purchased with great fanfare from one of Atlanta's most prestigious furniture dealers. The price had been over eight thousand dollars, a fact he had carefully concealed from Dr. Willingham. A skinflint, the old doctor, Alex thought, never willing to spend a dime more than he had to, so tight he squeaked when he walked. Alex paused a moment, needing some time to think, looked around his office, and took a deep breath: all those years are over now, he told himself; he would soon move into Doc Willie's office at the end of the hall, much bigger than his, but in dire need of renovation. But most important, he would now be able to make this antiquated organization into the global enterprise he wanted to run.

"Priscilla," he barked to his aging secretary, "get the funeral checklist file for me, and call all the senior officers to a meeting at 3:15 this afternoon. Tell everyone to be ready to work late tonight to set this thing up."

"Mr. Rumpkin, I don't think Mr. Scott and Mr. Wainwright are here. Their secretaries left word that they are out this afternoon—in mourning, you know. Something about it not being appropriate to be here under the circumstances."

Priscilla Alligood was a spinster in her sixties. She had worked at the clinic since the early forties, most of that time as an aid to Dr. Willingham, but Alex had inherited her when he was named executive vice president. He had never liked her, but he had no choice but to keep her as his secretary: the doctor liked her, and besides, she had bought stock in MedAmerica on a payroll deduction basis from the first day it went public. She had never sold a share, and with several splits, dividend reinvestment, and appreciation over the years, the woman was now worth nearly four million dollars. With the doctor out of the way, however, Alex knew he would find a way to get her out of his office, reassign her to something harmless where he wouldn't have to see her every day, but it would take a little time. She was an institution at MedAmerica, and he would have to handle the situation with kid gloves. Mustn't be impatient, plenty of time, can't do everything overnight, he kept telling himself.

"I don't give a hoot what those two think is 'appropriate,' Priscilla, call them at home and tell them to get over here *right now*, tell them I said so!" Grimacing, he muttered under his breath, "Before it's over, I'll give them something to mourn."

Alex picked up the phone and dialed Ethan Allday's extension. "Ethan," he said, "how about stepping down here?"

"Alex," Ethan said, entering the office, "I'm terribly sorry about Dr. Willingham. I know you and Annie must be heartbroken. Is there anything I can do?"

Alex stood and walked over to Ethan, putting an arm around his shoulder. "I know I can depend on you, Ethan. I'll need you to help me keep this organization together during the transition. I want you to know that I'll rely on your loyalty and support.

"That's gratifying to know," Ethan brushed a tear from his cheek.

"Well, let me tell you what I'd like you to do in the time we have before this afternoon's meeting. You know the financial records, annual reports, SEC filings that I've asked you to collect on the Panacea Company. Pull them all out and begin going over them. As soon as this funeral's over, I want to give some serious thought to a takeover."

"But Alex," Ethan protested, "I won't have time to do that. There's a long list of calls I need to return, well-wishers offering condolences, people like that."

"You let me handle the fuckin' well-wishers," Alex grumbled. "Just do what I tell you."

Shaking his head, Ethan turned and left the room.

Alex stayed on the telephone for the next three hours, pausing to nibble a sandwich between calls, executing his checklist like a well-worn script. First, the governor of Georgia, even though Priscilla pointed out before he made the call that they didn't have arrangements finalized for the service; in fact, hadn't even decided upon the *time*. "Well, it has to be Saturday afternoon—mid-afternoon," Alex snapped, "we can't afford to keep the clinic closed through Sunday. We'll go *broke*, for God's sake!"

"I have the governor on the line," Priscilla said.

"Governor, Alex Rumpkin here. How are you?"

The Governor came right to the point. "I'm afraid I know why you're calling, Alex. I can't tell you how terribly sorry I am to hear of Dr. Willingham's death. Please extend my heartfelt condolences to your wife, to everyone in the family and everyone connected with MedAmerica."

"I'll certainly do that, George," Alex responded, "and I know you must be making plans to attend the service. It would be fitting for you to be in attendance as the highest emissary of the citizens of this state. The service will be sometime Saturday afternoon. Maybe you can make a few remarks."

"There could be some scheduling problems for me," the Governor said, clearing his throat. There's a conference at Jekyll Island where I'm supposed to speak. Hope you'll understand. I will urge the Lieutenant Governor to be there, of course."

"George, before you make too quick a decision on this, you should focus on how important Dr. Willingham was to the people around here. It's really your call, but I believe your absence would be conspicuous. You know what I mean, a political albatross for you in years to come. You don't want *that*, do you? And, George," Alex added, "it would mean a hell of a lot to me *personally* if you're here. I'm sure you know who's going to be running MedAmerica now, and I'm planning to give you the company's support, support I'd have trouble justifying to the board if you didn't show up for the doctor's funeral."

After a long pause, the Governor assured Alex that he would find some way to attend. Variations of the same lines were used as Alex continued down his checklist: to the two Georgia senators, six members of the state's congressional delegation, the speaker of the Georgia House, and then to the governors of adjacent states. When he finally delegated the remaining calls to the public affairs people, Alex was pleased with the results. Commitments to attend the services had been received from nearly all of the political dignitaries. It would be a splendid turnout.

Plans for Doc Willie's funeral had been developed over the span of several years, sometimes prompted by the doctor himself. His wife's untimely death in 1954 in an automobile accident had caused the doctor to order the construction of a mausoleum in the center of the Shrewsbury Crossing cemetery. It was a massive, impressive tomb, shaped like a pyramid, with vaults for twelve members of the Willingham family. The facade was white granite and a French sculptor was commissioned to create a seven-foot statue of Dr. Willingham to guard the entrance to the crypt.

And then there was the funeral checklist. The preparation of the document was itself a testament to Alex's skills for planning and organization. Since the early eighties, Alex had convened regular meetings of the company's senior staff to develop a contingency plan for Dr. Willingham's death. After each meeting, the checklist would be revised and circulated to each participant for comments and further discussion in the succeeding meeting. No detail was too minute for inclusion in the discussion, and no wording so sacrosanct it could not be rewritten. The gravity with which Alex viewed these planning sessions for Doc Willie's last rites became apparent to all, and a participant's suggestion—actually offered as a joke—that the project was taking too much executive time was met with raised eyebrows and a cold stare from Alex.

Appended to the checklist was a batch of press releases with several blanks to fill in and released to the media within minutes of the doctor's death. These had been dutifully dispatched early on Thursday morning—well before Alex had returned to Shrewsbury Crossing. They quoted Alex profusely in his praise for Dr. Willingham, his legendary posture as a medical pioneer, his vision for the nation's healthcare. They placed emphasis on the harmony, the familial ties between Alex and his mentor, the altruism shared by the two men, and concluded with Alex's assurance that the work of MedAmerica would continue and flourish. A close observer of these bulletins or someone obsessed with detail would have found that the names of Charles Robert Willingham and Alexander Wayne Rumpkin received equal billing.

That Thursday after the doctor's death, the meeting of senior staff ran on and on—until nearly 9:00 p.m. It was late getting started to allow Alex's tailor to take final measurements for last minute alterations for the suit he would wear to the service. Morticians had been brought in from Tallahassee to prepare the doctor's body, which would lie in state for public viewing beginning early the next morning. Services would commence at 2:00 p.m. on Saturday and would be conducted at the First Baptist Church of Shrewsbury Crossing. Even though Dr. Willingham was Methodist, the Baptist church had a much larger sanctuary and, as Alex knew, the prevailing mood in Shrewsbury Crossing was ecumenical when it came to Doc Willie.

Telegrams of condolence began pouring in as the senior staff met, and Alex would interrupt the deliberations to read aloud those of importance. He smiled broadly as he read one from Billy Graham, who said he would send a representative to the funeral. Others came from eminent physicians, deans of medical schools and presidents of universities. The meeting proceeded at a snail's pace, especially when Alex kept insisting that the group revisit, time and again, the seating arrangements for the church.

It was nearly ten o'clock when Alex arrived at home. Annie met him at the door, tears streaming down her cheeks, and said: "Alex, why couldn't you have called? Priscilla kept telling me that you were doing something that could not be interrupted. I kept asking her to give you messages. Why didn't you call me?"

"Listen, Sweetheart," Alex said, "you have no idea how many details have to be worked out, the right people notified. You want everything to be perfect, don't you? You know your father would have wanted everything to be handled right. You'll be proud on Saturday that I've laid the foundation for a service befitting the man your father was."

"I would rather have had you here with me today. I've needed you so! Please just hold me." Annie's voice trembled as she held out her arms to Alex.

He pulled her close, kissed her cheek, and wiped her tears. "There, there, Sweetheart," he said, "it's all right! He was a wonderful man who lived a long and saintly life. We were all blessed by his life."

Annie rested gently in his arms for a moment. Then he stepped back and said, "Now, let's go over your wardrobe for tomorrow and Saturday. There'll be lots of big-wigs there. Mrs. Rumpkin has to look her best."

Dr. Charles Robert Willingham lay in state all day Friday and Saturday morning at the First Baptist Church of Shrewsbury Crossing. At times, a line two blocks long waited outside the church while hundreds of mourners shuffled by the ornate casket.

On the morning of the funeral, Jeremiah Goodwin had arrived in town shortly before ten. A three-hour talk with Sarah the night before had not persuaded her to make the trip, although she had agreed—once again—to try to preserve the marriage after he had promised—also for the umpteenth time—that he would stop drinking. At the Allday home, Jeremiah had coffee with Ethan and Irene, and the three then drove to the Willingham mansion to pay their respects to the family. Alex met and embraced each of them at the sitting room entrance and escorted them to Annie who sat surrounded by her two daughters and their husbands. C.R. Jr. sat across the room, remote, dazed. "Thank you so much for being here," Annie said to Jeremiah, her eyes swollen from crying. He leaned down to kiss her on the forehead and she grabbed him around the neck and pulled him to her. "And thanks," she whispered, sobbing in his ear, "more than you'll ever know, *thanks* for helping me find Alex."

Her innocent gratitude provoked an intense feeling of guilt in Jeremiah as he thought for an instant about the circumstances in the Crown Room that night and his own complicity in the matter. "It was nothing," he assured Annie, clearing his throat. "Nothing at all. You know you can always count on me."

"Jeremiah, can I speak to you privately in the study?" Alex quietly asked as Ethan and Irene came forward to comfort Annie.

"Of course," Jeremiah responded. Alex led him into the study, closing the massive door behind them.

Alex turned and faced Jeremiah. "Jero, aren't you a legal expert on mergers and acquisitions?"

"Yeah, 'M & A,' they call it in the trade." Jeremiah raised his eyebrows. "Why do you ask?"

"Have you ever heard of the Panacea Company?"

"I think you mentioned that name once, and I recall looking it up at the time, but isn't this an odd time to be talking about something like this?"

"Jeremiah," Alex said, "sometimes you have to seize an opportunity, you know, take charge of events—no matter what's going on around you. Do you know anything about Panacea?"

"Well, yes," Jeremiah said, "it's an old-line medical care company headquartered in Minnesota, isn't it? Hospitals and facilities in the upper midwest and northern tier of states. Seemed to be on the verge of bankruptcy for the last several years, right? Why on earth do you ask?"

"I've had my eye on taking over that outfit since the early eighties, but the old man wouldn't even consider it, said those operations would be out of our territory, stretch us out too thin, dilute the quality of our services. But he never wanted us to be aggressive about anything, Jero. I maneuvered our expansion in the Southwest and New England area all by myself. The man resisted like crazy when I argued that we needed to change the name of the clinic to MedAmerica in 1975. Back in '66, when Johnson signed Medicare into law, I was the only one here to foresee what a cash-cow that legislation would be for the medical care business. No one will ever know how hard Doc Willie fought me every step of the way."

"So what's your point, Alex? Why are you telling me this?"

"It's really simple, Jero, I want you to undertake a thorough analysis of the legal and regulatory barriers to MedAmerica's takeover of Panacea. You're one of the few people I can trust, and if this got out, Panacea's stock would go through the roof."

"Aren't you being a little presumptuous? You're not CEO yet, and how do you know the board will go along with the idea?"

"You leave the *board* to me, Jeremiah. I'll be appointed CEO next week at a special meeting. You just get busy on the project. I want to be ready to wrap this deal up within the next few months. Money's no object. Just keep a record of your time, and for God's sake, Jero, keep this under your hat. Don't let anybody know what you're doing."

"If I keep this close to the chest, I'll be limited on the research I can assign out, and I *do* have other clients, Alex, I can't just drop them. I almost lost a client this week fooling around with you at the airport."

"You just do what it takes, Jero," Alex said with a smirk, placing his arm around Jeremiah's shoulders as they walked from the room. "This deal's gonna be worth a lot to both of us. I've got complete confidence in you to help me pull it off."

❧ ❧ ❧

The funeral went smoothly, just as Alex had planned it. The church was not able to contain the throngs, but Alex had made sure that seats were reserved for the rich and powerful. A splendid organ pealed forth "Amazing Grace" and "Rock of Ages" after which a string of eulogists paraded to the pulpit to praise the fallen idol. Honorary pall-bearers, all carefully hand-picked by Alex, led the procession from the church. As hundreds looked on, the casket was placed in a golden Cadillac hearse for the cavalcade to the cemetery and the waiting tomb. At the cemetery, Jeremiah watched from a distance as Alex moved with his arms around Annie to rows of chairs under a canopy just outside the crypt. There they sat while streams of mourners walked down the line to offer their condolences. Watching Alex embrace and accept handshakes from well-wishers, Jeremiah mused silently to himself: "Wonder what he's *really* thinking about now? Doc Willie or Panacea?"

For Dr. Charles Robert Willingham, the patron saint of Shrewsbury Crossing and the founder of the Willingham Clinic and the sprawling MedAmerica Corporation, it was all finished. For Alexander Wayne Rumpkin, the doctor's protege, the good times were just beginning to roll.

CHAPTER 15

Ruler of the Queen's Navee

"I cleaned the windows and I swept the floor,
And I polished up the handle of the big front door.
I polished up that handle so carefullee
That now I am the Ruler of the Queen's Navee!"
W.S. Gilbert, *HMS Pinafore*

Jeremiah had been waiting twenty minutes at the passenger pickup island for the small airport serving Ludlow and Shrewsbury Crossing. It was late afternoon, but a hot July sun was still beaming down. He shuffled nervously on his feet. He had taken off his coat and loosened his tie, but that hadn't helped much; he was still miserable.

From his vantage point, Jeremiah could see acres of gently rolling farmland blending into the soft blue sky of the horizon. In early July of 1990, the fields on each side of the road leading from the four-lane to the airport were bursting with fecundity. From May through June that year, evenly-spaced rainfall on the rich, fertile soil of southwest Georgia had nurtured the corn, tobacco, peanuts, and cotton to brilliant hues of green. Monstrous tractors pulling two dozen plows could be spotted moving here and there in the fields, like giant beetles, uprooting weeds and loosening dirt between the rows so root systems could spread. The drivers sat in air-conditioned comfort in enclosed glass cabins, away from the dust, some listening to stereo. Amazing how farming had changed here since he was a boy, Jeremiah thought. Each tractor now able to perform in two hours the work a field hand could do plowing a mule for a week.

A big black Lincoln with darkly tinted windows suddenly pulled to a stop at the curb. "Hop in. Throw your stuff in the back seat." Alex Rumpkin called out through the lowered passenger-side window from his place behind the wheel.

Jeremiah opened the rear door and threw an overnight bag and two large briefcases into the seat. Then he sat down beside Alex, who reached over to shake his hand.

"Sorry I'm late, but you know how the five o'clock rush is in Shrewsbury Crossing." Alex grinned broadly.

Jeremiah's patience had worn thin waiting in the heat. "Look, Alex, don't give me that. I know damn well that Shrewsbury Crossing hasn't had a traffic tie-up since that propane gas truck turned over in front of the courthouse in 1953."

"You got me dead-to-rights, Jero," Alex chuckled. "Truth is, I had a half-dozen telephone calls just as I started to leave the office. Don't get pissed. It's good to see you."

"Good to see you too," Jeremiah softened his tone. "You know my theory about people who're consistently late—makes them feel important to have other people waiting. But you don't need that ritual to make *you* feel important, do you? How're things going?"

"Great! Absolutely great. Old Alex hasn't let any grass grow under his feet since I saw you at the funeral. Can't wait to tell you about everything, but before we leave the airport, I want to show you something." Alex pulled off on a service road leading to a hangar for a fixed base operator. Stopping the car, he said: "Come on, Jero, let's get out."

Alex led Jeremiah through a side door and inside was a sleek, twin-engine business jet, gleaming white with bold blue letters on the side reading **MEDAMERICA.** "How 'bout that, Jero!" he exclaimed as he bounced up the steps to the open door of the cabin. "Get up here, look at this layout."

As Jeremiah walked through the door and into the cabin, he saw the unmistakable signs of the newness of the aircraft: fresh paint, plush carpet, rich purple velour fabric and leather treatments everywhere. The airplane was a Gulfstream business jet, a G-4, designed to seat twenty passengers, but it had been reconfigured to make room for a private compartment with a bed, separate lavatory and wet bar.

"How much?" Jeremiah asked.

"Ah, not bad, Jero. Not bad at all. Probably less than you think. I told you the company needed one of these, and the Board voted unanimously for it when I explained how much executive time it would save. No more sitting around in some crowded airport waiting for a dimwitted agent to board a flight."

"But how much?" Jeremiah was persistent.

"Just a little over thirty-eight million, including the cost of reconfiguring the cabin."

"Doc Willie would turn over in his grave, you know that." Jeremiah said, "But it is a beauty, Alex. I'll give you that."

"Are you ready for dinner?" Alex asked, as they returned to the car.

"What about Annie? Are we gonna pick her up?"

"No, she sends her apologies. Says she's not feeling too good, but she'll see you at the house when we get there. You're spending the night with us, right?"

Alex had pulled the car onto a four-lane headed east, toward Ludlow. "I can stay at a motel, Alex, unless you're sure it's no bother to you and Annie."

"No bother at all," Alex said. "You remember how many bedrooms we've got in the old Willingham mansion, and Annie and I've done a lot of renovating since we moved in there with Doddy three months ago. You won't even recognize the place."

"So where are you taking us for dinner?" Jeremiah asked.

"My favorite eatery and watering hole around here," Alex answered.

"Yeah, where's that?"

"It's called the Moorings. It's on the Georgia Power lake south of Ludlow. They bring in flounder, mackerel, and oysters fresh from Appalachicola every day. Excellent food. Melts in your mouth."

"Sounds wonderful," Jeremiah said. "I'm starving."

Twenty minutes later, Alex parked in a handicapped spot just to the left of the entrance to the restaurant.

"Aren't you worried about towing?" Jeremiah asked as they got out of the car.

"You think these fuckers would tow the automobile of the damn Chairman, CEO and President of the MedAmerica Corporation? The owner knows I'd have this place shut down, but it ain't a problem. I been parking here since they opened this joint. Don't know why they don't just put my name on the spot."

Jeremiah smiled but said nothing.

"Your usual table, Mr. Rumpkin?" a pleasant looking man asked as they entered the restaurant. It was still early for dinner customers, only six o'clock. Alex nodded. "Of course, Roscoe, and send Tara over."

Within seconds after they were seated, a young woman in her early twenties came to the table. "Ah, Tara, my heart's desire," Alex said, smiling broadly. "Are you ready to run off with me to Antigua? You know, my favorite fantasy is to get you alone on my sailboat."

The girl blushed and said: "Mr. Rumpkin, how you carry on! You know we can't do that."

"How many times have I told you to call me 'Alex'? You make me feel like an old man." Alex glanced toward Jeremiah. "But I guess I'm being rude. This is my old buddy and cousin, Tara—Jeremiah Goodwin, born and raised over in Shrewsbury Crossing. We grew up together. Then he went off to Atlanta and became a high-powered lawyer." Alex paused to savor the blush on the girl's face. "And Jero, this is Miss Tara Fountain, and, I might add, the principal reason I patronize this joint. I want you to be honest: have you ever seen a more beautiful woman?"

Tara offered her hand as Jeremiah said hello. Her moist lips parted in a wide smile, revealing perfectly formed teeth. "I'm pleased to meet you, Mr. Goodwin." Jeremiah felt self-conscious, owing partly to the forwardness of Alex's remarks to the young woman but compounded by the fact that she *was* stunningly beautiful. She had long black hair cascading down her back, a face of unblemished, ivory-toned skin, a profile and body of classic proportions. Jeremiah caught himself staring awkwardly for an instant, then lowered his gaze.

"Bring me a Manhattan to get started, Tara, and I bet Jeremiah wants Jack Daniels on the rocks, right, Jero? Ain't that what you were drinking in Delta's VIP room that night?" Winking at the waitress as Jeremiah nodded, Alex said: "See, I told you, I know this fellow well."

As the girl turned and left, Jeremiah said: "OK, tell me what's been going on since they put you in charge of MedAmerica. Aside from spending a few bucks on that jet, of course."

"Boy! It's been a whirlwind five months, Jero," Alex said, resting his elbows on the table. "There was so much that needed to be done, and a lot of it had to be handled with kid gloves. You know, the ghost of the old man still hovers over everything."

"It always will, Alex," Jeremiah nodded. "Whatever the truth may have been, the perception is that he was a pioneer and a legend."

"Legends can screw up, Jero, and there were massive changes needed in the company. I guess the biggest challenge was to start bringing the doctors into line. Those fuckin' prima donnas are spoiled rotten, coddled from the start. Doc Willie gave them everything they wanted. Put two of 'em on the board. All that had to change."

Tara came with drinks, put them down and left.

"But I'm doing a lot of other good stuff," Alex went on. "Within the first few weeks after Doc Willie died, I doubled the PR staff from eleven to twenty-two people. Brought in a new guy, made him Vice President of Corporate Affairs reporting directly to me. Real hot-shot! Made a name for himself smoothing over an oil spill in the North Sea."

"What happened to the fellow that Doc Willie placed in the PR job many years ago, the early fifties, I guess? Did he quit?"

"Naw! I just demoted him, gave him a director title. He's still there."

"That didn't go over too well, did it? I guess he was furious."

"Hell! Nothing he could do about it. Where's he going to find a PR job in Shrewsbury Crossing—especially at his age? And I didn't cut his salary, that kept him from getting violent."

"What else?" Jeremiah asked.

"Damn, you're an inquisitive bastard, aren't you, but I like to talk about it." Alex took a long drink and wiped his lips with a napkin. "We've been modernizing a lot too. The old man resisted spending money on *any*thing he didn't understand, and he didn't have the foggiest notion about computerization. I brought in IBM people to revamp our entire set-up. We've got state-of-the-art capabilities now. Finance, accounting, billing, record-keeping. Each senior officer now has a computer at his fingertips, but I'll concede that most of the fuckers don't even know how to turn one on. That's gonna change, though. I'm gonna drag them kickin' and screamin' into the computer age, or I'll get rid of the bastards."

"How's Ethan feel about all this?"

"Worries all the time! But you know how he is—a team player. I'm sure I make him nervous as hell. In fact, I kinda' enjoy doin' it. But once that sucker knows I'm gonna do something, he always backs me up. He's one loyal son-of-a-bitch."

Jeremiah's drink was getting low. He caught Tara's eye and she came over.

"One for me too, sweetheart," Alex said.

"So what about Panacea?" Jeremiah asked. "Or I guess I should say 'Catnip'. Who came up with that code-name?"

"One of the damn investment bankers, but it's pretty catchy, don't you think?"

Jeremiah leaned forward and looked directly in Alex's eyes. "Alex, I hope you're not wedded to the idea of acquiring that company, 'cause I've dug up some pretty troubling things."

"Hell, Jero, that's why I hired you. I want to know everything, pro and con. You know the first thing I told my senior officer group when I took over? I said I don't want no 'yes men' around me. I told them I'd kick ass if I found anyone holding back. Don't want no noses up *my* butt."

"That's the way any good executive functions, Alex, and I always felt you had uncanny leadership skills. You remember how Ethan and I followed you around everywhere—believed everything you told us."

"Yeah, I always got a kick outta you fellows—even Beagle, I guess."

"I sometimes felt you mistreated us, but I guess that's just part of growing up. It was probably good for us in the long run."

"Hell yeah, it was good for y'all—made you better men. I deserve some kind of fuckin' medal, don't I?" Alex grinned broadly, his narrow eyes gleaming.

"Shit, Alex, you won't let me get serious about anything, will you?" Jeremiah slid his chair back from the table so he could extend his legs. "But back to Catnip: do keep an open mind tomorrow, 'cause I think I come down on the side of scuttling the deal."

"Don't be silly, Jero. This thing may have a few wrinkles in it, but hell, that's what challenges are all about. Sure, we'll do the deal, and I'm expecting you to help pull it off."

Jeremiah was feeling the buzz from the drinks. "OK, we'll see what tomorrow brings, but right now, I'd like to know how you feel about everything. I mean, Jesus, you've come such a long way since we played in the creek and jumped off the old sawdust pile. I'm sure you know that all the business gurus in Atlanta talk about you all the time—what a hell of a success story you are."

"Yeah, guess so." Alex took a deep breath. "It feels great, Jero, absolutely great, but don't make any mistake about it. It didn't come easy, not easy at all. I paid my dues. You'll never believe the things I did to make the old man feel good and keep him happy."

"Like what?"

"Well, shit, you can't even imagine. I stroked the old fart's ego every step of the way. Promoted his reputation and image lots of time when he didn't want to. Had to laugh at his half-ass jokes and nod like I agreed with his pious platitudes."

A couple sat down at a table across the room. Alex waved toward them half-heartedly, then gulped a long drink. He leaned closer to Jeremiah and said: "That's the damn preacher from the First Baptist in Ludlow. Can you believe it? Thinks if he and the old lady come out here early for dinner, nobody's gonna see them drinking."

"Getting back to Doc Willie. You were really like a son to Dr. Willingham, weren't you?" Jeremiah asked.

"Closer than his own son, for sure—that fucking alcoholic. You know, Jero, I've never told anyone about this, but there were times when I'd be alone with the old man and he'd put his arm around me and tell me how much he loved me. All the time saying I was handsome. Sometimes it made me nervous as hell."

"I guess you were just an indispensable part of his life," Jeremiah said.

"I ain't sure it didn't go even further than that. Once or twice—maybe even more often—I got this eerie notion when he was buttering me up."

"What do you mean?"

"Well, I don't really know. Kinda like he was getting aroused. Especially after his wife died. I don't know if he was kinky or something, but the way he looked at me, a kinda' glassy look—I swear I felt sometimes like he was on the verge of putting a move on me."

"My God!" Jeremiah exclaimed, "he never really tried anything, did he?"

"Naw, not really, and even if he had wanted to, he was probably too religious. Besides, he had to know I wasn't some kind of queer; but—just between you and me—I sometimes wonder now what I would have done if he'd tried something."

"Surely, you would have refused!" Jeremiah leaned closer and blinked.

"Oh, hell, yeah! You know I would, but I did everything else for the son-of-a-bitch. I'm just glad he never asked."

"What about Miss Emma? Were you upset when she got killed."

"Not too much," Alex puckered his lips, then cut his eyes toward his cousin. "I'll tell you the truth: I never really cared much for the woman, but I sure as hell had to play nursemaid to the doctor and Annie for months after the old battle-ax died." Alex tapped on the table with a fork. "Tell you what, Jero, that Emma—that woman was a first-class *bitch*, if I ever saw one."

"What do you mean? I thought she liked you, especially after you and Annie started dating."

"She did, yeah, I guess she did come to like me, but I had to work like hell for it. Emma was smart, *lots* smarter than the doctor, and she wasn't easy to handle, but I started working on it as soon as I began hanging out with Doddy. I mean, I'd dance with her at parties, smelling her nauseating tobacco and alcohol breath. The bony old bitch finally fell for it. I'd tell her how beautiful she was, rub up against her ass when we were alone—even told her several times I wanted to fuck her and the truth is I probably would have if it hadn't been for Annie. Emma loved the attention she got from me—just ate that shit *up*! Sometimes I nearly puked about how I had to flatter her, but I knew I had to keep her on my side. Yeah, I paid my dues, Jero, and sometimes they were pretty damn expensive."

"You're just saying some of this for shock effect, aren't you?" Jeremiah cleared his throat, then said, chuckling: "I used to believe all your bullshit, but now I know that half of what you say is just that—bullshit! I've always admired your drive and ambition, and you want to know something: I don't think for a second you're the unprincipled devil you've always pretended to be. It's just an act, isn't it—an act you perfected when we were growing up."

"Yeah, I'm just running on with you," Alex said, laughing. "But the fact is that I *have* made it to the *top*, nobody would deny that. Chairman of the board of one of the largest corporations in the world. Hell, Jero, MedAmerica has over one billion dollars in retained earnings. Do you realize that's more economic clout than about half the countries on this planet? And I control it. Heck, I'd rather be CEO of the MedAmerica Corporation than President of the United States. You know why?"

"Tell me," Jeremiah said, caught up in the fervor of Alex's voice.

"Shit, it's simple. The President has to watch every step he takes. He's got every politician in the country after his ass, can't move without some reporter hounding him. Look what they did to poor old Nixon. Me, all I have to do is keep fifteen directors happy, and that's *really* easy. I put most of 'em on the board, and they don't know shit about what's going on in the company. I tell 'em what I want 'em to know. Take Jesse Oldman, for example, the black on the board—you know, the one Carter appointed ambassador to Brazil. He doesn't know or care *anything* about MedAmerica. I put him on the board exactly for that reason. All he wants are the perks and the twenty-eight thousand dollars a year we pay him for attending four three-hour meetings and keeping his mouth shut. The others are the same way, especially the two females, you know, Agnes Blanchard and Rebecca Lewis, two fuckin' airheads. They're professional directors, you know, so-called feminists selling themselves to corporations like fuckin' whores at a convention."

"Sounds like you don't have a very high opinion of your directors."

"*Au contraire*, Jero, you misunderstand me. They're *perfect*. Exactly the kind of people a CEO needs."

The conversation got more boisterous as dinner and the drinking continued. They moved into the bar away from other diners. With the bar to themselves and interrupted only infrequently by Tara to deliver drinks, the two men reminisced about their boyhood—the initiation of Wilma as a wench, the greased pig contest, Rasty's wild tales in the Dixie Cafe, and the night they all rode in Doddy's convertible to see Alex's used condom. By the time they arrived at the Willingham mansion shortly before eleven o'clock, both men were sloppily drunk.

Annie met them in the foyer. Dressed in a terrycloth robe tied loosely around her waist, she gave Alex a perfunctory kiss on the cheek, and then she embraced Jeremiah warmly. Even in his inebriated condition, Jeremiah sensed a deep sadness about her. She was frail and thin, the once-rich glow from her big Kewpie-doll eyes was no longer there. As he held her, he could feel her tremble, and she nervously pulled away. Lines on her face and her ashen complexion made her appear at least ten years older than her fifty-three years. Indeed, just in the few months since her father's death, she seemed to have aged greatly.

Still grieving the loss of Dr. Willingham, Jeremiah thought, but he really didn't know the half of it.

CHAPTER 16

A Committee of One

"A committee is a group of the unwilling,
chosen from the unfit, to do the unnecessary."
Anonymous

"Did you fuck the preacher's wife?" Jeremiah asked.

"What the hell are you talkin' about?" Alex replied.

"You know, when we were boys. You told me and Ethan that you were going to fuck the revival preacher's wife. You must remember that."

"God, what made you think of *that*?" Alex asked as they pulled into the parking garage.

"I swear I don't know. I guess knowing I'll see Ethan today made me remember," Jeremiah laughed. "When we were boys, he and I used to debate that issue like crazy. I always said that I bet you did it, and he said even *you* wouldn't screw a preacher's wife."

"You two never had much to occupy your time back then, did you?" Alex chuckled, turning to face his cousin.

"Well, actually, the argument had religious overtones," Jeremiah said, grinning. "Ethan's position was that although we both knew you would screw almost any woman with a pulse, you wouldn't risk the hell-fire by banging a religious man's wife. I had more faith in you: I said you wouldn't draw any such line."

"So when did you have all these discussions about my sex life?"

"During the revival services and for many years afterwards. The subject kept coming up. You remember, you came to church that Monday night and the poor woman hugged your neck, you told us you would do it, and then you didn't come back the rest of the week. Aunt Pink and Mama made Ethan and me go every night, so we would sit there and study that woman, trying to decide if you would or wouldn't."

Alex had parked the car in his designated spot at the entrance to the elevator leading to the executive suites on the eighth floor.

"Well?" Jeremiah said.

"Well what?" Alex asked.

"Did you?"

"You'll never know, will you?" Alex grinned broadly, opening the car door. "Come on, Jero, let's get to work. This is gonna be a big day for both of us."

Jeremiah felt remarkably better than he had feared he would when he turned into his bedroom for sleep at the Willingham mansion the night before. He had lost count of the number of drinks he had consumed, but his head had been spinning when he placed it on the pillow—usually a sure sign that he would pay dearly for the alcohol the next day. But when he awakened, his head had been surprisingly clear, and he had seen only faint traces of redness in his eyes as he shaved. He and Alex had arisen at seven that morning, had coffee and Danish prepared by the maid, and left the house shortly after eight. Annie had not gotten up to see them off.

The complex of executive suites for MedAmerica on the seventh floor of the corporate headquarters had been known for years as 'Doc Willie's offices,' but had come in recent weeks to be called 'Marble Manor' by some of the staff because of the total refurbishing of every office on the floor when Alex became CEO. Alex had asked Jeremiah to meet that morning with MedAmerica's general counsel in preparation for the eleven o'clock meeting of the senior staff to discuss the Panacea acquisition. As he approached the spacious suite where his battery of three secretaries and two assistants waited, Alex pointed Jeremiah to a door down the hall and the two men parted company. The sign on the door read "G. Ernest Stodgley, Senior Vice President, General Counsel and Secretary." Carrying a pair of large black briefcases, Jeremiah set them down just inside the door and advised the secretary in the outer office that he was there to see Mr. Stodgley. The secretary disappeared for a moment, after which a sallow-faced man in his late forties came through the door, walking with a slight limp and extending his hand. "Hello, Jeremiah, I'm Ernest Stodgley. Alex told me to expect you."

"It's a pleasure to meet you in person, Ernest. I feel like I know you well after all our telephone conversations."

"Alex has talked a lot about you too and how much he admires your abilities. We need all the legal help we can get with this deal." Stodgley motioned for Jeremiah to come into his office. Picking up his briefcases, Jeremiah followed his host inside and sat in a large, straight-backed leather chair facing the man at his desk.

"Well, I'll do what I can. I've spent the last several weeks, as you know, looking through everything I could find on Catnip. SEC fillings, annual reports, contracts, personnel issues, and the like. But I guess I've mentioned most of that to you over the telephone."

"Yes, we were looking at the same things here." Stodgley pulled out a pipe, stuffed it with tobacco, but hesitated. "You don't mind, do you?"

"No, not at all," Jeremiah said. "I like the aroma."

"You grew up in this town, didn't you, Jeremiah?" Stodgley asked, lighting the pipe. "Lots of ties here, I presume."

"Yes, quite a few. Grew up with Alex and Ethan Allday, and I was a high school classmate of Annie Willingham. My mother's still here in the nursing home."

"Then you must be amazed to see what's happened to this institution. Dr. Willingham was a genius, wasn't he, and he was brilliant when he chose Alex as his successor."

"Yeah, I think he was. Lots of good careers have begun right here."

"Mine, for one," Stodgley said. "You'll never know what a dream come true it was when Alex asked me to join the company as Vice President of Legal Affairs…."

Jeremiah glanced at his wristwatch. "Listen, Ernest, I believe Alex wants you and me to spend some time going over the legal and regulatory issues so when the senior staff meets this morning, you and I will be singing from the same hymnal."

"That's my understanding too."

"Well, my thinking is that we've talked a lot by telephone and we agree on most things, don't we?" Stodgley nodded in agreement. "I've made a brief outline of the main points," Jeremiah went on. "Catnip is in extremis—cash flow is a serious problem with liabilities far exceeding assets. The company has labor difficulties by the boatload: adamant union resistance to wage increase deferrals or any other kind of cost-cutting, many lawsuits pending for malpractice and numerous violations of the bargaining agreements. Liens on everything. Facilities and equipment badly outdated and in need of repair. Some office buildings have already been foreclosed by creditors, and the ones they have left need major repair and renovation."

"Not a very pretty picture, is it?" Stodgley said.

"It gets even worse. I've had experts who used to work in the DOJ's antitrust division run the numbers, and MedAmerica's acquisition of Catnip would shoot the Herfindahl index into orbit. No way we're gonna pass antitrust muster, especially with that smaller TransMed Services out there with a competing offer."

"Yeah, I know we've discussed all this, and I think I'm pretty much in agreement." Stodgley fidgeted in his chair, staring out the window. "But, you know, Alex wants the lawyers to be *positive*—to find ways to do things, *legally*, of course."

"Most businessmen do," Jeremiah said, "but for the life of me, I can't see any way through this minefield. And even if we could work out the legal barriers, this thing's just a bad business decision, in my opinion."

"Tell you what, Jeremiah," Stodgley said, his brow furrowed. "I'd like for you to take the lead discussing the legal and regulatory issues when we meet this morning with the senior group. I know Alex respects your objectivity and honesty. You and I are in basic agreement on most things, so I'll just chime in where it's appropriate."

"Fine, if that's what you prefer, but please don't be timit. Feel free to disagree with anything I say or speak your own views at any point."

"Agreed," Stodgley said, rising from his chair. "We meet in just a little more than an hour, and I want to go over my notes and return a few telephone calls. Are you interested in having lunch after the morning session? I'm sure we'll adjourn at some point and resume this afternoon."

"Thanks, Ernest, but I think I'll go down to Ethan's office and see if I can talk him into lunch," Jeremiah smiled. "He's my first cousin, you know, and I haven't seen him lately. Lunch will be a good chance for us to catch up. I'll see you in the board room."

Jeremiah walked down the hall to Ethan's office. Ethan was standing in the center of the room, poring over charts spread over a large conference table, when Jeremiah entered. "Jeremiah," Ethan said, grinning broadly, "You're a sight for sore eyes. I heard you were here."

"Yeah, spent the night with Annie and Alex. How're you doing?"

"Just working my butt off. We seem to be going from one crisis to another around here—especially since Dr. Willingham died. Alex never quits. He's constantly jumping in and out of problems you wouldn't believe. And *now* this Catnip thing. I think it's going to kill us all."

"Ethan, I've looked at this proposal from every conceivable angle, and I can't see any sense in going forward with it. What's your take?"

"Couldn't agree with you more," Ethan said, "and the truth is it would be dead in the water except for one thing—one *monumental* thing."

"Like what?"

"Alex wants to do the deal. Simple as that. He's convinced that the company floundered for the last decade of Doc Willie's life—that our competitors left us in the dust. He sees this take-over as a way to make a quantum leap into the midwest and make MedAmerica the biggest health care company in the country. He seems oblivious to all the problems."

"I just came from Stodgley's office, and I think he knows the pitfalls. He told me on the telephone just last week that the deal is a 'no-brainer,' his words, a '*no-brainer*.' If the rest of the senior staff feels the same way, I can't believe Alex would insist on going forward."

"Well, I guess we should just see how the meeting goes," Ethan said. "I've got charts here which show that the acquisition will blow a hole the size of Georgia in MedAmerica's balance sheet. You can't imagine how much these things worry me, Jeremiah. I talk to Alex about them, but he's always too busy to give me time to discuss anything in any kind of detail. Just accuses me of exaggerating the problems. Calls me a prophet of doom. Thinks it's hilarious when he says stuff like that…."

"Yeah," Jeremiah interrupted. "His sense of humor was always a little weird, wasn't it?"

The senior staff for MedAmerica included six division heads plus the operational vice presidents from each division. At the meeting that convened that morning, Jeremiah was the only outsider. Alex said that legal and regulatory issues would be deferred until the afternoon session, but that each of the other senior officer would give a brief overview of the pros and cons of the acquisition. After this was done and without further discussion, Alex asked for a secret ballot from everyone but Stodgley and Jeremiah. The result: two ballots recommended "cautiously proceeding" with the deal; seven were against any further consideration of the proposal and one stated no position.

Alex stood and stared at the group after the ballots were read. "Gentlemen," he said, "I am fully aware that we face problems with this deal, but the alternative is to allow the company to stagnate. We just can't do that, in my view, so the task before us is to take the obstacles and turn them into opportunities. I've done that all my life, and I don't intend to let negative thinking sabotage this opportunity for MedAmerica. I want all of you to get some lunch, reflect on the issues, and come back here this afternoon with a new perspective."

Jeremiah and Ethan decided to get a sandwich in the company cafeteria.

"Looks like everyone but Alex wants to forget this thing, so he'll probably come around this afternoon, don't you think?" Jeremiah pulled a chair to the table where Ethan was placing his tray.

"I wouldn't bet on it," Ethan said. "I've heard Alex say more than once that he thought we *have* to do this deal if MedAmerica is to become a national player in the health care industry. He makes this noise about *critical mass*, bullshit he's heard from some of the economists and Wall Street experts he's talked to."

"What do you think?"

"You know what I think, Jeremiah. I think it would be *insane.* I worry enough already about the way Alex is spending money, and I'm scared shitless about sinking assets into Panacea's bottomless pit. It will cost millions just to rehabilitate their facilities where we can use them. One of our properties guys told me the roof leaks like crazy in the Minneapolis hospital. Christ! Can you believe that? Their frigin' flagship hospital! Alex wants to buy a company whose main hospital has a roof full of holes. No telling what nightmares we'll find in other locations."

"Well, it seems that the senior officers are almost unanimously opposed. Alex will just have to listen, won't he?"

"Jeremiah, you know what I think? I don't think Alex has any respect for any of the senior staff, including me. He thinks we're all a bunch of pansies, and there's some justification for thinking that. That's why I'm glad you're here. He has more regard for your opinion than for the entire lot of us. I know you probably find that hard to believe, but I think he's always felt you had good instincts—a certain intuitive intelligence. He just might believe what you say. I know he won't listen to the rest of us."

"I'm just a lawyer," Jeremiah said, taking a bite from his sandwich. "Alex didn't retain me to give him business advice. He asked me simply to explore the legal issues."

"You must, Jeremiah. You have to talk Alex out of this, and you're the only hope I've got. He thinks I'm just a nervous pessimist. He'll listen to you. Please, I beg you."

"Well, I'll do what I can. Stodgley has asked me to do the talking when we discuss the legal and regulatory issues, so maybe I can help focus the business issues—sorta indirectly. There's a lot of overlap. The legal obstacles are enormous, and it'll cost tons of money to clear them away. I bet it'll all go smoother than you expect. You know, Alex is right in a way: you always were a worry-wart."

Ethan looked at his watch, and said: "We better get back now, but one more thing, Jeremiah: you always underestimated Alex's determination, you know, and I'm afraid you are doing so today. I think he's hell-bent to do this deal and nothing's going to stop him."

Alex entered the room twenty minutes late for the afternoon meeting. He made no excuses for his tardiness, but walked in with an easy gait, confidently smiling and nodding to the group. Jeremiah, seated beside Ernest Stodgley, could not help but notice the mesmerizing effect on the others from Alex's entrance. At the morning meeting, there had been casual whispering and even loud laughter on occasion. This afternoon, Alex's entrance produced a palpable silence—a chill—over the gathering. Seating himself at the head of the large, mahogany table, Alex said nothing for several moments, peering into each face intensely. In the awkward moments while papers were shuffled and chairs pulled closer, it became clear to Jeremiah that the other people in the room were terrified of Alex.

"I guess we should get down to business," Alex said, clearing his throat. "How should we go about this? Maybe you should lead off, Ernest? Get all this legal shit out of the way."

"We'll be happy to begin, Alex," Stodgley said, cutting his eyes nervously. "Since you retained Jeremiah here to give in-depth study to the legal side, I've asked that he handle the presentation on the legal and regulatory issues. I'm sure you've seen the project paper we've prepared outlining what we believe are the significant concerns. There was an executive summary of that document attached."

"You know I don't have time to read all the paperwork crap y'all throw at me, Ernest. I don't know why you lawyers think that we have nothing better to do than to plow through all the legal double-talk. Hell, I haven't read any of that stuff. Don't plan to, either!"

"It was just intended as a frame of reference for you, Alex. Needless to say, we don't mean to take the focus off the business issues, so Jeremiah's going to give you a brief run-down and answer your questions. I'll help out where I can, of course."

Alex sat back in his chair, his hand cupped over his chin. "OK, Jeremiah, let's hear what you have to say." The tension in the room had increased dramatically with Alex's sardonic reaction to Stodgley's remarks. Jeremiah decided he would try an opening which would hopefully break the ice.

"Of course, I understand fully how much you respect the legal profession, Alex. And that's why I believe you're going to be gratified to know that the acquisition of Catnip will ensure battalions of lawyers a lifetime of full employment."

With the remark, Jeremiah had expected at least a few chuckles, if not laughter, but it produced no reaction at all from the group. Alex's face showed no emotion. The others stared downward blankly, rearranging their notes. Stodgley coughed nervously. Then Alex said, "Get on with it, Jero, let's cut to the chase. We don't have all day."

Jeremiah cleared his throat, then said: "Well, we've grouped the areas of concern into several different categories. They include personnel issues, properties and facilities, corporate and SEC concerns, and legal and regulatory matters, particularly anti-trust problems."

Alex interrupted: "Not '*problems*,' Jeremiah, '*opportunities*.'"

"'*Opportunities*' then," Jeremiah responded, "but these will be especially *challenging* 'opportunities.'"

"In the personnel area," Jeremiah went on, "we're going to have a hell of a time integrating the work force if we bring in any significant number of Catnip people. Of course, one of the benefits of an acquisition—as opposed to a merger—is that we don't have to integrate the employees of the two companies, unless we agree to hire some specified number in the acquisition agreement. We can expect the unions—especially the Teamsters—to raise cain, but I think everyone will agree that the fewest number of Catnip employees hired, the better."

"Is that really the lawyers' concern?" Alex asked. "That's why I have a personnel division, for Chrissake!"

"It becomes a legal concern when we have to face representation issues from the unions, not to mention lawsuits based on the integration decisions, seniority challenges, employment discrimination complaints, all of these things."

"Let's get on to the anti-trust stuff," Alex said. "Why would there be anti-trust problems if MedAmerica steps in and saves a company that's about to go under? Won't the government lawyers be happy, not to mention the general public, if MedAmerica comes to the rescue of this company which has provided medical care to the MidWest for decades? What about benefits to the local economies? The jobs saved?"

"Yes, those are all positive factors," Jeremiah countered, "but the DOJ and FTC look at other issues: the broad effects on competition, whether there are less anti-competitive alternatives, other mergers or acquisitions which might produce more public interest benefits. And there is one particularly troubling matter Ernest and I have discussed at length. The Washington regulators are wedded to a formula for testing the effects of a merger or acquisition. It's called the Herfindahl-Hirschman index, and I've had several economists perform the exercise—using hypothetical companies, of course, to protect confidentiality—and MedAmerica's proposed acquisition rockets the index into orbit. We can't see any way the DOJ and FTC will let this thing go forward. It would violate their established guidelines. It's as simple as that."

"So you're telling me some fuckin' formula is going to block a deal like this that's gonna' save a company from bankruptcy and give MedAmerica the chance to provide health care to a whole new region of the country? What kind of bureaucratic nonsense is that?"

Before Jeremiah could respond, Alex's secretary came into the room, apologizing profusely as she entered. "Mr. Rumpkin, I'm terribly sorry, but Wayne Elrod from Goldman Sachs called and insisted I give you this message. I've written it down verbatim. And, oh, Mr. Goodwin, there's a gentleman holding on my line from your firm. A Mr. Ansley. Says it's absolutely vital that he speak to you at once."

Alex's face flushed with rage as he read the note. "Goddamn! Goddamn!" he screamed. "There's been a fuckin' leak. Panacea stock has gone up twelve points since lunch."

"That's going to make the cost of this deal go out of sight," Ethan said. "We can't possibly buy the company at that price."

"You let me worry about what we can '*possibly*' do, Ethan," Alex said, grimacing. "Jeremiah, you take that telephone call while we mull this over."

The secretary pointed Jeremiah to a telephone as he left the conference room.

"Yeah, Ben, what's up?"

Ben Ansley's voice was filled with anxiety, a rare departure for him. "I guess you know by now that Panacea's stock shot up in the last hour."

"Just heard it," Jeremiah said. "The MedAmerica people just got the news from the investment bankers. It may queer the deal."

"Well, here's the *really* bad news. The leak was Kenneth Stripling. I've fired him."

"The hell you say! You must be kidding," Jeremiah stuttered.

"I'm not joking, Jeremiah. Michelle caught him rummaging around your desk yesterday afternoon after you left, and he got drunk last night and started bragging to some of the other associates that they could make a killing on Panacea stock. Told 'em to load up on it, said it was going sky high."

"So you *finally* fired him. Sorta late, wasn't it? *God*, Ben, I begged you to get rid of him months ago. Did he admit the leak?"

"No, *hell* no. He denied it, even though three of the associates said they heard him last night. I guess the bastard's a psychopath, just like you said."

"Well, firing him won't help us with Alex. He's going to be furious with *us*—with *me*, for God's sake. I thought those papers were secure—locked in my desk."

"Before I hang up, you need to know that Stripling blames you for all this. Says you were out to get him and framed him for the leak. Says he's going to get even. Mumbled something about his father's connections."

"I can't worry about that prickhead now. I've got to let Alex know what happened."

Jeremiah returned to the conference room just as Ethan was speaking. "If we assume a twelve dollar increase in the stock price, I estimate it'll add three-hundred million dollars to the cost of the deal. If it goes any higher, of course, that cost goes up."

"We can handle that," Alex said, "we can handle that, I think."

"I need to speak privately with you outside," Jeremiah said softly, leaning down behind Alex's chair.

"Can't it wait?" Alex asked.

"No, it can't wait," Jeremiah said, shaking his head.

Alex rose slowly from his chair and followed Jeremiah into the hall. "Alex," Jeremiah said, facing him squarely, "I don't know how to tell you this, but the deal was leaked to the market by an associate at the firm. We've already fired him."

"Somebody in your law firm? What the hell are you saying?"

Jeremiah stuttered: "A sorry son-of-a-bitch we should have never hired in the first place. I feel awful about it. I assume full responsibility for it. I know it's going to kill the deal."

"How did he get the information, Jeremiah? I told you to keep this thing close to the chest."

"I don't know for sure. Guess he rifled my desk. But the truth is I just don't know."

"I ought to sue you and your Goddamn firm for this! Do you realize what this is going to cost? Do you know what damage this does?"

"Sure, I do, Alex. Sure. I can't blame you for being angry, and I guess if you want to sue us, you've got good cause."

Suddenly, Alex smiled and placed a hand on Jeremiah's shoulder. "Hell, Jero, I'm not going to sue you. We go too far back, old Cuz. You know I couldn't get on the wrong side of a lawsuit with you, but you were being too damn negative about this deal. Tell you what. Get your butt back to Atlanta and let me handle everything here. We won't be needing you anymore. Just send me a bill for the work you've done."

"I can't do that," Jeremiah's eyes widened. "Under the circumstances, how on earth could I charge you? We've ruined your deal."

"Who says this deal is ruined?"

Alex smiled, turned and walked away. Resuming his position at the head of the conference table, he said: "OK, gentlemen, Jeremiah Goodwin has been called back to his office unexpectedly so we'll have to continue without him. Let's go on with the discussion of the legal issues. Ernest, you pick up where Jeremiah left off, please."

Part III

1996

CHAPTER 17

A Green Bay Tree

"I have seen the wicked in great power, and
spreading himself like a green bay tree."
Psalms, Ch. 37; v. 35.

The invitation was elegantly embossed in gold lettering. A calligrapher's masterpiece, it read:

The American College of Physicians and Surgeons
Cordially Invites You and your Guest to
A Banquet Honoring
Alexander Wayne Rumpkin
Chairman Of The Board, President,
and Chief Executive Officer of
The MedAmerica Corporation

Humanitarian of the Year

The Waldorf Astoria
New York, New York
March 20, 1996

R.S.V.P.
Five Hundred Dollars per plate
Proceeds to Benefit the ACPS Children's Research Hospital

A handwritten note was scribbled in the margin:

"Jero:

Don't do anything with this until you hear from me. I'll call in a few days.

Regards, Alex"

Three days later Jeremiah was standing at Michelle's desk, about to dictate a short letter, when the telephone rang.

"Well, hello, Alex, long time no see," Michelle stuttered, putting down her shorthand pad and eyeing Jeremiah uncomfortably. "Yes, it's good to hear from you too. When are you coming up our way?"

Jeremiah returned to his office, closing the door behind him. He had seen that his eavesdropping was distracting to Michelle. Several minutes passed and she finally buzzed him on the intercom: "It's Alex Rumpkin, Jeremiah, line two." As though he didn't know.

"Jero, old cuz," said Alex. "How's it going?"

"Great," Jeremiah answered, "and how's the 'Humanitarian of the Year'? That's some honor. You've come a long way since the sawdust pile."

It seemed like an eternity to Jeremiah since that chaotic day six years earlier in Shrewsbury Crossing when he had met with Alex and MedAmerica's senior staff. He had heard little from Alex since then but he had followed the roller coaster of MedAmerica's fortunes through the newspapers and occasional conversations with Ethan. He knew that the Panacea acquisition had been approved by the board of directors two days after he left town, and that the deal had been consummated three months later.

Inexplicably, the Department of Justice and the Federal Trade Commission had never raised a hand to prevent the takeover. No anti-trust objections had been voiced by either agency. A half-hearted complaint had been lodged with Justice by an obscure hospital chain, but that had been promptly dismissed. Ethan had confided that some people in high places wanted the deal to go through, telling the anti-trust watchdogs to back off. Jeremiah had been amazed that the takeover had avoided any regulatory barriers, and he had resolved at the time that he would never again attempt to predict what a federal agency would or would not do.

Jeremiah also knew that the Panacea deal had been a corporate disaster for MedAmerica. In the space of a few months, MedAmerica's financial posture had tumbled. In early 1990 the company had over one billion dollars in retained earnings and virtually no long-term debt. By the end of 1992, debt was greater than equity and MedAmerica's credit rating had been lowered to junk-bond status.

Timing could not have been worse. The recession of 1991 had exacerbated the built-in problems caused by the rapid expansion and spending binge that Alex had commenced when Dr. Willingham died. The bloated MedAmerica payroll had hemorrhaged badly when over two-thousand Panacea employees were added to the ranks. Lawsuits had been filed almost daily and dutifully reported in the legal media: three derivative stockholder suits, one in Delaware and two in New York; numerous employment complaints and several class actions running the gamut from sex and race discrimination to unfair labor practices; and myriad disputes and lawsuits involving lessors and suppliers of Panacea.

Before the bottom was reached, several major banks had withdrawn from MedAmerica's revolving credit agreement, making it virtually impossible to do any sensible long-term financing. By the end of 1991, MedAmerica had begun the painful restructuring and down-sizing process endemic to the American corporate world of the early 90's. Alex dropped from public sight during 1992 and 1993, shrouded from the shareholders and employees by his expanded public relations staff. Official statements released by the company stressed repeatedly that the Panacea acquisition had not caused the problem but was a necessary move to expand the company's geographic scope. The party line eagerly swallowed by the trade media was that MedAmerica was not immune from the market forces ravaging the health care industry.

But the facts could not be glossed over for the thousands of MedAmerica employees forced into early retirement or fired and there was a drastic shrinkage of the company's operations. The sterling reputation of MedAmerica—a name that had come to be synonymous with medical excellence—was sullied by poor service and incompetence. Employee morale plummeted. The log of malpractice lawsuits had bulged. Things were terrible.

Almost as quickly, the company's fortunes had turned around in 1994 and 1995. With an improving economy, profitability had returned. Stock prices for MedAmerica had soared, and Alex's name and picture reappeared in business publications and other news. He had survived the storm. And lo and behold: here he was in 1996—not only a survivor but "Humanitarian of the Year."

"So you got your invitation?" Alex said.

"Yes, I did," Jeremiah responded. "I'm trying to line things up so Sarah and I can be there."

"That's great, but I'd also like to see your firm buy ten seats for the banquet. Counting the two for you and Sarah, of course."

"My gosh!" Jeremiah gulped, "that's *five thousand* dollars, Alex. I don't think I can swing that with the other partners."

"I kinda think they better 'swing that,' if they know what's good for them."

"What do you mean?" Jeremiah coughed nervously into the phone.

"I'm just saying it would be a good business investment for your firm. You know how many boards I'm on, Jero? *Eight*, for God's sake—eight boards of the biggest companies in this country, and I have contacts in the business world you can't even dream of. If you and your partners want any damn legal work for the next ten years, you better shell out a few dollars for ten lousy tickets."

"That sounds like a threat, Alex." Jeremiah said.

"Let's just say I'm calling in a few chips for not suing your firm's ass when that little peckerhead leaked the Panacea deal. By the way, what did you ever do with him?"

"We fired him. I wanted to pursue criminal charges against him, but the other partners wouldn't let me. They were afraid of his father's connections."

"Whatever became of him?"

"Got a civil service job. Some kind of position with the Department of Agriculture. Landed on his feet, I guess."

"Just shows what contacts can do. More important than anything. That's your problem, Jeremiah. You always figured you had to play by the rules. Thought it was *what* you know that counts. That's bullshit! It's *who* you know, every damn time."

The nasal twang in Alex's voice became more pronounced as he pounced on the opportunity to lecture Jeremiah. Getting excited had always worsened the condition.

"So I'll put you down for ten plates, Jero. No problem with that, is there?"

"I don't think I have any choice, do I?" Jeremiah said with disgust.

"Oh, yeah, Jero, one other thing."

"What's that?"

"Do you remember the chick that waited on us several years ago when you came down for the Panacea deal? Tara Fountain. The Moorings Restaurant, remember? Gorgeous girl. Long black hair. Beautiful body."

"Yes, I think I remember. Why?"

"Well, I want you to give her a job."

"With the firm?"

"Yeah, with your firm, for God's sake. Where else?"

"Alex, you must be kidding. We're not hiring anybody now. In fact, we've been cutting back for two years."

"Jero, remember the damn Panacea deal. You keep forgetting that you and your firm *owe* me, big time. I want this girl on your payroll."

"May I ask *why*? Why on earth would you want her here?" Jeremiah asked.

"I've got to get her out of South Georgia. There's some talk around town about me and her, and Annie's suspicious. I can't afford a fucking divorce."

"So, what can she do? What are her skills? We don't have any jobs for waitresses," Jeremiah barked into the phone.

"Hell, I don't know. Receptionist or something. It doesn't matter. She won't need the money. I'll take care of that. I've bought her a condo down the street a couple of blocks from my place in Buckhead. I just want you to give her a job to occupy her time—you know, and so she'll be able to say she's got a job with a respectable law firm."

"All right," Jeremiah grumbled. "I guess I'll figure something out. When will she be here?"

"Toward the first of April. She's going with me to St. Thomas for the next two weeks. She'll call you when she gets into town. Arrange for an interview."

"OK," Jeremiah cleared his throat. "All I can say is I'll try."

"Good man, I knew you'd come through." Alex laughed. "I knew I could count on you. Good man," he repeated, and hung up.

It was a gala affair.

The hostess was Angela Goldman, a Miss America runner-up in the fifties and one of New York's best known celebrities. Married to a wealthy developer instrumental in the restoration of the waterfront district abutting Wall Street, she was a leading feminist and consumer advocate. She had championed women's rights issues across the board—abortion, sexual harassment, the ERA. She had testified before Congress and fought vigorously against the nomination of Clarence Thomas to the Supreme Court.

It was Angela Goldman's role tonight to introduce the guests, including the guest of honor: Alexander Wayne Rumpkin, humanitarian, public servant, and

Chairman of the Board, President, and Chief Executive Officer of the MedAmerica Corporation. He was a man Angela barely knew.

The chairman of the Humanitarian of the Year project had approached her several months earlier and asked her to officiate at the banquet. Stressing the limelight she would enjoy during the occasion, he provided her with a biography of Alex, a lengthy list of his corporate board memberships, numerous awards, and the humanitarian causes he had supported. By the time she took the podium at the banquet, she had familiarized herself with all the pertinent facts about Alex, but she didn't have a clue about who the man to her right on the dais really was. And she didn't care.

Alex rose from his seat as Angela Goldman proclaimed him the recipient of the Humanitarian of the Year award from the American College of Physicians and Surgeons. Over one thousand of the nation's elite stood in the cavernous ballroom and applauded this titan of the medical care industry. Alex paused to kiss Annie, then embraced Angela, who interrupted her own applause to receive the polite kiss Alex placed on her cheek.

As he moved behind the lectern, Alex made eye contact with each of the celebrities on the dais. Smiling broadly, and bowing slightly at times, Alex said nothing audibly as the thunderous ovation continued, but he mouthed several "thank you's."

Jeremiah and Sarah sat at the table with four of his partners and their wives. As he stood with the others and applauded, Jeremiah felt himself caught up in the drama of the moment. Hearing the thunderous ovation made Jeremiah think that maybe Alex *really* was a special human being and that the familiarity of their relationship had perhaps blurred his vision about Alex. As he glanced around the room, Jeremiah realized that the people applauding were the power brokers of American society; two former governors were in the audience, along with best-selling authors, several Hollywood celebrities, and throngs of wealthy businessmen. A lump rose in Jeremiah's throat as he realized that this adulation was directed solely at an individual with whom he had shared his boyhood.

At that instant, Jeremiah looked at Ethan, who sat at an adjacent table. He was not standing—was not applauding at all. His most distinctive facial feature was a sick smile.

Alex finally spoke into the microphone. "Thank you, thank you all very much. Please be seated. You are too kind." He smiled broadly as he scanned the audience.

"And, Angela," he went on, "I can't begin to tell you how your eloquent presence here this evening has transformed this night into a truly momentous occasion for me and all my friends. Thank you so much for your wonderful participation." As Alex turned toward the hostess, his standing position at the podium now allowed him to see for the first time the cleavage of her breasts beneath the sheer silkiness of her evening gown and the firm outline of her nipples. Even though she was approaching sixty, several facelifts and the cosmetic experts had preserved much of Angela Goldman's beauty, and Alex wondered how she would be in bed. He couldn't recall having slept with a dyed-in-the-wool feminist before, and certainly not one of this rank.

Alex's mental digression was imperceptible to the audience and he began his acceptance remarks. Never speaking with notes, he had determined years earlier that effective public speaking was the most sure-fire means of winning approval—an essential aspect of leadership. He always rehearsed each public appearance meticulously, working carefully on pronunciation, gestures, pauses, inflections, eye contact, the whole gamut of tricks he had been taught by speech consultants over the years.

One trick he had found especially effective for personalizing his remarks was to call someone from the audience—seemingly at random—to stand and be recognized for some achievement, and occasionally to make responsive comments. Recent presidents had used the same technique in nationally televised speeches or State of the Union addresses. Alex sometimes gave the individual advance notice that his name would be called when he asked for responsive remarks, but most of the time Alex gave no warning. Then the victim's stuttering, rambling comments would, by contrast, make Alex's delivery seem even more polished than before and would reinforce the audience's perception that Alex was an eloquent speaker, a brilliant thinker and totally in command of the situation.

Alex spent several minutes praising the physicians' organization for its charitable endeavors and support of the children's hospital. He called on several doctors to stand and be recognized, leading the applause each time.

Then he launched into a tirade against big government and the dangers inherent in government efforts to reform the medical care system. He knew the theme would play well with his audience, and there was a crescendo of applause as he ridiculed the efforts of Hillary Clinton to reform Medicare. He pounded the podium and lamented the decline of individual initiative and charity, and he urged everyone to help reestablish the traditional American values of hard work, honesty, loyalty and faith in God and the family.

"There can be no doubt," he thundered, "that forces of evil are intent upon destroying the social fabric of our country. Those who produce our entertainment, our movies, our books, our television, have abandoned the cherished values of our country in favor of greed and the quick buck. Too many politicians are no longer statesmen; they are charlatans, unprincipled disciples of the religion of power, of the doctrine that anything goes."

Alex paused, took a long sip of water from a glass, and cleared his throat again. Gazing directly at the audience and smiling softly, he went on: "I am often asked how MedAmerica came to be the magnificent edifice of health care that it is today, and I answer that question in one simple sentence. We took the bedrock principles of our founder, Dr. Charles Robert Willingham, and we live by them daily in our care of the sick and elderly and in our regard for all members of our organization. MedAmerica is a corporate family, an extended family, and the model for the kind of altruistic organization I hope will someday typify all of corporate America."

Applause rang out again.

"One of the most important members of the MedAmerica family is here tonight," Alex continued, "and I'm going to ask him to come forward so I can tell you a little about him. Ethan Allday, please join me here for a moment."

Ethan rose from his chair, smiled weakly, and threw his hands in the air to decline the invitation.

"Oh, no. Your modesty won't get you out of this that easily," Alex said, "and, besides, you don't have to worry about speaking. I'm not going to let you say anything. I'll do the talking." The audience laughed and applauded.

Ethan straightened his tie, buttoned his coat, and made his way to Alex's side at the podium. Placing his left arm around Ethan's shoulders and looking him squarely in the eyes, Alex repeated, "Now, as I said, you are forbidden to talk." Everyone laughed once more.

"Ladies and gentlemen, this is my friend and colleague, Ethan Allday," Alex said. "He is the Chief Financial Officer for MedAmerica. He's been with the company for thirty-eight years, and the greatest happiness for this man each day is to come into my office and plaster my walls with charts about the financial condition of the company." More laughter arose as Ethan shifted nervously on his legs.

"Now, I pulled Ethan," Alex continued, "who happens to be my second cousin, out of the backwoods of South Georgia, and gave him increasingly responsible jobs with MedAmerica. I thought I could make Ethan into a sophisticated individual, but I've completely failed. Even though he's been exposed to European cuisine and etiquette training, he still talks when he should listen." Ethan blushed and squirmed as the audience howled.

"But in all seriousness," Alex's expression turned dour, "Ethan is a fine member of our team at MedAmerica and exemplifies the work ethic and commitment I expect of everyone in the company." Ethan opened his mouth to speak, but Alex clamped his hand on the back of Ethan's neck. "Ethan, I told you not to say anything." Turning to the audience Alex said: "See, didn't I tell you? He talks when he should listen."

Ethan stammered, "But I…, I…." Alex tightened his grip, and said: "I said *no talking*! Didn't you hear?" The audience roared with laughter. Alex winked, patted Ethan gently on the shoulder, and sent him back to his table. As Ethan lowered himself in his chair, he muttered: "That son-of-a-bitch! Some day I'm going to kill him."

Alex paused after Ethan left the podium, took a drink of water, and resumed his address: "America is still the land of opportunity. Ethan and I are both living proof that people of the humblest origin can rise to the highest levels of responsibility through hard work and dedication. Let's all pursue the dream of making this nation better, a country where the lowliest citizen can rise to the pinnacle of success—a world where each human being is free to fulfill the noble destiny God intended." Looking toward an American flag standing by the entrance to the hall, Alex's voice broke as he said: "If we pull together as Americans and use our God-given talents to the fullest, we can make the lives of humankind better, healthier, stronger, happier, richer. We must all do our share, and toward that end, I pledge on behalf of MedAmerica that we will continue our quest to ensure the emotional and physical health of everyone in our great country." A tear ran down his cheek as he gazed toward the ceiling, raised his right arm and vowed: "So help me, God!"

The assembly rose in unison with boisterous applause and shouts of "Bravo!" and "Hear! Hear!" The acclamation was deafening as Alex returned to his seat. He stood, bowed gratefully, and waved with a flourish.

Then, while the applause continued, he sat down, leaned over to Annie, and kissed her on the cheek. Whispering in her ear, he said: "Your old shitass of a father would've *loved* that, wouldn't he?"

They caught the elevator together: Jeremiah, Ethan, Sarah, Irene and Annie. Alex was not with them. He had arranged for a reception after the banquet at

Club 21 for several dozen special guests. Jeremiah, Ethan and their wives had not been invited, and Annie chose not to go. They all had rooms at the Waldorf. Jeremiah and Ethan had adjoining rooms on the 38th floor, and Alex had reserved a penthouse suite.

When the elevator doors parted on the 38th floor, Jeremiah invited Annie to get off and join them for drinks. It was late, almost midnight, and Annie declined. "Thanks," she said, "but I'm pooped. It's been a long day. I will ask you for a big favor though, Jeremiah, if Sarah doesn't mind," she added. "Would you please see me to the apartment? I'm a little leery of going up by myself."

"Of course," Jeremiah said. "I'll be right back, Sarah. Y'all go on in and have a nightcap."

Jeremiah and Annie did not speak until the elevator doors opened again. Jeremiah held the "open" button as Annie walked before him into the corridor. He had looked closely at her in the garish light of the elevator. She looked tired, terribly tired, and not with just the kind of fatigue that came with a long, hard day. Her body seemed frail and fragile, a far cry from the rippling muscles of the robust young girl he had known in high school as the captain of the girls' basketball team. Her face was emaciated, lined with wrinkles, creases below her eyes, colorless cheeks.

As Annie unlocked her door, she said: "Please come in with me, Jeremiah, and look around for boogers." Giving a short, contrived laugh, she added: "Alex usually has a bodyguard who goes everywhere with us, but he gave him two days off while we're on this trip. Alex felt we'd be OK here with all the dignitaries, but I'm still nervous. You can imagine how many enemies Alex has with all the disruption at the company over the last few years."

"I'll be happy to go in with you and check everything," Jeremiah winked at her, "but I'm not sure what I'd do with an honest-to-goodness booger."

Jeremiah walked through the luxurious suite, its formal dining and living rooms, two bathrooms, one with a Jacuzzi, and two large bedrooms. He returned to the living room and found Annie sitting on a barstool near the kitchen. Seating himself across from her, he said: "No one's here. But what a layout! I've had the good fortune to spend the night in some pretty classy places, but nothing quite like this." Annie was oblivious to the comment.

"You know, Jeremiah," she said, lighting a cigarette, "there's one booger you can't do anything about." Her lips trembled.

"What are you saying?" Jeremiah asked.

"I mean the one who'll be staggering in here three or four hours from now."

"You mean *Alex*?" he asked, tentatively.

"Who else? Who else?" Annie's voice broke and tears ran down her cheeks as she blurted out: "Oh, Jeremiah, you were right! You warned me about this man. I should've listened to you. My life is miserable."

"Come on now, Annie, you can't be miserable. You have everything. A family, two wonderful daughters to be proud of—money, status, anything you want."

"You just don't understand. *Nobody* does. Nobody can understand." Annie crushed the cigarette in a gold-plated ash tray.

"Well, what is it? What's so bad?" Jeremiah wasn't sure he wanted to hear the answer.

"Look at me, Jeremiah," Annie said, "I look awful. I dread seeing myself in a mirror. I feel nauseated every time I'm in Alex's presence. My stomach stays in knots constantly and I can't eat. He was never easy to live with before Daddy died, but since then—well, it's as though he doesn't have to put up a front with me anymore. The only time he's half-way civil is when we're in public, and even then he cuts me down. We don't sleep in the same bed and haven't for years. He's completely aloof—so cold, so terribly cold. Can you imagine how it tears up the fiber of your inner being, Jeremiah? To hear over and over how you're no good—how you don't measure up? If he's trying to drive me crazy, it's working. He's never loved me. I know that now. I was just a pawn for him. I've been such a fool."

Annie reached over and touched Jeremiah's hand, tightening her clasp as she talked.

"You're just going through a phase, Annie—questioning everything." Jeremiah tried to smile. "Lots of couples do that after years of marriage."

Annie paused and took a deep breath, looking toward the ceiling. "I want to tell you something, Jeremiah—something I can't believe I'm saying…." Then, staring directly into his eyes, she said: "I think Alex may have caused my mother's death!"

"My God!" Jeremiah exclaimed. "You can't really mean that. You're just upset—you know, feeling down right now."

"I wish that were so," she responded, "but this has been gnawing at me for years. I know Alex wanted Mama out of the way. She had demanded that I stop dating him, and he was already talking about marriage. And for the wheel to just come off the car like that—a new car! It just didn't make sense—doesn't add up."

"Have you confronted Alex with your suspicions?" Jeremiah cleared his throat. "Wouldn't it be best to get it out in the open?"

"Yes, yes, I did confront him—a year or so after Daddy died. Alex denied everything, of course. I knew he would. He called me a fool for even thinking anything like that. He said I ought to see a psychiatrist."

"Look, Annie," Jeremiah sputtered, "I know Alex can be devious—even cruel at times, but surely he would never have harmed your mother. There must be some things even Alex wouldn't do."

"I hope you're right, but I guess it's almost beside the point now. The fact is my life with him is horrible—a nightmare. I don't see how I can go on living this way."

"What can I do?" Jeremiah asked.

"Nothing. There's *nothing* anyone can do."

"Why don't you separate? Just leave him for a while?" Jeremiah felt the clamminess of her hand. "And if you decide to make it permanent, a divorce should leave you very comfortable—you know, financially."

"I've thought about that a lot, but there are my children to consider. And I was brought up believing marriage is forever. An antiquated concept, I know, but it still torments me. You know, the 'better or worse' syndrome, as silly as that sounds."

"I can't stand to see you like this," Jeremiah said. "It seems to me that any change would be for the better. And you're wrong, I can understand some of what you're going through. Sarah and I are having problems, you know—have been for years."

"Why couldn't it have been *you*, Jeremiah?" Annie asked. "Why couldn't I have seen things better?" Tears were streaming down her cheeks, mascara streaking badly.

Jeremiah's arm was trembling as Annie pulled his hand to her, clasping it to her breast.

"I don't know what to say, Annie. What am I *supposed* to say?"

"You precious man! It could have been *us*, together all these years. I know you cared for me. It was obvious."

"Of course, I did, Annie. I still do, but everything is water over the damn now, isn't it?"

"That's the saddest part. You can't relive the past. I would if I could."

"Listen, I better go now," Jeremiah said, pulling his hand away. "Just call on me anytime you need me. Promise?"

"Yes, yes! I will. You can't know how important it is to me to know you're there."

With that, they stood up, facing each other. Annie cupped her hands on each side of Jeremiah's face. She pulled him slowly forward, kissing him gently but firmly on the lips. "I love you, Jeremiah," she said.

"I love you too," he answered, turning toward the door.

❧ ❧ ❧

Jeremiah returned to his room and found Ethan sitting alone, holding a drink, the TV on but muted. Jeremiah fixed himself a Jack Daniel's and sat down across from Ethan on the sofa.

"What took you so long?" Ethan asked.

"Annie needed to talk. She's not doing too well these days."

"I'll be frank with you, Jeremiah, I don't see how anyone lives with Alex—especially Annie. He changed completely when Doc Willie died. It's bad enough having to be around him at work. The only bright spot is that he's usually out of town, making speeches, strutting around as CEO. He loves the limelight."

"Speaking of limelight, how was it up there tonight?" Jeremiah asked.

"Not worth a damn! I may kill that son-of-a-bitch someday. Did you hear that stuff about my lack of sophistication? How he had tried to make something of me? That's his technique: always keep the poor bastards on the defensive. Never let 'em forget who's in control. Say something nice, and then slap the hell out of 'em."

"You sound bitter, Ethan."

"I am bitter!" Ethan walked to the bar and poured another drink. "But I've seen him pull that stunt a thousand times, and it makes me want to puke. I didn't think he'd use it tonight in front of that crowd though. Like when he's announcing a promotion in a staff meeting. He always makes the poor jerk feel like crap! So *undeserving* of the generous favor the all-powerful chairman has bestowed. So damn *lucky* to be in the good graces of Alexander Wayne Rumpkin. Makes the pretense that he's just joking, but he's serious as a heart attack. Like when he slaps you on the back—a good-natured gesture from most people, but not with Alex. Alex slaps the hell out of you. I've spent the last thirty years observing him, Jeremiah, and I can tell you—everything's designed for *one purpose*: to keep everyone else in suspense, wondering what he's going to do or say next. He's a master control freak: his words, body language, facial expressions, everything possible to let the whole world know he's in total control."

"Ah, you're just irritated that he singled you out tonight. It was his perverted way of paying you a compliment. You'll get over it."

"No. I won't get over it. You have no idea what damage he's done to MedAmerica."

"He's turned it around, hasn't he? Aren't y'all making record profits these days? I know the stock's doing great. Unbelievably well, especially after all the analysts thought the company was going belly-up with the Panacea debacle."

"Hell, Alex *caused* the Panacea debacle. It was all his fuckin' idea! Everybody in the company knew it would be a disaster. You were there. You saw it. You pointed out the problems. But he was hell-bent to do that deal."

"I read in the *WSJ* that the acquisition was unanimously approved by the board. I can't believe they did that without asking a lot of questions?"

"You should see Alex handle the board. Plays them like a fiddle. And the fact is that those pompous assholes don't really give a damn what happens to MedAmerica. He put them on the board, so they just take their forty thousand a year for four three-hour meetings, their perks, and they just rubber stamp everything he recommends. If things get too rough, or if they become concerned about legal exposure, they'll just bail out."

"You don't seem to have a very high opinion of corporate governance, do you, Ethan?"

"It's a lousy system. There's no accountability. The stockholders don't care what happens to the employees or the company's business so long as they get their dividends or make out well when they buy and sell." Ethan fixed another drink. "You want another, Jeremiah?" he asked. Jeremiah nodded, and Ethan picked up the Jack Daniels.

"We've talked about this before, Ethan. You and I have known Alex all our lives, and we both know his faults. But you've got to admire his drive, his determination, especially when you think about his origins. My goodness, who else ever achieved more than he has with sheer force of will-power and single-minded pursuit of a goal?"

Ethan glanced toward the ceiling. "Jeremiah, there's something that's bothering the hell out of me, and I can't talk with anyone else about it. I probably shouldn't say anything to you."

"Listen, Ethan, you know you can talk to me. We're like brothers. Hell, I'm closer than a brother: I can be your lawyer if you've done anything illegal," Jeremiah laughed, "and nobody can make me divulge anything. You know, attorney-client privilege and all that."

Ethan did not laugh. "You may be closer to the mark than you realize, Jeremiah," he said, somberly. "The fact is, I'm not sure whether I've done anything illegal or not."

"Aw, come on, Ethan. You're putting me on. You couldn't do anything shady if your life depended on it." Jeremiah punched Ethan on the arm.

"No, no, I'm serious." Ethan's voice quivered. "It all started with an IRS audit a year ago. They came in and tore the place apart. Examined every invoice we had, every transaction for the last ten years. I think we came out well on most everything, but there are several questionable checks for large amounts of money that were issued during 1990, when we were putting the Panacea deal together."

"Don't your records show what they were for?" Jeremiah asked.

"Yeah, but I couldn't find any supporting detail, no invoices, and the thing is that I signed them all. My name is on…."

"Well, at worst the IRS will just disallow the deductions if they were expense items and the company will have to cough up more tax money. No big deal."

"They're really *big* checks, Jeremiah. Two were for $375,000 and three were for a half-million, five checks in all. Total is two and a quarter million, and I signed the damn things. They were made out to MedAmerica's Washington office account, ostensibly for renovation of the suite of offices we have on Connecticut Avenue for our lobbyists. And the records on withdrawals for that account have mysteriously disappeared. The only authorized signature for withdrawals was a guy named Elmer Youngblood, and he can't be found anywhere. Disappeared two years ago."

"Well, you didn't get any of the money, did you?"

"Hell no! I've never taken one cent from the company I didn't earn, but the trouble is that I'm the only warm body they've found with direct ties to the checks. And now, to make matters worse, the IRS has turned their findings over to the U.S. Attorney's office for the southern district of Georgia, and they're poking around under a law that's supposed to insure accountability for this kind of thing. Foreign Corrupt Practices Act, they call it. I haven't hired an attorney yet, but maybe I need one? What do you think?"

"Yeah, the FCPA, I know a little about it. The penalties are severe, but I'm sure everything will come out OK. They're not going to prosecute you for some unintentional oversight."

"I wish I felt the same. You know, Alex has a pretty strong network of influence built up in Washington, so we can probably deal with the IRS, but this criminal business just scares the shit out of me. And they could take some of the stuff to the grand jury." Ethan's lips trembled and there was sweat on his brow. "And you know who the federal judge is down there—Beagle Williams. He's developed a reputation as a hanging judge and you know he's not going to wink at anything illegal."

"No, but on the other hand, Beagle has a high regard for you. He would be scrupulously fair if this thing ever came before him. He wouldn't allow you to be railroaded." Jeremiah stood up and leaned on the bar. "Do you have any idea what really happened to the money? Do you think Youngblood took it when he disappeared?"

"I really don't know. Youngblood was one of the high-powered people Alex brought into the company when Dr. Willingham died. Alex brought in a lot of new people in high level management jobs, especially after the Panacea deal got the company in such a bloody mess. He hired a bunch of expensive management consultants—McFriar and Associates—to come in and revamp the company. They were like a swarm of locusts, tore everything apart, had us firing people who'd been with the organization since Dr. Willingham opened the first clinic in the thirties."

"I've heard of McFriar. They've got a reputation for turning big companies around, and it seems they were successful with MedAmerica."

"Like hell they were. The main thing McFriar accomplished was the feathering of its own nest. Those people are in the same league as con artists and TV evangelists. They're all young MIT and Harvard MBA's, and they've been trained to use all the buzz words: 'empowerment, reengineering, restructuring, mission statements, outsourcing,' the whole pile of shit. And Alex bought it, hook, line and sinker."

"How does this tie in with the Washington bank account problem?" Jeremiah asked.

"Oh, it doesn't, I suppose. It's just that Alex started doing a lot of perplexing things after Dr. Willingham died. The Panacea deal was the worst, but there were other things. He told me to cut loose suppliers we had dealt with for decades. Cost and efficiency studies, he said, justified it, but I never saw the studies. I just don't know how things got so confused, Jeremiah. The whole environment seemed to change overnight when Alex took over."

"Well, Ethan, look at it this way: you're doing fine, a beautiful family, luxurious home, a comfortable lifestyle, the respect of everyone in Shrewsbury

Crossing. Not bad for an old redneck cousin, is it?" Jeremiah patted Ethan softly on the shoulder.

"All that won't help much if I'm in jail, will it, Jeremiah?" Ethan shook his head slowly as he poured another drink. "And I'm worried. Lord knows, I'm worried."

"We all worry too much," Jeremiah said. "Things'll look better tomorrow."

CHAPTER 18

The Princess of Spring

"But at my back I always hear
Time's winged chariot hurrying near;..."
Andrew Marvell,
To His Coy Mistress

The girl burst into Jeremiah's life like the first blossoms of a March dogwood: warm, radiant, promising, hopeful. Michelle had left for the day, so the young woman appeared in his office doorway unannounced. "Hello, Mr. Goodwin. I'm Tara Fountain. I believe Alex Rumpkin spoke with you about me." She moved forward, extending her hand over Jeremiah's desk. "You probably don't remember me, but we met once at the Moorings where you and Alex were having dinner. I was your waitress."

Jeremiah was thankful that she kept speaking, filling the void. He felt flustered, nervous like a schoolboy on his first date. Her beauty was more striking than he remembered. As he stood, reaching forward to accept her hand, he finally found his voice: "Of course, I remember you, Tara. That was about six years ago, wasn't it?"

"Probably so. I remember that night. You and Alex seemed so excited to see each other. You're friends from childhood, aren't you?" Her conversation was sophisticated and spontaneous, or so it seemed to Jeremiah. He had been told by Alex that she was now twenty-seven, but her maturity and poise made it difficult for him to believe that she was so young.

"Yes, we go way back, and we're related somehow—second or third cousins, I think. I've never been able to keep my family's genealogy straight. But I'm being terribly rude. Please be seated. Alex says you're looking for a job in Atlanta."

"He thinks your firm might have an opening, or perhaps you know a company or another law firm in Atlanta you could recommend." She crossed her legs, revealing shapely, tanned calves. He remembered how striking her legs were at the restaurant that night with Alex and how big she was—a woman of substance, not one of those flimsy, fragile females, looking as if they might break or bruise if you touched them. She wore an elegant, tasteful dress, a slit up the side—not the kind of dress for someone out of work.

"I'll certainly do what I can. What's your background, your experience?" Jeremiah asked.

"Mostly waitress jobs. Couldn't afford college when I graduated from high school, so I moved from Quincy, Florida, to Ludlow when I was eighteen and found a job at the Moorings. I had been there a year or so when you came in with Alex."

"How did you get to know Alex?"

"He was a regular customer at the Moorings when I started there. He would come in with big groups of business people, out-of-town guests. He began to ask for me to wait his table. Told me later that he liked to impress his friends. His tips were always generous, and he was terribly charming. I couldn't help but like him."

"When's the last time you saw him?"

"Oh, I've visited him at his Buckhead condo a few times over the last three or four months." Tara said. "Have you *seen* that place? It's fabulous. Unbelievable. I can't imagine how anyone affords something like that. It's in the same high rise where Elton John lives, did you know that?"

"I think Alex mentioned it. I haven't seen Alex since they honored him at the banquet at the Waldorf in March. I guess you know about that."

"Oh yes. He said he wanted to invite me, but he was afraid Mrs. Rumpkin wouldn't understand."

Jeremiah was uncomfortable with the conversation. He suddenly visualized Annie at home while Alex was meeting this girl at his condominium. He changed the subject. "You don't *really* remember me, do you? I mean, my goodness, that was six years ago."

"Absolutely, I *do* remember you," Tara said. "I remember thinking how polite and considerate you were that night—always said 'thank you' when I brought your drinks, and—I probably shouldn't say this—I recall how *handsome* you were."

"Goodness, how you talk! You've made an old guy's day." Jeremiah blushed. "I guess we better get back to why you're here. Do you have any other experience?"

"I was a receptionist for an insurance agency in Shrewsbury Crossing for a while, and I took several paralegal courses at the community college in Ludlow."

"Now, we're talking. What about typing, secretarial training?"

"Not much. Took typing in high school, but I haven't maintained my skills."

"Maybe we could send you to a refresher course. I think our reception area would be vastly improved if we placed you there to greet clients. Tell you what, it's getting close to happy hour. Would it be presumptuous to ask you to join me for a drink at the watering hole across the street? Some of my partners and I frequent the place, and it would be a good time to introduce you. They're suckers for tremendous looking females. Matter of fact, I am too." Jeremiah did not give the girl time to respond. "Let's wander over there; once the fellows meet you, I doubt I'll find anyone objecting to offering you a job here."

Just as Jeremiah expected, several of the firm's partners and a sprinkling of associates—all men—were at one end of the bar when he and Tara walked in. All eyes were on them. Ben Ansley, the managing partner, was the first to speak. "Well, well, Jeremiah, how did you ever persuade this lovely woman to enter a public establishment in your company? You must be her uncle."

"You're just jealous, Ben," Jeremiah placed his hand on Tara's back, gently moving her toward the group. "If you guys will clean up your act—and your language—there's a chance I might introduce you."

The charm and seductiveness of the young woman were palpable. She took a seat on the bar-stool offered by one of the lawyers, and they all drew around her in a semi-circle. Jeremiah stood to the side, mesmerized by her every move, listening with fascination to her banter, pretending not to notice as the slit in her skirt fell further away each time she laughed at a joke or leaned forward on the stool. Her conversation had an easy confidence about it, and Jeremiah knew she was secure in her understanding that any male there would take her to bed if given the slightest opportunity.

Abruptly she turned to Jeremiah and said: "Mr. Goodwin, I think I better be getting back to my place now. Will you walk me to my car?"

Jeremiah's ego swelled as he said: "I'd be delighted to, Miss Fountain." As she took his arm and they made their way toward the door, she looked deeply into his eyes, smiling and chattering.

At the staff meeting the next morning, there was no objection when Ben Ansley recommended that Tara Fountain be given employment with the firm. She was hired as the primary receptionist, and she reported for work the following Monday.

❧ ❧ ❧

Tara and Michelle quickly became friends. They ate lunch and took breaks together. Tara would come and sit by Michelle's desk to drink coffee each morning before the firm's office hours began, and Jeremiah could hear them outside his door whispering and laughing. It had been six weeks since Tara joined the office and several of the partners had admitted to Jeremiah that Tara made them giddy when she greeted them or relayed their calls. Clients had remarked what a lovely, personable receptionist she was.

Jeremiah sometimes wondered what she and Michelle discussed over their early morning coffee. Was it Alex? They both had notes to compare, Jeremiah knew for a fact. Or was it him? No notes there, and he felt that he was just flattering himself to think he might be part of the conversation.

It was a Wednesday morning in mid-May—well before eight o'clock. Tara came to Michelle's desk and found her chair empty. Peering through the open door at Jeremiah, whose view was hidden by the *Wall Street Journal* spread before him, Tara cleared her throat and said: "Excuse me, Jeremiah, is Michelle here today?"

"Good morning, Tara," Jeremiah said, putting the paper down. "No, as a matter of fact, she just called. One of her children has bronchitis, and she won't be in today. But you can drink coffee with me."

"What a nice invitation," Tara said.

Jeremiah's office was spacious: as one of the firm's senior partners; he trailed only two other members who had larger, better-appointed accommodations. Two richly clad leather sofas faced each other to the right of his desk near the window, with a marble coffee table separating them.

"Let's sit over here, Tara," Jeremiah said as he moved to a sofa. "We can enjoy the view of downtown 'Hot-lanta' while we take our caffeine hits for the morning."

"How do you think that name came about? I've always wondered," she said, seating herself on the other sofa, across from Jeremiah. "Everyone in south Georgia says it—never just 'Atlanta.'"

"Who knows? I've heard speculation that it goes way back to Sherman—who made things pretty hot from here to Savannah. That theory usually comes from a transplanted Yankee who knew nothing else about Georgia before he arrived here. Then, there's the weather—hot as hell, you know. My personal favorite is that it's the women—the sultry, sexy, hot women that are concentrated here." Jeremiah wet his upper lip with his tongue, and took a sip of coffee. "You know," he went on, "the South—and Georgia, in particular—has the most beautiful women on the face of the earth. I've traveled quite a bit, and I can confirm that firsthand. I'm always glad to get back to Georgia. By the way, what do you think of the 'hot women' theory?"

"Maybe it's the men, always in heat, you know," Tara smiled. "Or perhaps it's the two together, eh? Put the two together, and it becomes an incendiary city—a flammable town, don't you suppose? Scarlett and Rhett and all that."

The teasing in the beautiful girl's voice made Jeremiah feel the tinge of an erection building. He wondered if she could tell. She reached down and loosened a strap on one shoe, dropping it to the floor. The motion was casual, yet deliberate, and when she straightened up, she smiled and looked deeply into his eyes. "What time is it?" she asked.

"Damn it, Tara!" He blurted out the words. "You know what you're doing to me."

She remained calm. "I think I asked you the time," she said, smiling.

"Didn't you hear me?" he asked. "I said you're driving me nuts!"

"That's why I asked you the time. What *time* is it, my love? Do we have *time*, you know, time enough to fuck?"

Jeremiah got up, locked the door, and returned to her. "Yes," he said, his hands trembling as he reached for her. "Absolutely! We do have time."

As prearranged he boarded first. Feigning nonchalance, he smiled at the flight attendant as she tore his boarding card in half, giving him a stub with his seat selection marked. He walked down the long jet-way, following a woman and two young boys who paid no attention to their mother's numerous instructions for keeping the carry-on luggage out of the way of other passengers. Inconspicuously, he tried to eye the other passengers to spot any familiar face, any acquaintance who might innocently or deliberately share his secret with the wrong person.

Jeremiah settled down in a big leather seat, a window seat on aisle 4, in the first class cabin. The Lockheed 1011 was filling up fast, mostly through a boarding door in the side for the 200-plus coach passengers. A flight attendant offered to take his coat and get him a drink: he accepted both offers, specifying a Jack Daniels, on the rocks, twist of lemon. With the airplane virtually full, the gate agent made a final call for boarding, and Tara came through the first class door and sat down in the seat next to Jeremiah.

He reached over and squeezed her hand as she fastened her belt. This was it, he thought, the scheming and planning paying off. Everything was going smoothly, so far at least.

Since that first encounter in his office four weeks earlier, nothing in his life had been the same. His stomach had been constantly tied in knots. His mind had raced at full speed, trying to decide when next they could meet, how to minimize the risk of detection, whether an out-of-the-way rendezvous would be best, and the level of intimacy that would be safe to display in public. Between the two of them, he had been the most foolhardy, taking risks she cautioned him against, meeting at times in places where he was apt to be recognized, as though he wanted to be caught. When he was inclined to exercise caution, Tara had cooperated fully, assuring him that she understood the need for discretion. As for her, there had been only one major concern: arranging her schedule at work and with Jeremiah to accommodate several short, one or two hour visits from Alex in her apartment.

But everything seemed to be working out for Jeremiah now. He had announced his intent to attend the four-day anti-trust seminar in San Francisco in January: no one could be suspicious of a June business trip planned so much earlier. He had laid all the sensible foundations, with Sarah, with his clients, with the lawyers and associates, with his children. He would be out of town for most of the week at the Hyatt Embarcadero. He had advised them that the program would be a movable feast, some sessions and workshops to be staged at other locations and hotels, some night sessions planned. But messages could be left for him at the room, and he had assured them all that he would invariably return calls, though with how much delay he could not say.

There was a movie on the flight, but they scarcely noticed. Jeremiah did most of the talking, Tara hanging on every word. Her big brown eyes, deep and clear like some mountain pool at the base of a waterfall, glowed with joy and anticipation as he recounted tales of his youth: games he had played with Alex and the other boys, stunts they had pulled, lies they had told. She wrapped both arms around his right arm, guiding it firmly into the warm valley between her breasts, laughing softly at his stories. In his fifty-ninth year, he felt he possessed the fresh vigor of youth again in the company of this girl.

Leaving San Francisco International Airport, they drove directly to the hotel in a rented Cadillac. Jeremiah had reserved a suite facing the bay. From their window they could see the Oakland bridge and much of the bay. It was twilight when they checked in, and they ate in the room, made love, and went to sleep. Local time it was only eight-thirty, but body-time it was nearing midnight. It was the first night they had spent together.

At nine the next morning Jeremiah went down to the lobby to register for the seminar and pick up his name tag and badge. At the registration desk he was given written materials for the program, along with publishers' brochures advertising legal treatises and several hand-outs concerning up-coming seminars. There was also an attendee roster, and he sat in a lobby chair to study the names. A glance at the list suggested that more than one thousand would be in attendance. Looking for names he might recognize from the Atlanta bar and from the D.C. area where he spent much of his time, he found nothing to concern him. He went to a table of refreshments provided by the seminar sponsors, poured himself a glass of orange juice, and returned to his chair, this time scanning the lobby for familiar faces. Again, he recognized no one. Even if an acquaintance were here, he reasoned, there was slight chance they would meet in such a large crowd. Jeremiah breathed a sigh of relief and drank the remainder of his juice. Everything was working out for him just right—just right, for once.

Tara had showered and dressed when he returned to the room. They kissed, and then he asked her to stand back so he could admire her. She wore velvet pants that accentuated her long, shapely legs, and a yellow sweater with a high collar. She held a white windbreaker draped over her arm, for she had been warned of the Bay Area chill even though it was the middle of June. On her head was tucked a small white cap, somewhat like a sailor cap but bigger and adding a perfect touch of informality to her appearance—just the kind of unique headpiece someone of her generation would wear.

"Are you hungry?" he asked.

"Famished!" Tara said. "Did you eat anything downstairs?"

"I just had some juice," Jeremiah reached for a jacket while he talked. "Tell you what, let's drive to Fisherman's Wharf. There's a little restaurant on the pier overlooking the bay where we can have a Bloody Mary and brunch."

"Fabulous!" she said. "You always know the right thing to do."

They held hands waiting for the elevator, but Jeremiah let go as the doors parted with ten or twelve people inside—three men wearing name tags for the seminar, an elderly couple looking like tourists, and several teenagers with Notre Dame sweatshirts. Tara and Jeremiah said nothing to each other as the elevator descended.

Jeremiah had visited the Wharf twice before in his life, once with Sarah soon after law school, and again just two years ago with a young girl he had met on a cable car during a business trip. As they parked the Cadillac and walked up a flight of wooden steps into the restaurant, Tara beamed with excitement, her eyes sparkling. They requested a window table facing the bay and the request was granted. Afterwards, they strolled over the cobblestones and bricks connecting the antique shops, the hat boutiques, dress stores and jewelry shops of the Cannery and Ghirardelli Square. Tara went in each one, exiting some quickly but poring over the inventories of others.

It struck Jeremiah as odd that he didn't mind waiting on her—even enjoyed watching her browse. He had always detested shopping with Sarah: she always took longer than he thought necessary to make a selection and she was always buying things she later took back. It had been years, in fact, since he and Sarah had shopped together. With Tara, the waiting didn't seem to matter, and she bought very little: a bracelet here, a small bronze statue there. And Jeremiah didn't mind a bit. He studied her movements, her facial expressions, her banter with the clerks, as she moved through the shops; she was to Jeremiah a radiant, ephemeral vision that he still couldn't believe was his companion, his lover.

The afternoon came and they were getting hungry again. Holding hands, they sauntered down closer to the water, along the wooden paths by the hutches, nooks, and stalls of the Wharf where shrimp, oysters and clams were being cooked, the odors mingling in chaotic whiffs that confounded the sense of smell. They bought two baskets of grilled shrimp, ordered draft beer, and sat at a table to eat. It was an exquisite, clear, perfect day. Tara was beautiful and young, and Jeremiah gave no thought to his anti-trust seminar or to anything or anyone in Atlanta.

The next day they left the hotel early, driving north on Highway 101 in the direction of the California wine country. They crossed the Golden Gate Bridge into Marin County and took the road through Sausalito toward the Napa Valley. They rode through Sonoma and soon reached fields of vineyards endlessly stretching toward distant mountains. After touring a winery, they had a late lunch at a small cafe on the outskirts of Cloverdale.

After lunch, they continued north on 101, looping around the Mendocino region and cutting over to the coast where they took Highway 1 south. Navigating a road twisting by cliffs dropping hundreds of feet to the surging tide and rocks of the Pacific, Jeremiah became queasy, his knuckles white as he gripped the steering wheel with sweaty palms. As he steered around the winding curves, impatient drivers tailgating him to pass, Tara chattered away, urging him repeatedly to take his eyes off the road to take in a view. His nerves increasingly frayed, he finally glared back at her and spoke sharply to her for the first time.

She pouted in silence for a while, sitting close to her window and looking away from him toward the ocean. Jeremiah turned on the radio, picking up a soft music FM station just as one of his favorite songs, "The Way You Look Tonight," began playing. It was more than he could take, so he reached over and touched her shoulder, apologizing for his outburst. She smiled and squeezed his hand and moved closer to him again.

As they started the final leg of their journey back to the Bay Area late in the afternoon, Jeremiah persuaded a woman to snap a picture of them as they stood on a lookout point with their backs to the ocean. Afterwards, they stood together, holding hands, and watched the sun sink into the western sea.

It did not seem fair to Jeremiah that time had passed so quickly. After they had checked out of the hotel and were driving to the airport the next day, Tara seated silently beside him, he wondered why such transcendent happiness had to be so fleeting. Why couldn't he somehow capture Tara's vivacious, bright spirit and seal them tightly as though in a picture—some kind of time capsule, a protection against fading? He remembered the old saying, *carpe diem—*seize *the day*—but there was no way you could do it. Human beings could experience only some fragment of rapture and then watch helplessly as it slipped away. As he looked over at the radiant youth of the woman next to him, he thought of the poet's words: "Old time is still a flying, and this same flower that smiles today, tomorrow will be dying."

✦ ✦ ✦

Their first real argument came at the airport, waiting to board the return flight to Atlanta. Seated together in the first class lounge, filled to capacity with other passengers, Jeremiah blurted out: "Tara, I've decided that I want you to break everything off with Alex."

"What?" she asked, turning to face him squarely.

"I'm serious." Jeremiah squeezed her arm. "I just don't want to think about your being with him anymore. I don't think I can bear it, that's all!"

"Jeremiah, think about what you're saying. You know I can't do that, and you're in no position to ask me. You've known the bounds of our relationship from the start."

"Why can't you cut it off with him? I have money, not nearly as much as he does, but I can help you enough to get by."

"It's just not possible," Tara shook her head and glanced around the room. "Jeremiah, you know Alex, he's very possessive and demanding. He would never just go along with a breakup—especially if it's not his idea. He'd probably go off the deep end—wind up killing me and perhaps you, too, if he found out about us."

"Tara, Alex has lots of other women."

"I know that. Do you think I'm naive? I've always known that he has other women, but you don't understand his mentality. He would never let me go. Besides, I've gotten used to money—the car, the apartment, everything about my lifestyle. I don't think I could give it up, and you can't afford me."

"Maybe you don't *want* to stop seeing him? Maybe he gives you something you need besides money." Jeremiah was speaking louder than he realized, and several passengers seated nearby were staring at them.

"So what would you do?" Tara whispered, aware they were being overheard. "Leave your wife? Go through a divorce after several decades of marriage?"

"That could come later," Jeremiah said. "Right now, though, I need to know that you're not going back to Alex. I need to know that the last few days have been special for you."

"Don't be silly! You know what we've shared these last few days. I've never had anything like this from a man." Tara placed her hands in his. "Look, Jeremiah, we've got to take this relationship for what it is: a wonderful emotional and physical bond that few human beings ever find, but we can't ignore *reality*.

You're twice my age, and you have a wife who needs you. You can't lose your head."

His eyes fixed on the floor, Jeremiah gritted his teeth but said nothing.

"Besides," Tara went on, "I'll be there when you need me. Look at it this way: Alex is paying for everything while you eat the honey. Some deal, eh?" Jeremiah did not like the way she put it, but he said nothing. Cupping his chin with her fingers, she raised his face to hers, leaned forward and kissed him softly on the mouth.

Neither of them noticed the man on the far side of the lounge operating an idiot-proof Fuji camera with a zoom lens. In light bright enough to make a flash unnecessary, the lens opened and shut silently three times. The photographer was another attendee at the seminar, also waiting for the flight back to Atlanta. He was Kenneth Stripling, now an administrative law judge for the Department of Agriculture and formerly an associate with the law firm of Proctor, Bennett, and Goodwin. He grinned broadly as he placed the camera back in its case.

CHAPTER 19

Pandemonium

"Oh, life is a glorious cycle of song,
A medley of extemporanea;
And love is a thing that can never go
wrong;
And I am Marie of Roumania."
Dorothy Parker

The Federal Grand Jury for the Southern District of Georgia was in session, and Ethan Allday paced the floor. He had been subpoenaed, and he was nervous as a cat. He waited with his lawyer in the holding room off from the main chamber where the jurors met in the Federal Center of Shrewsbury Crossing.

"Take it easy, Ethan," Randall Murphy said. "This is not the end of the world. You'll get through it fine. There's nothing to worry about."

Murphy spoke with a lack of conviction which Ethan readily detected. Even though Murphy was the best criminal lawyer in South Georgia, he would not be permitted to accompany Ethan when he testified. They had rehearsed how he was to respond to certain questions, but Ethan knew that you could never be sure how things would go. The U.S. attorney would be there with a briefcase full of documents collected over the past two years from MedAmerica's records. Any one piece of paper could be a land mine: Ethan's initials scrawled in a margin, a mindless note made at the time which he could not possibly recall. The company's lawyers had repeatedly stressed the wisdom of an organized system of record retention and disposal, but Ethan had never had the time. In an environment where he was constantly buffeted by Alex's incessant and sometime irrational demands, he worked long hours, weekends and holidays just to keep up with whatever current crisis Alex generated. Ethan had been, as they say, so busy killing crocodiles that he had never found time to drain the swamp.

Ethan was almost relieved as the bailiff came to the door and told him that his time had come. The questioning went on for more than three hours. Ethan twisted and turned in the witness chair, staring at the ceiling uncomfortably at times, as he was asked the meaning of this or that notation in his own handwriting on obscure documents he could not recollect at all. Stuttering in response to questions which made no sense, he winced as glances were exchanged between the district attorney and the jurors, especially the foreman. Finally, mercifully, he was excused.

An indictment was returned four days later: Ethan Allday was charged with five counts of violating the record-keeping requirements of the Foreign Corrupt Practices Act and one count of Medicaid fraud. If convicted on all counts, Ethan faced as much as thirty years' imprisonment and a cumulative potential fine of tens of thousands of dollars.

Sarah Goodwin sat staring blankly at the clock as Jeremiah entered the den. She was full of rage.

It was after seven, and she had been drinking since three that afternoon. It was rare for Sarah to drink alcohol at all and getting drunk was almost unheard of, but tonight she was drunk. And she was furious.

Her vodka and tonic binge had begun only minutes after she had opened the odd envelope that had arrived in the afternoon mail. Her name was scrawled in large block letters and the words "Highly Personal" were printed in red ink and underlined to the side of the address. Inside, wrapped in a sheet of yellow, legal-size paper, were three color photographs. She had instantly recognized the male face on each picture. There was no writing or signature inside the envelope anywhere.

"Hello, Hon," Jeremiah said, walking into the den and eyeing the drink she held in her hand. "Are you celebrating something?"

Sarah threw one of the pictures toward him. It was the one of Tara kissing him. He missed catching it, and it fell to the floor.

"Pick it up, you bastard, and tell me who the slut is," Sarah yelled. "Was she one of the speakers at your seminar? Tell me, Jeremiah, *what* did she teach you?"

"Oh, my God!" Jeremiah said. "Where did you get this?"

"Someone was kind enough to mail them to me. *Anonymously*. Obviously, some friend or acquaintance of yours, or perhaps the girl's husband. I've already asked you once! Who the *hell* is she?"

"She's a girl I met in Ludlow. She came to Atlanta looking for a job and called me to see if I could help."

"And, of course, you're such a *fucking*, big-hearted gentleman that you *did* help, didn't you? And what you got in return was a piece of tail. What a *gem* you are."

"It's not what it appears," Jeremiah stuttered. "Give me a chance to explain."

"You'll get plenty of chances to explain—all you want—in a damn divorce court," Sarah said, slurring her words, her anger growing. "Get the hell out, Jeremiah, just get the hell out of my sight. You make me sick!"

He knew there was nothing he could say. Even sober, Sarah had little patience with him these days, and the truth was that she had caught him red-handed. And she was drunk—terribly, terribly drunk. He did not want to worsen the situation by trying to reason with her now. Better to let her sober up and simmer down. He packed a bag and left the house, stopping at a package store for a fifth of Jack Daniels. Using a public telephone to call Tara's apartment, he heard Alex answer. Jeremiah hung up. He then checked into a Holiday Inn Express three miles down the road from his home, drank three large glasses of the Tennessee whiskey, and drifted off to sleep. He would try to deal with all this tomorrow.

Judge Beagle Williams sat behind his desk, arms folded, listening dispassionately to the wrangling of the two lawyers. It was the third in-camera conference he had requested to be conducted in his chamber so that the prosecution and defense could iron out the disputes about discovery issues and pre-trial procedures. He had also urged both sides to work toward a plea bargain so he could clear this case from his crowded docket. This case, especially, he wanted off his docket.

Randall Murphy was complaining that the prosecution had held back on furnishing its witness list. The U.S. attorney, Ellis Peters, in his late twenties and fresh out of law school, was insisting that he had complied fully with the judge's orders.

"What about it?" Beagle asked. "You've both had time to prepare your cases, and this thing is set for trial after Labor Day."

"We've complied fully, your honor," Peters said. "If there are other witnesses not on our list that know something about this matter, the fault is the defendant's. I'm convinced he's hiding something and perhaps someone."

"What makes you say that?" Beagle asked.

"He doesn't have any basis for that asinine comment," Murphy said. "I suspect he's on some kind of punitive vendetta against my client. And as you know, Judge, Ethan Allday is one of the most respected men in this part of the state."

"My question was directed to the district attorney, Randall. Let him respond."

"As much as I am reluctant to admit it, Judge Williams, Mr. Murphy is partially correct. I don't doubt that the defendant is essentially an honest man, and there is no evidence that he profited personally from these transactions. But someone did come out with big bucks, and Allday is the only one we can identify with these payments—at least the only person we can find. The Washington lobbyist involved has disappeared, and Allday must know more than he's telling."

"And you're continuing to work on a plea?" Beagle asked.

"Yes, I've made several offers, your honor," Peters answered, "but it all has to be conditioned on full cooperation, and I just don't think they've been forthcoming with that."

"That's just a lot of bull, Judge," Murphy said. "My client can't remember every check out of the thousands he's issued for this big company during the last decade."

"These were pretty memorable checks he's been indicted for—two for nearly four hundred thousand and three for a half-million." Peters folded his arms and looked toward Beagle as he spoke. "Over two million dollars in all, your honor, and they weren't issued a decade ago. They were drawn six years ago—in 1990, about the time of the Panacea acquisition. Because of the regulatory issues that takeover raised in Washington, and since these large chunks of money disappeared there, there may have been some connection."

"Well, I want to dispose of this case without a trial," Beagle said, then added, laughing: "Hell, I want to dispose of all my cases without a trial." The two lawyers chuckled. "Randall," the judge went on, "talk to your client and tell him we need his full cooperation." Turning to the district attorney, he asked: "If Allday cooperates fully, what are you prepared to offer?"

"With a plea of guilty on one count, and a commitment to testify in any other proceeding that may grow out of this, five years on probation and a twenty-thousand dollar fine. I've made essentially that offer to Mr. Murphy before."

"And we've turned it down before, Judge," Murphy said, "and we'll have to refuse any plea bargain if it means that my client will have to fabricate testimony about facts he knows nothing about. How can the district attorney ask my client to go on the stand and perjure himself to stay out of jail?"

"I'm sure Mr. Peters doesn't want that," Beagle said, "but it does seem that Mr. Allday would have some recollection about transactions this big. Why don't you discuss it with him again, Randall, and stress the seriousness of these charges. My present thinking is that I couldn't accept any plea arrangement without full cooperation from the defendant." Beagle paused, then added: "In fact, whatever mood the prosecutor may be in later to accept a plea, I won't permit it until I'm satisfied—completely satisfied—that we know just how these funds were spent. And Mr. Allday, whether he likes it or not, is the only one who can lead us down that path."

"Your honor, I'm sure you're not suggesting that Mr. Allday lie to save his skin," Murphy said.

"Don't be absurd, Randall," Beagle snapped. "It's just that I won't let him get by with a memory lapse on this. You see, I know your client well, grew up with him, and I know he's honest and conscientious and probably didn't take a red cent that didn't legitimately come his way. But I also know he has a profound notion of honor and loyalty, and that may have led him to protect others in the organization. He's got to get over that and let the chips fall where they may."

"Judge," Murphy said, "you're not letting your personal acquaintance with my client color your thinking on this, I hope."

"Absolutely not!" Beagle turned on Murphy, eyes wide. "Randall, you've practiced here for years and you know how I am. Since I was raised here, I always put myself through a rigorous self-examination each time a case comes before me. It's pretty rare in this circuit to see a case where I *don't* know some of the parties—especially where an individual is a prominent citizen like Ethan Allday. And I certainly considered whether I should recuse myself when that indictment was returned. But the fact is that my relationship with Mr. Allday largely ended with our boyhood. In those days, black and white kids went their separate ways and the defendant and I have seen very little of each other these last thirty years. I have no doubt that I can preside over this matter in a totally fair and impartial manner. It's just that I want to see justice done, and if there was misuse of the corporate assets of this fine organization that so many citizens of this region poured their hearts and souls into, well, then—well, I intend to get to the bottom of it. And it appears that Ethan Allday is my only avenue for doing so."

"Yes, your honor," Murphy said, shaking his head. "You misunderstood me. I was not questioning your fairness at all. I might even add that I did discuss recusal with my client, and he insisted that we not raise any issue about that. He's convinced you'll be completely fair."

"*We* certainly don't have any problems with your presiding in this trial, your honor," Peters said.

"Well, that ends that," Murphy said. "I'll take up everything again with my client."

"OK, gentlemen, that's that." Beagle waved his hands, palms up. "If we can't get this thing settled, we'll plan to proceed to trial in September. If it must go to trial, please be ready. I want no delays."

❧ ❧ ❧

Jeremiah had arrived at Tara's apartment unannounced. He was unshaven and wore a loose-fitting, wrinkled shirt, stains on the collar. His failure to call ahead meant he was foolishly taking a chance on Alex being there, but it turned out she was alone. He had to see her. They had to talk.

"Jeremiah," she said, as she opened the door. "What's happened? Michelle said that she was telling everyone at the office that you are on a business trip, but three weeks? You've been out three weeks!"

"I'm holding together," he said, giving her a perfunctory hug. "But I've had to get away from everything and everybody to do some thinking. Things are a mess at home, Tara. Someone took pictures of us on the San Francisco trip and sent them to Sarah. She's demanding a divorce."

"Oh my God! Jeremiah, who would do such a thing?"

"I have no idea. Some anonymous asshole I guess, or someone just mean as hell. Whoever it was doesn't matter."

"What will you do? What about your children? Have they learned about this?"

"I don't know if Sarah's told them or not. This all happened about three weeks ago, a few days after our trip, and I've been living at a motel since then. Several times I've come within an inch of showing up here to see you, and I did call you once but Alex answered. I hung up."

"Will you consent to the divorce?"

"I don't know what to do, I swear I don't! When we returned from San Francisco, I felt like I could have given up anything to be with you. You have no idea how wonderful those days were for me. And if this picture thing hadn't happened, I don't know how I'd feel right now. But it has happened, and I've spent a lot of time thinking about the realities we face."

"What realities?"

"The main thing is that you're twenty-seven and I'm thirty-two years older. No matter how much passion we feel for each other, the fact is that when I'm seventy, you'll still be a vibrant, young woman. Aging has already taken its toll on me. I've tried to deny it—casting off notions about getting old like an uncomfortable pair of pants, but it just won't work. I guess I'm saying that being with me is not a future you want or need, and probably the same goes for me."

"Jeremiah, I hate to say it, but I'm not sure we've ever been on the same wave-length. I never wanted or intended a long-term relationship. You don't have to persuade me that we can't have a future together, and perhaps you're not really trying. Maybe you're just trying to convince yourself."

"That may be so, Tara. Maybe I was foolish to think about making this thing last. No, not *maybe*, I *was* foolish, I can see that now." His lips trembled as he spoke. "I've got to find a way to redeem myself with Sarah, but I don't think I can. I've hurt her too deeply. I'm afraid the scars are permanent."

"They may be," Tara said. "Most scars are, but that doesn't mean healing can't take place. And you're a wonderful, decent man, Jeremiah, full of love and kindness. I guess I'm beginning to feel guilty for my role in this affair. I should have just stuck with Alex. He's the kind of man who can play these games without hurting himself and he doesn't care if he hurts other people. They expect it of him. I guess that's his strength: he never makes apologies, no matter what he has to do. He sees an objective and goes after it. It's his nature. Maybe we should all be like him."

"Maybe so," Jeremiah said, a tear streaming down his cheek. "Sometimes I think my life would be easier if I were more like him. But damnit, I'm not!" He sighed deeply and gave her one last glance as he walked out the door.

CHAPTER 20

Friendly Persuasion

"Hello darkness my old friend
I've come to talk to you again."
Paul Simon, "The Sound of
Silence"

Eddie Cochran was well suited to his work. A burly brute of a man over six and a half feet tall, he had been a Navy Seal in the early Eighties before he was dishonorably discharged after beating an officer into a catatonic state one night at a dance hall in Tampa. After spending several years bartending in beachfront clubs in Pensacola and Panama City, he had arrived in Atlanta in 1989 to work as a bouncer in the Naughty Lady, one of Cobb County's upscale nude clubs. In spite of his violent past, evidenced by a scar that extended three inches down the right side of his face, he had a fair amount of charm, some personality, and enough intelligence to muster the polish required to deal with the high-brow executives who frequented the club. For the most part, the women who danced there were drop-dead gorgeous, and routinely made away each night with five-hundred to one-thousand dollars. The Naughty Lady was for high rollers, and Eddie Cochran was perfect as the guardian of the gate.

Alex Rumpkin had met Eddie Cochran at the club. In late September of 1989, Alex had come into town for a meeting of the American Healthcare Association's board of governors. Most board members, in Alex's view, were stuffed shirts; an inordinate amount of his will-power and diplomacy were required even to be civil to them, but one member was an exception: the chairman of the group was a doctor from St. Louis who was the kind of party animal Alex liked. They had gone drinking together many times after board meetings around the country, and the doctor's taste for women was the same as Alex's. The two men had a natural affinity for each other, with the money and aptitude for carousing all night and the discretion not to talk about it afterwards.

On the night he met Eddie Cochran, Alex and his drinking friend had gone to a lounge across from the hotel after they adjourned the board meeting, making prearranged excuses to leave the other members. After two drinks, Alex suggested that they visit the Naughty Lady. He was no stranger to the nude dance club, but he had never before encountered the bouncer. As they walked through a turnstile, Eddie rose up to block their path, greeting them with his immense torso and a broad smile: "Good evening, Gentlemen," he said with a coarse, raspy, high-pitched voice—a particularly incongruous sound from such a mammoth body. "Welcome to the Naughty Lady. We want you fellows to have a good time but just remember our 'touch and go' policy: you touch one of the ladies and you go!"

It was a line he had used with many customers, but Alex had not been amused. Extending his hand, he looked coldly into the bouncer's eyes and said: "My name's Alex Rumpkin. Don't believe I've met you."

"Eddie Cochran, Mr. Rumpkin. I just started workin' here, but I've heard your name. You're a regular, aren't you?"

"I suspect most everyone here would say that. Maybe it would be a good idea to find out who you're talking to before you start announcing club 'policies.'"

With a smirk on his face, Alex had shaken the bouncer's hand, pressing a twenty dollar bill into his palm. "Well, thanks very much," Eddie had responded, raising his eyebrows, "you just let me know if you need anything, Mr. Rumpkin. *Anything* at all!"

During the next two years, Alex had never again heard the bouncer mention any of the club's rules—nothing about the "touch and go" policy or any other club regulation. The relationship between the two men grew stronger as the denominations of the bills Alex gave Eddie grew larger—from twenties to fifties to hundreds. They usually exchanged jokes when Alex arrived at the club, and Eddie would then escort Alex to his favorite private room. Eddie selected the girls he knew Alex would prefer, always briefing them beforehand about Alex's status, his tastes and dislikes.

In early 1992 the director of corporate security for MedAmerica had a long conference with Alex about the need for a bodyguard. Alex had received anonymous telephone calls and unsigned letters threatening him and his family. The situation had become critical about a year after the Panacea takeover. At first, Alex had resisted any suggestion that he needed a full-time bodyguard. In spite of all the turmoil in the company—the furloughs, the firings—he felt that he was still warmly regarded in Shrewsbury Crossing and appreciated for taking the bold steps he had taken to hold the company together as much as he had. Moreover, there were many inside and outside the organization that constantly flattered him, congratulating him for his wise leadership, and assuring him that they supported him fully.

The turning point had come with the delivery of a small, innocuous-looking package to his office. Although addressed to Alex and marked personal and confidential, a mail clerk had opened it, losing both arms in the explosion.

So Alex had hired a bodyguard in December of 1992, and Eddie Cochran had been the choice.

On this August afternoon in 1996, Eddie sat nervously at the gate waiting the arrival of the flight carrying Judge Beagle Williams and his wife, Talisha. It was an important assignment. Alex had stressed that Eddie was not to be late for the arrival of the airplane under any circumstances and that every courtesy was to be extended to the judge and his wife.

Jeremiah fidgeted with the paperweight on his desk—a glass piece with the scales of justice engraved on top—as Ben Ansley read from the letter from Sarah's lawyer.

"This beats everything," Ben said. "The bastard thinks he can wipe you out just because he's got a couple of snapshots of you and your cutie in San Francisco. By the way, I'm *really* sorry we had to get Tara out of the firm. I had an eye for her myself."

"This is pretty painful for me, Ben," Jeremiah said. "Just tell me what Sarah wants."

"I can sum it up with one word: *everything*. They want your fucking soul, Jeremiah."

"What does the letter say, Ben?"

"Well, first off, they want the house on the river, *mortgage free*. Then they want the mountain home, along with the Mercedes, the Coca Cola and Georgia-Pacific stock, and one-half of all other assets—the CD's, the mutual funds, the bonds, the pension fund, everything."

Jeremiah looked at his colleague calmly, deliberately, then said: "Give it to them."

"What did you say?" Ansley asked.

"I said, give them what they want."

"You must be nuts, Jeremiah." Ansley rose from his chair and paced the room. "There's not a jury in this state that'll treat you this badly. Let them blow up the damn pictures life-size, if they want. We'll trot out testimony that'll show Sarah is no saint."

"I don't want to get into that kind of pissing contest," Jeremiah said.

"Well, we may have to," Ansley replied. "I'll discuss this with some of our people that specialize in this domestic relations shit, but I know we'll recommend that you tell your wife's lawyer to go to hell until he can come back with something we can negotiate. Otherwise, we tell them to get ready for World War III."

"Maybe you didn't understand me, Ben, I said give them what they want. Can't you prepare a short letter doing that, or do you want me to do it?" Jeremiah snapped, his voice breaking. He turned his head abruptly to the right to hide the mistiness of his eyes. After a moment of silence, Ansley walked behind the desk and placed a hand on Jeremiah's shoulder.

"Look, Jeremiah, I'm sorry. I know you're upset. This is probably not a good time to try to deal with this. I've never been in this situation, been lucky, I guess. But I have to tell you this. If you don't resist these ludicrous demands, you'll have to get someone else to handle this thing. Allowing you to give everything you have to this woman would be tantamount to malpractice, in my opinion, and I just can't do it."

"You don't have to represent me, Ben. I'll find someone else—or do it myself. Don't worry about it. I don't want to make you uncomfortable."

"Tell you what," Ben said. "Let's just talk about this later." He started to leave the room but turned at the door. Walking back to the desk, he tossed the letter down before Jeremiah. "Here," he said, "you can mull this over if you're inclined to. I have a copy."

As Ben Ansley closed the door behind him, Jeremiah stood and walked over to the couch where he and Tara had first made love. The scene was blurred in his memory—perhaps a fantasy that never happened. It took only an instant to realize that it was not a dream: it was cold reality, an undeniable part of his past, a brief interlude that had rocked the foundations of his life. And today, if he could, he would erase it all, wipe it away. "But, as they say," he mumbled aloud, "even the Almighty cannot change history."

* * *

The Atlantic Southeast flight had only six passengers, so Eddie Cochran had no trouble spotting Judge Beagle Williams and his wife as they walked off the jetway into the gate area.

"Judge Williams, Mrs. Williams," Eddie called out in his raspy voice, almost wheezing, simultaneously reaching for the two carry-on bags they held. "I'm Eddie Cochran, Mr. Rumpkin's personal aid and chauffeur. He's asked me to express his deep apology that he couldn't meet you himself, but he had a late afternoon business meeting."

Beagle and Talisha chatted with each other as they walked down the long concourse, Eddie Cochran leading the way a few feet ahead. After retrieving a checked bag in the main terminal, Eddie asked his guests to wait just inside the terminal door while he picked up the limousine. The car was parked illegally just off the main ramp, and was being watched by an Atlanta policeman to whom Eddie had given ten dollars for overlooking the infraction.

Within minutes, he returned to the terminal. Opening the limousine's rear door, he invited Beagle and Talisha to board. "And, what'll you have on the way into town?" he asked. "We have some very good cabernet or perhaps some liqueur? Any kind of mixed drink or beer, of course."

"I think we'll pass for now, thank you," Beagle said. "I'm sure there'll be other opportunities this evening."

Alex had planned this weekend since the day he was informed of Ethan's indictment. He had called Beagle several times, providing a number of open dates when he and Annie would be in town. The pitch was that Beagle and his wife would come to Atlanta for an evening on the town, a chance to renew old acquaintances and to relax away from the prying eyes of Shrewsbury Crossing. It would be a low-key, quiet weekend, Alex had promised.

Beagle kept putting off accepting the invitation. Without saying so to Alex, he had serious reservations about the propriety of the trip. He was a federal district judge presiding over the trial of the chief financial officer of the company Alex headed. How would it look, he wondered, if the press picked up the story? But as Alex's calls continued to come, Beagle became increasingly intrigued about the prospects of the visit. There would be something deeply satisfying, he felt, to be squired around Atlanta by a corporate titan who had been his nemesis as a boy. Besides, he told himself, the U.S. attorneys had never suggested that Alex was implicated in any of the transactions, and Ethan had testified before the Grand Jury that he could not recall that Alex was in any way involved with the transactions in question. Beagle was convinced Ethan knew more than he was admitting, but it seemed beyond belief that Alex would endanger his position and wealth as head of this major corporation with shenanigans this serious.

On the other hand, Beagle had reasoned, he and Alex had been childhood friends, even though there had been unsavory encounters. And beyond everything else, Beagle really admired the way Alex had lifted himself by his own bootstraps; in that respect, he felt, they had much in common. Their paths had crossed many times over the years. After Beagle returned to Shrewsbury Crossing as a judge, he was soon welcomed into the upper strata of the town's society. Even though he was the only black member of Crestview Heights Country Club, he had never considered himself a token or an Uncle Tom. He figured that he had paid his dues and entered the white world on his own terms, with his independence as a member of the federal judiciary reinforcing his belief that he owed nothing to anyone. He rationalized that he had worked hard, educated himself, and broken the racial mold that the community tried to force on him as a boy. Thus, he had the option of being a gracious participant in the life of the community that now, after all these years, welcomed him. And he and Talisha had worked hard to support various civic, artistic and charitable projects in Shrewsbury Crossing. Beagle was sure he was helping other blacks with his prestige and status in the social establishment: the more he enjoyed the fruits of his efforts, boldly and publicly, the more his life would inspire other blacks to enter the mainstream.

So finally, he had accepted Alex's invitation, and this evening found him and his wife riding in Alex's chauffeur-driven limousine through downtown Atlanta on the interstate toward Buckhead. It had been several years since Beagle had spent the night in the city. He had, of course, passed through the Atlanta airport many times on his way to other destinations, and he had attended numerous judicial conferences and one-day legal seminars in Atlanta; but his busy calendar had always made these trips hurried affairs which did not permit overnight visits. Beagle had come to love Atlanta during his college years; and even though the city had changed drastically since the early fifties, Beagle knew that Atlanta had always been hospitable for blacks—another reason Beagle finally accepted Alex's invitation for the weekend trip.

Their downtown route took them by the new stadium where the Centennial Summer Olympics had just been held. They rode past the State Capitol with its gold-plated dome glimmering in floodlights, past the massive Grady Memorial Hospital, and the soaring Atlanta skyscrapers: the granite covered Georgia-Pacific Building and the Peachtree Plaza hotel. Then they traveled north on the interstate toward Buckhead, passing Midtown riddled with new apartments and office highrises on their right—the imposing building where Jeremiah worked and a trinity of condominium complexes jutting dozens of stories into space.

Just before they took the 14th Street ramp off the interstate, Beagle saw the Varsity on the right. He reached over and squeezed Talisha's hand. "You know, sweetheart," he said, "there is no telling how many chili dogs and onion rings I ate there during those years at Morehouse. The place is world-famous," he continued, almost like a tour guide. "Presidents, governors, most any celebrity who comes to Atlanta—they all know the Varsity is a mandatory stop. But its really important contribution is that its low-cost calories and saturated fat literally sustained hundreds of thousands of students like me over the years—Morehouse, Emory, Georgia Tech, Agnes Scott, Georgia State, none of those schools would be here without the Varsity."

Talisha laughed, and said: "You speak of that place like it's some kind of shrine."

Beagle nodded and grinned: "Yes, I guess it is. I might even ask the driver to pull in for a chili dog, but Alex has told me that we should arrive with hearty appetites so we can enjoy what he called 'a spectacular dining experience.'"

As the limousine wound its way up Peachtree Street, Eddie Cochran opened the window separating him and his passengers and pointed out Alex's highrise in the distance. "Elton John has one of the penthouse suites near Mr. Rumpkin's," Eddie said, turning to face the couple. "I see him going in and out a lot when I'm escorting Mr. Rumpkin or his wife."

"Is that so?" Beagle asked. "I knew he had a home in the Atlanta area, but I didn't know where."

"He sometimes has freaky-looking guys with him. I guess y'all know that he's supposed to be gay, or maybe bi-sexual—or maybe y'all didn't know that." Eddie turned again to face the rear seats. "I hope my sayin' that doesn't offend you.

"Don't mention it," Beagle said. "We've heard those stories."

The elevator to the penthouse suites on the thirtieth floor stopped only two places: there and in the parking garage. Although the parking lot itself had a security guard, a special code was required to operate the penthouse elevator.

Alex and Annie met them at the door. "Beagle, how are you?" Alex said, as he reached to shake Beagle's hand. "And, Talisha, you're beautiful as ever," he added, leaning forward to kiss her cheek. "Don't you agree, Annie? Talisha just keeps getting better looking, don't you think?"

Annie looked worn, haggard, her eyes sunken in patches of dark lines and wrinkles, but she smiled and said, "Of course, Talisha always looks wonderful. And you too, Beagle. I'm so glad you could join us. Alex has been talking about the two of you visiting all week."

Alex took Talisha's arm and ushered her through the foyer and into a richly furnished sitting room. A magnificent fountain threw up a graceful spray, a silhouette of water outlined against the floor-to-ceiling windows revealing the galaxy of lights of the Atlanta skyline. The windows to each side were dressed with ornate, gold and lavender damask, and to the far right was a verdi marble fireplace. Leading Talisha to one of the several wing chairs in the room with an especially good view of the downtown and mid-town area, Alex said: "Here, Talisha, I want you to sit here—best view in the house. And what would you and Beagle like to drink? Annie and I were getting warmed up with a martini."

"A glass of chardonnay for me, thank you," Talisha said.

"A martini sounds fine," Beagle said. As Alex moved to the bar, Beagle added, "Alex, I can't begin to tell you and Annie how much Talisha and I appreciate…."

"Don't mention it," Alex interrupted. "I've been wanting to get you up here for weeks, you know that. If friends can't get together like this occasionally, what's life all about?"

"I certainly agree," Beagle said, "but I know what an effort you must have made to work us into your schedule. I can only imagine what a strenuous pace you keep."

"Same for you," Alex said, "and, by the way, I've told you before and I want to say it again, I'm damn proud of you and all you've accomplished. In fact, let's make that a toast: here's to Judge Beagle Williams and his beautiful wife, Talisha."

"Thanks very much," Beagle said, taking the first sip from the cocktail, "but let's not get maudlin here. Besides, I was lucky in a lot of ways. If Doc Willie hadn't been the kind of man he was, you know, taking an interest in me because of my grandma and paying for my tutoring and college, I would probably have wound up cutting pulpwood and drinking up my pay on Saturday nights." Nodding toward Annie, he said: "Annie, there could never be words to let you know how much I appreciated your father. I owe him everything."

"That's nice of you to say," Annie said, "but you deserve the credit for making the most of chances that came your way."

"Well, I'll always credit Doc Willie for making my life better, and I guess we have that in common, Alex. Doc Willie did a lot for you too, didn't he?"

"I don't mean any disrespect for my departed father-in-law, but I'm not sure he did me any favors getting me tied up with all the government interference and red tape that goes with operating a medical care company. Also, and you'll know what I mean by this, Annie, but most people don't appreciate what I did for MedAmerica long before the doctor died. I mean, that corporation would have remained a little back-woods operation if I hadn't come along."

"Well, my recollection is that MedAmerica was very profitable during the years we were growing up, and it was certainly robust in the late Fifties about the time you returned from Tech. It had become the leading health care company in America when Doc Willie died. Everyone knows how he put Shrewsbury Crossing on the medical map."

"That's just a myth, Beagle." Alex furrowed his brows. "By the time he died, Dr. Willingham had allowed the company to stagnate, no modern technology, computers, run-down facilities. People don't realize how bad things were."

Annie cleared her throat and said: "Look, let's not spend the evening debating about MedAmerica's past or future. I'd like to get away from that subject for a while."

Beagle stood and walked toward a painting on an easel to the right of the fireplace. He turned to Annie and said, "I've been admiring this painting. A Renoir, isn't it?"

"I hope like hell it is," Alex bellowed. "Annie paid over a half million bucks for the damn thing, and I don't particularly like it."

"How you talk, Alex!" Annie sounded exasperated. "He's just sounding off, Beagle, I think he really likes it."

"Well, *I* certainly like it," Beagle said. "I would guess that's a portrait of one of Charpentier's children, you know, the aristocrat who commissioned Renoir to paint his family members."

"Now, don't that beat all!" Alex said. "Listen to the boy talk. You take a black kid from south Georgia, send him off to college, and he comes back talkin' all this cultured shit!"

Beagle smiled, glaring directly into Alex's eyes. Talisha laughed nervously.

"It sorta' reminds me of that Sidney Poitier movie," Alex went on, "you know, where he was a Philadelphia detective—a smart-ass lordin' it over a Mississippi sheriff. 'Heat of the Night' wasn't it? Something like that."

"Well, maybe that's what I am," Beagle said, "a smart-ass. Is that what you're saying, Alex? You know, Alex, it's good to see that success and power haven't spoiled your capacity to be uncouth and proud of it. It's reassuring that there are some constants in the world."

"Come on, Beagle, I was just kiddin'," Alex grinned, jabbing him on the shoulder. "Let's get out of here, I'm hungry."

❧ ❧ ❧

Jeremiah returned to his hotel room shortly after eight o'clock. The telephone was ringing.

"Jeremiah, this is Ethan. I've been trying to reach you."

"Ethan, what's going on?" Jeremiah said. "Gosh, it's good to hear from you. How'd you get this number?"

"Sarah gave it to me. She said you and she are temporarily separated."

"Did she say 'temporarily'?" Jeremiah asked.

"I believe so. I think she said it that way, but I can't be sure. My mind's in a fog right now."

"Yeah. Mine too. I've heard about your troubles. I started to call you several times, but was afraid you'd think I was meddling, and that..."

"Well, I've been wanting to talk to you too, but my lawyer's been insisting that I talk to no one."

"Who's your lawyer?" Jeremiah asked.

"Randy Murphy."

"Heck, he's one of the best. A ruthless guy, but that's the kind you need when you're facing criminal charges. And I think he's right, Ethan, you probably shouldn't be talking with anyone right now—probably not even me."

"Yeah, I know, and I've followed his advice so far, but now—shit, Jeremiah—now this thing's so out-of-control I have no choice. I need your help."

"What can I do, Ethan? You know I've never handled a criminal case, and I wouldn't think you'd want me getting my education with your freedom at stake."

"It's not your legal expertise I need, Jeremiah. I'm asking you to talk to Beagle."

"Beagle's the assigned judge, isn't he, Ethan."

"Yeah, and he seems determined to nail my butt to the jailhouse wall."

"I can't believe that. He's always been fair, even though some of the good-old-boy lawyers down there don't like him."

"We've tried to plea-bargain, Jeremiah, but he just won't allow it. He says I'm holding back. Won't tell what I know."

"How does the U.S. attorney feel?" Jeremiah asked.

"I'm beginning to think he doesn't really give a damn. There are a couple of big murder cases he's working on, and my lawyer says he thinks the D.A. would go along with a plea if the judge would back off."

"What are you offering?"

"Randall says we can work out something like pleading guilty to one count, a twenty thousand dollar fine, and maybe two years of community service," Ethan said.

"Sounds stiff enough to me, but you think Beagle won't go along?"

"No, he says I've got to name names. He's convinced there were things going on at MedAmerica besides sloppy record-keeping on my part...."

"Were there?"

"I'm not sure, Jeremiah, honest to God, I'm not sure. The best I can recall, Alex didn't have any direct involvement, but I kept telling him that I was worried about how much money the Washington office was spending. He kept saying, 'Look, Ethan, Youngblood knows the law and he's not going to do anything to get us in trouble.' And I would say, 'But, Alex, he's asking for hundreds of thousands of dollars, supposedly to refurbish his suite of offices. That's damn high, I would say, even by Washington standards.'"

"So, did you ever ask Youngblood for details—estimates from contractors, invoices, you know?"

"Yes, yes, I did, and he would always promise that they'd be coming soon, but I never got them."

"Where do you think the money went?"

"I'm just not sure," Ethan said. "But I have suspicions."

"Like?"

"Well, the checks were all issued in late summer, early fall of 1990, just when we were trying to get approval of the Panacea deal. Remember, you predicted at the time there'd be objections from Justice and the FTC, and we initially heard rumblings but then nothing happened. Like the waters parted—you know, all the opposition seemed to disappear overnight. I have to think somebody got paid off."

"Well, why don't you just say all that? Youngblood has disappeared, right? So what can anyone do to you if you just say what you suspect?"

"I'm not worried about anyone doing anything in retaliation, Jeremiah. I'm just bothered by speculating about things I really don't know. What if Youngblood took the money and is spending it big time these days in Argentina or some place? And even though I want to kill the son-of-a-bitch on occasion, I don't want to harm Alex, and that might happen if I start speculating about the Panacea deal. My conscience won't allow me to get someone else in trouble, particularly when I'm just guessing."

"So what do you want me to say to Beagle?"

"Ask him to accept the plea-bargain. I'll resign from MedAmerica, take my retirement early, and we can put this whole thing to rest."

"Ethan, approaching a federal judge on this could get me in trouble, especially since I'm not your lawyer. Attempting this kind of influence, or whatever it would be called, is something you don't fool around with. Besides, I doubt it would change things with Beagle."

"I think it might, Jeremiah. Beagle's always thought the world of you. Used to stand up to Alex for you when we were boys. I'm desperate. If something doesn't change Beagle's thinking, I'm afraid I'll go to jail."

"Let me think this over, Ethan. You know, I'm sorta' in a daze myself. Sarah and I may not make it. I spent this afternoon going over a list of property settlement demands her lawyer has given us. And it's not just the financial stuff; ending our marriage seems like the end of everything to me."

"I can imagine what you're going through, and I hated like hell to bother you. But, like I said, I'm desperate." Ethan's voice broke. "Whoever thought life could turn out like this for either of us, Jeremiah, who would have thought?"

"You can't ever tell how life will turn out, can you, Ethan? You just can't ever tell."

The Williams were treated to a glorious evening on the town. After leaving Alex's penthouse, they dined at Hedgerose Heights Inn in Buckhead. In a loud voice, Alex had pretentiously pointed out what he considered the best items on the menu to Talisha and Beagle, and Annie had squirmed uncomfortably while he pounced on his guests to order the skewered buffalo meat as an appetizer. "Try it!" Alex had insisted. "Out of this world. They marinate it in some kind of shit before they cook it." Alex's language had become increasingly coarse with each drink. He stood clumsily and announced that he was going to the men's room.

After Alex departed, Annie said: "I hope Alex's profanity is not offending you, dear." Annie patted Talisha's hand. "He gets this way when he's drinking."

"Not really," Talisha said. "Beagle warned me about Alex and his language—that's it's just part of his personality. I know he doesn't intend to upset people. What raises my curiosity, though, is what he's like when he meets with his board of directors, or addresses dignitaries at the big medical conventions. I read where he makes speeches to groups like that all the time."

"You would not recognize him," Annie said. "I've attended those conventions with him, and he never fails to amaze me: his language is perfect and he makes quite an impression. Of course, he has had years of tutoring and taken workshops on public speaking. In fact, when he's before a large audience, he shows few traces of his Georgia accent. I frequently sit and wonder: 'Can this really be the man I'm married to?'"

Dinner was followed by a visit to a blues club on the lower southside and late night cappuccino at the Intermezzo on Peachtree Street. At every stop, the doormen, the maitre'd's, the waiters, the entertainers all knew Alex on sight.

It was almost 1:30 a.m. when the two couples returned to Alex's penthouse. The two women went immediately to bed, but Alex persuaded Beagle to have a nightcap. The men sat facing each other in the sitting room, the lights of Atlanta twinkling in the distance.

"How's this thing with Ethan coming?" Alex slurred his words.

"You mean the criminal charges? I really can't talk about that," Beagle shifted nervously in his chair.

"Why the hell not? Ain't I a close friend?"

"Being a friend has nothing to do with it, Alex. It's just that this is a pending criminal case, and as the judge, I'm not permitted to discuss it—not with anyone. It's a matter of propriety and ethics."

"Fuck ethics," Alex said, raising his voice, "Beagle, you've known Ethan since he was a boy—fact is, we were boys together, and you know he ain't never had a criminal thought in his life. But you got him scared shitless that you're gonna put him in jail."

"Alex, I said I can't discuss this case with you. But it's not just Ethan—there may be others involved."

"Involved in what?"

"Well, the charges stem from transfers of large amounts of money from MedAmerica for purposes Ethan can't—or won't—explain."

"What the hell do you think? Ethan's been stealing? For God's sake, you know him better than that."

"Alex, I really don't know what to think about this—that's not my job. But the prosecutor says he thinks Ethan's holding back, not telling all. He thinks the money could have gone to a Washington lobbyist, or perhaps someone in a government agency, but who knows? Besides, it's not up to me entirely. I just can't accept a plea involving minor penalties when there may have been others involved—you know, other major felonies committed like bribery."

"Bull-shit!" Alex leaned toward Beagle, shaking his finger in Beagle's face. "You're just riding a fuckin' high horse, tryin' to show how powerful you've become. A little prick-head in a black robe trying to get back at all the white folks. Ain't that right?"

Beagle furrowed his brow and hesitated before speaking. "Look, Alex, I realize you're drunk and you're letting alcohol talk for you, but you've said enough." Beagle stood up, and turned to leave the room.

"What you gonna' do?" Alexs followed him to the bedroom door where Talisha was sleeping. "You gonna hold me in contempt, your honor? Is that what the darky judge is gonna do?"

"Tell you what, I'm going to bed, Alex. I'll try to forget this conversation. I shouldn't have allowed you to open this discussion. In fact, I shouldn't even be here. Talisha and I will be leaving first thing in the morning. Don't worry about seeing us off. I'll get a taxi, so you can sleep it off in the morning."

"Pissed you off good, didn't I?" Alex laughed loudly. "Just like I did when you got smart with me growing up. I don't care how much you strut around thinkin' you're somebody—lordin' it over everyone in South Georgia. You know something? You ain't shit to me!"

"That's right. I think I've always known that, but I've avoided admitting it even to myself. The deep divisions between us just don't change, do they? All these years, I knew you thought I was dirt under your feet, and you've never let me forget it. I know I don't mean shit to you, but here's the shocker: you don't mean shit to me either. There's no love lost between us, right?"

Alex opened his mouth to speak again, but Beagle turned abruptly and walked away. As he entered the bedroom where Talisha lay sleeping, a tear ran down his cheek. He closed the massive door, turning the deadbolt behind him.

CHAPTER 21

A Wild Duck

"Always do that, wild ducks do. Go
plunging right to the bottom…as deep
as they can get…hold on with their
beaks to the weeds and stuff—and all
the other mess you find down there.
Then they never come up again."
Henrik Ibsen, *The Wild Ducks*

The telephone rang, instantly bringing a scowl to the face of Judge Beagle Williams, sitting alone in his chambers at seven twenty in the morning. Avoiding the phone and other interruptions had been his impetus for getting up at four thirty and reaching his desk shortly after five. He had been pouring over briefs and pleadings for the busy day of motion hearings awaiting him. The cases would be called, starting at nine, and he didn't think he would have time for breakfast. Now, the telephone was ringing, probably one of his clerks with some foolish question, and he was tempted to let it ring. But he picked up the receiver.

"Judge Williams here," he grumbled.

"Beagle," the caller said, "Sorry to bother you—hated to call this early. Talisha said you went to the courthouse before dawn. Oh, by the way, this is Jeremiah."

"It's a good thing you identified yourself, Jeremiah; I was about to slam the phone down. I have a hellacious day ahead, but you're probably the only human being I'm actually glad to hear from."

"It's been a long time," Jeremiah said. "We need to see each other more often."

"Couldn't agree with you more, but I know something's up. You didn't just wake up this morning missing old Beagle. Besides," he said, chuckling, "Atlanta lawyers, I'm told, seldom get out of bed before nine—much less do anything else before then."

"A famous jurist of your standing shouldn't generalize," Jeremiah joked, "but I admit, there are a few kernels of truth in what you've heard." Jeremiah paused. "Beagle, the thing is, I'm not sure I should be making this call, but I feel I have to do it."

"You sound too serious, Jeremiah." Beagle held his hand over the mouthpiece while he cleared his throat. "What's up? Are you OK? I heard you and Sarah were having problems."

"Well, yes, we are, but I've convinced her to try to reconcile. I'm back at home, separate bedrooms and all that, but we're seeing a counselor and trying to work things out. Some progress, I guess, but that's not why I'm calling."

"What then?"

"This trial next week for Ethan—it's tearing him apart, you must be aware of that. He's talked to me about the situation. He begged me to call you."

"Are you his lawyer?"

"No, I'm not calling in that role. It's purely friendship—you know, personal concern for his welfare—that kind of thing. He thinks that since you and I go so far back, maybe I can help you see what a mess he's in—how it's eating away at him."

"Jeremiah," Beagle said, "you know the rules. I shouldn't be talking about this with you."

Ignoring the statement, Jeremiah continued. "What he wants, Beagle, is that you reconsider accepting the plea. He says you're insisting he testify about stuff he doesn't know anything about."

"It's not just me, Jeremiah, the prosecutor also thinks he's holding out. You know what a rigid sense of honor and loyalty Ethan has—. Only God knows why he won't talk but he won't. We think he's protecting someone at MedAmerica, or perhaps someone else. I don't think Ethan took money himself—the IRS did a net worth on him and couldn't find any traces—but it doesn't square with what we know to believe that Youngblood took all this money and vanished. And it was a *lot* of money."

"What would it have been used for?" Jeremiah asked.

"I don't know, obviously, but it could have related to bribes on that Panacea deal—money for government contracts or perhaps administrative approvals of one kind or another. That's why we've got to get Ethan to tell what he knows."

"Ethan says they've offered a guilty plea on one count, some kind of probation with community service and a twenty thousand dollar fine. Seems to me that's a pretty stiff penalty for a first offense, and where you yourself say there's no evidence that Ethan himself took money—."

"It's not the penalty, Jeremiah, I have no problems with that. It's the refusal to talk. We just don't think he's opening up."

"He says he's telling all he knows."

"I don't think he is."

"Who do you think he's covering for?" Jeremiah asked.

"I think—" Beagle hesitated. "I think it could be other higher-ups at MedAmerica—even Alex."

"Alex! My God, Beagle, do you really think Alex would do something that stupid? Why on earth would *he* risk all he's got to do something that dumb—and illegal?" Jeremiah asked. "He certainly doesn't need money. I know he's no angel, but he's not an idiot."

"I don't know," Beagle said, "maybe it's not Alex, but I've got reason to believe he could have been involved."

"How's that?"

"Well, a few weeks back, he invited Talisha and me to Atlanta for a social weekend. I was hesitant about going, kept putting him off, but we finally went. The evening started out pleasantly enough, but he got dog drunk before the night was over. Started putting pressure on me to take a plea and get rid of the case. When I told him to shut up, that I couldn't discuss the case, he got really nasty—called me names, you know, the 'n' word like he did when we were boys and he couldn't get the best of me any other way. He turned into a mean-natured son-of-a-bitch, if you want to know the truth, Jeremiah. He tried to apologize the next morning, kept saying he had gotten out of line and was ashamed of himself, but it all made me think that he's trying to hide something and he's worried that Ethan's going to give something away."

"Well, hell, just let the D.A. subpoena Alex, get him before a grand jury and see what he knows, but you don't have to hold Ethan's feet to the fire."

"You'll just have to let me handle this, Jeremiah. I don't relish my job here, you know, presiding over this case. I even thought of recusing myself, but I wouldn't have any caseload at all if I dropped everything that comes before me just because I know the parties. Having grown up in Shrewsbury Crossing and all. Hell, you know that."

"I'm not suggesting you drop this case, and I know you're trying to be fair, but have you considered that you may be going harder on Ethan just because you *do* know him—you see what I mean?"

"Jeremiah, I'm going to forget you said that. Keep your head! You're losing your perspective trying to get Ethan out of this." Beagle's voice was angry. "Don't forget, damnit, I'm a federal district judge."

"I apologize, Beagle, you're right," Jeremiah said, realizing he had struck a nerve. "I shouldn't have said that. You know I think the world of you—your integrity, but I felt that this was a call I had to make. Please don't think I'm questioning your ethics."

"Enough said, let's just drop this subject now," Beagle said. "We'll see how this thing plays out. The trial starts Tuesday—after Labor Day—so maybe something will break over the weekend. Maybe the U.S. attorney will have a change of heart. We'll see."

"Well, I certainly hope so. I know you've got a lot on your plate. Thanks for talking with me. And give my best to Talisha."

"I will," Beagle said, "and I really hope everything works out for you and Sarah. You are a wonderful person, and I probably shouldn't talk this way, but you know, Jeremiah, I've always thought of you as a brother. You were an unusual friend when we were growing up. You treated me like a human being when I couldn't use the same water fountain as you and couldn't eat a meal at the Dixie Cafe. Don't think that I'll ever forget that. I won't."

"Now, you're getting maudlin," Jeremiah said, his voice breaking. "You take care of yourself, Judge Williams."

The afternoon wore on interminably. Alex had met with Ethan that morning, joining him in a conference call with Jeremiah, who had reported his failure to win Beagle over to a plea bargain. Afterwards, at Alex's insistence, Ethan had authorized his lawyer to make a last-ditch offer of forty thousand for the fine, five years' probation, and three months of actual jail time.

Ethan was now hearing the bad news from Randall Murphy. Late that afternoon, the prosecutor had turned them down, passing the buck to the judge, saying that Beagle was adamant about requiring a pledge of unequivocal cooperation from Ethan.

"What can we do, Randy?" Ethan asked. "My cousin, Jeremiah Goodwin, spoke with Beagle early this morning by telephone, and says he got nowhere. Says Beagle is convinced that I'm covering for someone."

"There's nothing we can do but prepare for trial," Murphy said. "Don't worry too much. These things have a way of working out. We can always sweeten our offer, but I'm inclined to just stand pat now. I want to see the jury pool and get into *voir dire* before I assess where we stand. You've got a sterling reputation in this area, Ethan, and I think we can get a sympathetic panel."

"Yeah, but what if Beagle's out to screw me?" Ethan asked. "How're you going to overcome that?"

"Well, he's got to worry about an appeal. Besides, I kinda think he's bluffing with this hard line on the plea bargain. When push comes to shove, he'll accept the plea. I think he likes you, Ethan. It's going to work out fine, trust me."

The day had turned out to be every bit as hectic as Beagle had expected: an endless parade of lawyers, mostly white, bickering before him, bowing and kowtowing, saying and doing everything conceivable to curry favor with him. It was past seven in the evening—no breakfast, no lunch, only two Snickers and some skim milk in chambers during the day. He was famished now.

Over the weekend odds and ends would have to be cleaned up before the trial could begin on Tuesday. Thank God, that could wait until Saturday or Sunday, or even Labor Day itself.

Beagle left his chambers at 8:10 that Friday night, the stress of the day weighing heavy, his brain numbed with a biting headache. He stopped at a water cooler and gulped down two extra-strength Tylenol.

Moving like a zombie, he locked his office door and stepped slowly toward the elevator. He mumbled a "good night" to a black janitor vacuuming the hallway. He was a man known to Beagle only as "Uncle Jack," a decent, church-going fellow who had been a fixture around Shrewsbury Crossing since Beagle's childhood. The man must be nearly eighty, Beagle figured, since he himself was sixty-one and Uncle Jack had been a grown man when Beagle knew him as a boy. Ancient, the man's ancient, Beagle thought, and here he is cleaning the floors of a damn building.

Beagle boarded the elevator alone, pushed the "P" button for the parking garage, and watched the doors close. Judges' chambers and the courtrooms were located on the fifth floor of the Federal Administrative Center, itself three blocks away from the massive complex of red-brick buildings comprising the general offices of the MedAmerica Corporation. The Federal Center was a drab, concrete structure built during the Carter Administration, now housing more than six-hundred government employees with such diverse agencies as the FBI, ATF, HUD, DOT, and Agriculture. The facility had been an enormous boost to the Shrewsbury Crossing economy: government paychecks were ubiquitous in local businesses on payday, and civil service employment was second only to the mammoth payroll of MedAmerica. Beagle had been the first federal judge to occupy the fifth floor, having been appointed to the bench to serve the newly created southwestern district of Georgia in 1978.

Beagle's Ford Taurus was parked, cater-cornered, in a spot with a "Reserved for Judge Williams" sign. As he unlocked the car door, Beagle noticed that he had parked with the rear a couple of feet over the line—intruding into another's space. He regretted for an instant that he had been so negligent: having lived most of his life feeling mistreated and misjudged, he had taken special care to avoid infringing on others. But tonight, he felt inclined to excuse himself. After all, he had put in a hell of a day, beginning before dawn, and he was only human. Damn it, he reasoned, he had a lot of pressures on him.

Beagle drove out of the parking garage and turned right onto Broad Street running through the center of town. For the last several years, downtown stores of Shrewsbury Crossing had been resplendently rebuilt; lining the street were quaint boutiques, specialty shops, and delicatessens where the rich doctors, MedAmerica executives, lawyers and their spouses, could buy antique furniture, wedding dresses, and the makings for gourmet cuisine. And now, Beagle told himself, he was one of them. His annual stipend alone—just over $100,000—did not qualify him as one of the wealthy, but the trappings of his life as a judge, holding the power of life and death over the citizens of southwest Georgia, had paved the way for his and Talisha's acceptance into the upper strata of Shrewsbury Crossing society. They now lived in a formerly all-white neighborhood, and were members of the most prestigious country club in the southeast, one founded by Dr. Willingham himself and built to its present elegance by generous endowments from Alex Rumpkin and other leading citizens.

There was little traffic on Broad Street as Beagle turned into the curb at the Dixie Cafe. It was almost closing time as he entered the restaurant where he had worked in his youth. The cafe had been renovated many times since then, and the menu had changed frequently to keep abreast of the times. It now included several vegetarian and pasta dishes, and, of all things, frozen yogurt and sorbet. The cafe was a busy place during weekday lunches—Beagle ate there sometimes with other judges and lawclerks—but few customers frequented the Dixie Cafe this late at night.

One thing had not changed over the years: Christina Rumpkin was still there, even though she now proudly wore a name-tag displaying her title: "Assistant Manager."

"Howdy, Judge," she said, as Beagle sat down on a stool at the counter near a successor to the sink where he had washed many dishes many years before. "We ain't got long before closin' time and the cook's turnin' off the stove, so if you want somethin' to eat, you better order it quick."

"I won't be long," Beagle said, "just a cup of coffee and a BLT. How long you been here, Christina?"

"Since seven o'clock this morning—just like every day—and I'm tired as all get out, Judge."

"No, no, that's not what I meant," Beagle chuckled. "How many years, that's what I intended to ask."

"Oh, since 1948, about the same time you started workin' here. When you was just a puppy, not meaning no pun, Beagle," Christina chuckled, proud of her wit. "But the fact is, I feel like I been here all my life, that's for sure." Christina turned and yelled toward the back: "One BLT for the judge, Lewis!"

"I must say, Chris, you're a fountain of youth," Beagle grinned. "You sound just like you sounded years ago—calling in your orders." But Beagle knew that Christina did not look the same: she was haggard and old, now in her sixties, her face reflecting the brutal history of her life. She had weathered three marriages: two of her husbands had wound up in jail, and one had left town—headed for Colorado, some said—many years earlier with another waitress, leaving Christina with two young children to raise. Withered away to ninety-five pounds, her eyelids sagging so badly they obstructed her vision, Beagle had said that he didn't think she had aged much at all. Some lies are good ones, he thought to himself.

"Well, thanks, Judge," Christina said, "that's nice of you to say. Lemme go see if your sandwich is ready."

The cafe was quiet, only two other customers, when Christina returned to the counter with Beagle's order.

"I've heard you may be runnin' for gov'ner one of these days, any truth in that?" she asked.

"Mere rumors," Beagle took a bite of his sandwich. "You know how people like to speculate."

"Shit, I think you'd *win*—excuse my French," Christina giggled. "They've registered enough blacks in the last two years to make you a shoe-in. Heck, I'd even vote for you, and I always said I wouldn't ever vote for no black."

"My goodness," Beagle said with a note of sarcasm in his voice, "you really have changed your thinking a lot if you'd do *that*. I remember you didn't seem to feel very kindly toward me when we had that sit-in here in '66. Fact is, you seemed about ready to shoot us all when we walked in that day and made such a ruckus that the cafe was shut down for weeks. I think I saw hatred in your eyes. I'm glad I don't see that anymore."

"Let bygones be bygones is my motto," Christina said. "I always figured you warn't doin' nothin' but what them outsiders was tellin' you to. You know how they flooded into town like a bunch of locusts. White women and niggers kissin' in public and havin' sex in the back seats of cars. That stuff was a disgrace, but I never thought you was doin' any of it. Heck, I knew Bootsie would give you a fit if she thought you was engagin' in immoral stuff with a white woman."

"Whatever," Beagle said, ignoring Christina's use of the epithet he hated. "In any case, those stories about me running for governor are premature at best. I have no plans for doing anything other than what I'm doing now. I'm not much of a politician—not sure I have the stomach for it."

Christina left to pour coffee for a customer and returned. Beagle asked, "You see much of Alex any more?"

"Naw, nobody around Shrewsbury Crossing sees him any more. He's too much a big shot now. I see his name in the Atlanta papers where he's talkin' to some bunch of doctors or politicians. Flyin' around in that fancy airplane. Real important, ain't he?"

"It doesn't sound like you've got much use for your brother."

"Shoot, since mama died, I don't reckon he's set foot in my house. Never gives me nothin'—him and all his money. Heck, he spends more on liquor every month than I make in a whole year."

"He's not all bad, Christina. You may not believe it, but he actually invited my wife and me to Atlanta a few weeks back for a weekend. Treated us very nice."

"Musta wanted somethin'. Alex ain't never done nothin' for nobody without expectin' somethin' back. And, no disrespect intended, Beagle, but I'm dead certain he wouldn't be spendin' no time with you and your wife—y'all bein' black and all—unless he needed a favor. I know him backwards and forwards."

"Christina," Beagle said, "I grew up with him too, and he has stuck out his neck for us several times since I returned to Shrewsbury Crossing. I finally accepted his invitation because I honestly thought he just wanted to get together—you know, for old time's sake."

"Hell! I'd bet it was connected to this mess about Ethan Allday and MedAmerica I been readin' in the papers. I bet Alex is nervous as a cat in the rain about that. Ain't you the judge?"

"Yes, I'm presiding over the case, but Alex isn't implicated, and I have no reason to think he will be."

"If it's crooked, I bet Alex had a hand in it."

"I don't think so," Beagle said, "but I don't really know how it'll all come out. I'm sure Alex wants the whole thing to be over. It's a cloud over MedAmerica, you know, but other than getting drunk and mouthing off about a few things, Alex treated us OK in Atlanta. Besides, there's a good chance this thing will be disposed of with a plea bargain next week. Then it'll be a closed case. We all want it that way. I know I do. I've been under lots of pressure with this case, not to mention the rest of my caseload."

Beagle finished his sandwich and all but a swallow of his coffee. Saying goodnight to Christina, he paid his check and left the cafe. He drove to the end of Broad Street and turned left onto the four-lane connecting Shrewbury Crossing to Ludlow and Interstate 75. When he came to the intersection where he usually turned to enter his subdivision, he continued on, quickly passing the Shrewsbury Crossing city limit sign. It was shortly after 10:00 p.m. and Talisha would be expecting him at home by now. He called her from his cellular telephone.

"Beagle, where are you?" she asked. "Do you realize how worried I've been."

"I'm sorry. I should have called earlier," he responded, lowering the volume of his radio. "Listen, Sweetheart, I worked 'til after eight and grabbed a sandwich at the Dixie Cafe. Got into a conversation with Christina—you know, Christina that manages the place—Alex Rumpkin's sister."

"Well, where are you now? On your way home?"

"Yes, I'm calling on the cell phone, but I don't think I'll come home right now."

"Why?"

"Talisha, please try to understand. I'm under tons of pressure—this Allday case, especially. Jeremiah Goodwin called me this morning to ask me to accept a plea and close the case, and maybe I *am* being too tough on Ethan. I'm not sure why I'm convinced he's got to talk. Maybe he really doesn't know anything."

"I know you're worried, Beagle, so come on home and we'll talk about it."

"Please don't take this the wrong way," Beagle said, "but I think I need to get away from everything for a little while, you know, be alone right now. I won't be decent company tonight. If you don't mind, I'm gonna drive over to Ludlow, find a quiet bar and have a few drinks."

"All right, if that's what you think you need to do, but don't drink too much and please come on home soon."

"I'll be home a little later, and don't worry: I know I can't afford a DUI. You know every redneck lawyer in South Georgia would celebrate if I got thrown in jail."

Reaching the outskirts of Ludlow, Beagle stopped at a Magic Market for gas. He paid the attendant and then went into the men's room carrying a large paper bag. Locking the door, he took off the white shirt and suit pants he had worn to the office, donning a light gray knit shirt and a pair of khakis. He washed his face, combed his hair, and splashed his face with Aramis cologne taken from the sack.

Walking briskly back to his car, Beagle cranked the engine and drove almost a mile, pulling the car into the parking lot of a Ramada Inn just off the interstate. He sat in the car for a few minutes, drinking vodka from a flask he pulled from the glove compartment. A half-moon flickered through the clouds, his radio playing softly from a Ludlow pop-music channel. He then left his car and walked through the Ramada lobby into a small lounge he had visited before.

Seating himself on a stool, he was greeted by the bartender, a woman in her mid-forties. "What can I get for you?" she asked. She wore a large, loose-fitting T-shirt, sleeves cut out and the midriff missing just below her breasts. Her hair, burned badly from years of peroxide, was pulled back in a ponytail, and pockmarks and lines dominated her face. Only three other customers, all white and seated at tables, were in the lounge. Before Beagle could reply to her question, she added: "Haven't I seen you in here before?"

"Yes, as a matter of fact, you have," he laughed, "they say all good bartenders have a photographic memory."

"For drinks and faces—not names." She held out her hand. "I'm Mona. What's your name?"

Beagle took her hand. "Phillip—Phillip Watson."

"Pleased to see you again," she said. "Vodka tonic, that's what you drink, ain't it?"

Beagle nodded and she mixed the drink. Setting it before him, she pulled a stool up, seating herself and facing him across the bar. "Ain't much going on in here tonight," she said, "I'm glad you showed up, Phillip. You a trucker or something?"

"No, not a trucker," Beagle smiled. "I sell insurance over in Shrewsbury Crossing."

"You married?"

"Yeah, yeah, I am," Beagle said, taking a drink.

"Why ain't you home tonight then," Mona asked, "or am I getting too personal? Just tell me to shut up if you want to."

"No, I don't mind. She knows I'm out for a drink. I've been under a lot of pressure. Needed a break."

"What kind of pressure? Money problems?"

"No, not finances so much. Just trying to know whether I'm doing the right thing on a particular matter."

"Heck, Phillip, don't do something you could go to jail for, it ain't worth it."

"I don't think I'll go to jail," Beagle smiled, "but someone else might if I make the wrong decision."

"Sounds serious," she said.

Beagle nodded in agreement. "Yes, it's very serious. I'll have another drink."

Shortly after 1:00 a.m., the bartender shook Beagle's arm. "Wake up, Phillip," she said. "I gotta close this place." Beagle was the only customer remaining, having fallen asleep with his head on the bar around midnight. As he roused himself, Mona said: "They tell us not to let the customers pass out on the bar, but you was the only one here and the manager's gone home for the night. I figured you needed the rest. You looked like you was real down when you came in."

Beagle stood up, weaving unsteadily. Thanking the bartender for her kindness, he paid for his drinks and walked shakily to his car, fumbling in his pocket for his keys. His car was parked next to a red Toyota pickup with oversized tires, splattered with mud. He cranked the car, put it in gear, and moved slowly toward the exit, grazing the pickup slightly with his bumper.

Back on the four-lane and heading west toward home, Beagle encountered a light fog mingled with smoke from forest fires that had settled on the roadway. His vision blurred, he was relieved that he met only two cars on the opposite side of the four-lane. He was careful to stay in the right-hand lane, and he drove slowly, the speedometer registering under thirty at times.

Five miles beyond the Ludlow city limits, bright headlights approached him rapidly from the rear, the beams flicking from bright to dim, blue strobe lights whirling wildly atop the dash inside the pursuing car. Beagle pulled to the side of the road in the emergency lane and the other car pulled close. An intense spotlight had now been aimed at him, making it impossible to see in his rear view mirrors the other vehicle's driver as the door opened and someone got out. Beagle lowered his window, leaning forward with his arms folded, resting his head on the steering wheel. Through blood-stained eyes, he was blinded by the glare of a flashlight fixed on his face, but he could tell that the person standing outside his car was a mountain of a man. "Officer," he pleaded, slurring his words, "I'm a judge—a federal judge. I'm so ashamed—so dreadfully ashamed. I been drinking and I ought not to be driving. I swear it'll never happen again. Can't you please just help me get home?"

"Yessir, your honor," a coarse, raspy, high-pitched voice responded. "I'm gonna help you. Fact is, I'm gonna help you a lot." The car door was pulled open and Beagle's left arm yanked savagely. As he sprawled on the pavement, Beagle heard his pursuer say: "And you're right, Judge, you're absolutely right. This ain't never gonna happen to you again."

CHAPTER 22

Limits

"You gotta learn they's limits.
People's got limits, Alex, everybody
has. Limits you gotta watch for."
Jeremiah, Chapter Four, *supra.*

The 1996 Mercedes-Benz S600 sedan topped a slight ridge on the road, and the frail, tanned body of a boy in his early twenties came into view. Weighing no more than one-hundred-fifty pounds, he had an army-green backpack lying on the sand beside his feet at the edge of the asphalt pavement. Sweat rolled from his forehead, his back gleaming with an oily Panama Jack luster as the hot Florida sun bore down unmercifully on him, draining him of energy in the mid-afternoon of this early December day. The environment inside the Mercedes offered a stark contrast: a perfect seventy degrees controlled by a battery of computers and resonating with Dolby music emitted in golden tones from the eleven Bose speakers fed by a compact disk—all included in the car's one-hundred-twenty-thousand dollar price tag.

Alex Rumpkin almost didn't stop. He was driving alone through the Florida keys, his destination Key West. He had managed to get off on a rare trip alone. Although his bodyguard had argued against it, he had adamantly insisted that he would be all right and that he could take the drive unrecognized. He felt he needed this chance to get away by himself, and he had spent the last four days driving through the Sunshine State, spending nights at Orlando, Fort Lauderdale and Miami.

His mind was miles away as he drove along that day, and he failed to see the hitchhiker until the car was nearly parallel to the spot where the boy stood. Slamming on the brakes, Alex pulled to a stop six-hundred feet down the road and watched in his rear-view mirror as the boy came running toward him, the backpack slung beneath his arm. Lowering his right-side window, Alex grinned broadly from the driver's seat as the boy leaned down and looked in. Speaking in a slow drawl, the boy said: "Mister, I cain't tell you how grateful I am for you stoppin'. Ain't nobody willin' to pick up a rider no more. Could you give me a lift into Key West, or however far you're goin'?"

The sweat on the boy's upper lip was matted in the faint fuzz of a mustache, and the biceps of his left arm bore a two-inch tattoo of what appeared to be some kind of fish—maybe a barracuda. He wore a soiled, loose-fitting sweatshirt, cut-off, badly frayed jeans with a jagged tear over the right hip, and flip-flops.

"Sure, hop in," Alex said. The boy seated himself and Alex put the car into gear, swinging it back onto the highway. "You got relatives or a girlfriend in Key West?"

"Naw, I don't know nobody down there. I'm just headed there to find work. I just got out of the Army and I ain't been able to land a job."

"What kind of job you looking for?" Alex lowered the volume on the stereo.

"God, it's nice to be in this air conditioning, I swear, it's hotter'n hell out on that road today." The boy was studying the array of instruments on the dash and the rich, burl walnut trim of the wood. He touched the grain of the supple, vat-dyed leather with his right hand, and said: "I bet this thing cost a pile of money. You must be *filthy* rich, mister."

"Some people say I handle my money well," Alex turned his face toward the boy. "I don't think you ever said what kind of job you're looking for."

"Oh, yeah, guess I didn't. I drove a big rig—you know, an eighteen-wheeler—in the service. Took auto mechanics in trade school. But, heck, I ain't particular, I'd take any kind of work that pays good."

"Well, I have friends in the Keys—maybe I can help you find something," Alex said, smiling. "I hope I'm not being too forward, though."

"Naw, man. Not a bit. I can use all the help I can get, and I can tell you got some pull somewhere." Alex wore a pale yellow golf shirt, open at the collar, and dark blue casual slacks. His loafers were of the finest calfskin and he wore no socks. Extending his hand, Alex said: "My name is Alex, by the way. What's yours?"

"Alph, sir—Alph Lokey's my name."

"And where are you from, Alph? Do I hear some Texas or Arkansas drawl?"

"Man, you are pretty damn *sharp*." The boy could see from Alex's broad grin that the remark had played well with his benefactor. "Yes sir, I was born in Lubbock and my mama moved to San Antonio when I was about four. We lived in this apartment about a half-mile from the Alamo. You probably know where that is. My mama worked as a maid in the downtown motels. Never knew my daddy. You know anything about San Antonio?"

"Yes, been there several times," Alex replied. "It's a nice town."

Alex had smoked marijuana several minutes before he stopped for the boy and the sweet pungency of the smoke lingered in spite of the automobile's state-of-the-art ventilation—an odor detected by the boy even before he had stepped into the car. The boy coughed nervously several times, cleared mucous from his throat and said: "You got a Kleenex or something? Don't know where I picked up this cold. Maybe from sleepin' on the beach the last three nights. I ain't had no money for a motel room."

Alex motioned toward a box of tissues on the driver's side of the console. "By the way," he said, as the boy reached toward the box, "would you like to burn one?"

The boy stared blankly toward Alex for a moment. "Man, you talkin' about pot? Heck, I don't do that kind of stuff. 'Sides, I don't know nothin' about you. You ain't no kind of DEA agent or something, are you?"

"Heavens no," Alex laughed. "Do you think a fuckin' cop would be driving a car like this? Not unless he's on the take, and if he were, you still wouldn't have anything to worry about. *Right*?" Alex opened the console and removed a foil pouch. Holding it out to the boy, he said: "Go ahead, Alph, help yourself. No strings attached."

The boy hesitated, then accepted the pouch. Alex gave him a light pat on the thigh as he used the car's lighter. As the boy drew the smoke into his lungs, Alex studied him carefully. Something about the boy reminded Alex of himself at that age. Although thin and somewhat emaciated, Alph had a handsome profile and rugged good looks with high cheekbones. His hair needed trimming but was still cropped close to his head—evidence of the final military haircut weeks earlier. But, unlike Alex, he was short—about five feet six. Too bad for the boy, Alex thought, since small men were at a disadvantage. With his own height just over six feet, Alex had always wanted to be even taller. He knew that a few short men—Hitler and Napoleon came to mind—had attained enormous power, but he considered them aberrations, and felt that they would have risen to even greater status if they had been tall. In Alex's view, being slightly taller than the average male had helped him rise to the top of the heap. People had to look up to Alex in more ways than one.

"I guess you don't have a place to stay tonight if you've been camping out on the beach," Alex said. "No place in Key West, I mean."

"Naw, I really don't know nothin' about the place, but I been told you can make money there. Lots of folks from Canada and the north come down there for the winter, I've heard. Lots of gays and lesbians too, ain't there?"

"My experience is that you can make money anywhere," Alex said. "Just depends on how smart you are and what you're prepared to do to get it."

"Shit, man," the boy said. "I'd do *anything*! Ain't nothin' I wouldn't do to have a car like this. I bet you get all the women you want. Hell, mister, you got it made in the shade, ain't you? What do you do for a living? Or, hell, you probably don't have to do nothing, you're so rich."

A road sign proclaimed that they were leaving the city limits of Marathon and another marker a few yards further down the road showed the mileage to Key West. The clock on the Mercedes dash read 3:18 p.m.

"You're getting a little personal, aren't you?" Alex said. "Are you always this blunt with someone who's done you a favor? You might want to use a little tact, you know." Hearing Alex's criticism, the boy fidgeted in his seat, beads of perspiration suddenly appearing on his upper lip. "I don't think you need to know a lot about me. Let's just say for now that I'm one hell of an *important* son-of-a-bitch."

"I'm sorry, mister. I didn't mean to upset you. Honest I didn't."

"Don't worry about it," Alex said.

"What's this gizmo here?" the boy asked, pointing to the center console.

"Oh, that's my dictating device, digital. I love that damn thing. I can use it riding along if I think of a memo I want to write or an action I need to take at the office. I just pick it up and talk, say whatever I feel like, and my secretary or assistant back there takes care of things. Sometimes I just call them on the cellular and transmit the messages directly to the office. Nothing like it. Cost over three thousand dollars, but worth every cent!"

"Well, ain't you a cool dude," Alph said, "riding down the road in your expensive car talkin' your head off into some machine, makin' people jump when you say so from miles away. You got the power, man, now don't you?"

Alex frowned, turning angrily toward the boy. "Listen, asshole, I don't need some shiftless turd like you ridiculing me. I'll put you out of this car right now!"

"Aw, I'm sorry, mister. I didn't mean to piss you off. I wasn't making fun of you no way. I *mean*, you *really* do have power, and I respect that."

"Well, just don't forget who's running this show. The wrong attitude with me will get you into the deepest kind of shit, and I'm deadly serious. You don't know who you're dealing with, Alph." The boy sank down timidly, silently in his seat. He was stunned by Alex's inflection and tone, the scathing, scolding, condescending manner—the piercing gaze of his squinting eyes and the raised eyebrows he had used for years to wither and dress down subordinates.

The car was nearing an intersection on the outskirts of Key West. All manner of garish billboards began to appear—advertisements for motels. condominiums, night clubs, t-shirts, tattoos, the Florida lottery. Suddenly, looming over the others, on the right side of the roadway was a giant, sixty-foot sign with MedAmerica's logo—a multi-colored crescent with an angel hovering above—and bold letters with the slogan: "WE ARE CAREGIVERS." Alex smiled broadly: he had concocted the slogan himself. It caught the essence of what the company was about, he thought, and he had hand-picked the team of professionals pictured on each side of the logo: a handsome, silver-haired doctor holding a stethoscope; an attractive nurse at his side holding an infant; a beaming, elderly patient in a wheelchair; and a smiling orderly holding the chair's handles. The team members, Alex felt, perfectly projected the company's image, all impeccably dressed in white, the nurse a young woman in her twenties, black hair under her cap and her wrinkleless white uniform covering a lithe, supple body. Alex remembered spending the night with the girl after she had posed with the others for the pictures. He could not recall her name but he did remember that she was good—almost as good as Tara.

Alex thought back to that day in his office when he gave final approval to the picture—later to be posted all across America. The advertising people had argued that the scene was too flat, mawkish, and syrupy. They advocated something novel—perhaps surreal—for the billboards to catch the public's attention and build a unique image for the company. Alex had vetoed the alternative ideas, muttering under his breath at the time that the trouble with the Madison Avenue types was they didn't know squat about human nature. He had also heard reports that his own marketing people were offended that the CEO was "micro-managing" the company and the ad programs in particular. He took special delight in such stories because, in Alex's mind, they simply meant that he had been spectacularly successful in keeping people on their toes. Making them all insecure was a major part of his job, he reasoned, since leaving them guessing was the best way to hold everyone in line.

As Alex and his companion rode through the streets of Key West, the boy said: "You can just let me out anywhere, mister. I don't have no place special to go."

"Tell you what," Alex said. "I know this little tiki bar right on the beach where we can get a cold beer. Ought to hit the spot on a day like this."

"Man, that sounds great, but—like I said—I'm flat broke. I cain't buy nothin' 'til I find me a job."

"Look, Alph," Alex smiled broadly. "Not to worry. Everything's on me."

Taking a left at the next light, they could see in the distance the clear, blue ocean glistening in the sun. Nearing the shoreline, the road took a sharp right, carrying them past new condominium developments punctuated with occasional rows of ancient one-story motels painted in pastels of blue, green and yellow, or in garish shades of orange and red and bearing names like the Mariner's Nest, Sandheaven, and Blue Tide. About a mile further on, Alex turned the car abruptly into a side road leading to a parking lot. On the edge of the lot was a building with a thatched roof, and over the structure a bamboo sign that said: "The Captain's Mate: Welcome To All Landlubbers."

Alex led the boy along a rickety boardwalk to the ocean-side of the building where a porch—raised high on pilings—overlooked the ocean. They found seats at the bar where a sun tanned girl with long bleached hair, her face riddled with freckles and pock-marks, came over and asked what they wanted to drink.

"What's your pleasure, Alph?" Alex nodded to the boy.

"You got imported beer?" Alph asked the girl.

"Tecate and Corona—the Mexican stuff—and Heinekins. I guess that's about it," she replied.

"Gimme the Corona," the boy said and added, glancing toward Alex as though seeking permission, "and a double shot of Cuervo Gold—if you have it."

Alex smiled and said, "That sounds good. I'll have the same."

The sun loomed like a giant orange beachball just over the horizon. It had been a fine afternoon. After the first two rounds of tequila and beer, Alex had begun buying drinks for everyone around the bar, including the girl bartender. His face reddened with the flush of alcohol, Alex had become increasingly rambunctious—so much so that one young couple, perhaps honeymooners, had made quick work of their drinks and left. But the other customers—three white males in their twenties and two middle-aged white females—listened raptly while Alex dominated the conversation. His opinions were boldly announced on wide-ranging subjects: Clinton, the economy, the breakup of the Soviet Union, the downfall of socialism. With a booming voice, he bemoaned the loss of family values—clear evidence, he said, that America was losing its greatness. From time to time Alph and the other customers nodded their heads vigorously in total agreement. Besides, Alex was buying the drinks.

"Did y'all hear the one about the three men killed in the same bus wreck who wound up together at the Pearly Gates?" Alex asked. Alph and one of the male customers shook their heads "No."

"Well," Alex went on, "one was a Jew, one, a Catholic, and one, a black man." Alex paused and grinned broadly. "St. Peter comes to the gate and says, 'boys, I can't let you three in because the gate's broke.' At that point, the black guy steps up and says, 'I believe I can fix it, but I'll have to charge six dollars for my work.'" Alex cleared his throat and took a drink.

"St. Peter says, 'Six dollars sounds fair enough,' but he turns to the Catholic and says, 'What would you charge?'" Alex folded his hands and leaned forward on the bar with his elbows. "'Oh, about twenty dollars,' the Catholic says: 'ten for the church and ten for me.' 'Glad to see you're thinking about the church,' St. Peter tells the Catholic and turns to the Jew. 'So what would you charge to fix the gate?' he asks. The Jew says: 'twenty-six dollars.'"

Alex took another sip from his drink. "'Twenty-six dollars,' St. Peter says, 'an interesting figure—how'd you come up with that?' 'Real simple,' the Jew says, 'ten dollars for me, ten for you, and six for the *nigger*.'"

Alex howled uncontrollably—more loudly than anyone else—slapping the bar with his hand as he delivered the punch line.

"Alph, why don't we get something to eat?" Alex bellowed. "I know a place where they've got filet mignon and lobster so damn good it'll bring tears to your eyes."

"Well, sure, Alex," the boy said, having started calling Alex by his first name. "Yeah, I'm starvin', but, like I said, I ain't got no money."

"Hell, I told you not to worry, boy," Alex said. "You're travelin' in style tonight with a fellow that's got more money than you ever dreamed of. You ain't been asked to pay for nothing yet, have you?"

Alex paid the tab at the bar, gave the girl a fifty-dollar tip, and he and Alph returned to the Mercedes. "Man," the boy said, "I saw you chunk down that big bill for that gal. Her eyes lit up like spotlights. Heck, I bet she would'a give you a blow job for that kind of money."

"No doubt she would have, Alph," Alex winked at the boy, "no doubt she would."

After their meal, they walked back to the automobile. Standing beside the car, Alex said: "Well, maybe we oughta find a place to spend the night?" It was twenty minutes past eleven. "There's an upscale hotel called the Golden Regent right on the beach where I've stayed before. It's five stories with a great view of the ocean if I can get one of the top floor suites."

"Heck, you ain't gonna get no argument from me," Alph said. "After spending the last three nights lying in the sand, I could sure use a shower and clean sheets."

They parked at the entrance to the hotel lobby. A bellhop opened the car door for Alex as he got out and walked to the registration desk. He and Annie had vacationed at the hotel several times, and the desk clerk recognized him. "Glad to have you back, Mr. Rumpkin. Your wife with you?"

"No, just a friend, and I didn't make a reservation," Alex said, "but I'd like my usual top-floor suite. Two bedrooms, of course."

"We can do that," the clerk smiled. "We're really slow tonight, and you'll have plenty of privacy. Only rooms occupied are on the ground floor, and you can use the reserved parking next to the elevator."

Returning to the automobile where Alph waited, Alex drove around the building and parked the car. Just as the boy opened the car door, Alex reached over, gave the boy's knee a firm grasp, and said "Wait a second." Unlocking the glove compartment, he reached inside. "I've got some stuff in here I want to take up with us." He then withdrew a revolver and a tin Band-Aid container. Alex opened the trunk with a remote switch, and the two men got out of the car and removed their baggage.

Alex led the boy to the elevator and jabbed the button for the fifth floor. As the elevator started to rise, Alph said: "Man, you *really* know your way around, don't you? And you ain't said much about yourself. I mean, heck, you know all about me, and I—er, I don't know nothin' about you."

"Could be I'll fill you in on everything before the night's over," Alex said, staring coldly into the boy's eyes.

"Why'd you get that gun outta the car?"

"I always keep it nearby when I sleep. Never can tell who might be out to get me. A man in my position makes lots of enemies. I have a bodyguard, but the fucker gets on my nerves being around all the time, so I like to get away by myself now and then."

"What kind of job you got?" the boy asked as the elevator came to a stop and the doors opened onto the fifth floor. "Just who are you, Alex?"

Stopping in the hallway, Alex winked, slurring his words: "I'm the *king* of the goddamn *mountain*, that's who!"

Inside the suite Alex casually tossed the gun and the tin container on the bed. "Hey, watch out!" Alph said, "that thing could go off." Alex shrugged his shoulders and went into the bathroom to urinate, leaving the door ajar. "Alph," he yelled, "go check out the balcony. You'll love it here. I like to sleep in the nude, leaving the balcony door open so I can smell the salt air, feel the breeze on my body, and hear the surf roar all night. Ain't this the fuckin' life?"

"It sure is," the boy walked to the balcony and stood there, looking out at the ocean, the wind blowing his hair. Alex came out to join him. "No kiddin' now, Alex," Alph said, "tell me *seriously* what you do."

"Ever heard of the MedAmerica Corporation?" Alex asked, staring directly into the boy's eyes.

"Some kind of hospital chain, ain't it?"

"Hell no! It's not just *some* 'hospital chain,'" Alex snarled, shaking his head. "It's the damn *preeminent* provider of all kinds of medical services—one of the biggest in the whole fuckin' world. Shit, we do it all—psychiatric therapy, retirement and nursing homes, in-home care, the best medical and surgical facilities and specialists."

"Yeah," the boy said, "now I remember. Y'all put on those TV ads about addiction, you know, drugs and alcohol. That line about if you don't get treatment from MedAmerica, be sure and get it somewhere else. That's a cool line, I think."

"A major profit center for us," Alex said, smiling. "If we can get some guy in for a free consultation, we convince him he's addicted—you know, we don't give a shit whether he really is or not—or maybe we persuade him he's got a son or wife who's addicted—then we've got him hooked. There's tons of money to be made with psychological counseling. That's why we spend so much damn money on television."

"And what's your job there?"

"I'm the top dog, Alph. You're in the company tonight of the damn CEO, for *chrissake*! The fuckin' *CEO*!"

"What's that mean?" the boy asked.

"I'll be damn, Alph, for God's sake!" Alex put his hand on the boy's shoulder. "CEO stands for 'chief executive officer' and I'm Chairman of the Board and President too. You don't know *shit*, do you?"

Alph turned away. He swallowed hard, lowered his head and stared out over the ocean. The pair stood silently on the balcony for a minute until Alph said: "Let's go back inside. I'm feelin' a little woozy from drinkin', and maybe I'm a little bit afraid of heights. It's a pretty bad drop to the beach." Alex suddenly grabbed the boy behind the neck and shoved his head forward over the railing.

"Heh, you *shitass*!" the boy shouted, pulling himself free and jumping back. "Don't do that, man. You scared the *hell* out of me." Alex grinned broadly.

They walked back into the room, Alex keeping one hand on the boy's shoulder. "Sorry, fellow," he whispered, "I didn't mean to scare you. I was just horsin' around." Alex stood by the bed, removing all of his clothes except for boxer shorts. He tossed his clothes in the floor, went to the kitchen, opened the courtesy bar, removed two small bottles of vodka and poured them in a glass. "Want something to drink, Alph?" he yelled.

"I don't know," the boy said, "maybe I've had enough tonight." The meal at the restaurant had sobered both men a bit.

"Well, I got some stuff here you might like," Alex said, walking back into the bedroom. He picked up the pistol from the bed and placed it on the nightstand. He then tossed the tin Band-Aid container to the boy, who examined the can with a puzzled look. "Open it," Alex said, "see if you want some. It's good stuff."

The boy opened the can, pulling out a plastic envelope of white powder. Sniffing the contents, he said: "Man, that is good stuff, ain't it? A load like this must have cost you several thousand dollars."

"Yeah, it would have cost plenty," Alex said, "but I don't have to buy it on the street. I own—and I mean that *literally*—I *own* several doctors who'll do any fuckin' thing I say. Get me any damn thing I want. And you want to know why? Because I've got something on some of them and the others just know I'll take care of them when they need it. It's the way the world works, Alph. As you get older, you'll learn that."

As the boy sniffed the powder, he said: "Yeah, man, that is *quality* stuff. Thanks for the hit!" He smiled broadly at Alex. It was well past midnight, and Alph's fear of heights was gone as he returned to the balcony.

Alex took his turn and inhaled some of the powder. Then he returned to the bed. He lay still a minute or so, allowing the ingestion of the drug to heighten the exhilaration he already felt. His mind raced euphorically through the afternoon's events. He kept thinking how he had transformed this young boy's life by simply picking him up, lifting him from the depths of being a nobody several hours earlier to the peaks of pleasure he was experiencing now. And, Alex kept telling himself, it was all because of his generosity in deigning to give the boy a ride. What sheer luck for the little turd! The bastard ought to get down on his knees and kiss my feet, he thought.

The December moon in a quarter crescent was hanging low over the water. A balmy wind whistled through the curtains on each side of the open glass doors and Alph turned, his back to the ocean, gazing into the dimly lit bedroom where Alex now lay, stretched out, on the bed. Floor-to-ceiling mirrors covered the wall behind the bed, allowing Alph to see his own image as he stood on the balcony framed by moonlight.

"Damn!" he called out to Alex. "What a difference a day makes! Twenty-four hours ago I'm sleeping on smelly beachsand, broke and hungry. Now, look at me: here I am, a belly full of food, high on coke, and enjoying the hell out of the good life. And this is the way you live *all* the time, ain't it?"

Alex did not answer but his eyes were glazed as he took a long drink from the vodka glass and grinned broadly. His head rested against two pillows.

"How'd you get to be the top man at your company?" the boy asked.

"I fought like hell for it," Alex sat up abruptly on the side of the bed. "I came from nothing, boy. I was always hungry when I was growing up. Didn't have shoes or anything decent to wear, and it killed me when I saw other boys skippin' along with happy families—goin' to the fuckin' church, seein' movies whenever they wanted to. I wasn't half-grown when I made up my mind that I'd have it all someday. And I set out to do it. The biggest thing in my hometown—Shrewsbury Crossing, Georgia—was a clinic started by a doctor named Willingham. I fought and clawed my way into it. Kissed asses, I mean—made friends with the doctor's son. Even married the old man's *daughter*, for *chrissake*! I worked my ass off to get where I am."

"It sure looks like it was worth it, man. You're livin' like a fuckin' king now, ain't you?"

"Yeah—shit yeah, it's worth it." Alex gulped down another big swallow of vodka. "You can't imagine how it feels to have this kind of power—what it's like to scare bastards *silly* just by raisin' my fuckin' eyebrows. I can ruin some turkey's life with a telephone call. I've done it many times, for God's sake. Do you see what I'm saying, Alph?"

"I reckon you mean you can get him fired."

"Hell yeah, I can fire him, but that's not the end of it. I can destroy a reputation just by wishin' it, and I've screwed wives and daughters of turds that tried to challenge me. I've got all sorts of ways to skin cats—hell, I'm a fuckin' *master* at skinnin' cats. Like I told you, boy, I'm *king* of the goddamn mountain! I really am."

"Doesn't it bother you sometimes when you cut people down?" the boy asked.

"Yeah, sometimes it really does." The boy had returned to the bedroom and stood leaning against the back of a recliner. "Yeah, sometimes it bothers me," Alex repeated. "But most of the time I get a kick out of it, like when I'm screwin' the ones who are trying to fuck with me, but I really don't relish shaftin' friends—you know, people who've helped me or stood by me, but that's when you have to be a strong-willed asshole. Any weakling can drop the hammer on his enemies, but it takes one tough son-of-a-bitch to kick a friend. That's what separates the sheep from the goats—being able to do whatever it takes no matter who suffers. I've had to do it, and yeah, it's worth it. Fact is, *anyone* who's made it to the top—whether it's the fuckin' Pope or the President—has to screw all kinds of people on his way up. That's just the damn *truth*!"

"You know, you're—you're the first big shot I ever met," the boy stuttered, "and I don't mind tellin' you—you're shockin' me some. You don't act like I figured somebody like you would act. Guess I just didn't know what to expect."

"I don't always talk like this," Alex replied. "You don't realize it, but I can be one smooth son-of-a-bitch when I wanna be. Right now, I'm kinda paying you a compliment—lettin' my hair down with you. I don't often walk around in my damn drawers either," Alex laughed. He returned to the kitchen, poured more vodka, and came back to the bed. Alph had seated himself in the recliner. Alex piled another pillow against the headboard, crawled back on the bed and sat with his legs spread apart, his limp penis and pubic hair slightly visible between the loose, unbuttoned folds of his shorts. "Why don't you get comfortable, Alph? Take your clothes off," Alex took another sip of his drink. "Matter of fact, maybe I could talk you into sittin' over here and givin' me a backrub. My back's achin' from the drivin'."

Alph removed his sweatshirt and cut-off's, turning to face Alex wearing discolored, sweat-stained briefs. The digital face on the bedside clock read "1:32 a.m." The boy sat on the side of the bed. "Never done much back-rubbin'," he said, "but you been nice to me, and I'm grateful for it. Tell me if I'm doin' it right."

Alex turned on his stomach, keeping the glass of vodka in his hand. Alph knelt beside him and began kneading Alex's neck, shoulders and upper back. "Oh yeah," Alex moaned, "that feels good. Can you get my legs now?" The boy changed his position and moved his hands down to the legs.

"Man, I guess from what you say that you've done some *terrible* things to get where you are."

"Not all terrible, maybe just things I wished I hadn't had to do." Alex raised his head and drank from his glass. "But there are always bad things that have to be done."

"Like what?" the boy asked.

Alex hesitated before answering. "Oh, I don't know. Maybe like handlin' a nigger judge who was tryin' to mess up my life, if you want me to be specific."

"What'd you do to him?"

"I ain't sayin' I did anything, but some of my friends got pretty upset with him for tryin' to fuck me, and they ain't no tellin' what *they* might have done. Doesn't really matter, I guess. The sucker disappeared about three months ago, and nobody's heard of him since."

"What happened to him?"

"Hell, nobody knows. There was a lot of talk—rumors, you know—and publicity when he vanished, but it's sort'a died down now."

"Was he killed?"

"They've never found a body, but I'll say this: he had plenty of enemies—I wasn't the only one. He was last seen gettin' drunk in a Ramada Inn, and some folks think maybe a drug dealer took him out. Others even think that maybe he took a payoff for something and is livin' like a king down in the Caribbean."

"What do you think?"

"Somebody probably blew him away, got rid of the car he was drivin' and hid the body. If I was guessin', I'd bet he's buried somewhere around Shrewsbury Crossing. Wouldn't shock me a bit if he was buried around the town's old abandoned sawmill. Nobody'd ever look for him there. It's too damn obvious."

"What was he after you for?" the boy asked.

"Shit," Alex said, "he was threatening everything I have. Had my company's finance man up on criminal charges, sayin' he was gonna lock him up if he didn't say all sorts of mess about me."

"Did you know him?"

"Yeah, I knew the nigger. Knew him all my life. Grew up with him. Played with him as a boy, but he was arrogant and headstrong even back then."

Alph inhaled more cocaine. In the bathroom, he urinated, flushed the toilet and returned to the bed. As he touched Alex's back to resume the massage, Alex said: "Tell you what. Why don't you reach down and massage my balls a little? And don't worry about touchin' my dick. I kinda like that."

"Wait a damn minute!" the boy jumped up, startled. "What the shit! What the shit's this—?"

"Come on, now, Alph. Calm down. Ain't nothing, Alph," Alex responded in a low, soothing monotone. "Hell, I'm just in the mood to feel good, and you can do that for me. Ain't I been nice to you today? Well, just let me fuck you in the asshole, or—if you want—you can suck my cock."

"Turn over, you son-of-a-bitch," Alph screamed. "What in hell do you think I am—I ain't gonna have sex with no man!"

Alex turned over, facing the boy. "Easy, easy, Alph. Take it easy. I never meant to upset you, but you said you'd do anything for a life like mine. Well, this is your chance. You take care of me now, and good things'll come to you. It's how you get ahead, don't you see that?" Alex reached out and grasped the boy's hand, attempting to guide it toward his erect penis. Alph jerked his hand away, grabbed the gun off the nightstand, and pointed it directly at Alex's head.

"You think I'm a damn *faggot*, don't you?" Alph shouted, his eyes filling with tears. "You brought me up here thinkin' I'm a *Goddamn faggot*!"

His eyes blinking wildly, Alex sat up in the bed, staring into the gun barrel. With alcohol and cocaine clogging his mind, he impulsively searched for a way out. Adrenaline pumped through his body and neurons fired randomly through the billions of cells in his brain as the primal instinct to survive became the dominant feature of his being.

"Alph, please listen," Alex begged. "Don't do something stupid. I was just horsin' around—you know, about the blow job and all. Hell, I could tell the minute we met that you ain't gay. Man, I could see you are a real macho stud."

"Like hell you say!" the boy shouted. "You thought I was some kind of *pervert* who'd let you fuck me in the ass. Well, I ain't a queer, and you ain't got enough money to make me one."

"No! That ain't true. I was just shittin' you. I never thought you'd do nothin' like that."

As the boy stood holding the gun, he sobbed and said: "Who's king of the fuckin' mountain *now*, Alex? How does it feel to crawl at somebody's feet? Maybe you know how that damn judge felt now.

"Alph, please calm down." Alex pleaded. "Listen, let's just forget this whole thing. Put the gun down and cool off. Shit, I've got over two-thousand dollars with me. Just take it all. You can have it—a gift from me, I want you to have it! All right?"

"You think your damn money can buy anything or anybody, don't you, cocksucker!" the boy cried, his lips quivering uncontrollably. "Well, I'll tell you this, you can't buy *me*. See how you like *this*, you perverted bastard—*a gift from me*!" The boy pulled the trigger and unloaded three chambers of the pistol, the first bullet striking just to the left of Alex's nose and the other two in the neck and chest. Blood spewed in all directions, drenching the bedsheets and splattering the wall of mirrors with crimson drops running down to the floor.

The boy's hands shook violently as he picked up his backpack. Placing the Band-Aid can and the gun in the bag, he pulled Alex's wallet from his pants on the floor and found twenty-two hundred dollar bills along with four or five twenties. Grabbing the keys to the Mercedes, he ran from the room, slamming the door behind him.

The Holiday Inn at Islamorada, one of the more innocuous Florida keys, was surrounded the next day at noon by state troopers, sheriff's deputies, and EMC vehicles. They had concentrated, front and rear, on room 118, which had been rented before daybreak that morning by a young man wearing a badly stained sweatshirt. A spanking new Mercedes had been sloppily parked at an angle outside the door. The innkeeper's suspicions had been aroused when the boy checked in, paying in advance for the room with a hundred-dollar bill. By the time the Key West police had been alerted, just before eleven that morning, Alex's body had been discovered by a maid in his room at the Golden Regent, and an all-points bulletin had been issued.

The standoff with police did not last long. The boy surrendered shortly after noon and hysterically told police a garbled story about defending himself against homosexual advances from an elderly man in Key West. And then he blurted out, "I did everyone a favor by killing him. He wasn't just a pervert—he was a damn *murderer*! He had a nigger judge killed somewhere in southern Georgia and buried around an old sawmill."

CHAPTER 23

Lamentations

"For in much wisdom is much grief,
and he that increaseth knowledge
increaseth sorrow."
Ecclesiastes, Ch. 1, v. 18

Melissa Goodwin sits in her wheelchair, beyond the hospital bed in the far corner of her sterile room. Brilliant sunlight floods through the window behind her, creating a surreal silhouette of her shriveled form and the snail-like arch in her back. Her hair is a silvery, tangled matrix, no longer the proud crown she has worn for the last several decades of her eighty-eight years. Unable to bear the pain of the shampoo chair and holding her crippled, arthritic neck back for the rinse, Melissa no longer cares that it has been weeks since she last visited the nursing home beautician.

As Jeremiah nears his mother, he calls out, loudly enough for her to hear: "Mama, it's me, Jeremiah." Bending down to kiss her cheek, he sees a weak smile break through her tightly drawn lips, erasing a few of the numerous wrinkles of her face.

"Baby, my baby" she says, patting his arm. "I'm so glad you're here. I been missin' you so bad."

"I'm glad to see you too, Mama," he replies. It is not true: it is the antithesis of gladness he feels; grief and sorrow are more accurate descriptions of his emotions. His visits, when he makes them, are now generated mostly out of guilt and an indefinable sense of responsibility. He can hardly bear looking into her pleading, searching eyes, eyes which never really demand anything but nevertheless seem to expect him to fix everything, to make it all right—to repair her body and restore her youth. He consoles himself that she is getting good care here, better care than he could provide, but the memory of what she once was—tall, vibrant, efficient, capable—haunts him constantly when he sees her now.

"Mama, I can't stay long." He is following his usual practice of preparing her early in his visitations for a quick departure. "You know, I really won't have much time to be with you today. I'll try to come back in a few weeks when I can stay longer," he says, reassuringly. "As I told you yesterday on the phone—I came down for the funerals. The first one—the one for Alex—starts at noon, and I have to get back to Atlanta tonight."

With her eyesight nearly gone, her hearing limited, and her mobility confined to the wheelchair, Melissa has one remaining faculty: her mind, still sharp, still lucid. Other than repeating herself and sometimes forgetting where she is, she shows no sign that her brain is not in good order. "Yes, I remember you told me that. It's Alex—and Beagle too, isn't it?"

"Yes, ma'am," Jeremiah responds. "From the time I was a boy—I think Grandma Goodwin's was the first one I ever attended—I've always hated going to funerals, but I felt I had to be here for these today. I decided I'd come early enough…."

"It's so sad. Both of them gone and still—really still young men, weren't they? And of course, you had to come. You need to do what you *ought* to do, Jeremiah, I always taught you that." Melissa's eyes twinkle as she waves her hand in his direction. "Fact is, I'da had to whip your fanny if you hadn't come." Jeremiah smiles inwardly as he hears once more the threat he has heard all his life—one his mother had rarely carried out, even when he was a child.

"Well, it's…it's an awkward situation, Mama," Jeremiah hesitates, groping for the right words. "The facts…the circumstances about Alex's death aren't really clear, and there's speculation you've probably seen in the papers that he was somehow involved when Beagle disappeared back in September."

"Well, that's all water over the damn, isn't it?" Melissa looks at her son intently. "Ain't no good to come from dredgin' up mud from the past and you ain't got no business spreadin' or repeatin' rumors. I'm so sorry about it all. You just go pay your respects like you should and do whatever you can to give comfort. Beagle and Alex were your friends, so pray for their souls, Jeremiah. We all stand in need of prayer."

Jeremiah silently wonders if Alex was ever his friend, or anyone's friend, for that matter, but he takes no exception to his mother's words. He never argues with her anymore. She has always seen the good in everyone and he knows there is nothing he can do—or wants to do—to change her now.

"Listen, you reckon you could go by and get Pink on your way to Beagle's funeral?" Melissa asks. "She wanted me to ask you." Pink lives alone. Both of the sisters' husbands had died the same year, 1979, and Melissa had moved into Pink's house, where they had lived together for ten years. Toward the end of 1989, Melissa had become so feeble that she had to be placed in the nursing home.

"Is Aunt Pink *able* to go?" Jeremiah asks, raising an eyebrow.

"Pshaw, I don't think so, and I told her that! She's not able to go, and she *ought* not to go, but she *says* she's goin'. Says she feels up to it. She wants to go to the one for Alex too, but I told her the papers are calling it a private service—that you had to be invited. She's gonna wish she hadn't gone to Beagle's either. There's gonna be a big crowd and it'll make her nervous. You know, Jeremiah, Pink gets real nervous these days—a lot more than she used to—but she's as hard-headed as they come. She's determined to stay in that house by herself. I keep tellin' her to move in here with me where they'll take good care of her, but pshaw, she won't listen. Grievin' her heart out over Ethan, too."

"Sure, Mama, I'll go get her. Don't worry. I'll see to it that she's all right."

"How's Sarah? And why isn't she with you?" Melissa asks, demandingly. "A wife needs to be with her husband at times like these."

"Well," Jeremiah pauses, his mind racing to find a response. "Er, she's…, she's not feeling well today, nothing serious, just didn't want to make the long drive." Jeremiah sees no need to worry his mother by discussing the foul-ups in his life.

"You be sure and let her know I asked about her, and bring her to see me the next time you come."

"Sure I will, Mama, I certainly will," Jeremiah answers, silently wondering if Sarah would ever be with him again.

"Look what I'm doing," Melissa says, excitedly, as she reaches down to a basket beside the wheelchair and grunts softly as she slowly lifts a large, grayish-colored ledger to her lap. With a frazzled binding, it seems to contain hundreds of pages, some of which are torn.

"What's that, Mama?" Jeremiah asks as he pulls a chair to her side and sits down.

"I'm writing a history of our old church—you know, the one out near the old homeplace we attended when you were a boy. I'm using old minute records to help me get the facts straight. One of the deacons at First Baptist asked me to do the history—said nobody in town knows more about that old church than I do. Wasn't that sweet of him?" Melissa's eyes twinkle. "I been workin' on it better'n two years now, but it's slow goin', you know, with my weak eyes and the arthritis in my hands."

Jeremiah takes the book from his mother's lap and starts turning the pages. In her familiar handwriting—now broken and shaky—are names from the past: preachers, deacons, genealogies of church members, all listed in sections chronologically arranged. Many names he recalls from boyhood, and many are unfamiliar. Then he comes across an entry reading "New Members, July through September, 1945." There he finds the name of "Ethan Allday" and in a column below, his own name, with a note in his mother's handwriting to the side: "My own son, who accepted Christ and was baptized."

Tears well up in Jeremiah's eyes as he pauses, reading and re-reading the note. Melissa has rested her head against the back of the wheelchair and says nothing, as if she does not want to disturb her son's reverie. Lost in his thoughts, Jeremiah silently wonders just how far he has come since the summer of 1945, or more accurately, just how far he has fallen. For some reason, the drunken scenes in the Crown Room with Alex and Michelle flash through his mind: images of the hurt and disappointment in Sarah's eyes when he stumbled in at midnight. The episodes with Tara, such a foolish adventure, he realizes now. Maybe he wouldn't feel the emptiness in the pit of his stomach now if he hadn't repudiated all he believed in the summer of 1945?

"Jeremiah, Jeremiah," Melissa murmurs, interrupting his musing, "Didn't you say that Alex's funeral starts at noon? You don't have much time."

"Yes ma'am, it does," he says, standing and looking at his wristwatch. His mother was right, he thought to himself: he didn't have much time left, not much time at all. He returns the notebook to her basket and bends down to kiss her. "I'd like to read more of that later, but now I better be running, I guess."

"You take good care of my boy," Melissa says, her voice breaking as she pats his face with her shriveled, trembling hand.

✤ ✤ ✤

Jeremiah parks the Jaguar on grass just off the driveway, directed to do so by a well-dressed man in his forties wearing a badge reading "Funeral Staff." The long, oval drive has ample room for the sparse number of vehicles already there. It is minutes before noon, and Jeremiah counts a dozen or so cars, including a hearse and two police cars near the entrance to the house. The colonnade of huge oak trees lining the driveway and the portico fronting the Willingham mansion don't seem to have changed much since Jeremiah first marveled at them as a boy. But he had learned from his visits with Alex and Annie that the rear of the estate had been dramatically altered in recent years. After Doc Willie died, Alex had embarked on an elaborate expansion of the house which had sadly obliterated much of the carefully cultivated gardens and the Japanese pool. An indoor swimming pool had been installed along with a new Olympic-sized outdoor pool, a luxurious bath house and bar, and an exercise room. Beyond the garden, a spacious guest house had been built, capable of accommodating at least ten people. There had also been a total renovation of the interior of the primary residence, which had allowed Alex to entertain frequently and lavishly in Gatsby style.

A policeman stands stiffly in the foyer as Jeremiah enters the house. The officer studies Jeremiah's credentials for a moment, and then directs him through double-doors to an ornately paneled sitting room with a twelve foot ceiling, where a dozen rows of folding chairs have been placed before a gold and silver-plated coffin. Everyone is seated: Annie and her two daughters with their husbands and children on the front row, and a sprinkling of mourners filling no more than half of the remaining chairs. Jeremiah finds a seat three rows from the rear just as a minister stands and opens a Bible. His face is enveloped in grim lines as he reads the 23rd Psalm. Then, in a halting fashion, and in a barely audible monotone, he speaks about Alex's life, his rise from obscurity, his stewardship of Dr. Willingham's legacy, the benevolent causes Alex championed, the wife and family he had left behind. The remarks are directed almost entirely to Annie, as though the speaker is oblivious to the presence of anyone else.

Looking around, it strikes Jeremiah as odd that the group is so small—even smaller than he had expected. Then he realizes that there are conspicuous absences: Christina, Alex's sister, is not there, and he sees no one from the ranks of MedAmerica's senior staff, insofar as he can remember those faces from his work on the Panacea deal. Doddy is also missing and there are no recognizable politicians or dignitaries. Perhaps, he muses, it is testimony to something he has long suspected: Even though Alex scrapped and clawed his way to the top of MedAmerica and Shrewsbury Crossing's social pyramid, no one—probably even Alex—had ever felt that he really *deserved* to be there. Alex was perhaps an abberation, Jeremiah thinks, some kind of miscarriage of the human species; but then again, maybe he was all too typical of people who are power-hungry and ruthless enough to rise to the top of whatever sawdust pile they're on. In any event, once gone, Alex had very few mourning his passing.

A demure woman dressed in navy blue with a veil covering all but her chin sits erect and rigidly alone ten seats over from Jeremiah. She never looks toward him and he wonders if this could be Tara. But why would she be invited, he wonders. And who would invite her? He never finds out.

The service draws quickly to a close. Following the coffin pushed along on its cart by the funeral director and an aide, six pallbearers leave in double file, trailed from a distance by Annie and her daughters. The procession moves slowly up the aisle, bound for cars which will form a cavalcade to the cemetery. As Annie passes Jeremiah's row, she stares straight ahead, cavernous circles of despair in her eyes, an almost lifeless, frail figure held upright by her two daughters. Jeremiah then decides that he will not go to the cemetery; he simply can't bring himself to speak to Annie while she is like this. After the room empties, he signs the funeral registry and walks outside, waiting just beyond the door until every car but his has left the grounds.

Finding a fast-food restaurant, he pulls a newspaper from a vending machine and gulps down a hamburger. In the *Shrewsbury Crossing Messenger*, he finds a three-paragraph obituary for Alexander Wayne Rumpkin. No picture of Alex is provided and no mention is made of the circumstances of his death, although the Atlanta papers have been headlining the murder since Alph's capture three days earlier.

Beagle's obituary is also there, covering nearly half a page. There are pictures of Beagle as a basketball standout, one at his graduation from the Naval Academy, and one of his swearing-in as a judge. Three columns are devoted to his career, and a final, short paragraph states that the police are still searching for his killer. "Several strong leads have surfaced recently," the article says. A final sentence reads: "A primary suspect is Eddie Cochran, a MedAmerica employee, but investigators are awaiting DNA testing results before making any arrests."

Shortly after two, Jeremiah arrives at Pink Allday's house. Bathed and ready, prim and proper in her flowered dress, an afghan shawl draped around stooped shoulders, she greets him from her rocking chair on her porch.

"Melissa called and said you'd be here at two, and here you are. You always did what you said you'd do, Jeremiah, so I knew I better be ready."

Jeremiah manages a weak smile, but his stomach churns as he hears his aunt's words. She has always believed he was better than he really was. He bends down, hugging her warmly and kissing her cheek. "You look wonderful, Aunt Pink. You're the only person I know who's getting younger every year."

"Pshaw, how you run on, boy. I wish it was so, but time's runnin' out on me. I'm still blessed with pretty good health, though, to be on the other side of ninety. The Good Lord's lettin' me stay on here for a reason, I reckon, but I'm not worth much. I'm workin' on some crocheting now I just can't seem to finish."

Suddenly furrowing her eyebrows, Pink asks: "Did you go to Alex's funeral?"

"Yes, ma'am. I did, but I didn't go to the cemetery. It was a pretty sad affair."

"Funerals always are, ain't they?" Pink shifts in her chair. "You know what worries me, Jeremiah? I can't understand all this stuff they're puttin' in the Atlanta papers about Alex and drugs and everything. They say he might have been connected with Beagle's death, too. How can they put stuff that ain't true in the newspapers? It makes me nervous readin' things like that."

"Me too, Aunt Pink." Jeremiah nods. "It makes me nervous, too." He decides to change the subject. "By the way, I'm going by Albany to see Ethan this afternoon on my way home. You need to send him anything?"

Ethan Allday is in jail in Albany—a city one hour's drive north of Shrewsbury Crossing. Just days after Beagle's disappearance, another judge had been assigned to Ethan's case and a plea-bargain had been quickly worked out. The sentence had been six months' imprisonment, a forty-thousand dollar fine, and three years' probation.

. "I've just baked a chocolate cake," Pink says, "and I'd be grateful if you'd take him a big piece. Would you like some too, Jeremiah?"

"Are you kidding, Aunt Pink? When did I *ever* turn down a piece of your world-famous cake?" Jeremiah laughs. "I've never found anything to equal it and I don't think I ever will. Some things about life just can't be improved, and your chocolate cake is one of them."

❧ ❧ ❧

The parking lot of the AME church is filled to overflowing and cars line sidestreets and alleyways, but handicapped spaces are reserved near the entrance to the church. While Jeremiah has no permit, he feels that his aunt qualifies them for a spot and he receives an understanding smile from a policeman as he helps Pink from the car. As they enter the crowded church, an usher whispers that there are seats near the front for the elderly, so Jeremiah and Pink take seats two rows behind and to the right of the section reserved for family members.

As the family enters the sanctuary from a waiting room beyond the pulpit, Bootsie Williams, now in her late nineties, is pushed along in a wheelchair by a tall, neatly dressed man, his hand on the chair's right handle revealing an ancient outrage—a missing middle finger. It is Leeman Williams, Bootsie's great-grandson, now a co-owner of the Negro funeral home serving Ludlow and Shrewsbury Crossing. Next comes Beagle's widow, Talisha; and then his sister, Wilma, now in her sixties but still grotesquely fat, wobbles along behind. By Wilma's side and holding Wilma's hand is a statuesque woman in her late seventies, with silvery hair, proud, high cheekbones, stylishly dressed.

Jeremiah turns to Pink and whispers: "Who is the woman with Wilma, Aunt Pink?"

"I'm not sure," she murmurs. "My eyes ain't too good no more, but I don't think I know her." She hesitates, then leans closer to Jeremiah. "Do you reckon it's Beagle's mama? She left town right after Beagle was born—left him and Wilma to be raised by Bootsie. I've heard stories she was dead, but then some said she moved to Detroit and married a rich man."

"Can you remember her name?" Jeremiah asks.

"Can't think of it right now," Pink answers, shaking her head. "Maybe it'll come to me."

Jeremiah looks down at the program, two pages of which contain a list of dignitaries, some designated as honorary pallbearers and others as eulogists. The service lasts nearly two hours, and when it ends, Jeremiah remains seated with his aunt while the sanctuary clears. With Pink hobbling on her cane and clinging tightly to Jeremiah's arm, they walk slowly up the aisle and leave the church. Outside, as they approach the parking lot, they find an elderly man, standing alone by the curb near Jeremiah's car, leaning unsteadily on a walker.

"Well, howdy, Miss Pink," Erasmus Bonobo says, tipping his hat. "Ain't this yore nephew you got with you?"

"Rasty!" Jeremiah exclaims, extending his hand, "My goodness! I can't believe my eyes! Good to see you—haven't seen you in years. How're you doing?"

"I reckon I'm OK, Jeremiah, considering how badly I mistreated my body." Erasmus coughs and turns to spit tobacco juice. "But I'll say this," he grunts, "I'm gettin' tired of funerals. Seems like I'm watchin' somebody I know get buried every day. I'm 'fraid these morticians are gonna run out and come after me, whether I'm dead or not." Erasmus grins as he grasps Jeremiah's hand. The man is now eighty-six, cancer of the lungs having devastated his health two years earlier. He is gaunt, thin, and weakened severely by radiation therapy. Two weeks earlier, he has been told he has six months to live.

"Erasmus," Pink says, "Did you notice the woman sitting by Bootsie at the service? Not Wilma now, I know her. The other one. I had a hunch that was Beagle's mama—was I right?"

"Yes ma'am, you was. It was Beagle's mama. I do believe it was," Erasmus replies.

"Well, what was her name?" Pink asks. "I used to know it."

"'Jasmine,' Miss Pink. 'Jasmine' is her name. Nobody's seen her in this town since the thirties but I remember her when she waited tables at the old Night Owl beer joint. A fine lookin' woman back then, and I reckon she still is."

"Oh yes, I remember now," Pink says. "People talked about her leaving town. Wondered where she'd gone. There was even a rumor back then—you know, when Bootsie took Beagle and Wilma to raise—that Beagle's daddy mighta been a white man. Did you ever hear anything about that, Erasmus?"

"Miss Pink," Erasmus looks down and shuffles his feet, "I ain't never said a word to nobody about this. I figured it warn't nobody's business, but I cain't see no reason to hold it in now. I know for a *fact* that Beagle's daddy was white. And shoot! Them boys is both dead, so it cain't matter no more. I'll just come out and say it: the boy's daddy was one of my buddies—Jesse Rumpkin, Alex Rumpkin's daddy. We worked in the mill together. Yes'm, Miss Pink, yes'm—I know for a fact that Jesse Rumpkin was Beagle's papa.

❦ ❦ ❦

Driving back to Pink's house, Jeremiah and his aunt say little. As the car pulls to a stop, Jeremiah turns toward her to see a tear trickle down her cheek. "What is it, Aunt Pink? Are you OK?

"Oh, I don't know. It just hit me all at once, I reckon." Pink brushes her face with a tissue. "Don't worry about me, Jeremiah. Just an old woman getting too upset, too emotional."

"Well," Jeremiah says, hoping to elicit a smile, "that was a really fine funeral, wasn't it? Did you ever hear such singing?"

Pink seems not to hear his questions and she does not smile. "My old eyes have seen a lot of sadness in this world and maybe I just can't take it like I used to—but sometimes it just seems too much—just the sadness of it all." Turning to face Jeremiah, she goes on: "So much waste in life, such foolish, *foolish* waste—especially with what Erasmus said about Beagle's mama. It breaks my heart to think about it. Do you reckon the only time she's been near him since he was a baby was when he was lying' in that casket."

"Why do you suppose she abandoned him and Wilma like that?" Jeremiah asks.

"Oh, I don't know, Jeremiah. I won't ever understand how a mother could leave her own youngun, but maybe she had to. Maybe she had good reasons. Maybe she thought her children would be better off—growin' up with Bootsie, especially with Beagle's daddy being white. Sometimes we can't understand how folks behave 'cause we don't know what's inside of them, or what things they've had to face. Who are we to judge? The Good Book says not to judge and we shouldn't do it! Not unless we want to be judged ourselves, and I sure don't." Her words spark a trace of amusement in Jeremiah. What on earth, he wonders, has this saintly woman ever done to make her fear the Judgment?

"We always wondered who Beagle's daddy was," Pink continues, "but it never dawned on me it coulda been Jesse Rumpkin. If anybody besides Erasmus knew, they hushed up pretty much about it, but now I wonder if it wouldn't have been better to get it all out in the open."

"Get what out?"

"You know, that Jesse was the baby's papa—with what they're saying in the papers and all, that Alex might have been mixed up in Beagle's death. What if that's true?"

"We don't know if that's true, Aunt Pink," Jeremiah says. "That's just the story that the hitchhiker told police. Nothing's been proven."

"If it *is* true, then Alex should have been told when he was a boy! That's all I know."

"Told what?" Jeremiah asked.

"That Beagle was his half brother. And with Jesse killing himself and all…."

"Killing himself? You mean Alex's daddy killed himself? Alex always said his father was murdered…, you know, ambushed by a gang of Negroes."

"Yes, that's the story some of them told, but Melissa and I always figured that wasn't so. Killed himself, that's what happened, and now with what Erasmus says, it makes more sense. Maybe he just couldn't face up to being with that colored girl and havin' a newborn child at home. And then Jasmine had Beagle. She must have known she wouldn't get no peace around here if folks found out she had a white boy's child, so she just left town. Left her younguns to be raised by Bootsie. 'Course, that's the best thing ever happened to Beagle and Wilma—thank goodness, they had that good woman to raise them. Lord knows what would have happened to them otherwise!"

Jeremiah puts his arm around his aunt. They sit silently in his car and he watches a fresh tear roll down her cheeks. "See, Jeremiah," she turns to him. "See the awful sadness! See how sad life can be? Ain't it a shame? The two of them was brothers, but they didn't even know it. They didn't realize that they carried the same blood in their veins."

The visitors' room at the Albany Correctional Institution is spacious, an open, well-lit area furnished with tables and reasonably comfortable chairs. The facility is new, a minimum security prison, reserved for white-collar, non-violent criminals serving five years or less. Since September, and for nearly three months, it has been home to Ethan Allday, formerly the Chief Financial Officer of the MedAmerica Corporation.

Ethan breaks into a broad smile as the guard leads him into the visitors' room and directs him to a table on the far side where Jeremiah stands, waiting. Prison regulations, carefully explained to Jeremiah when he signed in, prevent them from touching each other or shaking hands, but the warmth between them is palpable as they seat themselves, facing each other over the table while the guard retreats to a desk near the door.

"Gosh, I just can't believe you're here." Ethan leans forward and says, almost in a whisper. Muffled exchanges between other inmates and visitors filter in from other tables.

"I'm ashamed I haven't been here earlier. I should have, I know I should have! How long has it been, nearly three months?" Jeremiah asks, blushing.

"Yeah, seventy-two days, but who's counting? *Tempus fugit*, don't they say? Especially when you're having fun." Ethan folds his arms across his chest, awkwardly. "Guess you never thought you'd see your cousin sitting here in the can, eh?"

"No, can't say I did," Jeremiah says, nervously, "you certainly don't belong here."

"I guess the judge and the prosecutor felt differently about that, but it won't be too much longer now. I may even get to leave a few days earlier than my release date."

"When is that? February or March, isn't it?"

"March 12," Ethan nods.

"I can't begin to tell you how sorry I am this happened to you."

"Well, you did all you could, Jeremiah. You really stuck your neck out making that call to Beagle. My lawyer told me afterwards that you could have been disbarred. Made me feel like a fool for asking you to do it. But, I want you to know that I'll never forget that you made the effort. Besides, I have only myself to blame for this. I should have had more sense in the first place. I let Alex do things—and talk me into doing things—I should have known were shady."

"Yeah, he was pretty good at getting us both into trouble."

"Guess you've been to the funerals today?" Ethan asks, glancing toward the door where another inmate was being brought in.

"Yeah, I have. Didn't want to go. You know, those were pretty ugly situations—both of those deaths."

"Did you go alone? Sarah is not with you?"

"No, she stayed at home."

"So you went alone?"

"I went to Alex's by myself, but I took Aunt Pink to Beagle's 'cause she wanted to go. In fact, that's been the highlight of the day—just being around that wonderful lady for a while. I ought to be ashamed for not spending more time in Shrewsbury Crossing seeing our two mothers, Ethan."

"How's mama feeling?" Ethan asks. "I haven't seen her since I came in here. I *want* to see her, of course, and Irene would bring her if I asked, but I just can't stand to think of having her see me here."

"Well, she's worried sick about your being here, but otherwise she's just great, unbelievable really—for someone her age. She's a work of art and spunky as ever. I guess it goes to show that clean living has its rewards. By the way, she sent you chocolate cake—a big piece, but they made me leave it out front. Guess they'll x-ray it for a chain-saw or something."

"What about Aunt Melissa? I assume you saw her too."

"Yeah, spent nearly an hour with her this morning. Mama's wearing out fast—her eyes, hearing, all her systems just shutting down."

"I'm sorry to hear that. When I get out, I'm going to make a point of visiting her several times a week." Ethan hesitates, then added, tentatively: "And you and Sarah? How're things there?"

"We're together again, or living in the same house at least, and we're both *really* trying. If you want to know the truth, Ethan, I can't fathom why she's stuck with me this long—through everything. She must think something about our marriage is worth salvaging."

A long pause, then:

"And Annie, Jeremiah. How is Annie holding up with all of this?"

"Annie looked terrible at the funeral." Jeremiah shakes his head, his mouth drawn. "You know, she's been through hell. I don't see how can she go on with all this mess in the papers, the total humiliation, the effects on her girls and their families. She looks like she's near death herself—at least twenty years older than she really is. I never spoke to her at the service; she was stunned; just sat there, her face ashen white, staring blankly off into nowhere. I couldn't bear it, didn't know what to say, just signed the register and left. I decided not to go to the…."

"And Beagle's service?"

"Sad, of course, but totally different from Alex's. You know what black funerals are like—almost a celebration, and it was especially true because of Beagle's life, his achievements. Singing, shouting, clapping, the church overflowing with relatives and dignitaries, you can just imagine. And there was an air of optimism and hope mixed in with the grieving, like they really believe in all this heaven stuff. As a matter of fact, they *really* do, I guess. They *really* do, don't they?"

"Yeah, I think they really do," Ethan answers. "Beagle was quite a human being, wasn't he? You know, I never lost respect for him even when he was about to preside over my trial. My lawyer kept saying we ought to get him removed from the case, but I said no. I knew he would have been fair to me in the end."

"I believe he would have, at least in his own mind. Beagle had experienced enough injustice himself not to want to inflict it on someone else—especially someone he respected like you." Jeremiah suddenly grabs his chin with his right hand. "Oh my goodness!" he says, "that reminds me. You'll never believe what I've learned today!"

"Well, hurry up! Spit it out!" Ethan says, staring directly into his cousin's eyes.

"Let's see, it all happened after Beagle's service was over and Aunt Pink and I had left the church going to my car. There had been this woman sitting by Wilma and Bootsie during the service, and Aunt Pink had suspected that she might be Beagle's mother. Then we met old Rasty—you know, Rasty Bonobo—in the parking lot. He and Aunt Pink got to talking and he said the woman *was* Beagle's mother—a woman named 'Jasmine' who left town back in the thirties right after Beagle was born."

"Gosh!" Ethan says, furrowing his brow. "And so she came back for the funeral, after all these years?"

"But listen to this: here's the real kicker! Rasty says Alex and Beagle were really half-brothers—that Alex's daddy, the man called Jesse, fathered Beagle too. Remember, Alex always thought his daddy was murdered, but Aunt Pink says she knew Jesse killed himself right after Alex was born."

"Wait a minute now," Ethan gasps, shaking his head. "You're confusing me. How could Jesse have fathered Beagle if he was dead?"

"It must have been like this," Jeremiah replied. "Jesse must have slept with Beagle's mother just before he killed himself, and Beagle was born nine months later. The dates work out: Alex's birthday was in early April—I can't recall the exact date—and Beagle was born in December. Remember how he used to complain because he felt he got short-changed on presents from Bootsie because Christmas and his birthday were jammed together? And after Beagle was born, his mother left town—left her children with Bootsie."

"You can't be serious!" Ethan exclaims, wide-eyed. "Why didn't we know? Why didn't all this ever come out?"

"I guess folks just kept it all hush-hush. Aunt Pink said she and Mama knew about the suicide and had vague suspicions about a white man being Beagle's father, but they never made the connection. You know how things were in those days: being a half-breed was taboo for blacks as well as for whites. You got ostracized from both groups, so Bootsie was wise; she knew what she was doing. She took pains to raise Beagle as a Negro. She never let him cross the line, *never*." Pausing for a moment, Jeremiah adds, "And see, if you believe the hitchhiker, it means that Alex had his half-brother killed and that…."

"You don't need to fill in the picture," Ethan whispers with a grimace.

For an interminable moment the two men sit silently, searching each other's faces. "It's sorta unreal, isn't it?" Jeremiah says, hoarsely. "All those years growing up together, playing together, those two so competitive, hostile, not knowing they had the same father."

"Do you think either one ever suspected? You know, deep inside?" Ethan asks.

"I never saw any signs of it, did you?"

"Not really, but maybe if they had known, maybe there would have been less hatred—less rivalry, maybe—between them."

"I'm not sure," Jeremiah says, "Cain killed Abel, didn't he? We all seem to make life a lot harder than it has to be. At least, I know I have."

"You can put me in that category too," Ethan says. "What do you think drove Alex and Beagle to be the way they were with each other? And what made them both so hell-bent to get to the top?"

"I don't know," Jeremiah says, "I really don't pretend to understand it. In fact, I've decided that I don't understand much of anything—number one on the list being myself. Maybe something in the genes? Maybe someday they'll locate a stupidity gene in the DNA, you guess?"

"I guess you and I both got a little dose of that," Ethan smiles and nods.

"So what are your plans now?" Jeremiah leans back in his chair, raising the two front legs off the floor, the way he and Ethan did as boys at the table in Aunt Pink's kitchen. He folds his arms across his chest.

Ethan smiles again, tapping the table top with a finger. "You know, Old Cuz, from where you're seated, you ought to be able to make a fairly educated guess about my plans. The folks around here have my life pretty well structured for the next few months."

"Come on, smart ass! You know what I mean," Jeremiah says, "when you get out, when you leave here—what will you do *then*?"

"Well, the plea-bargain precludes my returning to MedAmerica even if they wanted me—so I guess my days for handling other people's money are over."

"So how will you get along?"

"I'm OK financially, believe it or not," Ethan says. "My conservative obsessions finally paid off: I have a fair amount of savings left even after the fine and legal fees, and I've got some stock options with the company that ought to be worth something someday."

"How will you spend your time?"

"This will sound corny to you, I guess, but I want to spend time—do things—with my family—Irene, my children and the four grandchildren. Through all of this, I've finally had the sense to examine my priorities. I guess I've come to understand a little better how precious life really is—how fragile, ephemeral."

"God, you sound like a preacher!" Jeremiah rolls his eyes.

"Well, you'll really have a belly-laugh when you hear this. When I get out, I'm going to join a Christian organization of ex-cons who visit high schools and grammar schools to warn kids how easy it is to get into trouble. I oughta' be great at that, don't you think? I broke laws I didn't even know existed. Imagine what a vicious criminal I could have been if I had tried."

"So you're gonna' be *The Catcher in the Rye*, eh?" Jeremiah chuckles. "Save the children and all that, huh? Boy, we could have used someone like that ourselves, couldn't we?"

"Do you think back to those days?" Ethan asks, wistfully. "You know, growing up—you, me, Alex, Beagle? There's one good thing about being in here: it gives you a lot of time to think—about all sorts of things, and I like to reflect on those days—how we were as boys."

"Yes, I do some of that myself," Jeremiah says. "Matter of fact, this morning on my way into Shrewsbury Crossing, I stopped by the old sawmill. I have no idea why I did it. Partly to see where Beagle had been buried, I guess, but it was more than that. I parked the car and got out—just stood there and looked around a few minutes. Not much left, really—only a decaying hump remaining of the sawdust pile. But it brought back a lot of memories. I could almost hear our laughter and screams the way we used to play around the sawmill, pushing each other off the sawdust pile. Remember how Alex and Beagle fought each other over who was gonna be king of the mountain? Alex and Beagle fought over just about everything, I guess."

"What was growing up like that all about, Jeremiah? Were we different from other kids or what?"

Jeremiah pauses. "No, I don't think so, Ethan, not really. Don't you imagine life unfolds in pretty much the same way whether you're a snotty-nosed boy growing up in south Georgia or a street-smart kid in Harlem—whether you're nobody or a celebrity. Don't you think we're all the same? The same needs, the same dreams—the same demons?"

"But somehow the four of us seemed different," Ethan says, insistently. "For sure, Alex and Beagle were different—possessed by some unyielding inner fire that drove them to break the molds, to challenge everything. They both came from absolutely nowhere and attained such heights, and then they came to incredibly tragic ends. Like figures out of Greek tragedies. As human beings, Alex and Beagle were unique?"

"Maybe so," Jeremiah shrugs his shoulders. "But perhaps that fire is buried deep in each of us. We *all* have it in varying degrees. We fight and scrape to get to the top of whatever heap we're on. Maybe *how* you get there depends in some way on how you grow up—not just money, necessarily, but a caring, nurturing family, a place in society, the opportunities given and denied...."

"Maybe somewhere in all that talking you're making a point, Cuz—maybe even an important point," Ethan wrinkles his nose, "but I swear, Jeremiah, it's just like the old days: you talk and talk and talk, and it sounds impressive; but when you finish, I still can't figure out what in the devil you've said."

Shortly before eight p.m., Jeremiah leaves the prison and finds his way to a four-lane running from Albany to Cordele where he takes the interstate back to Atlanta. It has been fourteen hours since he set out on the day's journey to Shrewsbury Crossing. He is weary but he feels a sense of relief, knowing he has met his obligations: spent time with his mother, attended the funerals, taken care of Aunt Pink, and visited Ethan. Now he is on his way home. He opens his car window for a while, breathing deeply the fresh, cool December air of the Georgia night.

It is nearly midnight when he turns into his drive in Roswell. Inside the house, he enters the kitchen for a glass of skim milk. He stands before the sink, drinking the milk, puts away the empty glass, and returns to the foyer where he ascends the stairs. He pauses for a minute at the top of the stairs. Putting his ear to the door, he can hear Sarah's breathing and soft snoring and he can picture her curled up and hugging the pillow in the bed he has shared with her for most of their married life. Then tears blur his vision and he realizes that it's no use: the bonds are gone. The long years of wear and hurt and turmoil have taken their toll, on him and on Sarah. In the future, he'll try to figure out what went amiss, how decades of life together finally tore them apart. And he'll have time to do that. But there is nothing left to connect them to each other now. It's over and dead.

He enters the guest bedroom across the hall, and quietly slips out of his clothes. He gets into bed, pulling the covers over himself. Before sleep finally overtakes him, he reflects on how things came to this complicated place in his life. He knows he must go on with life, with living, and he knows he'll have to do it without Sarah.

But he has survived before and he will pull through again. He doesn't know how, but he knows he will.

About the Author

Don Mobley Adams grew up in southwest Georgia and was an in house lawyer for a large Atlanta corporation for 25 years before retiring in 1993. His childhood and adult experiences provided the unique scaffolding for his novel. Living now in central Georgia, he continues to write humorous essays, fiction and poetry.

978-0-595-36011-6
0-595-36011-4